STILL TIME

Michael Llewellyn

For Doug —
All best wishes.

Michael Llewellyn

STILL TIME

ISBN: 978–1503226685

This book is a work of fiction. Names, characters, places, and
incidents are either products of the author's imagination or
are used fictitiously. Any resemblance to actual events,
locales, business establishments, or persons, living or dead, is
entirely coincidental.

Other Books
By Michael Llewellyn

Communion of Sinners

"Author Michael Llewellyn has cooked up a savory literary paella inspired by the hidden history of California's Spanish missions and flavored with a touch of investigative journalism and the beauty of the Pacific coast. Mysterious deaths, long held secrets, heartbreak and wonderful descriptions of food and wine combine in this compelling new novel to create a feast of a book."
— Anne Hillerman, author of *Spider Woman's Daughter*

Creole Son

"With skill and sensitivity, Llewellyn captures the interaction of art and violence, ugliness and beauty, the transition of an artist, a man and a world."
— Barbara Hambly, author of *A Free Man of Color*

"Llewellyn deftly imagines the beauty, peril, internecine struggles and seductiveness of late 19th century New Orleans as seen through the troubled artist's eye."
— Ciji Ware, author of *Island of the Swans*

"Llewellyn writes convincingly of a chaotic, sensual, dangerous and exotic city seething with racial tension, criminal politics, sexual license and moral ambiguity, and crafts a strong and persuasive argument for how New Orleans brought Degas to a new and daring way of painting. The descriptions of how Degas thought, observed and painted are finely wrought and very well written, showing detailed knowledge of the artist's style and methods. A book to be savored."
— Mary Burns, author of *Portraits of an Artist*

Twelfth Night

"Entertaining.—a solid sense of life in antebellum New Orleans."
— *Publisher's Weekly*

"Llewellyn has a real gift for atmosphere and characterization...exploiting the rich possibilities of the Quadroon Balls, the class conflict of Mardi Gras, and the voodoo legends of Congo Square and Marie Laveau... *Twelfth Night* will be the gilded bean in your king cake."
— *New Orleans Times-Picayune.*

"Accurately captures the atmosphere of New Orleans and Mardi Gras. The background material is well-researched, the spicy story is well-written and the pace is suspenseful."
— *The Jackson Clarion-Ledger*

Writing as Michel LaCroix

Alex in Wonderland

"Tennessee Williams meets Jackie Collins with a dash of Truman Capote...The perfect novel to read while sipping a mint julep and fanning yourself on the veranda."
— Michael D. Craig, author of *The Ice Sculptures: A Novel of Hollywood*

"A hilarious and utterly compelling story of one man's search for identity, independence and love, at the risk of rejection and forsaking a family inheritance. A sizzling mix of fast-paced storytelling and lyrical sexuality."
— Durell Owens, author of *The Song of a Manchild*

"Richly entertaining. Celebrates New Orleans in fine style. Fully loaded with plot, heart and rainbow-colored characters. Everything you could want is present and accounted for."
— *Edge Boston*

To Lola Leslie Jacobs
Confrere, confidante, fellow scribe and
Devotee of beach music,
With much love

STILL TIME

Scaramouche Publishing

"He was born with a gift of laughter and a sense that the world was mad."

Table of Contents

Part 1

"Everything in New Orleans seems worn out,
and the perfume of the past has not quite evaporated."

— Edgar Degas, 1872

1

Maddy said good-night to the last party guest and poured another glass of pinot grigio in hopes it would dull this latest disappointment. She glanced at the clock. Even close to midnight it would still be hot on the balcony, but fresh air might help sort her thoughts. A voice stopped her before she could reached the French doors.

"Want some company, darling?"

She spun, nearly spilling the wine. "My God, Paige! You scared the hell out of me!"

"Sorry."

"I thought everybody had left."

"I was powdering my nose." Paige looked bemused. "But how, pray tell, could you lose track of your best friend?"

"Maybe because it's been a—"

"Rough night?" Paige finished.

"How did you know?"

"Seth nearly knocked me down when he ran out of here."

"I'm sorry you saw that."

"Forget it, hon. Frankly I welcome any and all distractions from the fact that I'm turning forty next week, but what on earth got into that guy?"

"Who knows? I was joking with Karen Derdarian when Seth suddenly blew up and stormed out." Maddy grimaced. "It's not the first time he's misbehaved like that."

"Was he drunk?"

"He doesn't even drink. I swear. Every man I date is either a player or a psycho."

"I'm sorry. About Seth I mean."

"I'm not." Maddy sipped her wine. "I'm more relieved

than anything."

"Maybe we should face the fact that we both have rotten luck in the romance department."

Maddy looked pained. "I don't know if it's that or poor judgment or that I just screw things up, but after this newest fiasco I'm beginning to think Mr. Right is an urban myth."

"No, he's not, darling, and you'll find him. You're smart and pretty and young and—"

"I may be smart, but I'm not pretty, and thirty-three is hardly young."

"I was that age when I found my third husband."

Maddy smiled. "Yeah, and I think you got my share of available men."

Paige chuckled but kept the conversation on course. "You know you can go the glamour route when you want to. How about that costume ball when you dressed as Eleanor of Aquitaine? You were gorgeous!"

"Probably because I looked like someone else."

Paige snorted. "For God's sake, Maddy. I'm the one turning the big four-oh, but if you want to throw yourself a pity party, go right ahead. But I can't understand why you hide your curves under shapeless clothes and wear your hair in that tight-ass bun. I know you're a librarian, dear, but you don't have to dress like their damned poster child."

"My hair's straight as a stick, Paige, and a bun's the easiest way to wear it. Besides, I want it off my neck in this heat."

"But if you'd only let me take you to my hairdresser—"

"I know you mean well," Maddy said tiredly, "but please don't start that again."

Paige retreated. "I'm sorry. I didn't mean to get too personal."

"Forget it. Now let's go outside and enjoy what's left of the evening."

As they stepped onto the small balcony overlooking Royal Street, Maddy's face blazed as heat and heavy humidity swarmed over her. She closed the door to keep the air conditioning inside and joined Paige at the iron railing where she leaned into the night and filled her lungs with New Orleans's damp, languid breath. Streetlights were fading behind deepening fog, and the sidewalks were oddly deserted for Saturday night in the French Quarter.

"Wonder where everybody is," Paige muttered, as if reading her friend's mind.

"Probably that big masked ball at the Roosevelt."

Maddy absorbed the comforting vista of ornate Victorian shotgun homes, simple Creole cottages and elegant townhouses swathed in iron grillwork. The latter were her favorites because they faced the centuries with rouged patinas she found oddly empowering. She also welcomed the Quarter's unique susurrus marrying muffled laughter with the creak of carriage wheels and clip-clop of hooves, the lonely hoot of a riverboat and a distant trumpet courting the blues. Maddy loved that these sights and sounds hadn't changed in two centuries.

"It amazes me," she said as memories of Seth were erased by the moment, "that even in this awful August heat, the old gal still works her special magic."

"Old gal? You mean the city."

Maddy nodded. "No matter how bluesy I get, New Orleans always picks me up."

"Not me. This damned heat still wears me down."

"After eight years, you're still not used to it?"

"I'm from Oregon, remember? You grew up with this torpor. It's in your DNA."

There's more to it than that, Maddy thought. As she studied the thickening fog, made to dance with gusts from the Mississippi, New Orleans's heartbeat merged with her own. It was like this the first moment she saw it, brought to town by her shrimper father to see the Christmas lights. The little Cajun girl from nearby Westwego had been saucer-eyed with wonder, dazzled and frightened by the incredible sprawl of Canal Street, the widest thoroughfare in America, lined with glittering stores decorated for the season. Maddy was particularly awed by a fifty-foot-tall snowman suspended across the front of Maison Blanche department store. He wore an ice cream cone hat, striped mittens and an enormous red bow tied under his chin. Most amazing of all, Maddy thought, were his wings made of holly. He took her breath away.

"Papa!" she cried. "Who is that?!"

"Mr. Bingle," Emile St. Jacques replied with a smile. "All the children in New Orleans love him."

"I love him too!"

"I'm sure he loves you back, *cher.*"

Despite her father's good intentions, Maddy had felt patronized, as if Mr. Bingle's affection was shared only with local kids, and, although barely six years old, she promised herself that some day New Orleans would be her home too. Her secret desire became reality when she won a scholarship to Tulane and moved into a campus dormitory. A dedicated history major, she immersed herself in the city's exotic past and never permitted its unending problems to tarnish deep love for her adopted hometown. That passion saved her in the wake of Hurricane Katrina which unleashed horrors that brought the city to its knees and made it synonymous with government inefficiency and man's inhumanity to man. Like many other locals, Maddy ignored the harsh reality that New Orleans was America's most flagrant act of civil disobedience, preferring to think about the next Mardi Gras or Jazzfest or the daily wonders that came simply from living in a place celebrating life like nowhere else in the country. Maddy was comforted by that jingoistic notion as she leaned over the railing. Down below, three amorphous forms sharpened into caped, hooded figures and emerged from the fog like floating specters. They huddled at the corner of Dumaine Street and spoke in hushed whispers. Maddy wondered if they were lost.

"Wish I had my camera!" she whispered to Paige. "They look like they're from the nineteenth century!"

"Or maybe they're guides for one of those awful haunted tours."

"Probably going to a party." Those were reasonable enough theories, but Maddy grew dizzy when the wind gusted and fog swirled around the cloaked trio. "How strange they look. It's…it's as if—"

"As if what?"

"I…I don't know, but all of a sudden I've got a peculiar feeling."

Paige sniffed. "It's this damned heat. I'm going back inside. You coming?"

"In a minute."

Left alone, Maddy realized her feet were rooted to the balcony, just as her gaze was commandeered by the tableau below. A hot wind arose, dizzying her as the fog whirled feverishly fast. She grabbed the railing for support and watched two of the enigmatic trio head down Dumaine Street while one looked up toward Maddy. A hand pushed back the hood enough to reveal a man's shadowy face. His deep voice rose through the fog, eerily commanding.

"*Bon soir!*"

Maddy gulped the steamy air and called back. "*Bon soir.*"

"Will you join us, *mademoiselle?*"

"Where are you going, *monsieur?*"

"On a journey."

"What sort of journey?"

He shrugged, pale hands palms up. "Who can say?"

Maddy frowned. "Do I know you?"

"Not yet." He indicated his companions. "Will you join us, pilgrim?"

"I'm sorry, but I can't." Maddy trembled with a tide of desire, but something kept her chained to the balcony. "Not tonight."

"*Les vrais paradis sont les paradis qu'on a perdus.*"

Maddy translated quickly. "True paradise is the one that you have lost." Good Lord, she thought. This guy's quoting

Proust. She was more intrigued than ever but still unable to move. *"Je regret, m'sieur."*

"Moi aussi."

"Another time perhaps?"

"Perhaps." The man bowed low, cloak rustling in the murky air. *"Bonne soirée, mademoiselle."*

"Please don't go yet!" Maddy cried. She didn't know why, nor did she know why she felt abandoned when the stranger tugged the hood over his face, whirled abruptly and vanished into the fog. With his disappearance, her will to move returned and she went back inside to find Paige pouring a fresh glass of wine.

"My God!" Paige gasped. "You look like you've seen a ghost."

"I'm...I'm not sure I didn't." Maddy waved away more wine and sank onto the couch. "It was the oddest thing."

"Tell me." Paige was nonplussed when Maddy finished describing the interchange. "What's so odd about strangers asking you to a party? It happens all the time in the Quarter."

"This was different. Different and confusing. Disturbing even."

"Was the man creepy?"

"Not really, but he was speaking French."

"What's odd about that, Cajun girl? So do you sometimes."

"This wasn't Cajun. It was dialect, something from the *ancien regime.*"

Paige made a face. "The what?"

"France before the 1789 revolution."

"I'm not following you and I don't think it's the alcohol."

Maddy shook her head, drowning in a wave of disbelief. "The man was speaking the sort of French that died out in New Orleans over a century ago."

2

Maddy awoke with a headache, not from too much wine but from yakking until all hours with Paige. When she finally got to bed, instead of sweet dreams she was plunged into a surreal odyssey that left her exhausted. She concentrated until enough crystallized to reconstruct the nightmare.

"It was that guy in the street," she muttered, sitting up and rubbing her temples. "With the hooded cloak."

Maddy closed her eyes and leaned back into the pillows as shards of the dream shimmered and sharpened. She heard the mysterious stranger's alluring voice and took a smooth gloved hand as he led her into a tangible fog. She smelled cool water as a steamboat churned by and felt warm flesh between her legs as she mounted a horse and galloped through a forest of sugar cane. The slashing stalks drew blood before her steed disintegrated, and Maddy tumbled into a cascade of silk and velvet pillows. She feared she might suffocate until the stranger reappeared in fancy dress as a nineteenth century *boulevardier* and took her hand again. The moment they touched, a stately saraband rose from nowhere.

"Come, pilgrim," he said in French. "Come before the music stops."

Maddy struggled to escape the voluptuous pillows. She remained paralyzed, limbs heavy and unresponsive. As she struggled for breath, she was overwhelmed by a familiar fragrance, the sort of old-fashioned perfume Grand-mère Aglaé might have worn. Was it rosewater? She couldn't think, didn't know and couldn't move.

"Come," the man entreated again.

"I can't," Maddy gasped. "I can't!"

"Celui qui obéit est presque toujours meilleur que celui qui commande."

"He who obeys is almost always better than he who commands," she whispered in translation.

"Exactemente."

Maddy was distraught as the stranger withdrew his hand and stepped away before slowly evaporating inside a blue nimbus. *"Mais, non!"* she cried. "Don't go!"

She fell back asleep and was awakened by her own moans of despair. She tested her consciousness by taking inventory of her bedroom, relieved to see the familiar Degas print by the door and her grandfather Armand's antique clock on the dresser. The last of the distressing dream fled when she saw it was almost ten.

"Damn," she muttered, throwing back the covers. "Paige's salon!"

With no time for coffee, Maddy grabbed a cool shower which vanquished her headache along with memories of the troubling dream. She hastily toweled off and ran a comb through her dark brown hair. As she pulled it into her trademark bun, she remembered Paige's criticism and let it fall to frame her oval face. She'd done this before but never liked the result. Now, with no boyfriend or prospects for one, she decided Paige might be right about a less severe look. She applied more than her usual hint of mascara and eyeliner and reddened her lips before hunting for a dress that had hung unworn in her closet since Paige gave it to her last Christmas. It was a white gauze sundress with spaghetti straps and a lacy front that hugged her flat tummy and showcased breasts usually hidden under loose blouses and bulky sweaters. A critical look in the mirror, however, and she lost her newfound nerve.

"It's not me," Maddy muttered. She was reaching for the zipper when she heard the stranger's voice.

"Come, pilgrim. Come before the music stops."

Ignoring her instincts, she grabbed the straw picture hat

hanging over her dresser and plopped it on her head. She had bought it for room décor and was surprised to learn that it fit. Afraid to look in the mirror again, she fled her apartment as though pursued by the Furies and made the short walk to Paige's home on Ursulines Street without breaking a sweat. She paused at the front door of the 1848 Creole townhouse, enchanted as usual by ornate iron gates and high walls dripping orange trumpet vine and purple oleander. In marked contrast to her small one- bedroom apartment, here was one of the French Quarter's largest homes with gardens to match, won after Paige's third divorce last winter. Its splendor was often on display as Paige was one of the city's great hostesses, especially celebrated for Sunday brunches mixing people who might otherwise never meet. Where else, Maddy wondered, could she discuss politics with an African-American sculptor, an opera singer and a gay street poet or hear a recitation of Russian fairy tales or a jazz jam session? These vibrant gatherings had become known as "Paige's Sunday Salons," and she worked hard to make them memorable.

The gates buzzed open and the door swung wide to reveal a hulking black man. Jesse Fox, Paige's major domo, was the picture of menace, but Maddy knew his heart was as big as his grin. Maddy adored Jesse, but he truly became her hero a few months ago by disarming her would-be mugger and strong-arming the guy to the Royal Street police station. She returned his warm smile and blushed at his unexpected comment.

"Hey, pretty lady! What'd you do with Madeleine?"

"Stop it, Jesse. You know it's me."

"Lookin' good this morning!"

"Thanks," she said, blush deepening.

"Miss Paige has been looking for you."

"I'll bet." Maddy welcomed the air-conditioning as she stepped into the chilly marble foyer. "No doubt she said something about my being late."

Jesse gave her a conspiratorial look. "No doubt."

"It's her fault for keeping me up half the night talking."

"I hear you."

As Jesse responded to another ring of the doorbell, Paige burst into the foyer, shimmering in cool peach silk. Frosted blonde hair hung in a single braid down her back, and a ghetto-made tin necklace danced across her bosom. Maddy had envied Paige's slightly offbeat style since they met some years ago at Jazz Fest, rhapsodizing together when Aaron Neville unexpectedly took the stage in the gospel tent and melted the crowd with "Ave Maria." The bookish librarian and flamboyant divorcée were an unlikely pair, but they discovered they had a surprising amount in common and soon became devoted friends.

Paige's blue eyes widened as she took inventory. "Wow!"

Self-confidence boosted again, Maddy executed an impromptu pirouette. "You like?"

"Love it!" Paige bussed her cheek before giving her outfit another appraisal. "What prompted you to burst out of the wallflower closet?"

"Last night's nagging of course, as if you didn't know."

"All I can say is I sure wish nagging had worked on my husbands." Paige hugged her again. "You'll be the belle of the ball."

"Thanks, Paige." Although grateful for the flattery, Maddy changed the subject. "How's your head this morning?"

"Don't ask," Paige moaned. "I should've cut myself off like you did. That last glass of Pinot grigio put me over the edge." She looped her arm around Maddy's waist and ushered her toward a noisy parlor. "You know where everything is, darling, so help yourself while I circulate."

Maddy poured a cup of coffee from a vintage Russian samovar and threaded the crowd, nodding politely to people she didn't know and accepting compliments from those she did. She drifted from one group to another, catching up on the latest French Quarter gossip until Carlota Romero cornered her. She wasn't surprised when Carlota said nothing about her new look and began whining about the miserable contractor repairing her roof. Maddy tried to be attentive, but when she glanced toward the foyer she locked eyes with a stranger talking to Jesse. She blushed and looked away when he waded into the crowd and made straight for her. Carlota was still complaining when the man introduced himself as Henri Chabrol.

"A pleasure to meet you," Maddy said. "I'm—"

"Madeleine St. Jacques," he finished. "Please don't be embarrassed. We met once before, a few weeks ago."

Maddy took quick inventory while racking her brain to remember. The man was short and stocky, early forties probably, and wore bifocals. She wouldn't call him handsome, but he was attractive in an academic sort of way. A thick reddish moustache obscured his upper lip, and wavy brown hair streaked with silver needed a trim where it curled over his collar. A worn linen jacket, rumpled white shirt and corduroy trousers unseasonable in this heat gave him a comically professorial air, but she was more puzzled than amused.

"I'm afraid you have the advantage, Mr. Chabrol."

He smiled disarmingly. "You work at the Wilkins Research Center, do you not?"

Maddy brightened, relieved. "Ah! You wanted information on the Cane River colony."

"You have an excellent memory."

"Except for names I'm afraid."

"I'm Carlota Romero," Carlota blared, unhappy at being ignored. She took Henri's hand and held it longer than necessary. "I've been telling Maddy about the miserable contractor working on my house on St. Philip."

"Yellow with jungle green shutters, across from the school?"

Carlota beamed. "Why, yes. How did you know?"

"I've admired it for years and was pleased to see someone working on it. It's one of the finer Creole cottages in the

Quarter. Almost completely intact, isn't it?"

"Almost," Carlota replied proudly. "We're still repairing roof damage after the storm."

Like all New Orleanians, Carlota referred to Hurricane Katrina as "the storm."

"Are you an architect?" Maddy asked.

"Physicist, actually. Architecture is one of my avocations, along with history."

"Two of my interests also. I know nothing about physics, though, and we certainly don't have many inquiries about it at the Center."

Henri grinned. "I shouldn't think so."

"Do you live in the Quarter?" Carlota persisted, again stressing her presence.

"The Lower Garden District. Orange Street actually."

"Next time you're in the neighborhood I'd be happy to give you a tour of the house."

And anything else you'd care to see, Maddy thought. She looked away, embarrassed. Carlota was a famously free spirit whose sexual appetite, along with that of her husband Joe, kept local tongues wagging. It was no small accomplishment in a neighborhood famed for overindulgence and sexual high jinks.

"I'd be honored, Ms. Romero. How shall I—?"

Carlota pressed a business card into his hand. "Call whenever you like."

"Thank you," he said with an old-fashioned bow. When he turned back to Maddy, Carlota took the hint and excused herself as Maddy changed the subject.

"How do you know our hostess?"

"Paige saw my article in *Scientific American,* got my number off the Tulane website and asked me to give a little talk today."

"So you *are* a professor," Maddy blurted.

Henri smiled. "The clothes, right?"

"I'm sorry. I didn't mean to think in stereotypes."

"Don't apologize. It's sort of an act."

"Pardon me?"

"People seem to pay more attention if I dress the part." He tapped a pipe poking from his lapel pocket. "I don't even smoke this thing, and frankly, in this god-awful heat I'd much rather be in tee shirt and shorts."

"Me, too." Maddy mirrored his grin. "Please tell me about your article, Professor Chabrol."

He leaned in and whispered. "Actually it's Dr. Chabrol, but I wish you'd call me Henri."

"Only if you call me Maddy."

"Would you mind if I called you Madeleine? It's such a beautiful name, and one you don't hear much any more."

"I don't mind at all. My grandmother insisted that the grandchildren have old French names, maybe because she was saddled with one. Her name is Aglaé. Talk about a name you don't hear any more."

"It's unusual for a grandmother to choose the names. She must be a formidable lady."

"She is indeed," Maddy said. "I come from a long line of formidable ladies, at least on her side of the family."

"What about your grandfather's side?"

"Oddly enough, *Grand-mère* can trace her side of the family back to *Le Grand Dérangement* when the Cajuns were thrown out of Canada, but I know almost nothing about my grandfather's people."

"I assume you've tried the internet."

"I can't get any further back than my great-grandfather Louis. It's as if the St. Jacques family didn't exist before him."

Henri winked. "Maybe he sprang fully grown from Zeus's head like Athena."

"That's as good a theory as any. Now then. About your article?"

Before he responded, Henri glanced over Maddy's head and scanned the parlor. After a moment, he blinked and said, "Forgive me, Madeleine. I'm afraid my mind has a tendency to wander before a speech. It's been my *bête noir* for years, but lately it seems worse."

"Would you like some water or coffee or something?"

"No, no. Thank you. It's passed already. Now what were we talking about?"

"Your article in *Scientific American*," Maddy answered, wondering if he was the quintessential absent-minded professor.

"Oh, yes. Nothing earth-shattering. A piece on Hugh Everett." His penetrating stare made her wonder if he was about to embark on another flight of fancy. She was relieved when he stayed on course. "He was a physicist, 1930 to 1982, whose claim to fame, one that remains supremely controversial, was a conviction that our vast universe is one of many."

"What's so controversial about that? It's a huge conceit to believe otherwise, like those people who insist Earth has the only intelligent life."

"I quite agree, but that's not what Everett was getting at. In 1957, he theorized that these universes, or multiverses as he called them, existed side by side and were in a state of constant flux, splitting like protoplasm. It was an interpretation of quantum mechanics asserting the object relativity of the wave function."

Maddy gave him a droll look. "Surely you don't think I followed that."

"I confess I was testing you a little. Let's say Everett espoused more than one version of history in these parallel universes, an alternate reality if you will. There was one where Vesuvius didn't bury Pompeii and another wherein Einstein's theory of relativity remained undiscovered." He smiled sadly. "And one leaving the World Trade Center intact."

"Those are certainly intriguing notions."

"True. I can't imagine living without antibiotics and computers, but how splendid to be rid of Al-Qaeda and scientology."

Maddy chuckled. "I take it you're not a fan of L. Ron Hubbard."

"Or rabid dogs," Henri grunted, "but that's a topic for another time. Today is all about parallel universes and how, why and if they might intersect."

"Do you believe such things are possible?"

"It's what Dr. Everett believed that's important."

An evasive answer, Maddy thought. Dismissive even. She was about to ask why a history and architecture buff would write about such a peculiar theory when Henri looked over her shoulder again. Paige was approaching with a big smile.

"Here you are, Dr. Chabrol. Again, let me thank you for agreeing to speak today. I see you've met Madeleine."

"Actually we've met before. At the Wilkins Center."

"What a small world."

"It's about to get smaller," Maddy said with a glum nod toward the parlor. "Seth's here."

Paige acted fast, taking Henri's arm and steering him toward the dining room. "Brunch is served, doctor. I'm sure some grits and grillades will provide solid fuel before your talk." She glanced over her shoulder at Maddy and mouthed, "Good luck!"

3

Well over six feet, Seth Marcum had no trouble spotting Maddy in the crowded parlor. As he made his unwelcome approach, she saw he wore his the usual scolded puppy look. Not this time, she thought. No matter what Seth pulls from his tired bag of tricks, I'm not going to get suckered back onto that rollercoaster.

"Hey, babe," he said, as casually as if discussing the weather. "How's it going?"

Maddy noted the Saints tee-shirt, frayed jeans and backwards baseball cap. Dear God, she thought. What was I thinking? A thirty-three-year-old librarian and a twenty-five-year-old perennial frat boy? She knew of course. When she met Seth at the Spotted Cat, a jazz joint in the Faubourg Marigny, she'd been totally disarmed by a sweet goofiness and zest for life making her ignore both the age difference and educational disparity. Before she knew it, they were back at her place, and, although the sex was initially rewarding, after a few months it disintegrated like everything else. Out of nowhere, Seth's fun-loving nature was bulldozed by mood swings as volatile and unpredictable as the hurricanes that roared out of the Gulf. It was, Maddy decided, time to board up the house and get the hell out of Dodge.

"What do you want, Seth?"

"Just wanna talk, I guess."

"After last night I think we're through talking."

His pale face went ruddy as reality scratched his brain. "Uh, yeah. Sorry about that."

"That's the problem. You're always sorry and you always say it won't happen again and it always does."

"But last night was different because I was bummed. See, that job I applied for over at—"

"It won't work, Seth. I've heard all the excuses. You got fired and can't make rent. Your family doesn't understand you. *I* don't understand you." Maddy shook her head. "You're right. I don't understand you, but I do understand that I can't handle the mood swings and that there's no point in talking about it, so why not do the gentlemanly thing and leave me alone?"

"You don't mean that."

"Yes, I do. And the sooner you agree, the better for both of us."

Seth's face hardened and his eyes shrunk to angry pinpoints. "Since when are you calling the shots?"

Damn, Maddy thought. Here we go again. Not about to let Seth's temper spoil Paige's salon, she headed for the front door. Her only hope was Jesse, and she buzzed with relief when the vigilant butler stepped from the shadows. He instantly assessed the situation and moved between her and Seth.

"Everything alright, Madeleine?"

She threw a warning glance toward Seth. "I'm fine, Jesse, but Mr. Marcum is leaving."

"Says who?" Seth grunted.

"Says me," Jesse replied.

"Bullshit!"

Maddy knew Seth's protest was only bluster. So did Jesse. "Use common sense, kid. You may be twenty years younger, but I outweigh you by fifty pounds of pure muscle."

"He's a bouncer at House of Blues," Maddy warned.

"So what?" Seth sputtered, louder this time.

Paige overheard from the hall and hurried into the foyer. "Is there a problem?"

"No problem, Miss Paige," Jesse said coolly.

"Good." Paige grabbed an oversized bicep when Jesse took a menacing step toward Seth. "Are you alright, Seth dear?"

The soothing tone and term of endearment caught Seth off guard. Anger morphed into confusion, and his face contorted with shame. "I'm...I'm sorry, Paige." He looked at Maddy. "Okay. I'm leaving."

When Seth bolted through the door, Maddy blinked with relief. "I'm sorry, Paige. I'm so embarrassed."

"That boy's bad behavior is hardly your fault, and he was an invited guest after all." Paige patted Jesse's arm. "Anyway, crisis averted courtesy of this gentleman."

"Just doing my job, Miss Paige."

"Your job description hardly includes wrangling rowdy guests. I owe you one." As Jesse smiled modestly and resumed his post by the door, Paige tucked Maddy's hand inside her elbow and nodded toward the dining room. "Now let's eat. I'm dying for you to try my new twist on oysters Bienville. They're too divine."

Maddy burst out laughing. "Sometimes you amaze me."

"What do you mean?"

"You're absolutely amazing in a crisis. One minute you're facing down violence, and the next minute you're talking about food."

"But, darling! That's what we do in New Orleans!"

"I suppose you're right." Maddy was grappling with that bitter reality when she spotted Henri Chabrol carrying a plateful of food toward an empty corner. "It looks like your guest of honor is eating by himself."

"Oh, dear. And me with a thousand hostess-y things to do. Would you be a doll and keep him company?"

"Sure. But that reminds me—"

"Of what?"

"Do you honestly think these people will pay attention to a lecture on quantum physics? And since when do you read *Scientific American*? You're my best friend, and I know damned well you don't read anything more challenging than French *Vogue*."

Paige cackled. "I'd be offended if that weren't true. The truth is there was a copy of *Scientific American* in my dermatologist's waiting room, and when I saw a cover story on Henri and Tulane, I couldn't resist looking inside and...oh, I don't know. There's something about a man in a lab coat. Don't you think he's dreamy?"

Maddy didn't see that coming. "You sound more like Carlota every day."

"Nonsense. I'm just between husbands. Now answer my question."

Maddy glanced in Henri's direction and opted for diplomacy. "Oh, I don't know."

"Of course you do. You said I'm your best friend, so tell me the truth."

"Alright. He's bright and certainly polite, but don't you think he's a bit professorial?"

"I hardly intend to sleep with his mind, darling." Paige gave her a quick buss on the cheek. "And as far as this quantum physics business is concerned, I'm guessing the good doctor will surprise us all."

4

Paige was right. Once Henri began, Maddy lost herself in his speech and forgot about Seth. What she feared would be either bone-dry or overly erudite teemed with color and humor and more than a few jolts. The biggest revelation was Henri's smooth segue from Hugh Everett's parallel universes to an enthralling discussion of time travel. When he began drawing things to a close an hour later, he had everyone's full attention, even those who had overindulged in Paige's trademark Bellinis.

"Fascination with the phenomenon is almost as old as recorded history and continues to pervade our culture," he concluded. "The *Mahabharata,* a Sanskrit epic of ancient India possibly dating to the eight century B.C.E., traveled into the future. Time travel became an especially popular plot device in nineteenth-century novels which are still widely read. As kids, we studied Washington Irving's *Rip Van Winkle* and H.G. Wells's *The Time Machine* and saw the movies too. Ensuing generations flocked to the *Back to the Future* films, and even Harry Potter got into the act with his *Prisoner of Azkaban*. My personal favorite is *A Christmas Carol* with Ebenezer Scrooge traveling back and forth in time. True, he couldn't interact with what he saw or heard, but it could be said that Charles Dickens was arguing the existence of Everett's parallel universes. Dickens, however, might not have been so daring had he been familiar with the Grandfather Paradox." Henri closed his folder of notes and scanned the room, eyes flickering from one face to another before lighting on Maddy. "Let's assume a man travels back in time and kills his grandfather before his father is conceived. That would mean he and his father are never born. Of course, if he were not alive, he couldn't have traveled back in time and dispatched poor old granddad in the first place. Therein lies the paradox." Henri smiled and looked at his watch. "Now, at the risk of making a bad joke, I'm out of time."

Everyone laughed, and Paige glowed as Henri got a standing ovation, a first for her salon speakers. Her guests were so enthusiastic that they insisted on a question and answer period resulting in a lively debate about time travel. The discussion might have continued into cocktail hour if she hadn't shaken her famous elephant bells to end things.

"That's enough, everyone. You'll wear the poor man out."

"Let us have one more question, Paige," Joe Romero insisted.

She glanced at Henri who nodded agreement. "Alright."

"I'm sure we'd all like to know the professor's personal opinion on time travel."

"For now, I'm afraid it must remain the domain of science fiction writers," Henri replied. "If it were possible, wouldn't we be overrun with visitors from the future?"

"How do you know we're not?" Joe pressed.

"That's a good question, sir, and the answer is, I don't."

"Then why—?" Joe persisted.

Noting Henri's look of desperation, Paige rattled the bells again. "Okay, folks. Show's over. Thanks for coming everyone." As the party exodus began, she motioned Henri over. "Madeleine and I are having cocktails in the library, Dr. Chabrol. Please say you'll join us."

When he hesitated, Maddy said. "If you stay, we promise not to talk about time travel."

He smiled impishly. "On the contrary, I promise to leave if you don't."

"You're not tired of the subject?"

"*Mais, non.* Why would I tire of my favorite subject?"

Maddy's eyebrows rose. "Do you speak French?" Henri nodded. "Then I have something to talk to you about, something that happened last night."

"Oh?"

Paige gave them a gentle push toward the library. "You two go ahead while Jesse and I get rid of the hangers-on. I'll join you in a jiffy."

Maddy led Henri down a long hall to double cypress doors gleaming with ormolu and swung them back to reveal an opulent private library. Mahogany shelves rose twelve feet on every wall, filled with rare and expensively bound books and dotted with strategically spaced authors' busts. An enormous Aubusson carpet sprawled across a parquetry floor, and a wheeled ladder waited to bring the most inaccessible volumes within reach. Oversized leather chairs flanked a fireplace, and a nineteenth century Spanish credenza sparkled with crystal decanters.

Henri looked envious. "I could spend the rest of my life in this room."

"Me too. It was Paige's second husband's idea. They spent hours in here, talking and reading together." Maddy expected Henri to ask what happened to the marriage, but he was staring so raptly at a bust of Dante she wondered if he was listening. "It's beautiful, isn't it?"

"They all are, but Dante is one of my favorite writers. In fact, *The Divine Comedy* was what first whetted my interest in time travel. I yearned to tag along with Dante and Virgil, especially on their journey through hell."

"Really?"

"Really."

She smiled. "What would you say if I confessed that I wanted to be Beatrice's best friend?"

"I'd say we have something very unusual in common."

"Indeed." Maddy ran a fingertip across brass labels on the decanters. "Brandy? Sherry? Port?"

"Brandy, please, and forgive me for that digression. You said you have something to tell me about last night?"

"Yes, I do." Henri listened closely as she described the caped figures in the fog and how they appeared to hover between reality and illusion. "I know that's nothing unusual in this old carnival city, but one of the figures, a man, called out to me in nineteenth century French."

"How do you know?"

"My master's degree is in French, and because my undergrad degree was in history I made it a point to study some of the older dialects."

"Did you answer him back, this stranger in the street?"

Maddy nodded and handed him the brandy. "At first I thought he was asking me to a party. You know. The way people do in the Quarter. But this was...different."

Henri sipped the brandy and set the snifter aside. "How so?"

Maddy took a deep breath. "He returned in my dreams last night. Of course I often dream about things I experience right before bedtime. A movie I was watching or book I was reading. Conversations sometimes."

"Nothing odd about that," Henri insisted as they sat in the big chairs. "I've read a good deal about dreams and dreamers and find them endlessly fascinating."

"Then you're going to love this one. The guy asked me along on another journey, and this time I went. It's funny that you should mention *The Divine Comedy* because he reminded me of Virgil with his long robes."

"Where did he take you?"

"I pieced some of it together after I woke up, but now I don't remember much."

Henri leaned toward her and rested elbows on his knees. "Please try, Madeleine."

"Why?"

"Please," he said again.

Maddy was unnerved by the urgency in a voice more telling than asking, but wasn't eager to reveal the disturbing dream to someone she just met. Yet, under Henri's mesmeric stare, her reluctance eroded. As inchoate images stirred in her head, she closed her eyes to better concentrate on the flickering fragments. She described them as they became sharper and continued her recitation until her guide vanished back into the fog.

"Open your eyes, Madeleine."

Maddy obeyed and squinted at Henri's blurred image. She was woozy and disoriented. "What...happened?"

Paige floated grandly into the room but stopped abruptly when she saw Maddy's ashen face. "Good heavens! What on earth have you two been talking about?"

Henri ignored the question and knelt at Maddy's feet. He took her hands and whispered. "Please tell me you're alright."

Maddy slowly grasped the situation. "I'm...fine."

"You don't look fine." Paige looked from one to the other, concern turning into annoyance. "Well? Are you two going to tell me what happened or not?"

"I was telling him about a dream and I...I sort of blacked out for a moment."

"That must've been some dream."

"It was about that guy in the street last night. The one who asked me to a party." She pulled away from Henri and leaned back. "Wow."

Paige poured a shot of bourbon. "Here, honey. This ought to perk you up."

Maddy waved it away. "No, thanks. The moment was a little intense, that's all."

"Suit yourself." Paige downed the whiskey and smiled. "Waste not, want not."

Henri sat again. "What happened isn't so unusual, Madeleine. One of New Orleans's many unique charms is her talent for conjuring the past. I experienced something similar in Venice once when I wandered the city alone. I was listening to my footsteps echo alongside some foggy, deserted canal when the echoes changed to voices. Venice can be dicey if you stray too far from the Piazza, and I was deep in the Cannaregio *sestiere*." He looked from Maddy to Paige and back again. "What unnerved me far more was that I was hearing Renaissance Italian. It was like eavesdropping on the Medicis."

Coolness crawled down Maddy's spine. "My God!"

Paige looked at Maddy. "Like the fellow speaking old French last night."

"Yes."

"Did you talk to them?" Maddy asked.

"I never saw them. They and their voices were swallowed by the fog, and it was as if I had imagined the whole thing."

"Did you dream about them afterward?"

"I'm afraid the similarity ends there."

"I had a similar experience at Baton Rouge," Paige said. When the others looked in disbelief, she smiled. "Oh, don't be silly. I only wanted to lighten the moment."

Maddy got slowly to her feet. "I'd better be going, Paige. It's been a long day and I'm suddenly very tired."

"May I walk you home?" Henri asked.

Maddy responded without hesitation. "Thank you. I'd like that." After the unpleasantness with Seth, she worried that he might be waiting outside to pick up where they left off. "I live a few blocks up Royal, near Dumaine."

"What happened to our little cocktail hour?" Paige protested.

"Forgive me, but I'm a bit tired too," Henri said.

Paige immediately retreated. "No, no. You should forgive me. You must be exhausted after your speech and all those questions. I'll see you two out."

Henri bowed. *"Merci, madam."*

5

Maddy and Henri headed down Ursulines toward the river. As they approached the corner of Royal Street, a tourist carriage drew up alongside the curb, close enough for them to hear the driver's spiel. Henri paused to listen.

"In 1728, girls from fine Paris families were imported as wives for the Louisiana colonists. They were called casket girls because they brought their dowries in caskets. Or so everyone thought." When the man paused for dramatic effect, Henri's face darkened. "Historians now believe those caskets were used to transport vampires from the old world to the new. If you've read any of Anne Rice vampire novels, you already know that—"

Henri gave Maddy an apologetic look before yelling at the driver. "Why are you lying to these people?" Totally blindsided, the driver was speechless as Henri marched over to address the bewildered tourists. "I'm a professor at Tulane University, ladies and gentlemen, and I assure you those girls' trunks were filled with clothing issued by the Mississippi Company which underwrote their journey. Granted the odd-shape trunks resembled caskets, but the similarity ended there." He glared at the driver. "Unless you prefer to believe in vampires and that every other house in the French Quarter is haunted."

Embarrassed and angered, the driver told his fares to ignore Henri. "The Quarter is full of crazies and drunks, folks."

Henri stepped closer, fists on hips. "You're opening yourself to a slander suit, pal."

The driver's face blazed, and for a moment Maddy worried he might throw a punch at Henri. Instead he mouthed "Asshole!" and flapped the reins hard against the mule's back.

Henri jumped back as the carriage lurched away from the curb and headed down Royal. He turned to Maddy, eyes narrowed with outrage.

"Do you believe that philistine, concocting such a ridiculous tale?"

"I'm afraid so. I hear those guys below my balcony all the time, spouting ridiculous things. If they did their homework, they'd know our history is a lot more colorful than anything they can make up." She paused to ponder the unexpected show of bravado. "I must say that was very impressive, sir. Like watching someone being challenged to a duel."

Henri was still seething. "My temper is a genie I try to keep in the bottle. I apologize, my dear."

"For what? Being my hero?" She calmed him by taking his arm as they turned onto Royal Street. "No apology needed."

My dear, Maddy thought. She couldn't remember when a man had called her that and certainly not one this appealing. She wondered why she had dismissed him at first, especially after Paige's gushing, and now found herself wanting to lean against his shoulder as they walked on. Instead, she changed the subject.

"What did you mean earlier today, when you said you were testing me?"

"I was curious to know if you were as intelligent as I suspected."

"Am I?"

"Absolutely." He smiled. "Not about quantum mechanics perhaps, but I suspect you're more cognizant of parallel universes than you think."

"Maybe so. When I see videos of flood victims in Peru or suicide bombings in Iraq, I feel like I'm not living on the same planet as those people."

"Tell me more."

"Alright. Something even more unsettling happened when I came back to New Orleans after the storm. I entered a world as unfamiliar as it was familiar. Everyone walked around in a sort of daze, praying we'd wake up from the worst imaginable nightmare. I read up on post-traumatic stress syndrome, but I kept thinking this was something more, almost an out-of-body experience." She squeezed the inside of Henri's elbow. "Is that strange?"

"To the contrary, it's very perceptive." Maddy was about to ask him to elaborate when he stopped at the front door of her apartment building. "Here we are."

She smiled and released his arm. "Thanks for the most interesting day I've had in a long time."

"I might say the same thing." He retrieved a small package from his coat pocket and held it out. "I hope you won't think me presumptuous."

"Is that a gift?" He nodded. "But you don't even know me."

"The truth is I planned to give it to Paige, a sort of hostess gift."

"Why didn't you?"

"She's a wonderful hostess and I mean no disrespect, but after meeting you I decided you would appreciate it more."

"I still don't understand," Maddy protested.

"See for yourself." Henri pressed the little box into her hand. "Please."

Maddie hesitated, staring at the package a long moment before opening it to find a silver lady's wrist watch. She noted the delicate marcasite insets. "It's art deco, isn't it?"

"Indeed it is. From 1939 to be precise."

"It's lovely, Henri, but I can't accept it."

"If it gives me pleasure, why not?"

"Because I don't know you well enough and because it's a bit too intimate."

"Ah. An old fashioned girl, eh?"

"About some things, yes."

Henri looked pleased. "You've no idea how much I respect that, Madeleine, but perhaps we can strike a compromise. Keep the watch for now. If, after a time, you're overwhelmed with impropriety, feel free to return it."

"Alright." Maddy blushed. "You win."

"Hopefully we both win." Henri took her hand, leaned down and brushed it with his moustache. "Until we meet again, Mademoiselle St. Jacques."

"Indeed," Maddy replied, hoping his old world manners weren't some kind of act.

He turned to go, reconsidered and looked back. "May I tell you something, strictly *entre nous?*"

"*Bien sûr.*"

"What I told those people about time travel was a lie."

Maddy was taken aback. "What do you mean?"

"Exactly what I said, my dear."

Before she could question him further, Henri executed another trademark bow and bustled toward Canal Street. Maddy considered going after him but caught herself when a more immediate mystery washed over her.

She hadn't told Henri Chabrol where she lived, so how did he know to stop at her front door?

6

Maddy adored lazy Sunday mornings, especially those cool enough to enjoy on her balcony. Taking advantage of a sweet river breeze, she lingered over beignets and café au lait and finished the *Times-Picayune* crossword puzzle before the heat drove her back inside. She cranked up her antediluvian a/c a couple of notches, stretched out on the couch and was immersed in a movie on television when the phone rang. She noted the caller ID before answering.

"Hi, Paige."

"Hello, darling. I've been perusing my engagement book and realized I have absolutely nothing on tap for this afternoon. How about cocktails at the Roosevelt and dinner at the Palace Café? My treat."

"Sounds lovely. I'll see you at the Sazerac."

"What's your rush?" Paige protested. "We haven't chatted in days, and I promise there's lots to talk about."

Maddy was anxious to get back to the movie. "Can't it wait until this afternoon?"

"I suppose so, as long as you're not interested in my 'almost' date with Dr. Henri Chabrol."

At the mention of Henri, Maddy glanced at the antique watch he gave her a week ago after Paige's salon. She'd worn it every day but decided to leave it home tonight. With her eye for jewelry, Paige was sure to notice, and Maddy didn't want to flaunt a gift originally intended for her best friend. "What's an 'almost' date?"

"I'll tell you if you turn down that damned TV."

"I'm watching *Chocolat,*" Maddy protested.

Paige's groaned. "Good lord, child! How many times have you seen that thing?"

"You know it's my favorite movie."

"Yes, yes. And I also know you identify with that Julia Binoche character who longs to be...how did you put it? 'A wanderer blown by the north wind.'"

"So? What's wrong with a little fantasizing?"

"You got me there. And I guess if you prefer old movies to me, there's nothing I can do about it. Ciao, darling."

"Ciao." Maddy chuckled at Paige's shift to drama queen mode and returned to the film. She was drooling over the confections in Juliet Binoche's *chocolaterie* when her ancient air-conditioner rumbled, clanked loudly and wheezed into silence. "Oh, no! Not in this damned heat!"

Maddy turned the control off and on again before pounding the unit with her fist. Sometimes that jolted it back to life, but the air-conditioner was dead as a doornail. Worsening matters, she knew it would take her a while to track down the off-premises super. She adored Jedediah Jefferson, but since Saturday was his night to howl, she knew he'd be sleeping it off on a Sunday morning. She looked at Henri's watch.

"Almost noon," she muttered. "Maybe he's up by now."

As she punched Jedediah's number, Maddy glanced at the overhead fan. Its weak breeze might help if she couldn't find the super, but it wouldn't guarantee a good night's sleep in this sticky heat. She was further discouraged when Jedediah's cell phone went straight to voice mail. She left an urgent message and went back to the movie.

New Orleans' summers are as debilitating as they are fierce, and without air conditioning the heat in Maddy's apartment rocketed fast. She fought it by stripping to khaki shorts and tee shirt and downing a constant flow of iced tea. That helped a little, but by the time Juliet and Johnny Depp were heating up the screen, Maddy was drowsing. She clicked off the television and stared at the overhead fan until its steady whirring and rotation grew hypnotic and lulled her toward sleep. As she began to drowse, the walls of the apartment wavered, retreated and rushed back with a ferocious whoosh. The impact startled her eyes shut, and when Maddy opened them again she was and was not where she had been. The room was familiar, but geometric wallpaper now covered the walls, and she was on a black tufted couch with mesa-flat arms. Maddy sat up and caressed the sofa back, and when she recognized it as art deco, she jumped up like she'd been stung.

"What the heck—?"

Other art deco furnishings crowded the small room, chairs, tables and a pair of torchiere floor lamps. Maddy was drawn to a tall cabinet in the corner which turned out to be a Philco floor model radio. She marveled at the waterfall motif and flashy gold speaker cloth and couldn't resist turning the on switch. The Bakelite face lit up, and when almost a full minute passed before she heard music, she remembered Grandmama Aglaé saying the old radios needed to warm up before playing. The top of the chassis was cluttered with photographs of Greta Garbo, Mae West, Charlie Chaplin and other long-dead film stars Maddy couldn't identify.

"Wow," she muttered. "Somebody's a movie fan."

Maddy moved trance-like around the room, startled to spot something familiar propped in a chair. When she moved into the apartment, she'd found a souvenir pillow from the 1939 New York World's Fair on the top shelf of a closet. Except for the faded silk and tarnished gold fringe, it was in surprisingly good shape, prompting Maddy to have it cleaned and re-stuffed and given a place of honor on her bed. Now here it was again, bright and brand new with gleaming fringe and, she guessed, placed there by its original owner. Maddy picked it up and was unnerved when she went weak in the knees. She settled back on the couch, closed her eyes again and lost herself in Tommy Dorsey's Song of India. She was drifting toward sleep when she heard a strange clicking sound. She got up and turned off the radio, cocking her head as she tried to determine the source of the noise. It grew louder as she approached the front door and louder still when she went into the hall. She followed it to the base of a narrow flight of stairs leading to the third floor. Although she'd been in this apartment building almost six years, Maddy had never been to the top floor, and, until now, assumed it was an empty attic. She grabbed the banister and swung onto the stairs, taking them two at a time. The heat soared with each step, and by the time she reached the door at the top, the air was stifling and the peculiar clacking was louder than ever. She knocked. The noise stopped and a man's voice rang out.

"Come in please!" She pushed the unlocked door and winced as rusty hinges protested. "Isn't that sound dreadful? I can never seem to get around to fixing it."

The man faced her as he stood, a quizzical expression on his pale moon face. He looked to be in his late twenties, short and slender with unruly brown hair and a neat moustache. He wore a white, short-sleeved shirt with suspenders and a pair of dark trousers hiked above his waist. He'd been sitting at a small table by a dormer window, the only one in the tiny garret room, and what perched on that table was the source of the clacking noise.

A typewriter! Maddy thought. She'd never seen or heard one except in movies and on television and couldn't imagine why this man used one in the age of computers.

"I'm Tom," he said finally. His frank appraisal reminded Maddy she was naked under the tee shirt. "Are you a neighbor?"

She nodded. "I'm Madeleine. I live on the second floor."

"Oh, dear. I hope my typing didn't disturb you. These old typewriters are awfully loud." His shoulders rose and fell as he looked at the antiquated machine. "It looks like it was purloined from the *Musée Mechanique*, doesn't it?"

Maddy had no idea what he meant. "Your typing didn't bother me, but I got curious when I heard it. I didn't know anyone lived up here."

"I've been here about a month." Tom gestured helplessly

around the room. Aside from the battered table and folding chair, the only other furniture was an equally derelict chest of drawers and a single unmade bed. A bare light bulb hung from the ceiling. "I'm afraid it's not much, and I know it's improper to ask a lady into one's bedroom." He stepped aside and offered his chair. "But would you like to sit down?"

"Thanks." Maddy sat by the open window, grateful for a fitful breeze off the Mississippi. "How can you work in this awful heat?"

"That thing helps a little, and when it doesn't, I get as cross as ten flies." Tom nodded at an old fashioned fan wheezing atop the chest. "Of course at night the mosquitoes nearly eat me alive, but I occasionally scrounge a citronella candle from one of the bars." He reddened slightly. "I go out whenever I can afford a drink."

"Sounds like you're the quintessential artist starving in his garret. Living *la vie Bohème* and all that."

"To be perfectly frank, Bohemia ain't all it's cracked up to be. It would sure be nice to have three squares a day. Then again, I'm not looking forward to the day I stop suffering because that will mean I'm dead!"

Tom chuckled, rather nervously, Maddy thought. She glanced at the sheaf of papers beside the typewriter and read the title aloud.

"*Moth*? That's an interesting name for a book."

Tom smoothed the rumpled sheets and sat down. "Actually it's a play."

"Your first?"

Another nervous laugh. "At the rate I'm going, my last."

"You're much too young to be discouraged," Maddy insisted. "I want to write but don't have any real flair. That's a nice way of saying I don't have any talent."

"I'm sure you're being modest." Tom looked flummoxed. "My stars! I wish I had something cold to offer you, Miss Madeline."

Maddy smiled at the little formality. "My, but you have

beautiful manners."

Tom's cheeks went russet. "Miss Edwina says there's no excuse for bad manners, even if you're poor white trash."

"Miss Edwina?"

"My mother." He glanced at the ceiling. "I can just hear her now, saying she can't stand a naked light bulb any more than she can stand a rude remark or vulgar action."

Maddy considered the deep drawl. "Are you from Mississippi?"

"Why, yes. Columbus in fact. Why do you ask?"

"You don't have a Louisiana accent, and Mississippians are unusually polite."

"That's sweet of you to say so."

"Where's Columbus?"

"Up on the Delta."

Maddy pursed her lips. "I've heard about the Mississippi delta all my life but never knew exactly where it was."

"It stretches from the Peabody Hotel in Memphis to Catfish Row in Vicksburg."

"But why do they call it a delta? It's on the Mississippi, not at its mouth."

Tom gave her an impish look. "You're sure full of questions, Miss Madeleine."

"I'm a librarian."

He looked pleased. "How wonderful! Where do you work?"

"At the Wilkins Research Center on Chartres Street."

"I don't believe I've heard of it."

"Then you must come by some time, especially if you're writing about Louisiana. Our collection of local research material is the best in the country."

"Thank you. I promise I'll do that."

Maddy patted the manuscript. "Do you mind if I ask what *Moth* is about?"

"I'm not sure myself since it's in the very early conceptual stage, like one of several I'm working on." Tom gave her a quixotic smile. "Would you like to guess?"

"I'm sure I'd be wrong."

"Well, in all fairness it's allegorical. The play isn't about moths at all, at least not the six-legged variety."

"I don't understand."

"My heroine has a delicate beauty that must avoid strong light. Her uncertain manner and penchant for gossamer clothes suggest a moth, you see."

"That's fascinating." Maddy thought a moment. "And a little familiar."

Tom looked displeased. "How so?"

"Oh, I don't mean it doesn't sound original, only that— oh, my Lord!" Maddy jumped at the sound of screeching metal and loud clanging in the street below. "What was that?!"

"Good heavens, Miss Madeleine. That's nothing to be afraid of. It's just that rattle-trap streetcar that bangs through the Quarter, up one old narrow street and down another."

Maddy's forehead erupted with sweat. "What…what did you say?"

"I said it's the streetcar." Tom cocked his head. "Is something wrong, ma-am?"

Maddy got shakily to her feet. "What's a streetcar doing on Royal Street?"

"It's been there for years as far as I know."

"But the streetcars were taken out of the Quarter before I was born."

Tom looked confused. "I'm afraid I don't know what you're talking about."

Maddy flinched when the streetcar clanged again and rumbled down Royal Street. She listened closely, terrified and confused, until it faded away. "Dear God! How is this possible?"

"How is what possible?" When Maddy didn't respond, Tom said, "Do you want me to get you some water or help you back to your apartment? It's probably the heat, but I'm afraid you're looking a little piqued."

"All I want," Maddy said slowly, heart pounding in her ears, "is for you to tell me the name of that streetcar."

"Why, that's the streetcar that goes out to Desire Street, Miss Madeleine. Everyone in the Quarter knows that."

Maddy turned toward the fan, blades lazily whup-whupping through the heavy air. It was the last thing she remembered before collapsing in Tom's arms.

7

Maddy sat up and rubbed her eyes, promptly falling back against the couch pillows when she was swamped by a wave of vertigo. The stifling heat didn't help as she struggled to grasp what had happened. The last thing she remembered was growing faint before falling into her neighbor's arms. Tom, she thought foggily. His name was Tom, and he was certainly nice enough, but something unpleasant drove Maddy into her memory bank. Her apartment was hushed except for the monotonous whir of the overhead fan. She glanced up but quickly looked away when it bothered her eyes. After a few cloudy moments, Maddy realized it wasn't images she was trying to invoke but sounds, ear-splitting screeches accompanied by loud clanging. It rushed back, hurting her ears before melding into something more immediate and recognizable. Her cell phone was ringing inches from her head.

"Damn!" She grabbed the phone, wondering why she chose Ride of the Valkyries for a ringtone. Her brain cleared further when she heard a familiar voice.

"Hey, Maddy. I got your message."

"Jedediah. Thank God!" She sat up again, relieved when there was no dizziness. "I'm burning up over here. How soon can you come over?"

"I'm downstairs. Thought I'd give you a heads-up."

"Great. Come on up." Maddy barely had enough time to splash cold water on her face before answering the superintendent's knock. Jedediah Jefferson was an affable middle aged black man who, like a lot of New Orleanians, worked and played hard, believed life was one long celebration and never apologized for it. One look at his bloodshot eyes told

Maddy it was business as usual. She smiled. "Hmmm. Some-body's been partying."

He chuckled. "Reckon I got me a touch of the French Quarter flu."

"Oh?" Maddy chuckled at the local slang for hangover.

"Sure enough, we hung out on Frenchmen Street last night, listened to some music and had a few drinks." Jedediah rolled his eyes. "Now, I'm gonna tell the truth and shame the devil. It was more than a few drinks."

"I'm betting you and Serena had yourselves a time."

"Indeed we did."

"That's all that matters then." Maddy didn't care how much the guy boozed as long as he did his job. She nodded at the air-conditioner. "Think you can fix that old relic?"

"One more time I reckon. Then you better talk to the landlord about a new one."

Maddy snorted. "You know what a tightwad MacGruder is. Every time I've asked him he says you'll fix it again."

"I'll talk to him. This thing's on its last leg, and he knows I won't bullshit him."

"You're an angel, Jedediah. I don't know what I'd do without you."

"You'd burn up, that's what." Jedediah pulled a bandana from his overalls and mopped his forehead. "I swear it's hotter inside than out. A man could die of thirst."

Maddy took the hint. "How about a beer?"

Jedediah beamed. "Now who's the angel?"

"Sandwich too?"

"No, thanks. I grabbed an oyster po' boy at the Nelly Deli."

Suddenly ravenous, Maddy made a sandwich from some leftover chicken salad and kept Jedediah company while he worked. "How's it look?" she asked between bites.

"Downright pitiful. This old thing belongs in a museum."

Maddy munched thoughtfully. "That reminds me. Did you ever hear of something called the *Musée Mechanique*?"

"Sure enough. It was a place in the Quarter that had coin-operated mechanical toys. I remember my daddy talked about looking in the windows. Black folks couldn't go inside back in those days." Jedediah took a healthy swig of beer and probed deeper into the air conditioner. "I think if I grease this old motor real good, it just might come back to life."

Maddy only half-heard, still thinking about the *Musée Mechanique*. She excused herself and went to her laptop in the bedroom. A quick search took her to a website for the *Musée Mecanique* in San Francisco but returned nothing about New Orleans. She was about to try an alternate spelling when Jedediah called from the living room.

"Yo, Maddy! We're back in business." He nodded at the humming air-conditioner when she returned. "For the time being anyway."

"Think it'll get me through the night?"

"It's good for a few days, but I'll call MacGruder first thing in the morning." He drained the beer and handed the bottle to Maddy. "Thanks, lady. That hit the spot."

Jedediah was halfway across the room when her voice stopped him. "What do you know about the tenant upstairs?"

Jedediah cocked his head. "What tenant?"

"Tom. The guy in that garret at the top of the stairs."

Jedediah laughed and mopped his forehead again. "I think the heat's got you."

"What's that supposed to mean?"

"There's nothing up there but an unfinished attic."

That wasn't what Maddy wanted to hear. "Are you sure?"

"Sure I'm sure. I've managed this building for twenty-three years, ever since McGruder restored the place, and I guarantee there are only four apartments. Two on this floor and two downstairs." He looked suspicious. "Did you hear noises up there or something?"

"I thought I did," Maddy said slowly, increasingly unsure.

"Could be pigeons if there's a broken window pane. Or rats. Want me to check it out?"

"Please. I'll come too."

Maddy's knees were a little rubbery as she followed Jedediah up the narrow stairs. His bulk blocked her view until he reached a flimsy wooden door at the top and pushed it open. She followed him inside and looked around. The place was empty, long-dead air smelling of must and age, and there were no signs of animal intrusion. The lone window overlooking Royal Street was opaque with dirt, panes filthy but intact.

"If there were animals, they didn't get in that way." Jedediah inspected the tiny, blazing hot room, searching for rat droppings and finding none. Satisfied there was no vermin infestation he turned to go until something caught his eye. "I'll be damned. I never noticed that before."

"Noticed what?"

"That." Jedediah pointed to an empty socket hanging from the ceiling. "I never knew there was electrical wiring up here, so I guess—"

Maddy's heart began racing. "You guess what?"

"This might've been an apartment at one time, but it would've been a long time ago. The thirties or forties maybe."

Defeated and confused, Maddy started back down the steps. "I'm sorry I dragged you up here, Jedediah. Obviously I was imagining things."

"Like I said before, it's probably the heat."

"Yeah. Probably."

8

After Jedediah left, Maddy paced like a caged animal, restless with confusion as she struggled to comprehend what happened on the third floor. Had she actually chatted with a young man named Tom or merely fever dreamed about it? She tried to convince herself that Jedediah was right about the heat, that she had succumbed to torpor intense enough to trigger a nightmarish fantasy. Frantic to make sense of things, she scoured the internet for information on day-mares. She felt better after reading case histories of troubling sensations spawned during wakefulness and decided to leave early for her rendezvous with Paige. If nothing else, she could lose herself in her favorite cocktail lounge in the city.

Like most of New Orleans, the Fairmont Hotel had been slammed hard and shut down by Hurricane Katrina. After four years and $145 million, it had been reborn as the Roose-velt, its name from 1923 to 1965, and was once again the epitome of bygone glamour. Entering the Sazerac Bar was like walking into the 1920s when Governor Huey Long was a regular and male customers helped the mixologist by pass-ing cocktail shakers the length of the bar. Maddy was espe-cially fond of Paul Ninas' dazzling art deco murals and the gracefully curved bar of African walnut. To her surprise, the notoriously tardy Paige was perched at the bar, cocktail in hand.

"Darling!" Paige smiled and waved before bussing Mad-dy's cheek. "I do believe we're making history."

"How so?"

"Two women meeting for cocktails and both of them ear-ly. It's positively revolutionary!"

"I'm early because I need a drink."

Paige's eyebrows soared. "You? The president of the Eve-rything-In-Moderation Club? I'm reeling!" She patted the bar stool beside her. "Climb aboard."

Maddy scanned the room. "Let's grab that corner ban-quette. I also need to talk and I want total privacy."

"Sounds serious." Paige picked up her glass and followed Maddy.

"It is." Maddy nodded at Paige's colorful drink. "What're you drinking?"

"A Sazerac of course. New Orleans' official cocktail and *la especialité de la maison.*" She looked puzzled. "In all the times we've been here, don't tell me you've never had one."

"Never. But since today is a day of firsts, bring it on."

Paige gave a waiter their drink order and leaned close when she and Maddy were alone. "What's this about a 'day of firsts'?"

"You want the long version or the short?"

"Let's start with the short."

"Okay." Maddy took a deep breath. "I'm losing my mind."

Paige reconsidered. "Hmmm. I think maybe I'd better have the long version."

"And I think I need that drink first."

Over Sazeracs, Maddy reiterated the encounter with the mysterious Tom and the trip to the attic with Jedediah. Paige listened closely, and, when Maddy finished, said, "I think Jedediah's right. I'll bet the whole thing was brought on by the heat. I've had some pretty crazy daytime dreams myself."

"I need to believe that, but what happened was too damned real. I could close my eyes right now and hear the screech of that old streetcar. The clanging bells too. I can even smell that apartment upstairs, everything from the stale bed sheets to the young man's sweat. Are your dreams that vivid?"

"No. And I barely remember them afterwards."

"So what do you think happened?"

"I don't know, darling, but I learned a long time ago that

not everything has an explanation."

"I wish I believed that." Maddy sipped the smooth blend of rye, bitters, sugar and absinthe. "Because I'm terrified about what might come next."

"Why should anything else happen? I'll bet this was a one-time thing."

"Then you'd lose the bet."

"What do you mean?"

"It wasn't the first time something like this happened."

Paige's blue eyes widened. "Now *I'm* the one who needs another drink."

"It was before Katrina hit," Maddy explained. "I was watching the Weather Channel and, like everyone else, trying to decide whether to evacuate or not. They were still predicting the storm might come up the mouth of the Mississippi and—"

"I remember all that," Paige interrupted. Like all New Orleanians, she was bone-weary of Katrina stories and urged Maddy to get to the point.

"I was listening to Jim Cantore's speculation about where the thing would make landfall when my apartment turned suddenly dark and the wind started gusting. I knew it couldn't be Katrina because she was two days out, and since the weather guys had forecast clear, sunny skies I went outside to see what was going on. And that's…that's when it happened."

She and Paige sipped their drinks.

"It was like that tornado scene in *The Wizard of Oz* with all sorts of things flying by. Chunks of metal flashing and shingles and trash cans. Palm fronds and tree limbs. The combination of wind and things crashing everywhere was deafening."

"Maybe it was a freak tropical storm like the one back in '98. I remember Nash Philips saying if that thing had hit during hurricane season it would've had a name."

"C'mon, Paige. You and I evacuated together, so I know

you were still here. You don't remember anything like I described?"

"Sorry, honey, but I don't. Why didn't you mention it when it happened?"

"Because everyone thought Katrina was the Big One, and I figured I'd hallucinated out of pure fear." Maddy closed her eyes a moment. "So much stuff was flying by that I could barely see across the street, but there's something else I remember. The cars."

"What cars?"

"The ones parked across the street. They were old, every one of them. I saw a 1962 Buick Electra and was thinking my rich Uncle Carl had one when I almost got hit by a limb and ran back inside. I started watching Cantore again and whatever was going on outside stopped. It didn't die down slowly either. It just stopped." She picked up her drink and studied Paige over the rim. "Those old sixties cars were gone too, and it was as if nothing unusual happened."

"Like what happened this morning?"

"Exactly." Maddy drained her glass and waved away the waiter's offer of another. "I keep thinking I'm overdue for a physical and should maybe get some tests done. Who knows? Uncle Carl's son Rudy has a screw loose. Maybe I do too." She grabbed her vibrating cellphone and checked the caller ID. "Oh, God. Not again."

"Seth?" Maddy made a face. "You're not going to answer it, are you?"

"Absolutely not. He's left apologies every day since making that scene at your brunch, but I meant what I said about ending the relationship. The guy's too unpredictable."

"Speaking of unpredictable." Paige looked mischievous. "I never told you about my 'almost' date with Henri Chabrol."

Maddy forced a smile. "I'm all ears."

"I invited him to Arnaud's for dinner and was all buffed and fluffed and waiting for the doorbell when the phone rang instead. It seems the good doctor had to go out of town on some last minute emergency or other."

"Since when do scientists have emergencies?"

"He didn't say, but the poor fellow apologized all over the place and promised another dinner after he gets back."

"When is that?"

"Sometime tonight he said." Paige took a final sip. "Know what I think? Before you go see your doctor, I think you should talk to Henri about these hallucinations."

"No way. It was hard enough to tell you, much less a virtual stranger."

"He's hardly a stranger," Paige insisted. "He's smart and sympathetic and kind and divinely sexy."

Maddy grinned. "And you're high as a kite."

"Right you are, darling." Paige flagged the waiter for the check. "It's time to get to the Palace and get some food in this tired, old carcass. Those damned Sazeracs went right to my head."

"Mine too. I'm not used to hard liquor." Maddy felt unsteady when she stood and turned the wrong way when they left the Sazerac Bar. "Whoa!"

Paige chuckled. "Canal Street's this way, darling."

Maddy grinned tipsily and took Paige's arm. She couldn't resist seizing the moment to emote with mock drama. "Whoever you are, I've always depended on the kindness of strangers."

Both women cackled and lurched down the Roosevelt's block-long lobby of gilded columns and crystal chandeliers, giddily unaware that they were being closely watched.

Part 2

"Don't you just love those long rainy afternoons in
New Orleans
when an hour isn't just an hour,
but a little piece of eternity dropped into our hands
— and who knows what to do with it?"

— Tennessee Williams, *A Streetcar Named Desire*

9

Maddy threw herself into work, determined to forget yesterday's puzzling events and railroad her life back on track. Luckily, Mondays were crazy busy at the Center and, working from her desk in the main reading room, she assisted a steady stream of locals and tourists researching everything from Sophie Newcomb pottery to Bourbon Street stripper Blaze Starr. She was hunched over her computer, scouring the catalogue for material on the 1988 Cabildo fire when she heard her name.

"Hello, Madeleine."

She looked into a pair of intense brown eyes. "Dr. Chabrol! Hi."

"Henri," he corrected. "How are you?"

"Fine." This time he was dressed for the heat in khaki shorts and a short-sleeved white shirt, and she liked the look. "I'm a little swamped this morning, but otherwise fine."

"I don't want to interrupt, but I was hoping we could have a chat."

Maddy motioned him to lean down again and whispered. "Conversation unrelated to work is seriously discouraged. Maybe you didn't notice my watchdog when you were here before." She discreetly indicated Georgia Warren, the head librarian monitoring staff activity from a far corner. Only this morning Warren had criticized Maddy for swapping her trademark bun for a trendy new haircut, and her gaze was now fixed on Henri.

"See what I mean?"

Henri pretended to shudder. "Will you join me for lunch at the House of Blues?"

"Thanks, but I brought my lunch today and planned to

eat it here."

"How about Woldenberg Park instead. We can watch the ships while we eat."

Maddy was more than tempted. Henri had mature charm to burn and exuded an unexpected sensuality that made her neck tingle. "I'd love to."

"Wonderful. I'll grab a muffaletta at Central Grocery and meet you back here at—?"

"Twelve fifteen sharp," she mouthed. "Ms. Warren's very strict about lunch hour."

"I'll be out front."

Maddy intentionally fueled her boss's disapproval by tossing Henri a saucy smile. As he walked away, she remembered Paige's suggestion to discuss her phantom upstairs neighbor with Henri. She remained reluctant until he met her outside and she suddenly found herself telling him everything, including the esoteric episode as Hurricane Katrina approached the city. Henri was silent until they found a shady spot by the Mississippi. His opening salvo was a shocker.

"Would you like to know more about Tom?"

"Are you saying he's real?!"

"He was."

"But how do you know?"

"What matters is that I do."

Her spirits plunged. "I don't understand."

"He died in 1983, but before I tell you more I need to know if you were wearing the watch I gave you when you met him."

She thought a moment. "In fact, I was."

"Do you know what watch you were wearing when you saw those old cars?"

"What do watches have to do with anything?"

"Please answer my question."

"God only knows, Henri. That was years ago."

"Do you have a lot of watches?"

"Three, counting the one you gave me."

"Think back."

"Okay. I wore a Relic back then, but it could have been my mom's old one."

Henri looked pleased. "Do you know when her watch was made?"

"Sure. 1965. It was a wedding gift from Daddy. He bought her a more expensive one for their silver anniversary, and I got her old one because I admired it so."

"You said those old cars dated from the sixties?"

"They might have been older. I don't remember."

"Let's have these later." Henri set his sandwich aside, prompting Maddy to do the same.

He took her hands and looked deep into her eyes. "I want you to give me something, Madeleine St. Jacques."

She was unsettled by his urgency and the use of her full name. "What do you want?"

"Don't be frightened," he said when her hands begin trembling. "Just look into my eyes and give me your resistance."

"My...my resistance? To what?"

"To the truth I'm about to tell you. Look in my eyes please."

Maddy recoiled. "Are you going to hypnotize me?"

"I promise I know nothing about hypnosis." Henri's voice was deeper now, more insistent as he gently squeezed her hands. "Please do what I tell you and...yes, that's it. I can feel the resistance flowing from your body into mine."

"You can?" Maddy asked in a small voice.

"Yes, indeed." An encouraging smile flickered across his lips before he grew serious again. "It's growing stronger by the second. There. You feel it too, don't you?"

"I feel something," she confessed.

"Can you describe it?"

"It make me heady, strong even, but at the same time I want to jump out of my skin."

"That's good. Very good."

Henri's grip tightened as he looked deeper, as if searching for something. Through the trees behind him, a monstrous Chinese freighter swept down the river, gathering speed as it caught the current and hurtled toward Dead Man's Curve. The eight-story leviathan turned Henri into a silhouette while everything else retreated into the shadows. Maddy shrank with fear when the noonday sun was obscured by a menacing cloud bank, but the moment she feared it would swallow them, it evaporated as though sucked out a window. The park and river grew bright, edges razor sharp, colors blindingly brilliant.

Henri released her hands. "How do you feel now?"

"More wide awake than I've ever been."

"What do you see?"

"It's like looking through a magnifying glass. Things look...surreal."

"Can you hear me alright?"

"Clear as a bell," she replied in a steady voice.

"Then you're right where you need to be. Now then. Shall I tell you about Tom?"

"Perhaps I should tell *you* about him."

Henri looked pleased. "You're ready to do that?"

"Oh, yes," Maddy replied dreamily. "Tom isn't his name, is it?"

"Yes and no." Henri's eyes gleamed with anticipation. "Go on."

"That play he was working on, the one called *Moth*. It's wasn't finished until years later, and he changed the title to *The Poker Night*. True?" Henri nodded. "Later on he changed the title again and his name too."

"Go on."

"The play became *A Streetcar Named Desire*, and Tom became Tennessee Williams." Maddy glowed with excitement. "My God, Henri! I met Tennessee Williams, didn't I?"

"You did indeed," he assured her.

"And that storm with those old cars was—?" She closed her eyes as the unfathomable truth rushed over her. "It was Hurricane Betsy!"

"Which hit New Orleans in 1965."

Maddy gasped as more reality dawned. "The same year that watch was made!" Henri nodded again. "But how…how is this possible?"

"Because you're a Courier, Madeleine."

"Courier?"

"I'll explain later, about the watches too. For now, I'll only say that if you choose a Courier's path, it will lead you on a journey beyond anything you could imagine."

"I believe you," Maddy said without hesitation.

"I'm deeply pleased."

"But—"

"But what?"

Maddy blinked, face awash in sunlight as the Chinese ship finally passed, taking the cool shadow with it. She waited until it disappeared around the great bend in the river before turning back to Henri and staring until comprehension gripped her. As she was drawn back to the here and now, she leaned toward Henri, driven by a force stronger than herself. Their lips were inches apart when she breathed her ultimatum.

"Tell me you know," she breathed.

"Of course I know," Henri replied warily. "I just didn't expect—"

"Expect what, *mon cher?*"

Henri swallowed hard. "I didn't expect it to happen so fast."

"That's a good thing, isn't it?"

"I don't know yet, but—"

"No 'buts,'" Her fingers touched his mouth. "Say it."

"Say what?"

"Say that we've had this date from the beginning."

"C'est vrai," Henri sighed as their lips met. "It's true."

10

Henri's house on Orange Street conjured fairy tales in Maddy's mind. A one-story raised cottage built in 1846, it floated on a cloud of banana trees, Chinese fan palms, and elephant ears making it invisible from the sidewalk. As she trailed him through the lush green maze, Maddy felt like she was in the tropics when a parrot screeched from a towering palm. On the small front porch, all but obscured by an arch of Carolina jasmine, Henri lightly kissed her cheek.

"Are you sure about this, Madeleine?"

"I've never been so sure of anything in my life."

Henri took her hand. "Come along then."

Once inside, Maddy scarcely saw her surroundings, aware only of Henri's touch as he led her toward a door at the end of the hall. He opened it and stepped aside. Beyond waited a bedroom dominated by a tall mahogany tester bed draped in a gauzy *mosquitaire.* She paused to absorb the dreamlike setting, pleased that it continued the ongoing fantasy.

"Perfect."

Henri squeezed her hand. "I hoped you'd think so. *Un moment.*" He drew heavy draperies across a pair of French doors and threw the room into deep shadow. "I sometimes have trouble sleeping. These curtains keep out the light." He started toward her, hesitated and stopped at the foot of the bed. "Forgive me, *chéri,* but I should warn you about something."

"Oh?"

"I was in a fire some years ago, and my back is badly scarred."

"I promise it won't bother me." Maddy sat on the edge of the bed. "Come here."

Henri perched obediently beside her as Maddy unbuttoned his shirt. When she pushed it off his shoulders, the clean, grassy scent of *vetiver* rose from his skin, a cologne she knew only from historical novels. She took a deep breath before leaning around to see his back. The scar was a trail of reddened, cruelly gnarled flesh reaching from shoulder blades to the base of his spine. Even dimly viewed it was gruesome, and in spite of her promise, Maddy caught her breath.

Henri trembled. "I'll put my shirt back on."

"No!" She leaned around to look at his face. "Does it hurt?"

"Sometimes."

"I won't ask what happened, but I do want you to open the curtains."

"Are you sure?"

She gave him a sweet smile. "You keep asking me that, Henri."

"I want everything as it should be. *Est-ce que tu comprends ce que je dis?*"

"*Oui, mon cher.*" Maddy adored that he spoke French. "*Moi aussi.*"

Henri yanked the draperies wide to flood the room with afternoon sunshine. He paused, caught by the light and seemingly unaware of the rustle of clothing as Maddy undressed. When he turned around, she was naked against the white pillows, one hand behind her head, the other resting discreetly in her lap like a modern day odalisque.

"*Sacre bleu!*" Henri whispered, shedding the rest of his clothes as he crossed the room. "You take my breath away!"

Maddy shivered with anticipation as he nestled naked beside her and kissed her with a gentleness as sweet as it was fleeting. Desire stirred quickly in both, and, at Maddy's urging, Henri took her fast. She rode with him as they mounted a rapturous wave and shook hard as both were delivered. When she returned to reality, Henri, body bathed in sweat, face glowing with satisfaction, was gazing into her eyes.

"Welcome back, *ma cher.*"

Maddy blinked away mental cobwebs. "Why do I keep fading in and out around you?"

"You've not experienced *le petit mort* before?"

"*Jamais!* I've only read about it."

Henri smiled. "Good. I'm honored to be the first man to take you there."

"I'm honored too, although it was a little scary." When Henri started to pull away, Maddy kissed him until she felt him stir. "You're ready again, my darling!"

"Yes!" he murmured, investigating her flesh as well. "So are you."

They took longer this time, striving for a release even more intense and exhausting. Henri arrived first and gasped hard before growing still. "Now I'm the one experiencing the little death." He held Maddy close, kissing her eyes, nose and lips until the last erotic shudder coursed away. "You're magnificent, Madeleine St. Jacques. Dear God, what a day of revelations!"

"For me too. You continue to give me memorable moments." Maddy sighed again and stretched like a contented cat before resting her head on Henri's chest. She shut her eyes and let her mind drift. How different this man was from her other lovers, especially Seth. Something, maturity perhaps, had taught Henri how to please a woman, how to raise her to a certain plateau and hover until she was ready to descend. The fact that they attained this release together made it beyond satisfying. How, she wondered in amazement, had an innocent lunch by the river led to such passion, in an enchanted little cottage no less. "Henri?"

"*Oui?*"

"Kiss me."

He grinned. "Haven't you had enough kissing for one afternoon?"

"Jamais," she whispered. "Never."

11

At dusk, Henri's bedroom came alive with shadows. Filtered through nodding banana fronds, exotic birds fluttered across the wall and Venusian flowers bloomed on the floor. Freshly showered and wrapped in his robe, Maddy watched the chiaroscuro from bed, sipping fragrant *café au lait* and listening to the baritone in the shower. She couldn't recall when she had been so content and blew the man a kiss when he emerged with a towel around his waist.

"You know of course that I have a million questions to ask you."

"Considering what I told you by the river sounds like science fiction, I should think you would." Henri padded barefoot to an armoire and rummaged for his spare robe. "Go ahead."

"Suppose we start with this business of old watches."

"That's perfectly logical." Henri pulled on a robe. "We'll begin with my library. It's nothing like Paige's but...well, you'll see." He held out a hand and helped her from the high bed. "Come along, *mon petit ange.*"

Maddy was thrilled to be called his little angel. It wasn't the sort of endearment a woman over thirty heard, and it stoked childhood memories. "Papa used to call me '*mon petit choux.*'"

"My little cabbage."

"*Oui.* And when he was being playful, *mon petit choux-choux.*" Maddy cocked her head. "Where did you learn such beautiful French and acquire those old world manners? At first I thought you were just being professorial and formal, but now I think you might be the real deal."

"First things first, Madeleine." Henri put a hand on her

shoulders and gently steered her down the hall. He opened a door, then threw his arm wide. *"Voila!"*

"My God!"

The sound hit her first, the cacophonous ticking of more clocks than she'd ever seen in one place. Tucked atop mantle, table and desk and alongside books filling shelves on all four walls, they came in every shape, size and age. There were grandfather, grandmother and granddaughter clocks, wall clocks and table clocks and bracket clocks, even a Black Forest cuckoo clock. Maddy inspected them one by one before pausing by the mantle where twin candelabra flanked an ornate bronze clock.

"Gorgeous!"

"A Napoleon III Doré garniture," Henri said as Maddy gingerly caressed the clock face. "Garniture?"

"A Middle French term meaning a grouping of *objets d'art.*"

Maddy gave him a saucy smile. "You're teaching me all sorts of things today, professor."

"Touché." Henri nodded toward the corner. "That cabinet is my real pride and joy." Maddy inspected a case gleaming with rows of antique watches. "There are exactly one hundred, one for every year from 1850 to 1949. That empty slot held your 1939 Bulova until last week."

"What a fantastic collection." Maddy studied them a moment, then gestured around the library. "Isn't there a room like this in *The Time Machine?*"

"Indeed there is." Henri pulled a book off the shelves, deftly flipped the pages and held it out to Maddy. "I believe this is the passage."

Maddy read aloud about the clock-filled room before inspecting the winged sphinx on the cover. "I adore publishers who reprint classic with their original dust jackets."

Henri smiled. "Perhaps you didn't notice the slight foxing on the cover. Look inside."

Maddy was stunned by the publication date. "1895! My

Lord! This is a first edition!"

"They're all first editions, my dear."

Maddy closed the book and, like all conscientious librarians, carefully slid it back into its place on the shelf. She noted the titles flanking it, and read them aloud. "*Time and Again, Time Travel in Einstein's Universe: The Physical Possibilities of Travel Through Time, Time and Space, Time's Arrow and Archimedes' Point, Time Traveler: A Scientist's Personal Mission to Make Time Travel a Reality.*" She looked at Henri, face flushed with anticipation. "We'd better get back to the watches before I get overwhelmed."

"Fair enough." Henri glanced at the room's lone window and noted the deepening twilight. "I'll pour some wine and we'll sit outside. The back porch gets magical this time of day, and I can't think of a better place for what I have to tell you."

"Sounds perfect."

Your favorite wine is Pinot grigio I believe."

"How did you know?" Maddy thought a moment. "And how did you know where I live? That afternoon you walked me home from Paige's, you—"

"All in good time, my dear. No pun intended."

"Lead on, MacDuff."

Still in Henri's robe, Maddy explored the back porch and found it as charming as the cottage. Old fashioned white wicker chairs and a settee with a riot of curlicues reminded her of Grand-mère Aglaé's sun room, as did pots of hibiscus and flamingo plants. A grove of banana trees flaunted brilliant purple blooms and stalks of bright green fruit. Dutch pipes tangled at their feet while butterfly ginger cologned the air. As Henri said, the ambience was magical, and once Maddy settled on the love seat with a glass of wine, he took a chair and began.

"I must ask you again to keep an open mind like you did this afternoon. Otherwise you will find my words beyond incredible."

"I promise."

"Good." Henri took a sip of wine. "When I called you a Courier, I meant that you're in an elite group with the ability to move through time. Neither you nor anyone in your family knew you were born with this gift. It first manifested itself in dreams and later in the elaborate fantasy world you created as a child. I know, for example, all about Zenobia."

"No!" Maddy gasped. "My imaginary playmate? The one I believed was—?"

"Cleopatra's long lost cousin."

"My God, Henri! This is getting scary."

He patted her knee. "I promise there's nothing to be afraid of."

Maddy waved for silence while she sorted her cluttered thoughts. After a few moments, calm spread through her body like mulled wine. "Alright. I believe you. But even my mother didn't know about Zenobia, so how could you?"

"Because I'm the Marshal instructed to memorize you. It's no accident that I knew your address, your preference in wine and secret playmate. Nor is it an accident that you studied French and history or that I was schooled in the same things, along with physics and architecture. All was in preparation for us to meet once they decided you were ready to travel."

"They? Who are they?"

"The August Ones, those who guide our destiny by instructing us in our dreams. I know only that they are ageless and timeless and simply *are*." Henri flicked a mosquito from his forearm. "You must understand that time is connected by an infinite number of waves that occasionally erode and threaten to snap. There are Couriers all over the world whose jobs are, among other things, to keep these waves from breaking and altering the course of history. Owing to the current miserable state of global affairs, you're probably thinking that changing history is not a bad thing, that it could prevent global warming, war, poverty, hunger, disease and so forth. Sad to say this is not the lot of us Homo sapiens. Time has proven again and again that man was put on Earth to wreak havoc, with an occasional burst of splendor to keep us from sinking into utter madness and chaos."

"Hellenic Greece," Maddy murmured softly. "The Renaissance. The Maya."

"Among others." Henri studied Maddy as she absorbed her destiny and hastened to address the doubt flickering across her face. "You know you have the power, Madeleine. You felt it this afternoon by the river. There's no other explanation for your knowing, without my coaching, that you'd met Tennessee Williams and experienced a hurricane that existed forty-five years ago. It's an exhilaration you'll never forget. I know."

Maddy's eyes widened. "You're a Courier too?"

"I'm a Marshall." He gave her a wry smile. "We know similar sensations but are only the supporting cast. You, my dear, are the star."

"The star in what? Why do I have this special talent? Am I part of some big overall plan?" Urgency riddled her voice. "And do I have any choice in the matter?"

Henri was schooled to soothe her. "Certainly. The choice is yours alone, Madeleine. You can walk away right now and forget this ever happened."

"And forget you too, I suppose."

"As I said, the choice is yours."

Maddy shook her head. "The way I feel right now, I'm not sure I believe that."

"Then please hear me out. It will be a while before you go anywhere because I don't know what sets your journey in motion. There are two given elements. The period watch is one, but there's a missing piece that acts in tandem. As yet, I haven't been told what it is."

"Why not?"

"It's simply part of their plan."

"The August Ones, you mean."

He nodded. "But I may be able to isolate it if you describe what you were doing when you traveled back to meet Tom and when you saw the hurricane. It would help to know what those incidents had in common."

"Both times I was watching television. That's pretty much it."

"What were you watching on television?"

"Before I met Tom, it was a movie. *Chocolat,* to be exact. With Hurricane Betsy it was the Weather Channel."

"Obviously there's a link between the two storms, but I can't connect Tennessee Williams with a French film about food." Henri paused. "Were you eating or drinking anything? Wearing anything unusual? An antique cameo or ring perhaps? Was it the same time of day?"

When none of Maddy's responses helped, Henri said, "In that case, we can only wait until it reveals itself. Besides, we've had enough excitement for one day, don't you think?"

Maddy toasted Henri with her wine glass. "Not to mention indoctrination."

"You don't miss much. That's another thing I adore about you."

They sat in silence as the purple martins began their nightly aerial ballet, swooping and diving to gorge on mosquitoes. Despite the tranquility of the moment, Maddy's mind vacillated between the thrill of what she had discovered about herself and fear of what this great unknown might bring. The heavy stillness was eventually broken when "Ride of the Valkyries" burst through the bedroom windows.

Henri was incredulous. "A Wagnerian ringtone?"

"Don't tell me you didn't know?" Maddy teased.

"Nope," Henri confessed. "That's one thing I missed."

"Good." Maddy bussed his cheek before going to answer the phone. "A girl needs *some* secrets."

When she returned a few minutes later, Maddy's mood had soured. She sank tiredly onto the settee, turned her phone off and finished the last of her wine.

"What's wrong, darling?"

"That was my boss, Ms. Warren. She hung up before I got to the phone but left quite a message."

"Uh-oh."

"Uh-oh is right. She asked why I didn't come back to work after lunch and wants to see me first thing in the morning. She said if I expected to keep my job, I'd better have a very good explanation." Distress deepened as Maddy replayed the phone message in her head. "Decent jobs for librarians are hard to come by, Henri. As it is, I barely make ends meet."

"It's completely my fault of course."

"What're you talking about? I'm the flake who took six hours for lunch and was too caught up in the moment to call with some sort of excuse."

"And I'm precisely the reason why."

"So what?" Maddy set her wine aside and crawled into Henri's lap. She nuzzled his throat and whispered, "Those six hours may be the best spent of my life."

12

Henri put Madeleine into a cab and went into the library. Suddenly exhausted, he collapsed in an overstuffed chair and tried to lose himself in the mechanical monotony of the clocks. Most people would've dismissed the ticking as distracting or annoying, but he found solace as he sorted through the last twelve remarkable hours.

It had begun well enough with Maddy believing the unbelievable and embracing truths that could have unraveled a less stable soul. He was greatly relieved, knowing her reaction would please the August Ones, but then Madeleine, without warning, challenged their ambitious plan with a single kiss by the river. That loving gesture, which Henri should have avoided, spawned something powerful enough to bring her into his bed. Memories of that vivid moment thrilled and frightened him, and he closed his eyes to escape deeper into the dense library cacophony. The ticking finally began to soothe him before merging into a singular rhythmic boom. Instead of tick-tock, tick-tock it thundered loss, loss, loss, eventually conjuring a long forgotten passage from, appropriately enough, Tennessee Williams. Henri was buoyed by both deafening din and the quote as Williams' prophetic words overrode everything.

"Time is short and it doesn't return again. It is slipping away while I write this and while you read it, and the monosyllable of the clock is loss, loss, loss, unless you devote your heart to its opposition."

My heart, Henri thought. What about my poor heart? After all that's happened, can I let myself be separated from Madeleine? Can I send her to places filled with terrible unknowns that may take her from me forever? Can I lose a treasure so recently found?

The more Henri pondered his dilemma, the more troubled he became and the deeper he combed the past for answers. Eventually his own voyage of time travel transported him back to those earliest moments when he, like Madeleine, was chosen for this special journey. He was thirteen-years-old, at his grandparents' house outside Paris, when the dreams began. Fascinating at first, they flooded his young mind with dazzling images and tempting notions, but as he matured they contained more serious imagery and promises of power. Henri remained mystified, telling no one, not even his beloved grandparents, about his nocturnal visitations. Finally, on his twentieth birthday, the August Ones revealed his destiny. They never told him why he was chosen, only that he *was*, but despite being strongly intrigued, Henri resisted. Since childhood he had yearned to be an archeologist exploring the exotic extremes of the globe and was reluctant to pursue another career. His hesitation, however, was deftly deflected when the August Ones asked how an archeologist, without so much as lifting a trowel, could make a discovery superior to what he was being offered. Surely shepherding someone into a time corridor eclipsed unearthing the treasures of Tutankhamen or the gold of Troy or stumbling upon Machu Picchu. That seminal moment, twenty-two years ago, had compelled Henri to sublimate personal desire and accept his altered fate. Once he capitulated, Henri was designated Marshal and rigorously instructed in every aspect of the so-called Madeleine Project, trained to answer her questions and calm her fears while shepherding her toward the past. He was schooled to remain stalwart and impersonal, to distance himself from his assigned Courier and to never surrender to emotions. Henri believed himself capable of following these dictates until Madeleine's fateful kiss by the river.

"She's changed the rules!" he shouted to the thundering clocks. "What am I to do now?"

Henri's first impulse was to take Maddy and flee New Orleans, but there was no escaping the inevitable because he had committed himself to the August Ones and exchanged irrevocable promises. Because these ethereal beings inhabited his mind and were as much a part of him as this newfound love, his only choice was seeking their verdict. Perhaps there might be compromise. Perhaps they might even permit him to accompany Madeleine on her journey or send her on a trip with safety guaranteed. If he had learned anything about this esoteric endeavor, it was that nothing was impossible.

Henri was further heartened when the clamor of the clocks faded, and they resumed their harmless ticking. He left the library and crawled into bed exhausted. The clean scent of Maddy's perfume lingered on the pillowslips while more evocative reminders emanated from the sheets. He immersed himself, seeking strength as he closed his eyes and waited. But sleep remained elusive, and for long hours Henri tossed and turned on sheets that grew damp with the sweat of anxiety. He pounded the pillows and begged the August Ones for reprieve.

"Please!" he pleaded. "Please speak to me."

Time and again, Henri squinted toward the window, fearful that dawn would announce his pleas had gone unanswered and that he would face a day of uncertainty. He groaned at a faint shard of light, but as he prepared for defeat, a hot frisson prickled his shoulders and plunged him into a deep, all-consuming sleep. With it came the voices he desperately sought. At first, the August Ones were smug and playful, refusing to coalesce as they danced through his brain. Knowing his dilemma, they taunted and teased, asserting their powers before revealing themselves. Just when Henri feared he might lose his sanity, the dream message emerged full force and with surreal clarity.

He was alone on the ferry crossing the Mississippi from New Orleans to Algiers. The great river was wrapped in pale mist and teemed with traffic, a raucous crush of steamboats,

barges and pleasure craft. The water grew restless, then began to pitch and heave. Henri grabbed the rail to keep from
being tossed overboard and looked up in horror when an
enormous freighter exploded through a mountain of spray
and threatened to swamp the little ferryboat. On the prow of
the freighter high above, Henri spotted Madeleine, a tiny
figure waving frantically and yelling words he couldn't understand. His feet left the slippery deck and he was hurtled
free as the two vessels continued their collision course.
Higher and higher he soared, grasping frantically for Maddy's outstretched hands, but when she was almost in reach
the metal freighter morphed into a juggernaut of whirling
foam. Sucked into its wake, Henri shot like a juggernaut
through watery blackness before washing up on Venice's Ac-
cademia Bridge. The Grand Canal was deserted except for a
gondola bearing a lone passenger in a dark hooded cloak.
Madeleine was unhearing as Henri called out, and her figure
grew smaller as she was rowed around the *Punta della Doga-
na* where she disappeared from sight.

Henri awoke in a sweat, shivering with the icy clarity of
the dream message. There was no longer any question that
his sacred duty was facilitating Madeleine's journey into the
past, and that irrevocable truth left him with a melancholy
he could scarcely bear.

13

Maddy whispered a quick prayer before entering her boss's office to explain yesterday's disappearance. She wasn't optimistic. Georgia Warren had zero tolerance for deviation from library rules and was quick to admonish her staff for the slightest infraction and upbraid visitors using a ballpoint pen instead of the requisite pencil. All Maddy could do was claim it was a personal emergency, but when she finished apologizing, Warren pursed her lips into an ugly smirk.

"I lunched in Woldenberg Park yesterday, Miss St. Jacques. I wasn't more than thirty feet away, but you and your gentleman friend were much too preoccupied to notice. Am I to assume he was your 'personal emergency'?"

That witch spied on me, Maddy thought. She knows damned well I was with Henri and is torturing me plain and simple. "Miss Warren, I—" A poisonous glare silenced her. "Sorry."

"I saw the two of you, shall we say, 'carrying on' before catching a riverfront streetcar, so it seems that you're guilty of three infractions. You left work mid-day, did not call to explain your absence, and subsequently lied about it."

Maddy bristled at the accusation. "I didn't lie, Miss Warren. I did have a personal emergency and I've apologized for my behavior. I don't know what else I can do."

"You might consider telling the truth."

Maddy was usually even tempered, but this woman was pushing her buttons fast and furious. "The fact is that my emergency concerned the gentleman you saw me with. I'm not at liberty to say more, only that it kept me from returning to the Center and was, frankly, beyond my control." When Warren glowered, Maddy added, "It is *not* what you are implying."

Warren wasn't buying it. "Surely you don't expect me to accept such a vague explanation."

"Owing to my excellent work record here at the Center, I would hope so."

Warren muttered to herself as she grabbed Maddy's employee file and noisily flipped the pages. She sucked her teeth as she examined the evaluation record, ignoring Maddy's superb performance marks and focusing on her lone weakness. "Your attendance record is borderline at best, Miss St. Jacques."

"Please remember I was tending critically ill parents, Miss Warren, and was the only one there to drive them to doctor's appointments, do their grocery shopping and make sure that—"

Warren was unhearing. "Triple infractions this serious are not to be repeated. If something like this happens again, I will bring you before the board. Do I make myself clear?"

"Very clear." To keep her temper in check, Maddy reminded herself she was as guilty as Warren was duplicitous. "And I assure you it won't happen again."

"See that it doesn't."

A dismissive wave sent Maddy back to her desk on the library's main floor where she pondered her boss's ugly threat. Warren had been at the Center over thirty years and could easily have her fired. On top of what had happened with Henri, concern for her job made it difficult to focus, and Maddy spent the day on autopilot, mechanically answering questions and supplying people with research material. Staying busy helped pass the time, but when she left to meet Paige for dinner at Galatoire's, Maddy was exhausted. She told herself she was too tired to be good company, but the real reason she wanted to go home was because she had slept with a man her best friend was interested in. She hoped Paige had already forgotten about Henri and set her romantic sights elsewhere, but when she walked into the restaurant and saw Paige's scowl, that hope evaporated. She squared her shoulders and soldiered into the lion's den.

"Hi, Paige."

"It's about time," Paige said coolly. "I assume you know that the only acceptable excuse for standing me up is a man."

"What're you talking about?" Maddy glanced at her watch as she took a seat. "I'm right on time."

Paige said, "For dinner, yes. For the theater, no."

Maddy was so tired it took a second for Paige's words to register and she remembered they were scheduled to meet last night at *Le Petit Théâtre du Vieux Carré*. Clearly, Henri's powerful presence had made that, and everything else, slip her mind.

"God, Paige. I'm so sorry."

"You should be," Paige sniffed. "I was mad as hell but now I'm just glad you're alright.

"I couldn't reach you because your phone was turned off, and if you hadn't shown up for dinner I was going to start dragging the river. Where the devil were you?"

"Home," Maddy lied. "Work yesterday was such a bear that I went home, nuked some jambalaya and went right to bed. I slept badly, and I'm still tired."

"You do look tired," Paige conceded. "In fact, you look like you've got jet lag."

"That's not far from the truth. It was like being on another planet."

Paige's eyes narrowed. "What do you mean?"

"Nothing."

"Nonsense. I know you like a book, my dear, and can tell when you're hiding something." Paige's coolness melted beneath a sweetly suspicious smile. "Did some randy gentleman invite you up to see his etchings?"

"A clock collection is more like it," Maddy blurted in a weak moment.

"You and Henri finally got together!" Paige clasped her hands. "Wonderful!"

Maddy's cheeks blazed. "You don't mind?"

"Heavens, no!"

Maddy was foundering. "But I thought...no, wait! How did you know it was Henri? And what do you mean 'finally'?"

"Brace yourself, sweetheart." Paige whispered, barely able to contain her excitement. "I've known about him from the beginning. I also know about Tennessee Williams."

"What?!" Maddy reeled as Paige's incredulous admission gave her precarious new world another jolt of the insanely far-fetched. It took her a moment to find her voice and work to restore reason. "Alright, Paige. If you knew where I was last night, why all that business about dragging the river?"

"Role-playing, darling. I had sworn to Henri I wouldn't show my hand until you were ready to see it. Your remark about the clock collection was the sign I was waiting for because, whether you realized it or not, it told me you wanted to talk. Am I wrong?"

"No." Maddy smiled with relief and reached over to take Paige's hand. "I made a vow of silence too. It's the hardest promise I've ever made because I was dying to tell you everything. We've never had secrets, you and I, but as you know this one is huge."

Paige nodded. "To put it mildly."

Maddy struggled to put things into perspective. "I'm dying for details, and I know you are too, but Galatoire's is the eyes and ears of the city and it's hardly the place to discuss time traveling."

"True, but tell me one thing. What was it like to meet—?" She gave Maddy a theatrical wink. "Your upstairs neighbor."

"Too late, honey child." Maddy lowered her voice. "The mouth of the South just took the table behind you."

"Fran McDonough?" Maddy nodded. "Damn! That woman has ears like a fox and she'll repeat every damned word we say."

"Then let's toss her a bone to chew on." Maddy returned McDonough's saccharine smile before raising her voice. "Oh,

Paige. I forgot to tell you about my new kitten. His name is Tom, and he's sort of shy but very well behaved."

"I can't wait to meet him," Paige said, continuing the game. "Tell me more."

"Let me see. Oh, yes. He loves playing with the keys on that old antique typewriter."

Paige chuckled. "Maybe he'll write something some day."

"Maybe." When Maddy noted Fran's befuddlement, she pushed the joke another notch. "He might even win a Pulitzer Prize or two."

14

When they left Galatoire's, Maddy suggested switching from Bourbon Street to Royal Street. It was far less crowded and would be fine for discussing Henri.

"And we can window shop along the way," Paige said giddily.

Maddy was amused but wondered if Paige was too tipsy to discuss anything serious. "Maybe we should talk about this another time."

"Oh, no you don't! I've been waiting for months for you to hook up with Henri and I can't endure another moment without comparing notes." She nudged Maddy with her elbow. "I'm buzzed, not blitzed, darling."

"Alright then, but you start since you met Henri first. Exactly how did you two connect?"

"Well, I think of him as the man of my dreams because that's where I first met him."

Maddy thought of the dream she had discussed with Henri when they met at Paige's salon and her shock last night to learn he had a hand in it. To prove his involvement, he cited the quote from Ernest Renan: "He who obeys is almost always better than he who commands." His revelation nearly caused Maddy to swoon.

"Go on," she urged.

"There's not much to tell," Paige said. "Henri, in one guise or another, began appearing in my dreams and when we finally met I knew I would do whatever he asked, just as I knew I was safe and reasonable in doing so. I know that sounds bizarre but—"

"Not to me it doesn't. When did you actually meet him?"

"He phoned one day, introduced himself as a Tulane professor and asked if he could see the house. It happens all the time because it's the second biggest piece of private property in the Quarter, so I didn't find it an odd request. Anyway, he told me to confirm his identity on the Tulane website, and I nearly fainted when I saw a photo of the man I'd been dreaming about. Since Jesse was there to protect me in case the guy was dangerous, I invited him over and was charmed from the moment he walked in. Jesse brought drinks, and next thing I knew Henri said he'd been observing you for years and needed to meet me because we're best friends. I accepted everything he said, without question."

"Because your dreams had prepared you to play along."

"Exactly. He said they were a sort of brainwashing and explained about you being a Courier and him being a Marshal and the multiverses, and I bought the whole package. I begged him to let me be a Courier, too, but I don't have the gift. Instead I'm to be a Colleague, which is sort of your personal assistant. I was thrilled because I so want to be a part of all this."

"I'm sure you'll make the best assistant ever."

"Frankly, I never imagined myself playing such a part, but we Colleagues do have our perks."

"So now the truth comes out." Maddy smiled. "What sort of perks?"

"The day after our meeting, a package arrived from Dr. Chabrol who obviously knew my passion for vintage jewelry. It was a pair of garnet earrings that belonged to Lola Montez. The ones she's wearing in that famous portrait in the Tate, no less. Henri even included proof of provenance from a Munich antiques dealer no less."

"My God!" Maddy laughed. "All I got was an old Bulova watch. I'll bet you knew about that too, didn't you?"

Paige took her arm as they continued down Royal. "All part of the plan, dear. In fact, I threw that particular salon to introduce you two and provide Henri with the opportunity to give you that old watch. As you now know, it was critical in transporting you upstairs to meet Tennessee Williams in 1939." Paige sighed. "I was so worried you'd see through the whole charade when I claimed to be reading *Scientific American*. Me, of all people!"

"So this business of you being attracted to Henri was—?"

"Another part of the plan, silly girl. You know I prefer younger men." She squeezed the hand inside her elbow. "As for what happened last night. I'm happy for you both."

"You really mean that?"

"Of course."

"But I never do things like that, sleeping with someone I barely know. Good Lord!"

"Henri's not like any man we've ever met, Maddy, and this...um, situation is hardly the norm. Besides, you know him better than you think. And now it's time to change the subject." Paige paused before a shop blazing with lights. "I adore the Harouni Gallery. You like David's work, don't you?"

"Yes, I do." Maddy was studying an oversized portrait when an unwelcome reflection appeared in the glass. "Seth!"

"How're you doing, Maddy?" He smiled at Paige. "I haven't seen you since you threw me out of your house."

Paige ignored him and remained focused on the paintings.

"I'm fine," Maddy said tiredly.

"How come you haven't returned my calls?" Seth moved so close that she felt his body heat. "I must've left a dozen messages."

"Because it's over between us, Seth. How much plainer can I be?"

"You don't mean that." Seth put a hand on her shoulder, but Maddy pushed it off.

"Leave me alone, Seth."

He ignored her. "You can't dump me like that. Have you forgotten all the good times we had? I mean, we really had it going on, babe."

What Maddy once considered cute now repulsed her. "You walked out on me once, Seth. I accepted it gracefully, now why can't you be a gentleman and do the same?"

Seth glowered, countenance changing as Maddy knew it would. "What's the problem?"

"You're the problem."

"Aw, don't be like that, babe."

Seth tried to put his arms around her, but Maddy stepped away. "Don't touch me."

"You heard the lady," Paige said. "Leave her alone."

"Screw you, Miss Rich Bitch!" Seth growled, turning ugly right on cue. "This is none of your business."

"Then I'm making it my business," Paige shot back, all trace of tipsiness gone. "Now back off, asshole!"

"Go fuck yourself!" Seth grabbed Maddy's arm and pulled her along the sidewalk. He'd gone only a few steps when someone stepped from the shadows.

"You heard the lady. Back off!"

Powerful hands yanked Seth away and sent Maddy reeling into Paige's arms. The women stared in relief as Seth was strong-armed down Royal Street.

"Are you alright, darling?" Paige asked.

"I'm fine." She watched Seth disappear around the corner of St. Philip Street. "Where the devil did that guy come from? Was he following us or something?"

"A good Samaritan I guess."

"Mmmm. Maybe chivalry isn't dead after all." As Maddy rubbed her sore arm, she noticed something in Paige's hand. "Oh, my God! You were going to mace him?"

"Damned right I was. Seth's lucky I left my Lady Derringer at home. Now come along. I'll walk you home."

Maddy's mind was elsewhere else. "On second thought, there was something familiar about that guy."

"Your good Samaritan?"

"Yeah. I've heard that voice before."

15

Maddy was still shaken when she got home. Paige wanted her to file assault charges against Seth and, seething at being called a rich bitch, eagerly volunteered to act as a witness. Maddy thanked her but said no. Instinct said that her rescuer would punish Seth enough, but where, she wondered, had she heard that voice?

She took a leisurely soak, pleased when the hot water and fragrant bath beads calmed her nerves. She forgot about Seth and thought about Paige and Henri and how deftly they had manipulated her. She ignored a twinge of resentment, realizing both had her best interests at heart and was excited again that her best friend would participate in whatever the mysterious August Ones had in store. As she finished bathing and toweled off, she thought about last night's abundant surprises, especially Henri's prowess as a lover, and decided to call him. The phone sounded when she reached for it, and she smiled when she saw Chabrol on the caller ID.

"I was about to call you. Is e.s.p. part of our new arrangement?"

Henri laughed heartily. "I have a few special talents, Madeleine, but being psychic isn't among them."

"So it was only a coincidence?"

"I'm afraid so."

"Well, it's a very nice one." Maddy flopped onto her bed, pleased at how happy his voice made her. "Did you have a good day?"

"Fine, but tell me how things went with your boss?"

"She let me off with a reprimand," Maddy replied, not wanting to go into detail. "The big news is Paige. We had dinner at Galatoire's, and you can guess the rest if you haven't already."

"Then I'm guessing she told you."

"Yes, indeed, and I must say you two busy bees put one over on me."

Concerned filled Henri's voice. "You're not upset, are you?"

"Mmmm, I was a little resentful in the beginning because I felt manipulated."

"I'm sorry, darling. We didn't have any choice."

"I understood after I thought about it. In fact, I took a long hot bath and sorted through things and—"

"You took a long hot bath without me?"

She enjoyed a naughty chuckle. "You're incorrigible."

"Would you have me any other way?"

"What do you think?"

"I think you're the most desirable, most understanding woman in the world."

"Why did you say 'understanding?'" His long silence made her uneasy. "Henri? What are you trying to tell me?"

"I'm sorry, darling. It's more like what I'm trying *not* to tell you."

Maddy's heart sank. "Okay. I'm a big girl so let's have it."

"I've been summoned by the August Ones."

"Go on."

"I've been told to take a leave of absence from the university, nothing more."

Maddy accepted what would've been unacceptable coming from anyone else. "Can you at least tell me what's happened?"

"You, *ma chérie.*" Henri's long sigh was riddled with melancholy before he added, "*You* have happened."

Part 3

"Perhaps only in the Rome of the Caesars
did people love holidays as much as the citizens of
New Orleans."

— Robert Tallant, *Mardi Gras*

16

Few New Orleanians remembered a more brutal summer. Maddy was wondering if the heat would linger forever when November came to the rescue with cold rains and plunging temperatures which, unfortunately, made her yearn for Henri's warmth. It was four months since his abrupt departure, made worse because she didn't know his destination, return date or how to reach him. Her only solace came at Thanksgiving when he fulfilled a promise to appear in her dreams and reassured her with a visit so real she awoke feeling his breath on her throat.

Unknown to anyone, even Paige, Maddy tried to discover the missing element Henri needed to transport her back in time. She repeatedly used his 1939 Bulova in an effort to conjure Tennessee Williams, but even after recreating every detail of that first encounter, down to wearing the same clothes and renting *Chocolat* to watch on TV, nothing materialized. By year's end Maddy despaired of seeing Henri again and feared the whole situation was a cruel hallucination. As her Colleague, Paige did her best to banish her worries with frequent lunches and shopping sprees. She even asked Maddy to co-host her fabled New Year's Eve bash, bribing her with a sassy beaded gown from Fleur de Paris which she insisted be accessorized with Lola Montez's earrings. Maddy conceded that celebrating with a hundred people was better than singing Auld Lang Syne alone.

The night of the party, Maddy wished Henri could see her ongoing transformation. She still lacked self-confidence but felt better when she looked in the full-length mirror and preened in her glitzy finery. She nodded at her reflection.

"Hmm. You're cleaning up pretty good these days." Her

phone sang as she tucked it in her purse, and she braced herself when she saw the Out of Area caller ID. Even on New Year's Eve, it was probably a telemarketer, but she prayed it was Henri. "Hello."

"Happy New Year, darling!"

"Henri!" she cried. "Happy New Year to you too! How are you? Where are you? When are you coming home? What's going on that's kept you from—?"

Henri's deep laughter crackled over the line. "If you stop talking, I'll tell you."

"I'm sorry. It's just that I haven't heard anything since Thanksgiving and I'm so happy to finally hear from you that...oh, dear! I'm doing it again!"

"Except for missing you, I'm fine. I welcomed the New Year all by myself in Venice. After all, where else can one spend thirty bucks for a glass of Prosecco?"

"Venice?!" Maddy glanced at her watch. "What time is it there?"

"Two-thirty."

"Why are you up so late?"

"Because I'm a fool in love, my dear. I went to bed right after midnight, and when I couldn't stop thinking about you I had to call and wish you a happy new year."

"You've no idea how much I've missed you. If it hadn't been for that beautiful dream—"

"I was worried it might not reach you."

"It did. In fact, the dream and Paige's support are what have kept me going."

"So she's performing her duties as Colleague?"

"She's the best."

Henri turned serious. "I'm truly sorry things had to be this way, Madeleine, but I'll make it up to you. For starters, we'll be in each other's arms within the week."

Maddy gasped. "Promise?"

"I leave Wednesday the fifth and will fly home via Atlanta. I'll get to New Orleans around six in the evening."

"I'll be there with bells on!"

"Which I fully intend to remove the moment I get you alone," Henri teased.

"I can't wait." Maddy blinked tears when she realized their conversation was ending. "Hurry, hurry home!"

"Bon soir, mon ange. Je taime!"

"Bon soir. I love you too."

Maddy went into the bathroom and burst out laughing at her mascara-streaked cheeks. She quickly repaired her make-up and hurried out the door. The star-filled night was crisp, not bitter, and she was a thousand percent better after hearing Henri's voice. She all but floated down Ursulines Street, smiled at the security guard on duty outside Paige's house and beamed when Jesse answered the front door.

"Hey, Jesse."

"Hey, Madeleine," he said, flashing his usual big grin. "Happy New Year."

Maddy surprised the big man with a hug. "My friend, you have no idea!"

17

Maddy slaved to make everything perfect for Henri's return. Knowing his favorites, she splurged on a bouquet of stargazer lilies and stocked up on so much food and wine there would be no need to leave the apartment. She was thrilled when he praised her attention to detail and even happier that, despite his jet lag, their first night together was pure joy. Maddy let him sleep late the next morning, waking him with croissants and chicory-laced coffee. Henri insisted he'd never been more content than in their little love nest, but by late afternoon said he needed to face the outside world.

"Why?" Maddy protested. "I'm finally on such good terms with my boss that she gave me tomorrow off. I made gumbo yesterday for us to have tonight."

"It'll be even better tomorrow, *cher.* I appreciate all you've done but after four months I need to go home and check my mail. Besides, aren't you forgetting something?"

"What?"

"There's a bed on Orange Street too."

Maddy blushed and gave Henri's bare bottom a playful swat as he slipped from bed and headed for the kitchen. "I just realized something," she called after him.

"What's that?"

"You haven't told me what you've been doing these past four months."

"Not my fault!" he called back. "You've kept me busy with other things."

"I'm serious, Henri."

"First things first, my dear," he said, returning with a bottle of champagne and two glasses. He poured the wine and settled in beside her. "After our first night together, I was truly confused. You have to understand that my training as your Marshal forbade me from falling in love, and when the unthinkable happened I went wild with worry about what might happen once you crossed into another multiverse."

"Good heavens, Henri. Where are they planning to send me?"

"That's something else I needed to know, along with the missing element to get you there. The August Ones only reveal information when they deem it necessary. My journey these past four months is emblematic as I was sent to one place after another. Uxmal, Petra, Karnak, Angkor Wat, and finally Venice."

Maddy's eyes widened at the litany of exotic names. "Why Karnak, for example?"

"Because of a tomb recently unearthed there. It belonged to a mysterious noble and its door bears the most intact, most complex hieroglyphics yet found."

"I read about that in the *Picayune*. The ancient Egyptians believed it was a portal for the spirits of the dead to travel to and from the underworld."

"I believe it too, but now isn't the time to discuss it. What's important is that the key to your journey will be revealed soon and that you will be going back to nineteenth century New Orleans. 1861 to be exact."

Maddy took a moment to digest that. "What do I do when I get there?"

"That too will be revealed."

"You're beginning to sound like Hercule Poirot with this 'all will be revealed' business. It's not very reassuring."

"Sorry, my dear. That's how the August Ones operate."

"Can you tell me how they reacted to you falling in love with your Courier?"

"They confirmed that we can't change our assigned roles but, as I explained that first night together, you can refuse the journey if you choose."

"And I told you that I didn't believe I had that choice. Despite my love for you, or perhaps because of it, I still don't." She shrugged helplessly. "In fact, I'm burning to get started."

Something dark crossed Henri's face but didn't surface. "The August Ones have done their jobs well, my darling. On both of us."

"I suppose." Maddy pressed his hand against her cheek. "But remember they also brought us together. Before them I was living life by rote."

"So was I," Henri conceded. "Although I didn't know it."

"Then let's continue with our lives and deal with the consequences as they arise." She smiled. "Like any other loving couple."

"You make it sound so easy."

"I have to, *mon cher*. The truth is I'm all jelly inside."

"Moi aussi."

"Then we better make the most of our situation. I have a confession to make. While you were gone, I used your watch and tried to contact Tennessee Williams again. I failed, but it made me wonder if I should try other things. Do you know how other Couriers trigger their trips?"

Henri nodded. "Colors, sounds, clothing, scents, that sort of thing. Coupled with the appropriate timepiece, of course."

"Should we experiment?"

"I'm afraid the August Ones have already set our course, so all we can do is wait."

"That reminds me." Maddy recounted the incident with Seth and her mysterious Samaritan. "While I was telling you this, I remembered where I heard that stranger's voice. He was the one who called to me in old French, and his appearance was so timely it was like he'd been watching the whole thing. Maybe even following me. Why the long face?"

"I wish the August Ones would keep me better informed."

Maddy sighed. "It's all so complicated, isn't it?"

Henri set his wine aside and nestled Maddy's head against his shoulder. He stroked her hair and spoke in soothing tones. "There will be moments when you feel overwhelmed. Things will get easier when what we've discussed becomes reality. A big reason you were chosen as Courier is that you're smart, Madeline, so I have every confidence you'll find your way."

"I hope so. I want to make you proud of me. Paige and the August Ones too of course."

Henri kissed the top of her head. "Okay. Time to change the subject. Do you realize this is Twelfth Night? How about we grab the streetcar and party with the Phunny Phorty Phellows?"

"You always know the right thing to say." Maddy smiled and breathed in the scent of his bare chest. "Those goofy guys are just what we need."

An hour later they caught a specially decorated streetcar at Lee Circle and joined a group of costumed revelers celebrating Twelfth Night, the first day of Mardi Gras. Called The Phunny Phorty Phellows, they heralded the arrival of the carnival season from a streetcar complete with jazz band. By the time Maddy and Henri traveled uptown on St. Charles Avenue and got off at Felicity Street, their spirits were soaring. Maddy even hummed a little as they walked to the cottage on Orange Street.

"It's so clear tonight," she said, looking up through the gnarled branches of a rambling live oak. "Check out all those stars."

"I want to show you something." Henri pointed up. "Do you see that one there, through the crook of that big limb? Right below the North Star."

Maddy followed his lead. "Yes, I do, but it's strange."

"What's strange?"

"I found the star alright, but when I look at it directly it disappears. I'm a little near-sighted, but—"

"There's nothing wrong with your eyes. There are a few

places where another universe is visible to everyone. That's one of them."

Maddy studied the heavens. "It keeps appearing and disappearing."

"Because it is and it isn't," Henri explained. "Like that car that's in your rear view mirror one minute and gone the next and you didn't see it turn off."

"Absolutely amazing. All this time I've glimpsed other universes and never knew it."

"And soon you'll visit one in person."

As they continued to the cottage in silence, Maddy speculated about the unknowns ahead. The more she thought, the more exhilarated she became. "I don't know about you," she said as Henri opened the front door, "but this has been a pretty perfect day."

He eyed a stack of mail on the entrance hall table and noted an elegant, oversized envelope. "It's about to get even better."

Maddy watched him open the envelope and smile. "What is it?"

"How would you like to attend the Olympus Ball?"

"No!" Maddy was floored. "That's the hottest Mardi Gras ticket in town."

"I take it you want to go," he teased.

"What do you think, silly boy?" She grabbed the engraved invitation and was disheartened by the date. "January twenty-ninth! That's only three weeks to find a costume!"

"I'm way ahead of you, sweetheart. My old friend Anne Petree is a costume designer for the movies, and your outfit is almost finished. She can arrange for wigs too."

"Wow! You think of everything."

"I try, but it was the August Ones' idea for you to costume as a nineteenth-century courtesan."

Maddy's jaw dropped. "Me? A courtesan?!"

"Truth is, it's perfect. The ball is at the Bourbon Orleans Hotel where the old Quadroon balls were held. You know.

Where courtesans made arrangements with rich gentlemen."

"Rich *white* gentlemen, you mean. And those women were ladies of color, remember?"

"Of course I remember. I also know some of them were even lighter than you."

Maddy reconsidered. "I guess it could work, but I hardly see myself as a courtesan."

"Don't sell yourself short, my dear. I guarantee every man at the ball will be wowed."

"You're sweet, but what about those period hair-dos and accessories and—?"

"Anne can arrange everything. She's making my costume too."

Maddy grinned with excitement. "And?"

"When I was growing up in France, I wanted to—"

"Aha! So that's where the old world manners come from. Why didn't you tell me?"

"All in good time, my darling." Henri smiled. "Anyway, when I studied American history, I fantasized about being a nineteenth century Louisiana gentleman, and here's my chance."

"So we're going to the ball as an antebellum couple, huh? Sounds to me like the time traveling is going to start with or without the August Ones." When Henri gave her a long look, she hastily added, "On second thought, maybe not."

18

"You look beautiful, Madeleine," Henri said. "Absolutely beautiful."

"No one has ever told me that before," she confessed. "Thank you."

Maddy blinked away tears of happiness, not wanting to spoil Anne's expert maquillage. For the first time in her life, she was thrilled with her appearance. Her hair was swept high in an elaborate coiffure with corkscrew curls and ostrich feathers designed to dance. A swan's down fan hung from a velvet ribbon around her left wrist, a vintage reticule from the other, and a wool shawl was draped over bare shoulders. Her ball gown was an exquisite confection of pale yellow watered silk showered with ivory Chantilly lace. Cut in extreme *décolleté*, it was by far the most revealing dress Maddy had ever worn.

"I feel a little indecent though."

"Better late than never."

"You're a shameless flatterer." Maddy waved a hand at his old fashioned black tuxedo with high collared shirt and white tie, top hat and gleaming boots. "You look pretty snazzy yourself, and with that rented carriage I'll be like Cinderella going to the ball."

"All the better for making an entrance, my dear."

Maddy grinned. "You sure have a flair for the theatrical, professor."

"It comes in handy. You'll see."

By the time they pulled up in front of the Bourbon Orleans Hotel, Maddy was giddy with anticipation. She gasped at the throngs of locals and tourists jamming the sidewalks, cameras and iPhones aimed at those lucky enough to be invited to the exclusive ball. Ordinarily she would have been daunted, but instead tingled with newfound confidence as Henri stepped out and extended a gloved hand. She took a deep breath and felt her breasts strain at the low neckline as she leaned out of the coach. The crowd responded with applause and an explosion of camera flashes. Maddy ignored a flush of embarrassment when she remembered Paige's advice: "Don't put it out there if you don't want it looked at."

Henri beamed. "As I predicted, you've wowed the crowd."

"Something else I've never been told," she said as they ran the gauntlet of gawkers. "It's sure a night of firsts."

"Good. I want it to be."

Henri flashed their invitation at a security guard and ushered Maddy into the hotel. The lobby was a crazy collision of time periods. Cleopatra, Elizabeth I and Cher rubbed shoulders with Napoleon, Alexander the Great and Czar Nicholas II while clowns, harlequins, vampires and warlocks stirred the colorful mix. Maddy and Henri headed upstairs where a sterile conference space had been transformed to a glittering ballroom. Tall windows were draped with the purple, green and gold bunting of carnival, and Mardi Gras flags hung everywhere. Hot jazz blasted from the Red Pepper Pods, and the dance floor rocked with giddy revelers.

"I've been to a few carnival balls," Maddy said excitedly, "but nothing this fabulous. Thanks again for bringing me."

"*De rien.*" Henri took her hand and bowed to brush it with his lips. "*Je taime, bébé.*"

Maddy gave him a sly look. "I love you too, but isn't all that hand-kissing just so you can peek at my boobs?"

"What a bourgeois thing to say," Henri retorted, feigning insult. "I can assure you, *mademoiselle,* that I was in no way attempting to—" He burst out laughing when his fib fell apart. "Yeah, I was copping another peek."

"I knew it!" Maddy rapped his shoulder with her fan. "A wolf in gentleman's clothing."

"You must allow me to atone," Henri said, playing along.

He scanned the crowded room until he found a bar. "Would *mademoiselle* care for a glass of wine?"

Maddy leaned closer to be heard over the blaring music. "Bet your ass, *monsieur*."

"Coming right up."

When two rowdy musketeers moved into Henri's vacated space, Maddy retreated to an uncrowded corner to people-watch. She was fascinated by the sea of revelers, marveling at a towering Marie Antoinette holding a basket with her own talking head and a caped phantom of the opera balancing a four-foot-tall chandelier on his head. When crowds at the bar delayed Henri's return, Maddy's heavy costume grew uncomfortably hot. She waved her fan through air thick with perfume and body heat, but the exertion only made things worse, and when sweat beaded her forehead she went looking for fresh air. She fought her way to the upstairs lobby and continued down a hall where she found a janitor's closet with the door ajar. Spotting a utility sink, she slipped inside, peeled off her long gloves and, forgetting about her make-up, splashed cold water on her face.

"Ahhh!" She braced her hands on the sink as the refreshing water trickled down her face and the nape of her neck. "Much better."

After a moment, Maddy pulled a compact from her purse and studied her face in the small mirror. As she repaired the water damage, her hand rubbed against the antique watch pendant Henri gave her when they left for the ball. He had clasped it around her neck so fast she hadn't examined the delicate cameo on the backside. She took a moment to admire it before opening the watch with a flick of a fingernail to find a daguerreotype of a dashing nineteenth century gentleman with dark hair and eyes and a thick moustache. Some lucky belle's Rhett Butler, she thought. Maddy closed the watch and was checking the time when she realized the water was still running. As she reached to turn it off, a faint, distant humming bloomed in her head and increased to a roar as she stared at the tiny whirlpool in the sink. The noise grew deafening as the drain hole yawned into a dark tunnel and sucked Maddy inside. There was no free fall, only a backward slide as a rush of air propelled her against the wall. She braced herself for a jolt but was instead cushioned by red velvet draperies trimmed with gold fringe. As she nestled against them, the thunderous din was replaced by masculine laughter and the sound of shuffling cards. Blurred surroundings began sharpening, as did the voices around her, and she found herself in a small, lavishly appointed room filled with tobacco smoke, the smell of whiskey and four elderly gentlemen playing cards.

"Dear God!" she breathed. "What's happened?!"

The curtains rustled as someone joined her, and she looked into the greenest eyes she'd ever seen. A young woman in an emerald ball gown smiled. "*Bon soir, mademoiselle.*"

"*Bon soir,*" Maddy managed, struggling to make sense of what was happening.

"I have not seen you here before," the woman continued in cultivated French. "May I introduce myself?"

"*Bien sûr.*"

"I am Félicité Chevalier."

"Madeleine St. Jacques."

Félicité leaned closer, radiating the scent of Florida water. "You look a bit wan, my dear. It is the cigar smoke, *non?*"

Maddy nodded, trying desperately to register the unreality of the moment. Her insides turned to jelly when she realized this woman was no reveler in a rented ball gown. As she battled a wave of nausea, she finally comprehended that she had gone back in time, but how and why? Surely the watch pendant was a contributing factor, but what had happened in the janitor's washroom to trigger its powers?

"I loathe it too," Félicité continued, nodding at the formally dressed gentlemen playing poker. "Besides, there's no one here worth meeting tonight, *n'est- ce pas?*" Maddy shook her head no. "Then shall we go outside and take the air?"

"Yes, thank you. That's a wonderful idea."

Félicité smiled sweetly and took Maddy's arm, escorting her past a maze of smoky gambling rooms into a bustling vestibule infused with the gleam of marble floors and flickering gold chandeliers. They continued to a grand staircase sweeping up the second floor, deliberately wide enough to accommodate women passing in hoopskirts. As they rose higher, Maddy heard violins playing the waltz and the swish of swirling hems.

"You have an unusual accent," Félicité said as they continued their slow ascent. "Are you from *La Nouvelle-Orléans?* No, don't tell me. It will amuse me to try to guess."

Oh, boy, Maddy thought. I'm definitely not in Kansas anymore!

19

Maddy battled hyperventilation when she reached the top of the stairs. Any doubt that she had retreated in time was vanquished by a glamorous spectacle that could have existed only in 19th century New Orleans. The Bourbon Orleans Hotel had vanished and she was now in the old *Salle d'Orléans,* host to the city's infamous *Bals du Cordon Bleu,* commonly called the Quadroon Balls, where white men chose mistresses of color. The system was called *plaçage,* from the French *placer* meaning "to place," and the women were called *placées.* Well-educated and famed for their beauty and grace, they comprised a unique tier in a complex Louisiana caste system composed of the *gens du coleur libres,* the free people of color. The celebrated quadroons were one quarter black and three quarters white, while octoroons were only one eighth black and the *sang-mêlées,* or mixed bloods, were so pale they could often *passe blanc.* Such people considered themselves neither black nor white but literally a world apart while disdaining *mulattoes, saccatras, griffes* and other darker skinned brethren as beneath them. Félicité, Maddy guessed, was an octoroon, and as they passed under the blaze of chandeliers she saw the woman was almost as fair as herself, an illusion enhanced by Félicité's auburn curls.

Maddy struggled to not stare at a tableau straight out of Anne Rice's historical novel, *Feast of All Saints.* These exotic women, reminiscent of tropical birds in their jewel-toned ball gowns, and urbane white gentlemen belonged firmly in the nineteenth century, as did their manners, dance steps and music. They waltzed on the finest dance floor in America, triple-thickness cypress polished by slaves to resemble glass, and sipped *eau de sucre, ratafias* and absinthe. Even the air seemed from another era, thick and heady with a fusion of flowers, long forgotten *parfums* and the sweet-sour underlying odor of sweat. Maddy's wonder grew as she passed walls paneled in expensive woods and hung with finely executed oil paintings. Only the marble female nudes seemed in questionable taste, but at least they were discreetly tucked in niches. She and Félicité skirted the whirling dancers and approached French doors to a small terrace overlooking Orleans Street. A liveried servant moved swiftly to open the doors and was rewarded by a nod from Félicité.

"Oh, yes." Félicité breathed in the cool, damp air. "This is much better."

"Indeed, it is," Maddy agreed.

She was as captivated by what she saw outside the *Salle d'Orléans* as what she left behind. To the right, the Rue Orleans stretched toward *La Cyprière*, the trackless swamp between the city and Lake Pontchartrain. In the twentieth century it would be drained, cleared and filled with houses below sea level, but tonight it was an empty sea of darkness. To the left was St. Louis Cathedral, its triple spires silhouetted against the stars, and St. Anthony's Garden teemed with palmettos and enormous live oaks. The great trees gave Maddy a twinge of nostalgia since she knew they would be destroyed by Hurricane Katrina. On the street below, a crush of coaches, carriages and hacks picked up and delivered the *demi monde* beneath the golden glow of gaslight. Maddy took a deep breath while absorbing the astonishing tableau.

"Better?" Félicité asked.

"Much. Thank you."

"Your gown is lovely." Félicité leaned closer, admiring the delicate needlework. "Is it by Madam Gautier?"

Maddy thought fast. "My Tante Anne makes all my clothes."

"Her work is superb. Does she take clients outside *la famille*?"

"I'm afraid not." Maddy felt those green eyes studying her. "Is something wrong?"

"Forgive me. I was admiring your height. Perhaps 'coveting' is a more honest word. I see certain advantages to being as tall as most gentlemen." Maddy's cheeks grew hot as the woman continued. "I'm still trying to identify your accent. It's a little hobby of mine, but I must confess you have defeated me."

"I grew up in Natchez," Maddy said, beginning to build her lie.

"Ah. That explains it."

"And you, Félicité? Are you from *La Nouvelle-Orléans?*"

"*Mais, non.* I was raised on an upriver plantation called *Belle Rêve.* Are you familiar with Cane River and the people of the Isle Brevelle?"

Luckily Maddy had helped a novelist research this peculiar Louisiana subculture which remained largely ignored by historians shying away from a caste system based on lightness of skin. Maddy wondered if it were mere coincidence that Henri was researching the Cane River colony the day they met.

"I know only that the island plantations are owned by free men of color."

"*C'est vrai.* And of course, being one of us, you know those planters are adamant in arranging marriages for their children."

One of us, Maddy thought. Oh, my God! Félicité believes I'm a person of color since white women are barred from these balls. "Of course," she agreed, recalling the intricacies of the Ile Brevelle's rigid social structure. "Only one of our many unwritten laws."

"Then you must consider me a criminal of sorts because I broke that unwritten law when *mon père* tried to force me to marry a man twice my age. Yes, the gentleman was rich and of a good disposition, but that hardly compensated for lack of love." Félicité shivered when a river breeze chilled her bare shoulders. "Besides, I was in love with someone else from the island. His name was Philippe Dupre, and he was my age, handsome and full of life. We ran away together, here to New Orleans." She cocked her head. "You look shocked by my confidence, *mademoiselle*. Surely you know there are few secrets among those attending the balls. Indeed, my story is an open book."

"To the contrary, I think it's thrilling!" Maddy smiled at the timelessness of the love story but was puzzled by Félicité's presence at the Quadroon Ball. "Where is Philippe now?"

Félicité shuddered again, but not from the cold. "He's dead."

Maddy didn't see that coming. *"Mais, non!"*

"Mais, oui. Like some five thousand others, he was carried off by yellow fever three years ago, in the Great Plague of Fifty-Eight."

"I'm so sorry."

"Merci. I grieve for Philippe every day, but what is one to do?" Félicité lifted and dropped her shoulders in a purely Gallic shrug.

"What brought you to the balls?" Maddy pursued.

"Eh, bien. What other choice did I have? I had fully disgraced myself and could not go back to the island. As I have no skills other than the obvious and was branded 'damaged goods,' my path led to the *Salle d'Orléans.* Rather inevitably I suspect."

"You don't see your family at all?"

"Maman makes the occasional secret visit, under the guise of shopping, but to Papa I am dead. I sneak back to *Belle Rêve* when he is away on business, but—" Her voice trailed away.

"How sad."

Félicité mustered a weary smile. "You mustn't fret over my misfortunes. Life is not unendurable. For three years, since I was nineteen, I was with a young white protector who left last Christmas because it was time for him to marry. I knew from the beginning that such a day would come. He was sweet and gentle and kind enough to leave me a little money, and of course, I own our house in the Rue Rampart and have a Negro girl to do the work. I am secure for now, but who can say what will happen now that Louisiana has seceded?"

"Who indeed?"

Maddy's knowledge of the future alarmed her with its inestimable responsibility. Standing on this terrace, she realized she was a potential Cassandra on the walls of Troy, screaming doom and warning of America's coming civil war. It was a power she must rein carefully to avoid interfering with the flow of history.

"Madeleine?"

Maddy was lost in thought. "Forgive me, Félicité. My mind tends to wander."

Frightened or not, her historian's curiosity hungered to know the political views of a nineteenth-century courtesan. Unfortunately, such conversation became impossible with the arrival of a young blonde gentleman who bowed with an extravagance Maddy found almost comical. She intuitively concealed a smile behind her fan as he spoke in heavily accented French.

"My apologies for the intrusion, ladies. Please allow me to introduce myself."

Félicité discreetly whispered to Maddy. "*Americain.*"

"Joseph Moran," he said with another bow. "Whom do I have the honor of addressing?"

"Félicité Chevalier." She dropped a deep curtsy. "And Mademoiselle Madeleine St. Jacques."

"*Enchante, m'sieur,*" Maddy said, passably imitating Félicité's graceful bow.

"Might one of you do me the honor of a dance?" Moran asked.

"You go, Félicité," Maddy insisted. "I'm a bit feverish."

"So I see." Félicité drew a lacy handkerchief from her

cleavage and dabbed Maddy's damp forehead. "There now. That's better." She pressed the handkerchief into Maddy's hand. "We will talk again later, eh?"

"I hope so."

"Bon soir," Moran said, offering his arm to Félicité.

As they walked away, Félicité whispered something that brought a smile to his face, then delivered a throaty laugh. Wow, Maddy thought. That girl has got some act.

But fascination quickly faded when her new friend disappeared and Maddy realized how utterly alone she was, the proverbial stranger in a strange land. She had been so swept up in the magic of her journey that she hadn't considered the desperateness of her situation. Now it hit her hard. I don't even know how I got here, she thought, much less how to get back home!

20

Maddy leaned against the balustrade, mind racing. Maybe if I return to the scene of the crime, she thought. If I go back to that room where I arrived and hold this old pendant watch like before, maybe I can trip back to the present. Hope faded as she rushed back downstairs and wandered the labyrinth of private rooms. They were more crowded than ever, and with all of them looking alike, she had no idea which had been her landing point.

"Oh, Henri!" she moaned. "What do I do now?"

Heart pounding, Maddy chose flight. Running a gauntlet of men ogling her as a potential *placée,* she made her way outside where she dodged a sea of carriage traffic and found refuge across Orleans Street. She paused before a pharmacy and peered through the windows at the strange display of bottles, posters for all sorts of cure-alls and rows of apothecary jars including one teeming with leeches. Repulsed, she turned around and faced the *Salle d'Orléans* for the first time. The three-story building was as plain on the outside as it was glamorous inside, giving no hint of the opulent harbor for men and women seeking sexual liaisons. She was watching a coach discharge three inebriated gentlemen when a shift in wind brought an unwelcome surprise.

"What on earth—?!"

Maddy fumbled in her reticule and grabbed Félicité's handkerchief, pressing it to her nose as she was swamped by odious smells. She had read about the wretched conditions of nineteenth-century cities with their inadequate sewerage systems and lack of sanitation. New Orleans, below sea level with a high water table, was doubtless one of the worst, and she was grateful Félicité had generously perfumed her handkerchief with the citrusy Florida water.

Increasingly frightened and alone, Maddy leaned against the door of the apothecary and clutched the pendant, praying for a miracle as she listened to the jangle of harness and the shouts of drivers navigating the traffic jam. As the noise grew louder and more insistent, Maddy became mesmerized by the revolving spokes of landaus, broughams and rockaways as their wheels turned the street into one great whirring blur. Her head throbbed and she grew faint as the *Salle d'Orléans* began vibrating, as though taking a deep breath before rushing to the horizon and disappearing. Maddy retreated too and held her breath when the building came hurtling back and the thundering carriage wheels morphed into cars and cheering carnival crowds.

"Oh, my God!"

She was back.

A few rocky seconds passed before Maddy grasped that she had catapulted from one universe to another. The somber *Salle d'Orléans* was once more the lively Bourbon Orleans Hotel with Mardi Gras flags flying and throngs of revelers. Giddy with relief, Maddy raced across Orleans Street only to face a security guard demanding her ticket. Henri had kept it, and she was close to tears when the other guard remembered her extravagant costume. He grinned and waved her in.

"Go on in, Miss Scarlett."

"Thank you!" Maddy cried. She raced upstairs to the spot where Henri had left her and arrived as he was returning with the wine. He gasped when he saw her flushed face.

"Are you alright?"

"You didn't even know I was gone, did you?"

"Gone where?"

Maddy smiled as she lifted the pendant watch and dangled it in Henri's face. "Guess!"

"You didn't—?!" When Maddy nodded, Henri set the

glasses aside and hurried her to an uncrowded corner. "Where did you go?"

"Technically, nowhere. I was here in the hotel the whole time, except it was the old *Salle d'Orléans,* the year was 1861, and I was at the Quadroon Ball."

"How do you know?"

"Because an octoroon courtesan named Félicité Chevalier told me her lover died of yellow fever three years ago, in the Great Plague of Fifty-Eight." Maddy remembered the lacy handkerchief. "Here. This is what she smelled like."

Henri ignored the handkerchief and grabbed Maddy's shoulders. "You did it, Madeleine! You went back!"

Maddy shook hard with raw excitement. "Yes, I did."

"How do you feel now?"

"Relieved to be back!"

"It wasn't supposed to happen, you know. Not yet anyway. I still haven't been told the purpose of your journey, much less how to initiate it. My God, Maddy! What did you do?!"

"I honestly don't know."

"Then you must tell me everything that happened, down to the tiniest detail. We'll compare it to your other trips and see what they have in common." Henri's enthusiasm prompted him to grab Maddy and hold her tight. "Shall we go to Orange Street and sort things out?"

"Could we take a walk first? I'm still a little fuzzy, and the night air might help."

"Anything you say, darling. We'll go to the Moon Walk."

As they walked down Pirate's Alley and around Jackson Square to the Mississippi, Maddy and Henri were stopped half a dozen times by tourists wanting photos of the beautifully costumed Southern belle and her dashing beau. They were as cooperative as possible but glad to find the Moon Walk deserted except for a black saxophonist wailing the blues. They swept passed him and took a bench overlooking the inky Mississippi. Henri took Maddy's hand.

"Whenever you're ready, *ma cher.*"

Maddy began haltingly at first and then rushed with the speed of the river at their feet. Henri listened intently, filing every detail as precious information before giving an analysis.

"Now I know what you meant about being in the hotel. The janitor's washroom is where that card room was located in the old *Salle d'Orléans.* You reappeared precisely where you disappeared, which is why you disappeared and reappeared on the sidewalk when you came back. But I'm still baffled as to why. The only thing your transitions have in common are those old watches. Think again about what you did right before these last two journeys. We're missing some significant detail."

"I splashed cold water on my face before I tripped back."

"And when you returned to the present?

"I was watching the carriages."

"Carriages and sinks." Henri was totally frustrated. "I cannot fathom a connection."

Maddy reconsidered. "Actually, it was wheels more than the carriages themselves. There were so many I got sort of hypnotized and then they turned into a blur."

"Wheels?" Henri frowned. "Wait a minute! When you tripped back in your apartment, weren't you lying on the sofa looking at the overhead fan?" Maddy nodded. "And the hurricane symbol on the weather map was—"

"Spinning like the fan and the carriage wheels!" Maddy finished. She grabbed Henri's arm. "And the sink in the janitor's closet. I was watching water circling the drain!"

"Rotation!" Henri cried. "It's rotation that triggers the antique timepieces!" He threw his arms around Maddy. "Now that I know how to send you back, we only have to wait for the August Ones to reveal your mission."

His exhilaration was contagious. "I think my heart's going to jump out of my chest."

"Shall I take you home?"

"No, no!" Maddy jumped to her feet. "I want to celebrate. Let's go back to the hotel and dance the night away. I've wanted to attend the Olympus Ball as long as I can remember." She did a little spin. "And I certainly don't want to waste this beautiful dress."

"Whatever you wish, *mon amour.*" Henri rose too and gave her a deep kiss that prompted the watchful musician to improvise a sexy riff on his sax. "That gentleman deserves a handsome tip!"

21

Maddy cuddled closer in Henri's bed. She'd never been with a man whose body fit hers so perfectly. She inhaled his scent and made it a part of her before stretching extravagantly.

"After everything that happened tonight, I should be exhausted, but I feel oddly awake."

"It's probably nervous energy." Henri stroked her bare shoulder with his fingertips. "Do you want to tell me more about this Félicité?"

"Sure. She befriended me as soon as I tripped back and she was fascinating. Her father's a planter on the Cane River, and she ran away when he tried to force her to marry some old rich guy. She was in love with someone else, but when he died of yellow fever her only option was becoming a courtesan. She's had an amazing life for someone so young. I mean imagine going from spoiled belle to prostitute."

"A stranger told you all that?"

"She said the courtesans' lives are open books and naturally I was dying to hear everything. In spite of all that bad luck, she has a very positive attitude. She's also gorgeous with auburn hair and deep green eyes. I swear, under the chandeliers she looked as light as myself."

"Were the women as beautiful as the books say?"

"Actually there were quite a few plain Janes, but they were so lavishly turned out that...well, their business is illusion I guess it didn't matter. What surprised me most was their height. I'm only five-six, but I was the same height as the men. Félicité even commented on it. The women are tiny, around five feet."

"What did you tell her about yourself?"

"Only that I was from Natchez. I figured it was safer than New Orleans in case she started quizzing me about who I knew. I've spent a lot of time up in Natchez so I know the town pretty well. Hey, I was so nervous I'm lucky I didn't tell her I was from Dubai!" She and Henri shared a laugh before she turned serious again. "I'll admit it was a thrill going back, but it's also damned scary. I had to be on guard every moment to keep from giving myself away, especially after Félicité assumed I was a woman of color."

"Naturally she would, considering where you met." Henri thought a moment. "That could be complicated if you want to see her again."

"Oh, I definitely do. And I'll tell her I'm white the first chance I get."

"Since you know white women are banned from the place, will you look for her at the *Salle d'Orléans*?"

"If I'm questioned I could claim to be looking for my cheating husband."

Henri laughed. "You are one fast-thinker, my dear."

"I'm sure that's not the solution but, I'll think of something. I have a good feeling about this woman."

"You know what, Madeleine? I'm sure the August Ones arranged this accidental trip to prepare you for what's coming and are pleased with how you acquitted yourself."

"I hope so, but there were moments when I was caught off-guard. When Félicité mentioned that Louisiana had seceded, for example. I immediately thought about the civil war and what she and New Orleans will face when it comes."

"Knowledge of history is both boon and bane for time travelers and requires constant vigilance to resist its power. I'm sure you'll master it, and lots more besides."

"There's something else bothering me. I was in the past for a couple of hours, but you didn't know I was gone. How was that possible?"

"Times are not synchronized among the multiverses. You could be gone a month and no one here would be the wiser.

You return to the time you left. If you leave at noon on June 17, 2012, you'll return at that time and on that date."

"No matter what time or day I leave the past?"

"Correct."

"What if I'm gone a year or ten years? Will I have aged when I return?"

"No. You will appear as you were when you left. Unless you physically alter yourself in the past. That sort of thing is self-made and has nothing to do with time."

"It's getting complicated again." Maddy yawned. "Suddenly I'm tired again."

"Me too. Shall we get some sleep?"

"Mmmm." Maddy turned onto her side, facing away and waiting for him to nestle behind her, spoon fashion. "Do you think the August Ones will speak to you tonight?"

"They promised as much." Henri drew the sheet and blanket over them and cozied up to Maddy as she hoped. "And they've yet to break a promise."

22

Maddy was so exhausted she slept well into the morning. When she stirred, she found Henri at the sunny kitchen table, sipping coffee and perusing the Sunday *Times-Picayune.* He beamed when she padded over and gave him a kiss.

"Good morning, sleepyhead."

"Morning." Maddy poured a cup of coffee and joined him. "I'd forgotten how exhausting travel can be."

He liked her joke. "You're certainly in good spirits."

"Because I'm excited about another trip. Any dreamy itineraries I need to know about?"

"As a matter of fact, yes."

"Great." Maddy yawned. "I feel like a secret agent waiting for the next assignment."

"Are you awake enough to listen?"

"Are you kidding? I've been waiting for this all my life. I just didn't know it."

"As I suspected, what happened last night was a sort of dress rehearsal because you're going back to 1861. You'll need to spend the next few evenings with Anne Petree."

"Oh?"

"She's agreed to see you this afternoon, to measure you for an eighteen-sixties traveling ensemble out of *Godey's Lady's Book.* It was the *Vogue* of its time. Anne will also whip up a morning dress, a walking dress, and something glamorous for evening. That will tide you over until you can visit a dressmaker."

Maddy's pulse quickened. "When do I leave and what do I do when I get there?"

"You'll leave a week from today," Henri said, pleased by her eagerness. "While you're seeing Anne, I'll visit Sam

Canales, a designer friend who also works for the movies and is an expert at reproducing historical documents. He'll create calling cards and fake letters of introduction which will bear an untraceable Natchez address." Maddy nodded. "After that, we'll pay a call on Paige. She's got the currency for your trip. I stashed it at her house because she's got a safe and a great security system."

"Currency? You mean the nineteenth-century kind?"

"God, no. I wouldn't dare give you counterfeit money. You'll carry a small fortune in jewelry instead. Sam will forge proof of ownership papers for those too, and once you're settled you'll visit Menard Jewelers on Canal Street. Etienne Menard will find buyers for your jewelry."

"Won't that take a while?"

"It shouldn't. Cotton was king back then, and two-thirds of America's millionaires lived in New Orleans or on the river plantations. There were plenty of rich men buying baubles for their wives and mistresses, and when M'sieur Menard, pays off, *voila!* You'll be a very comfortable lady."

Maddy smiled and sipped her coffee. "Sounds good to me."

"You'll stay at the St. Louis Hotel, the best in the city. It was torn down in 1917 and eventually replaced by the Royal Orleans. It will also be your bank since women couldn't enter banks in 1861, much less have accounts. You'll keep your money in a safety deposit box in the hotel, drawing what you need as you need it."

"I'm getting more excited by the minute," Maddy enthused. "Tell me more."

"After Menard, you'll call on Madam Poulard, the finest *modiste* in the *carré de la ville.*"

"Oh, that's right. The French Quarter wasn't called the *vieux carré* back then."

"No, and you must remember endless similar details to keep from giving yourself away.

Madam Poulard's salon is called *La Belle Creole* and is at

the corner of Royal and Dumaine Streets. She'll provide you with a new wardrobe, everything from petticoats to corsets."

"No corsets," Maddy announced. "They're barbaric."

"I understand that, but if we're to be absolutely authentic—"

"I'm in too good a mood to argue, darling. I'm sure Anne can come up with some sort of compromise."

"That's my girl." Henri leaned across the table to claim a kiss. "On a more serious note, now that we know that the combination of watch and rotation triggers your journey, we'll combine both elements in a single unit. We'll replace the daguerreotype with another watch with hands that, once you trigger them, spin abnormally fast to give you a jolt of rotation. It's to be kept with you at all times." He took a breath. "And now you'll want to know why you're doing all this."

"Go ahead, chief. What's my mission?" she asked with mock seriousness. Henri frowned. "Did I say something wrong?"

"I'm no longer talking about fancy dresses and grand hotels, Madeleine." He looked so stern that she felt like a scolded child. "This is no joking matter."

"I'm sorry." She pretended to lock her lips and throw away the key. "Please go on."

"Ordinarily these journeys are about righting wrongs, about gathering information that won't change the past but can alter the present before it becomes history. Other times they're without specific goals, and I'm pleased that the August Ones have chosen this path as it's the easier of the two. Now, I know that with everything I've told you this morning it seems like you're preparing for a play complete with costumes, props and so forth, but what you'll be doing must be as authentic and real as your audience. What happened with Félicité was merely a taste as you face the same problems as everyone else living in 1861. Every day will present new challenges, new dangers too, and you must be constantly vigilant to keep your identity a secret. As a Louisiana historian you already know plenty about New Orleans, but I want you to spend the next few days reading everything you can about that particular year."

Maddy knew he was trying to soothe her fears, but instead they bloomed again. "Oh, Henri. I do want to make you proud of me, but I'm—"

"Nervous? Worried? Frightened?" He squeezed her hands. "That's normal, my darling, but you'll be fine because you have the gift. Remember you'll be guided by the August Ones."

"So I simply put myself in their hands and trust them to take me where I need to go?"

"As you have done with me."

When Henri opened his arms, Maddy hurried to curl up on his lap and nuzzle his shoulder while he held her close. At this moment, she knew that she never wanted to be anywhere else, in this universe or any other, without him. She also knew that, because of him, such things were beyond her control.

23

"Darling!" Paige greeted Maddy with hugs and kisses. It was only a week since they had seen each other, but she behaved like it was months. "It's been forever."

Maddie chuckled. "I've missed you too."

"Then we'll spend the afternoon catching up before Henri comes over." She led Maddy outside where Jesse had set up drinks and hors d'oeuvres. A sudden warm front drenched the courtyard with sunshine, and it washed Maddy's face as she settled into a chair. "Now then. What's the big news you mentioned on the phone?"

Maddy poured some iced tea before explaining about her accidental trip to the Quadroon Ballroom. Paige hung on every word, occasionally shaking her head and muttering "Oh, my God!" When Maddy finished, Paige was breathless.

"What was it like? I mean, really."

"Vibrant. Surreal. Dreamlike. And damned scary when I thought I couldn't get back."

"Do you sense that the August Ones were watching over you?"

"Somebody sure was."

Paige reached for the martini shaker. "If I were in your shoes, I'd be counting the hours before I could go again. What an incredible adventure!"

"I know. I'll miss you and Henri of course, but it's comforting to know I can pop back here whenever I like."

"That Félicité creature sounds fascinating."

"Doesn't she? I plan to look her up first thing when I return next week."

"So soon?" Maddy nodded. "Are you going back via the

Bourbon Orleans?"

"Henri says it will be the Royal Orleans this time. It's on the site of the St. Louis Hotel where I'll be staying. Did you know there are the remains of a sign from that old place, at the corner of Chartres and St. Louis?"

"Why, no. How did I miss that?"

"I don't know, but that's where I'll go back, at one in the morning so hopefully no one will see me disappear."

"I don't suppose Henri would let me come to see you off."

Maddy burst out laughing. "You? At one in the morning?"

"You're right. Who am I kidding?" Paige sipped contentedly. "Okay then. Want to see your jewelry?"

"I thought you'd never ask."

"It's right there." Paige nodded at a blue velvet bag by the cocktail shaker. "There's some serious bling in there, my dear."

Moments later Maddy squinted at a collection of rings, brooches, diadems and necklaces gleaming under the sun. "Wow! You weren't kidding!"

"That's my favorite." Paige indicated a bow brooch of gold filigree set with diamonds and pearls. "Isn't that divine?"

"This is more my style." Maddy picked up a pair of earrings of stamped gold and cabochon garnets and held them up to her ears. "How do they look?"

"Fabulous, of course."

Paige was much more knowledgeable about antique jewelry than Maddy and explained why some pieces were more valuable. "This shell cameo of Queen Victoria was made for the 1851 Great Exhibition in London. It's exquisitely detailed, but this little item will really bring the bucks." She picked up a bracelet with diamond flowers, pearl buds and emerald leaves. "Fit for a queen I would say. Knowing Henri, I wouldn't be surprised if it didn't belong to one."

Maddy shook her head. "Where do you suppose he gets all this stuff?"

"I'm not one to ask questions, particularly after getting Lola Montez's earrings."

"You're right." Maddy slipped everything back in the velvet bag. "I've learned it's best not to think about things too much. No matter how you look at it, none of this is especially real."

"No kidding."

They spent the rest of the afternoon catching up on local gossip and discussing the new restaurants. Paige was singing the praises of a Mideastern café called Palmyra when Henri arrived. He bussed both women on the cheek and accepted Paige's offer of a martini.

"Excellent," he pronounced after a long sip. "Did you see the jewelry, Madeleine?"

"I'm still drooling. I've never seen things like this outside of a museum."

"Which is exactly where they came from. But before you think I'm a cat burglar, rest assured the owners were handsomely compensated." He pulled something from his pants pocket. "I picked this up on the way over."

"My watch pendant!"

"Look inside. As we discussed, that old daguerreotype has been replaced by a watch face and a special second hand."

Maddy hesitated. "Remind me again what I'm supposed to do."

"Simply press the knob on the side of the new watch face, and the second hand will start spinning fast. Once that happens, grip the watch tight and you'll slip between universes."

"Such a delicious man of mystery," Paige said. "You don't have a brother, do you?"

Henri chuckled. "I'm afraid not, my dear."

Maddy looked lovingly from one to the other. "I'm really going to miss you two."

"Nonsense, darling!" Paige insisted. "You'll be so enthralled by so many new people and experiences that you won't give us a second thought."

"Don't be silly." Maddy turned to Henri. "I was just telling Paige it's a good thing I can travel back and forth and see you whenever I like."

"I only wish that were possible, my dear."

"What do you mean?"

"I mean that I took a nap this afternoon and was visited by the August Ones."

"And?" Maddy asked, heart sinking.

"They've altered the parameters. Once you go back you're allowed only one return."

"But—"

"And it's forever final."

Part 4

"Why is it that while the most thrifty and neat
and orderly city
wins our approval and gratifies us intellectually,
such a thriftless, battered and stained, and lazy old place
as the French Quarter of New Orleans takes our hearts?"

— Charles Dudley Warner, *Harper's New Monthly Magazine*,
January 1887

24

A sudden cold wave rushed down the Mississippi Valley, plunging temperatures near freezing and chilling Maddy to the bone. She was grateful for the heavy wool traveling ensemble and layers of clothing, but they didn't stop her shivering as they rode up Royal Street. The sensation intensified when Henri turned onto St. Louis Street and drove past the Royal Orleans Hotel, and by the time he made a left onto Chartres Street, Maddy felt like she might explode. She checked her pendant watch for the umpteenth time. Only a few minutes before one in the morning.

"Oh, Henri," she groaned. "I wish it was like last time, when I didn't know it was coming."

"You'll be fine, *ma cher*." He took her hand as he parked by the curb. "Check one more time to make sure you have everything."

Maddy stroked her waist where the velvet jewelry bag nudged her ribs. Letters of introduction and other official papers were in her portmanteau along with her new clothes. Against Henri's wishes she was wearing a front-zipping bustier from a popular French Quarter boutique called Trashy Diva. It was a comfortable alternative to the torture of a boned corset, and although he worried she was asking for trouble, Maddy promised no one would see it except herself. After that testy interchange, she decided not to tell him about her secret stash of L'Oreal cosmetics. That decision came after Paige declared that no woman should face the nineteenth century without decent make-up.

"I'm good to go," she announced, inspection complete.

"In that case—" Henri reached for her, but Maddy pulled away. "What's wrong?"

"Enough good-byes, my darling. I can't stand any more tears."

"I understand." He looked through both windshields and surveyed the street. "Once those people go inside the Napoleon House, Chartres will be clear in both directions."

"Then I'd better go." Maddy opened the car door, gathered her long skirts and bag and stepped onto the sidewalk. "Good-bye, my love."

"Au revoir, mon amour." Henri blinked away tears. *"Bonne chance!"*

Maddy walked away without looking back. She was afraid if she saw Henri's sweet, sad face she'd run back and never make the journey. Instead she squared her shoulders, took her place beneath the faded hotel sign and reached for her pendant watch. At exactly one o'clock, knowing she'd lose her nerve if she hesitated, Maddy pushed the knob and watched the black second hand begin spinning against the white face before whirring into a mesmeric blur. Beneath her feet, the sidewalk shuddered and popped as concrete melted into wooden planks. Maddy recoiled from another, more forceful trembling and a great roar as old walls replaced new and the massive St. Louis Hotel swallowed the smaller Royal Orleans, swelling to four stories and sprouting a dome eighty-eight feet high. Electric streetlights flickered and died before morphing into gas lanterns dangling from ropes strung across the streets. Cars, trucks and vans, including Henri's Subaru, evaporated, and Chartres Street now had a farm wagon, a cruising hackney and a few late night pedestrians. The last murky details settled and sharpened into place, and the roar ebbed as the time transfer was complete. In its wake, Maddy's breath was sucked away, and her lungs filled with the heavy, pungent air of times past.

"Dear Lord!" she gasped.

She was still marveling at the transformation when a door swung open and a pair of flamboyant dandies burst from the hotel's side entrance. The moment they saw the

132 | Michael Llewellyn

smartly dressed young woman, they held the door and tipped their stovepipe hats as she nodded her thanks and swept inside. Heart racing, she didn't dare pause to admire the hotel's lavish décor but hurried to the lobby where a solicitous clerk beamed as she introduced herself.

"Ah, yes. Mademoiselle St. Jacques. We were expecting you tomorrow, but fortunately the hotel is not full." Maddy masked her surprise, assuming this was an action by the August Ones. "As requested, we reserved a room on the third floor with a view of the Cathedral."

"Très bien," she said, relieved that her voice didn't tremble.

He offered a fountain pen and turned the registry in her direction. "Will you sign in, please?"

Eager for privacy to sort her thoughts, Maddy quickly signed and surrendered her portmanteau to a sleepy bellboy. She trailed him up a grand curving staircase to the third floor and was ushered into small but handsomely appointed quarters. The bellboy gave her the key, bowed politely and closed the door behind him.

"I did it!" Maddy whispered to herself, heart racing. "I've gone back again!"

She explored the room, noting the brass double bed, armoire, wash stand and a writing table and chair by the windows. She peeked through curtains and looked across Toulouse Street where the Pontalba Apartments and the spires of St. Louis Cathedral glowed beneath the winter sky, and the Cabildo looked close enough to touch. The flicker of myriad candles and gaslights mirrored the sparkling stars.

"How magical!" she breathed.

Maddy wanted to enjoy the view a while longer but tended to more pressing duties instead. She unpacked and hung up her dresses, tucked her stockings and undergarments on shelves inside the armoire, and set her make-up case and toiletries on the wash stand. She slipped on a nightgown and was brushing her hair when she drifted back to the window for a last look at the cathedral. After committing the view to memory, she turned down the gaslights and crawled into bed, enjoying the smell of freshly ironed and starched sheets and the feel of a mattress firmly stuffed with Spanish moss.

She was asleep before she knew it.

25

Maddy slept late and awoke ravenous. Breakfast was usually an English muffin eaten on the run, but she couldn't resist a room service menu offering oranges, oatmeal with cream, *pain perdu* with Louisiana cane syrup, *omelette aux confitures* as well as broiled trout with duchess potatoes and the ubiquitous *café au lait.* She was glad Paige couldn't see her devour French toast and eggs and speckled trout caught that very morning. Like everything else, it was notably fresher than what she was used to.

What an amazing difference, she thought.

After such a big breakfast, Maddy knew a walk was in order. Besides, she was eager to explore the city and re-immerse herself in the sights, sounds and, to some degree, the smells of a mid-nineteenth century city. She would, as planned, visit the jeweler and the modiste, but the rest of the day would be serendipitous. She donned Anne's walking dress, a smart outfit of fawn merino with a short brown satin cloak trimmed with fringe. A deep green bonnet added the jaunty touch Maddy wanted, and she was admiring herself in a standing mirror when she heard a loud knock.

"Who is it?"

"Telegram for Madam St. Jacques."

Well, Maddy thought. The August Ones aren't wasting any time. After sending the bellboy on his way, she opened the telegram and read aloud.

"My darling Madeleine, I regret that La Sirene *keeps me from your arms until this evening. Until that moment, you rule my heart and thoughts. Yours eternally, Jean Noël."*

"Wow!" she muttered. "That's some welcome to New Orleans!"

Assuming the mysterious communiqué would eventually be explained, Maddy tossed it atop the writing table and concentrated on business at hand. She was heading for the door when she was startled by another knock, louder and more insistent this time.

"It's Madeleine St. Jacques, you imposter! Open up!"

Dear God, Maddy thought. What now?

She opened the door enough to peer into the hall. A gloved hand pushed it back, and a wildcat in red velvet exploded into the room. The young woman planted hands on her hips and glared while angrily tapping the toe of her boot.

"Well?" she demanded. "I'm waiting!"

Maddy was thrown. "Waiting for what? Who are you and why are you in my room?"

"I already told you my name, madam! A better question is why you're in *my* room! I arrived at the hotel this morning only to be told I had checked in last night, and that some imposter used my name to usurp a room I reserved weeks ago." She glowered. "It was hardly what I wanted to hear after traveling all the way from Port LeBlanc!"

Maddy felt a chill when she remembered Port LeBlanc would become Westwego. Hearing that long forgotten name deepened suspicions already stirring in her soul. Could this woman sharing her name be an ancestor?!

"Port LeBlanc?" she asked haltingly.

"I live on a plantation near there, but what has that to do with why you purloined my favorite room?" The glower intensified. "I demand an explanation!"

"But, my name is also Madeleine St. Jacques," Maddy insisted.

"Impossible!" The woman paced the small room, ostrich plume on her bonnet jerking with fury. "Absolutely impossible!" Maddy remembered her calling cards, pulled one from her purse and held it out. The other Madeleine gave it a cursory look, expression switching from rage to bewilderment as the name and town registered. "Natchez? *Mais,* I don't understand."

"Apparently it's only an incredible coincidence," Maddy said, relieved when her visitor began to calm down. "We live in different cities but have the same name and happened to book the same hotel. I was also confused last night when I checked in and was told that I was a day early. I was further bewildered when—"

"What's this?" The woman stopped pacing when she saw her name on the telegram. She snatched it up and read it, anger now forgotten and replaced by disappointment. She shook her head. "A word of advice, mademoiselle. Never become involved with a riverboat captain."

"I beg your pardon?"

She waved the telegram in Maddy's direction. "I assume you read it too. *Eh, bien.* Naturally you would since it has your name on it." She thought a moment. "Your middle name isn't Anne too, is it?"

"Marie."

"Thank goodness that much is different." She looked back at the telegram. "I suppose you have deduced this is not from my husband."

"I deduced nothing of the sort, although I suspect few husbands write their wives with such passion. Either way it's none of my business."

"C'est vrai." The woman tucked the telegram into her purse and grimaced. "This is all so embarrassing."

"As I said, it's none of my business."

"That's not what I meant. I'm referring to my outrageous behavior. Bursting into a stranger's room, calling her names, making accusations. It's inexcusable."

Maddy smiled. "It was all a terrible misunderstanding. Consider it forgotten."

"I'll do nothing of the sort. Let me think. Ah, yes! You must let me take you to dinner, my dear. It's the very least I can do." Before Maddy could reply, Madeleine waved her hand. "It's utterly *comme il faut,* and I will not take no for an answer."

Maddy had never received, much less accepted a dinner invitation from a total stranger and reminded herself that 1861 manners were far more formal and complicated than she was accustomed to. Besides, she wasn't about to miss the chance to know more about this feisty, outspoken woman with the same name. "It would be a great pleasure."

Madeleine instantly brightened. "*C'est bien.* The Ladies Table here is quite good and is set at five. Shall we say five thirty at the entrance to the restaurant?"

"That will be fine. I look forward to it."

"As do I." Madeleine smiled for the first time, dimpling prettily to reveal how attractive she was when not in a rage. "*A bientot!*"

"*A bientot.*"

The woman vanished in a flurry of velvet and plumes, leaving Maddy momentarily drained. Well, she thought. Day One certainly began with a bang. I can hardly wait to see what else is in store.

26

After a rewarding visit with Etienne Menard, who assured Maddy he had several rich clients eager to purchase such extraordinary bijoux, she left his Canal Street store and headed for Madam Poulard's shop in the Rue Chartres. It was a cool, sunny February morning that invited strolling, so Maddy took her time to absorb an environment both familiar and alien. As with her first visit, she was shocked by the noise. Nineteenth-century New Orleans throbbed with the racket of wooden and metal wheels on cobblestones, shouting drivers, the clang of forges, clip-clopping hooves and whinnying horses. A more pleasant surprise was public politeness prompting her to nod pleasantly to gentlemen tipping their hats or touching the brims if they were in a hurry. The awful stench she experienced on Orleans Street was erased here by the mouth-watering smells of *charcuteries, boulangeries* and *pâstisseries,* and she was thrilled by a constant array of colorful characters. She passed black women balancing baskets on heads wrapped in scarves of dazzling colors, praline *vendeuses* singing the praises of their sweet candies, a Greek organ grinder with a dancing monkey, a pair of Ursuline nuns and, inexplicably, a Moroccan in flowing robes and scarlet fez. By the time she reached the cathedral, Maddy was so mesmerized she decided the *modiste* could wait while she explored Jackson Square. It remained her favorite spot in the French Quarter, and because it was so familiar, its newness was a jolt. The mansard roof on the Cabildo, installed in 1847, gleamed brightly, as did the Pontalba Apartments completed only nine years ago. Maddy almost laughed at their freshness since she knew them as America's oldest apartment buildings. If only Henri could be here to share all this, she thought wistfully.

Dizzied by the spectacle, she found an empty bench inside the fenced, formally landscaped park and studied the unique potpourri of humanity. Stationed at intervals around the square were a dozen uniformed City Guards sporting cutlasses. Less obviously armed was a trio of dashing *boulevardiers* with elegant *colchemardes,* or sword-canes, clanking against their thighs as they promenaded like musketeers. The preening dandies were distracted by a stunning, tawny-skinned quadroon who drew stares from everyone, including Maddy. Followed by a mulatto *domestique* laden with brightly colored packages, she seemed indifferent to the stir she was creating. Maddy thought her supremely insouciant in a deep blue merino ensemble with hat and ostrich plumes dyed to match. Gloved hands twirled a parasol that seemed out of season until Maddy reminded herself that such ladies prized and protected pale skin as diligently as white women, perhaps more so.

She's lovely, Maddy thought, wondering if she, like Félicité, was a *placée* or another wellborn lady of color. Either way, she trailed a wake of desire as she traversed the park and exited at the *Rue de le Levée*. Maddy gasped. Until she turned to follow the girl's progress, she didn't realize she hadn't looked toward the river. In place of Woldenberg Park and the Moon Walk was a crush of ships unlike anything she'd imagined. Going for a better look, she was dazzled by magnificent, smoke-belching, fire-breathing steamboats, Indiamen from the Caribbean and New England coasting craft moored five and six deep. Where the Aquarium of the Americas would rise in 1990, a majestic clipper ship poked masts sixty-five feet into the air and was far more graceful, Maddy thought, than any engraving Currier & Ives rendered. Scrambling along the waterfront was an army of sailors, passengers, merchant marines, roustabouts, gamblers, medicine pitchmen, banana peddlers and Choctaw squaws selling woven baskets. Maddy was enthralled by the raucous spectacle but hurriedly retreated when a shifting river breeze brought the noxious smells of fish, smoke, brine, tar and rot. Time to move on.

Maddy window-shopped down Royal Street and found Madam Poulard's shop, *La Belle Creole,* at the corner of the *Rue du Maine.* She admired a stylish oil-painted sign depicting a lady in *costume de bal* and another in *costume de promenade.* A bell whispered discreetly as she entered a quiet, perfumed, very feminine oasis in the middle of the boisterous city. A smartly dressed woman her own age rose from behind an ornate *escritoire.*

"Bonjour, mademoiselle. I am Madam LaCroix. How may I be of assistance?"

Maddy introduced herself and explained that she needed a few dresses for spring and summer. The woman appraised her with a critical eye. "Madam Poulard is very busy at present, but you may be in luck. Please." She indicated a *bergère* chair, and Maddy sat. "A client who ordered a new wardrobe has, alas, a husband who refuses to pay the bill. It leaves us in a most awkward situation, but since you appear to be her size I see no reason why you shouldn't see the clothes. They include some of Madam Poulard's finest creations for next season."

Maddy tingled with excitement. "I'd love to see them."

"Bien."

Maddy examined one exquisite ensemble after another and decided the luckless customer had far better taste in clothing than husbands. After selecting five dresses, she stepped into a curtained alcove and stripped to her corset cover and waist petticoat. When she emerged to try on clothes, she faced a woman as formidable appearing as Georgia Warren. Short and stout, hair pulled into a tight bun, her black dress was relieved by a garnet brooch pinned to an ample bosom. She nodded briskly.

"Je suis Madam Poulard," she announced. "And you are

Mademoiselle St. Jacques?"

"Oui, madam." Maddy instinctively dropped a curtsy. "It's an honor to meet you."

"Yes, I should think so," Poulard replied. "Now let me get a look at you."

Maddy froze while the woman circled her, inspecting first with her shrewd *modiste*'s eye and then with her fingers. She caressed Maddy's back and shoulders and cupped hands around her waist. "The clothes should fit perfectly. Indeed, I see no need for any extensive...*mais,* what's this?" A shudder shot down Maddy's spine when the woman tugged at the front of her corset cover and pointed. "Eh?"

Henri's warning about authenticity replayed in her head. "You mean my corset?"

"I mean *this!*" She tapped the zipper with a long finger-nail. *"Eh, mademoiselle?"*

Damn, Maddy thought. This old gal doesn't miss a thing. Her mind sped with possible explanations before she blurted, "It's called a zipper."

Madam Poulard pursed thin lips. "Zipper? What does it do?"

"It opens and closes the front of the corset," Maddy explained, lowering the zipper a few inches and sliding it shut again. *"Voila!"*

"Voila, indeed," the woman snorted. "I know of something similar made by Elias Howe, but it's nothing like this." She grabbed the zipper and yanked it down, oblivious to Maddy's exposed cleavage as she repeatedly opened and closed it, like a child with a new toy. "Where did you get this, may I ask?"

"It was a gift," Maddy replied without thinking.

The *modiste* was shocked. "Corsets as gifts? Unthinkable!" Suspicion arose as she reassessed her new client. "Unless you are...*mais, non!*"

Maddy instantly read the innuendo. "I assure you I am no fallen woman, Madam. I should have said my mother saw it in a shop in London and thought it so innovative she bought one for each of us. It's ever so comfortable."

"Then I shall trouble you for the name of this London merchant, if you please." When Madam Poulard pursed her lips, Maddy saw the wheels turning. "This will revolutionize haute couture and make someone a fortune. I see no reason why it should not be me."

"I'll try to find out, but my poor *maman* is so forgetful that I—"

The *modiste*'s beady eyes narrowed even more. "I assure you I will make it worth your while, Mademoiselle St. Jacques. Now then. Shall we begin?"

"*Bien sûr,*" Maddy replied, relieved as a white linen batiste dress was slipped over her head. Another crisis averted, she thought.

27

Maddy was still shaking from her close call with Madam Poulard when she returned to the St. Louis Hotel. With a few minutes to kill before meeting Madeleine, she went exploring. She was impressed by lavish public rooms appointed with chandeliers, gleaming brass fixtures, sumptuous French furnishings and forests of potted palms. The only blot on such elegance was a row of cuspidors where the floor was stained by wayward tobacco squids. This is worse than a cigar bar, Maddy thought with disgust.

She lifted her long skirts and breezed by the spittoons, following signs reading "To Rotunda." Maddy was eager to see this architectural wonder, described in the hotel brochure as a "magnificent dome sixty-five feet in diameter, soaring to the breathtaking height of eight-stories and boasting a modern glass skylight." She was soon engulfed by a crowd flowing toward the site but didn't notice she was the only woman until she inhaled the stench of cigar smoke and unwashed bodies. She grabbed her scented handkerchief and craned her neck for a look at the great dome, but something else caught her eye. A forest of top hats and clouds of cigar smoke made visibility difficult, but Maddy's height revealed something that would haunt her the rest of her life. A crowd of men formed a semicircle around a wooden platform holding a well-dressed white gentleman and a quadroon woman Maddy's age wearing a garish red and yellow striped robe and blue peaked hat. Hands hung at her sides and she stared at the floor until the man rapped a gavel and barked at her to look up as he sang out her housekeeping skills, her obedience and deep piety. Maddy cringed as she registered the horror of the moment. Not only was she witnessing a slave auction but, in keeping with the carnival season, the woman wore a Mardi Gras costume! She looked away only to see a wretched cluster of black men, women and children whose destinies would also be dictated by the gavel. Gorge rising, she whirled and pushed her way through the enrapt crowd.

"Pardonnez-moi!" she cried again and again. *"Pardon! Pardon!"*

Maddy fled like a woman possessed and didn't stop running until she reached the lobby. She sank into a chair and fought a wave of nausea, dabbing a damp forehead with her handkerchief until the wave passed. She closed her eyes and took a deep breath, and when she opened them again Madeleine was standing over her, face taut with concern.

"Are you alright, my dear? You're pale as a ghost."

"I was feeling a bit faint." Maddy got shakily to her feet. "If I could step outside for a moment and get some fresh air—"

"Bien sûr!" Madeleine gave her a supportive arm and steered her through the front entrance. "There now. Is that better?"

"Yes, thank you." Maddy took a deep breath and filled her lungs with cool air gusting off the river. "This is so unlike me, but I…well, I saw something very upsetting."

Madeleine cocked her head. "Oh?"

Maddy reminded herself that since this woman was plantation-bred she surely bought the system that built her family fortune. She probably also believed it was the sacred duty of white Christians to rescue black heathens from pagan hellfire and damnation, and that if slavery was accepted by Abraham and Saint Paul that was alright with her too. Still, she waded deeper.

"Have you seen the hotel rotunda?" she asked cautiously.

Madeleine sniffed. "Once was enough, my dear. Jean-Noël and I walked in there one morning last fall, rather by accident. *Tiens,* a slave auction is not something a lady wants to see, especially not right after breakfast."

"You're not an abolitionist, are you?"

"Heavens, no, but I agree with President Jefferson that slavery is like holding a wolf by the ears. It's equally frightening to hold on or let go, and without it the Southern economy would collapse. Either way, I don't need to witness such spectacles."

"Especially not when they dress the slaves in Mardi Gras costumes."

Madeleine made a face. "For heaven's sake, that would've upset me too. I wonder what enterprising gentleman dreamed that up." Before Maddy could respond, Madeleine said, "Are you up to eating something now?"

"Oddly enough, I'm famished."

"Moi aussi." Madeleine ushered her back inside the hotel. "I arrived early and peeked at the menu. The *specialite de la maison* tonight is broiled sheepshead."

Maddy hadn't eaten that particular fish since she was a teen. It was delicious to be sure but rarely found in New Orleans restaurants because it was difficult to bone. Once again she was awed by an extensive menu offering oysters on the half shell, Spanish mackerel, lamb cutlets, green turtle soup, teal duck stuffed with truffles and sweetbreads *a la Creole*. Desserts included nesselrode pudding, cocoanut custard pie, sponge cake and petits fours.

"I could almost gain weight by reading this menu," Maddy laughed.

"That's a peculiar way to put it," Madeleine said, "but I know what you mean."

"If you'll pardon my saying so, you look to be the perfect weight."

"You're sweet," Madeleine said, "but I must exercise caution as the ladies in my family are given to *en bonpoint*."

Charmed by Madeleine's smile, Maddy could hardly believe this was the furious shrew who burst into her room that morning, face contorted with rage. With features relaxed and spirits high, Madeleine was another person altogether and,

146 | Michael Llewellyn

Maddy noted, had turned prettiness into beauty with chic clothes and a smart coiffure. As for make-up, Maddy knew that Creole women disdained *maquillage* and admitted only to coloring gray hair with coffee grounds. A close look debunked this myth although Maddy conceded Madeleine's make-up was as skillfully applied as her own *L'Oréal*. After ordering dinner, the women began getting acquainted. Madeleine turned out to be as genial and vivacious as she was attractive, but she was also guarded until she learned more about Maddy.

"Please tell me something about yourself, my dear. I've never been to Natchez, but I understand it's lovely."

"It is indeed." Maddy thought of modern Natchez's treasure trove of urban villas and pillared plantation houses. It boasted more antebellum architecture than any city in America, most of it new in 1861 as Natchez rode a vertiginous wave of cotton wealth. "It sits on the highest bluff on the Mississippi and has glorious views of the river."

Madeline nibbled an olive. "I envy you. We're so abysmally low-lying and flood-prone here it's no wonder the first colonists called Louisiana *la flottant*." The floating land, Maddy translated. She couldn't think of a more appropriate label, especially in Katrina's wake. "*Mais*, tell me what brings you to New Orleans. Shopping? The opera? And who is your traveling companion?"

Knowing the proprieties and protocols of the time, Henri had anticipated this question and devised a response. Because she believed Madeleine to be a woman of courage and independence, Maddy presented her alibi as though it was a serious confidence.

"As a matter of fact I'm traveling alone, and, if I may be frank, I suspect you don't find the idea scandalous."

Madeline took the bait. "You're very perceptive. I assume you're unmarried as well."

"I am indeed and have no family to speak of. I was orphaned at seven when my parents were killed in a steamboat explosion. I was raised by a maiden aunt who died last year and left me with the means to do as I choose. I'm afraid I shocked Natchez by taking a steamboat to Vicksburg alone last fall and so enjoyed myself I decided to visit New Orleans."

"How deliciously bold!"

Maddy pursed her lips. "And not a little satisfying."

"It would seem you and I have much in common, my dear, and I sense a peculiar kinship, considering you're a stranger." Madeleine stopped talking while the waiter delivered crawfish bisque for Maddy and okra gumbo for herself. She continued over the soup. "It will sound most peculiar, but I even think there's a bit of a resemblance."

"I'm flattered."

Madeleine smiled. "You have no idea how much I'm enjoying this moment. My husband doesn't permit entertaining, you see, so I—"

"*Mais,* what sort of husband would do such a thing?"

"One who is evil personified, that's what sort." Madeleine's face darkened. "Jules didn't want a wife. He wanted a subservient to dominate and humiliate, and it is precisely that situation that drove me to take a paramour."

"*Mon dieu,*" Maddy breathed. "I'm so sorry."

"*Moi aussi.* I've been living a nightmare these past few years. Out of desperation I confessed the truth to my priest, but he only insisted my duty was to remain with my husband. I felt so trapped that I wept in the confessional."

What bullshit, Maddy thought, struggling to conceal her disgust with the papacy's eternal aversion to reality.

"You must forgive me. I have no business burdening you with my misfortunes. You see, the only women I'm ever around are servants or shopkeepers, and I yearn desperately for a close female confidante."

"Another coincidence," Maddy said, seizing the moment. "I feel the same way."

Madeleine's face flooded with relief. "Truly?"

"Truly."

"Then we must make the most of our time together. My hateful husband has allotted me exactly two weeks to finish my shopping, and during that time I insist on showing you the city. You've no idea how much that would please me."

"But what about Jean Noël?"

Madeleine looked resigned. "As I told you, he's a steamboat captain and finds time for us whenever he can. They're a busy breed, meaning this morning's telegram was, although disappointing, not unusual. I've learned to accept the situation since we must grab happiness whenever possible. Having you to keep me from being alone would be absolute bliss."

"I'm certain I'll enjoy it too. I wish there was some way I could reciprocate."

A gleam appeared in Madeleine's blue eyes. "In truth, there *is* something you could do. The circumstances of my liaison with Jean Noël dictate that we not be seen in public. That could change if he was with another woman and I was perceived as their guest, if you know what I mean." Madeleine wrinkled her nose. "You must find me terribly wicked and selfish."

Maddy chuckled. "To the contrary, I find you terribly clever."

"You're not offended then?"

"Not in the least. I'll be happy to help out with Jean Noël but with your husband on the plantation why the need for such secrecy in such a big city?"

"Because Jules is here more than he's home. You see, he's also a riverboat captain."

Maddy blinked. "Is there a possibility he and Jean Noël might cross paths?"

"More than a possibility, my dear. They're business partners."

Dear God, Maddy thought. This sounds like a plot from Desperate Housewives!

28

Both women were in high spirits when they left the ladies' dining room. Not since meeting Paige had Maddy bonded so quickly with a new acquaintance. She didn't know if it was the work of the August Ones, but she was definitely less anxious about being alone in another century and was grateful for that. She was about to excuse herself so she could return to her room and begin her travel journal when she was overwhelmed with déjà vu. The discomfiting sensation deepened as a tall, uniformed gentleman approached across the lobby. He had a thick head of wavy brown hair and muttonchops, and smiled broadly as he touched his hat brim. Maddy's heart fluttered when she thought he called her name.

"Madam St. Jacques! How delightful to see you!"

It took Maddy a second to realize it was Jean Noël playing his usual public role as he took Madeleine's proffered hand and touched it with his moustache. Maddy didn't know how even a casual observer could miss the electricity when the secret lovers gazed in each other's eyes. She smiled at the charade but grew embarrassed when he addressed her.

"I don't believe I've had the pleasure, mademoiselle."

Despite knowing he belonged to another woman, Maddy blushed when the handsome riverboat captain turned his full attention on her. He smelled faintly of tobacco, bourbon and leather and had a deep voice reminding her of James Earl Jones. Madeleine's laughter brought her back to reality.

"Brace yourself, captain. The lady and I share the same name." When he stared in disbelief, she said, "Allow me to present Mademoiselle Madeleine St. Jacques. Madeleine, this is Captain Jean Noël Baptiste."

Maddy was a little wobbly as she dropped a curtsy and rose to find the man's gaze more intense than ever. "Captain Baptiste," she managed, thinking he looked even more familiar than Madeleine.

"*Mais,* how is this possible?" he asked incredulously.

"A grandiose coincidence," Madeleine explained, "and a rather awkward one. I should begin by telling you the lady is from Natchez and her full name is Madeleine Marie St. Jacques. At least our middle names differ." Jean-Noël laughed heartily as she explained the confusion over the hotel reservation and the extravagant scene she made that morning. "But as you can see, things turned out very nicely, and we have become friends."

"*C'est bien.*" Jean-Noël looked from one to the other. "But won't it be confusing with two Madeleines?"

Maddy found her voice. "All my friends call me Maddy."

"Then Maddy it is." Madeleine gave Jean-Noël a mischievous look. "Maddy has agreed to keep me company when you're otherwise engaged." She leaned close and lowered her voice to a whisper. "She's also agreed to accompany us in public as your lady friend which means we can finally share those places we both love." His raised eyebrows triggered a hasty addendum. "She got your telegram by mistake, so she knows everything."

Jean-Noël was skeptical. "You're trusting a perfect stranger?"

"I'm from Mississippi," Maddy interjected. "I've never been to New Orleans, so I know no one with whom to share your secret."

"That's a relief." Jean-Noël gave her a dazzling smile as his eyes flickered to her pendant.

"What a lovely cameo. Is it a watch as well?"

"So you noticed it too," Madeleine said. "I thought it was the one you gave me last summer, the one I lost, but Maddy showed me there's no daguerreotype inside, only a funny sort of extra watch."

"An extra watch? May I see it?"

"Bien sûr, m'sieur." Maddy popped open the case to reveal the inside compartment. *"Voila."*

Jean-Noël scrutinized the watch face added by Henri. "I've never seen anything like this. What is the purpose of two watches?"

Maddy thought fast. "Insurance in case the first one stops, of course."

Jean-Noël seemed satisfied. "What will they think of next?"

When he looked from Maddy to Madeleine, there was no mistaking the longing in his gaze. Maddy took that as her cue to say good-night. "If you'll excuse me—"

"Not quite yet," Madeleine said. "We must ask Captain Baptiste if he's free for dinner tomorrow evening. I understand Antoine's is *très amusante.*"

"And quite fashionable too." Jean-Noël brightened at the prospect of dining publicly with his secret love. "In fact, M'sieur Antoine Alciatore is an acquaintance of mine. He and his wife sailed on *La Sirene* some months ago."

"*The Mermaid* is his ship," Madeleine explained.

"He was most gracious and asked me to be his guest at the restaurant sometime, an invitation I'd forgotten until now."

"Then Antoine's it is." Madeleine happily turned to Maddy. "Now I will let you say good-night." She surprised Maddy with a kiss and whispered, *"Merci beaucoup."*

Maddy was halfway to her room when she realized why Jean-Noël looked so familiar. It was his face in the daguerreotype Henri had replaced in the watch's second compartment!

"I'll be damned!"

She was amazed yet again by the machinations of the August Ones and by Henri's slyness in giving her something from someone in the past whom she was destined to meet. As she sank in the chair to contemplate things, she was thrilled when Henri became an almost palpable presence. She took this as a sign he was with her in spirit.

I'm with you, too, my darling, she thought. And you've no idea how much I miss you.

29

The night they met, Maddy recalled Félicité telling her she lived on Rampart Street. Except for the occasional dinner at Meauxbar, this was a street she avoided, a dicey strip bordering the Quarter with mostly dilapidated apartments and sleazy bars. She knew, however, that it had a proud past and saw proof as she walked wooden sidewalks which, in 1861, were lined with raised cottages, handsome one-story affairs of woodlap siding or stuccoed brick with chimneys piercing the center of the roof. Built by white men for their mistress of color, most were turned into boarding houses when the liaison ended and their female owners retired as courtesans. This was the vista she enjoyed as she strolled Rampart from the *Rue du Maine* toward Esplanade Avenue. At Hospital Street she encountered a mulatto *marchande* balancing a basket on her head and sing-selling her wares.

"Belles des figues!" the woman trilled. "Beautiful figs!"

Maddy approached her. *"Pardonnez-moi, madam.* Do you know which house is the residence of Mademoiselle Félicité Chevalier?" When the woman looked dumbstruck, Maddy worried that she had addressed her too formally. She was about to continue in more common terms when the *marchande* pointed down Rampart.

"At the Rue St. Philippe. Two orange trees and a blue door." Before Maddy could thank her, she charged down the street, pausing twice to look over her shoulder. Not until she turned a corner did she resume her strange song. *"Belles des figues! Belles des figues!"*

Maddy chalked up the vendor's odd behavior to her own ignorance of local customs and continued down the wooden *banquette.* She paused before the only corner house flanked

154 | Michael Llewellyn

by orange trees and was about to knock on the blue door when it swung open. Another *marchande* was leaving, this one carrying a basket filled with pralines and pecans. She curtsied and hurried away to reveal a familiar figure loomed in the doorway.

Maddy smiled. "Mademoiselle Chevalier?"

The woman smiled back. "Mademoiselle St. Jacques? Is it truly you?"

"Oui. C'est moi."

"What an unexpected pleasure. I thought you'd fallen off the face of the earth." She stepped aside. "Won't you come in?"

"Merci."

"But how did you find me?" Félicité asked as she ushered Maddy into a small parlor. It was sparsely furnished, but the few pieces were extremely high quality. A sand-filled pot containing palmettos stood in one corner, reminding Maddy of her grandmother's old-fashioned *éventails lantaniers.*

"I recalled you said you lived on Rampart, so I asked a woman selling figs and she directed me here. She acted most strangely."

"Was she wearing an indigo *tignon?*" Maddy nodded. "Ah, yes. That would be Iris. She and her circle are the only ones to wear that particular color. Rumor has it they're *voudouiennes,* but who can say? In any case, all *marchandes* know me since the world of us octoroon *placées* is rather small." She indicated a chair and Maddy sat. "Now then. To what do I owe this unexpected pleasure?"

"This." Maddy drew Félicité's fancy handkerchief from her reticule. "I didn't want you to think me a thief."

Félicité laughed, the throaty sound Maddy remembered from the *Salle d'Orléans.* "I thought no such thing, mademoiselle, although I have turned this house upside down looking for it." She pressed it against her cheek. "It belonged to my grandmother, you see, and I have precious little to remember my family by." Maddy wanted to pursue that line of conversation remembered from the night they met, but chose to keep still. "Please tell me what happened. I sought you out after a few dances with M'sieur Moran, but you had vanished."

Maddy began the speech she and Henri had prepared for this occasion. "I was afraid of being exposed."

Félicité's frown ruined a perfect face. "I don't understand."

"I'm not a *femme de coleur.*" The green eyes widened. "When I began getting suspicious looks, I worried that someone might demand my papers and decided to flee."

Félicité was shocked. "*Mais,* why would a white woman attend our balls?"

Maddy decided her claim of looking for a wayward husband would only complicate matters, so she opted for a simpler explanation. "Because I wanted to." She expected Félicité to be further appalled, even insulted, but to her surprise the young beauty laughed again. "You find it amusing then?"

"To the contrary, mademoiselle. I find it both refreshing and bold. I admire any woman who dares challenges the social status quo."

"I'm delighted to hear that," Maddy said, relieved.

Félicité seemed genuinely pleased. "Will you have tea with me?"

"I'd be honored."

"A white lady honored to keep company with a woman of color? You are daring!" Félicité addressed a Negro girl hovering in the hallway. "*Thé et crullers,* Zaza."

While they waited for refreshments, Maddy answered questions about who she was and why she was visiting New Orleans. She kept her story as close as possible to what she told Madeleine, adding only that she wanted to experience those freedoms denied women afraid of flouting convention. She was not, she assured Félicité, concerned with what people thought here or in Natchez. "Or, for that matter, any and all points in between."

"I admire your courage," Félicité said, "and confess to chafing at the strictures of society, especially since I'm fairer than most white women but must carry official papers declaring my lineage. I never imagined I would say as much to a white person, but I despise the old dictum that one drop of Negro blood makes one all Negro." She toyed with her auburn curls. "Especially when I'm living proof that it isn't true."

The way Félicité scorned the word "Negro" supported what Maddy knew about the elaborate New Orleans caste system and the loathing by those with light skin for those darker than themselves. "Forgive me for being so personal, but have you considered going somewhere that such a law does not exist?"

"You mean *passé blanc*?" Félicité waved a hand airily. "Certainly I have considered it, but being an octoroon is more than light skin and commingled blood. What's outside and what's inside are very different things. Besides, something strange binds me to Louisiana, some unknown energy I've never understood. Not family certainly, but who can say?" Like a high-born white woman, Félicité discreetly waited until her servant delivered the refreshments and left before continuing the conversation. "Our world, that of free octoroons and quadroons, has always been fragile, but these days it is more tenuous than ever."

"What do you mean?"

"Everyone knows that our rights are rapidly disappearing. Have you not heard the latest, that we can no longer worship without white supervision?"

Maddy's shock was genuine. "No!"

"Or that we can no longer operate coffee houses, much less those places serving liquor."

"I suppose I don't pay much attention to such things," Maddy managed, ashamed of her lame excuse. Luckily Félicité was too distracted to notice.

"If the Union doesn't allow the South to leave in peace,

our fate hangs with that of the Confederacy," Félicité continued. "If it is defeated, so are we free people of color. Of course we must pray that this does not happen."

"Of course."

Maddy sipped the fragrant tea, struggling to appear sympathetic while knowing the newborn Confederacy was doomed and Louisiana's caste structure with it. President Lincoln's Emancipation Proclamation would free some four million slaves, the vast majority illiterate and unskilled, who were then left to fend for themselves as the war raged on. The rigid social barriers between them and Félicité would begin to dissolve, and, with Appomattox, the educated and professional free blacks would be on equal footing with the lowliest, most ignorant slave. It was a prospect Maddy knew would devastate and humiliate Félicité.

"Have you considered what to do if that day comes?"

"*Bon dieu!* It's too dreadful to think about. For now I must continue going to the balls and hoping to find a protector."

"What about M'sieur Moran?"

"Oh, I considered him a serious suitor at first, but now I don't know. He's come calling a few times but made no mention of an arrangement. Dealing with the unknown on a daily basis is so frustrating, and the threat of war is no help. Some days, I think I...oh!"

To Maddy's surprise, Félicité buried her face in her hands and began weeping. Although she scarcely knew Félicité, she could not resist embracing this poor exotic creature. Félicité seemed embarrassed by the comforting gesture.

"You are too kind, mademoiselle."

"Please call me Maddy."

"Will you be likewise familiar and call me Félicité."

"Of course, Félicité. I only wish there was something I could do to help."

"*Mais,* you are helping by merely being here and listening to me." Félicité dabbed her eyes with her grandmother's handkerchief. "I have so few friends these days."

"I don't understand."

"It's not unusual. You see, once a liaison is formed we courtesans are devoted to our protector, with little time left for ourselves, much less our friends. I was with Randolph four years and only recently returned to the balls where I found myself isolated and ignored by other women. That is why I approached you so readily, a stranger looking as lost as myself." She took Maddy's hand. "I've never had white friends, but, as you are flouting convention and inspire me to do likewise, may I consider you as such?"

As Maddy looked into Félicité's eyes, she attributed this second bonding with a stranger to more intervention by the August Ones and decided that the coincidence of so easily engaging Madeleine and Félicité, both women without female friends, meant that they were designated touchstones for her timeless odyssey. She smiled and squeezed Félicité's hand.

"Indeed you may."

30

With Jean-Noël between them, a lady on each arm, Maddy and Madeleine leisurely strolled the few blocks from the St. Louis Hotel to Antoine's restaurant. Because she was dining in public with her secret paramour, Madeleine was in exuberant spirits. Her peach taffeta gown with matching plumed hat dazzled passersby, feathers dancing as she chatted away, eyes sparkling as though drunk on life. Jean-Noël was equally lively, Maddy noted, and quite dashing in a black derby, gold silk vest and tobacco-colored frock coat. She sparkled too in a silver-gray silk evening ensemble with contrasting cape. As they garnered more admiring stares, Maddy wished she'd stashed a tiny digital camera to capture the moment, but Henri had been so adamantly opposed when she suggested as much, she didn't dare risk it.

In 1861, Antoine's was smaller and a block away from the one Maddy knew on St. Louis Street. She found it much nicer without the usual crush of noisy tourists and, because Jean-Noël was a guest of the owner, more welcoming as well. Given a superb table and fawned over by a host of waiters, she envisioned a memorable evening, but her focus shifted elsewhere when Madeleine peeled off her gloves. The centuries merged and hummed in Maddy's brain when she saw the woman's right hand, and her reaction did not go unnoticed.

"My dear!" Madeleine said. "You looked so startled."

"It's your ring," Maddy gasped. "I've never seen anything like it." It was a lie of course. Blinding her with memory and glamour was something she had been secretly promised as a child—Grandmother Aglaé's ruby and sapphire ring. It was the final proof she needed that Madeleine was an ancestor, and the realization was stunning. She steeled herself against the sort of unsettling moment Henri warned about and mustered restraint to keep from blurting the astonishing truth. "It takes my breath away," she managed finally.

"Mine too." Madeleine twirled the ring on her finger. "When my parents honeymooned in Paris, Mama found it in a shop in the Montmartre and begged papa to buy it. The shopkeeper claimed it was made for a Sultana, but I suspect the truth is less romantic. I don't wear it often because it's a bit gaudy, but with mother and father gone now, it's become especially dear to me." She smiled. "Would you care to try it on?"

"Oh, no, thank you," Maddy demurred, fearful that contact with something she had touched in the future might trigger some sort of time rupture. The threat mercifully ended when waiters delivered a cornucopia of dishes from oysters on the half shell and green turtle soup to delicate river shrimp and sweetbreads *à la Creole.* Jean-Noël marveled at Maddy's healthy appetite while Madeleine daintily nibbled a tray of Spanish olives, celery and pickles before picking at a lamb cutlet. Embarrassed by Madeleine's restraint and reminding herself she couldn't work off any extra pounds at Curves, Maddy put down her fork and said she could eat no more. Her resolve lasted until Antoine himself sent over *pouding a la reine,* queen of all puddings. She couldn't resist the rich layered confection of egg whites and jelly laced with raisins, currants and lemon zest, but stopped when her zippered bustier protested.

"Enough," she proclaimed. "I cannot eat another bite." When Madeleine and Jean-Noël swapped amused looks, she knew they were wondering if she meant it this time. "I must say Natchez has nothing to compare with this."

"I've visited the town many times and wondered about the paucity of good restaurants," Jean-Noël offered.

"Especially since Natchez has more millionaires than New Orleans," Maddy teased.

"Touché," he laughed.

"I know something else we have in abundance," Madeleine interjected. "Fortune tellers!"

"What on earth made you think of that?" Jean-Noël asked.

"I've no idea." She turned to Maddy. "Have you ever had your fortune told?"

"No," Maddy confessed, remembering the ever-present cluster of tarot card dealers fleecing the tourists on Jackson Square. "I admit it intrigues me."

Madeleine clapped her hands. "Then it's decided. We'll go see one tonight. It could be an amusing way to end our lovely evening."

Jean-Noël was unconvinced. "What if she makes unpleasant predictions?"

Madeleine gave Maddy an exasperated look. "Steamboat captains are such a superstitious lot."

"Maybe he's right." Suddenly Maddy was afraid of anyone discussing her future, even a charlatan, but Madeleine would have none of it.

"Nonsense. I've been to this woman before, and she's never disappointed me with gloomy prophecies. She has a place in the Rue Burgundy, and there's a lovely *patisserie* along the way that has the most divine almond macaroons."

Jean-Noël was bemused. "But you didn't even try M'sieur Alciatore's pudding."

Madeleine said nothing, merely gave him a look announcing her mind was made up. The message was driven home when she stood and smiled, indications that she was ready to leave and expected the others to follow.

Wow, Maddy thought. If she's really my ancestor, why didn't I get some of that iron will?

Fifteen minutes later, macaroons in hand, the trio was ushered into the fortune teller's dilapidated shotgun house and told by a fat Negress that Madam Iris would receive them directly. While she waited, Maddy checked out a small, crazily cluttered room reeking of cheap incense, dead flowers and must. Sweating walls bore swags of dirty draperies contributing to the ancient smell. Candles flickered everywhere, dripping wax on tables and floors, and small altars were tucked against opposing walls. One venerated the Blessed Virgin, St. Peter and a black saint Maddy had never seen, and the other held a cluster of grotesque animal figures, seashells, rocks, antlers and bones. The place was so creepy she was about to plead a headache when a pair of dusty portieres burst open and the fortune teller appeared. Maddy was startled to see the mulatto woman she'd encountered yesterday on Rampart Street, the same Iris whom Félicité suspected might be a *voudou* priestess. The blue tignon was gone, replaced by a white turban and yellowed robes in need of laundering. Enormous gold hoop earrings swung from her ears, and some sort of amulet hung around her neck. She looked, Maddy thought, much harder than before.

Madam Iris said nothing, only pointed at Maddy and motioned her inside a smaller, darker, even more malodorous room. The portieres closed with a dull whoosh as the woman indicated a small table. Maddy sat and took such a deep breath that the bustier pinched her flesh. The fortune teller opposite, eyes narrowing, stare intensifying. "I know you, mademoiselle."

"Of course you do. I stopped you yesterday and asked for directions?"

"That's not what I meant, is it?"

Maddy was been leery of people who answered questions with questions. "I don't know what you mean."

Madam Iris fixed Maddy with a malevolent glare. "Do not think to manipulate me or the spirits, gal, as neither of us are to be trifled with. You came here for the truth, and I expect nothing less from you."

Maddy bristled. "I came here only because my friend asked me to come along while she had a fortune told."

"Nonsense. We both know you're here for a special reason."

"Then please reveal it."

"Not until you concede that we know each other."

Gambling that this was a challenge from the August Ones, Maddy said. "Very well, madam. We know each other."

"In this and other lives," Madam Iris said.

"In this and other lives," Maddy echoed, not knowing why.

"Your name?"

"Madeleine St. Jacques."

The woman's countenance flickered from threatening to smug to unreadable before she continued. "I confess to being bewildered by your presence, Mademoiselle St. Jacques. I will not attempt to explain it and can say only that your search for the man is coming to an end."

Maddy frowned. "The man? What man?"

"A Spaniard."

"His name?"

The woman gave her a toothless yawn. *"Je ne sais pas."*

"But if you don't know, then how will I—?"

"You will find him in the last possible place you would think to look." Rheumy eyes narrowed to slits as the woman reiterated. *"The last possible place."*

Maddy's annoyance flared. "You're talking in riddles."

Madam Iris stood abruptly, rounded the table and yanked the curtains aside. "We're finished here." She glowered at Madeleine and Jean-Noël. "Finished!"

Responding to an unheard, unseen signal, the corpulent Negress opened the front door from the street and beckoned them all outside. Maddy, Madeleine and Jean-Noël had no sooner stepped onto the sidewalk when the woman went back into the house and slammed the door.

"Mon dieu!" Jean-Noël grunted. "What on earth happened?"

"I wish I knew," Maddy confessed.

"Mais, Madam Iris looked enraged. What did you say to her?"

"Nothing. In fact, she did all the talking." Maddy didn't mention that she had encountered Madam Iris before and certainly said nothing about her prediction about the Spaniard. "It was mostly mumbo jumbo, but it's still very upsetting."

"And it's all my fault for insisting we come here," Madeleine cried, taking Maddy's arm as they walked toward Bourbon Street. "Please forgive me."

"There's nothing to forgive. You couldn't have known that old crone would act so crazy."

"But the whole thing was my idea, and you must let me make it up to you."

"Seriously, Madeleine, there's no need to—"

"I know!" As was her fashion, Madeleine wouldn't be stopped. "You must let me entertain you at Five Oaks!" She glanced at Jean-Noël. "I grew up there and, granted everything is not as I wish, but it's lovely and quite peaceful when Jules is on the river."

"*D'accord*," Jean-Noël affirmed. "That's a splendid idea."

Maddy jumped at the chance to see what might have been her ancestral home and to move her time odyssey outside New Orleans. "That's very kind. I'd love to."

"*C'est bien!*" Spirits restored, Madeleine squeezed Maddy's arm and leaned close. "We'll have a wonderful time. I promise."

As they walked back to the hotel, Maddy weighed the events of the day. Her reunion with Félicité was bright with promise, as was the deepening likelihood that Madeleine was her antecedent. And although Madam Iris's bizarre behavior had upset her, she was exhilarated by the fortune teller's prediction about a mysterious man and wondered if it were another step on the path blazed by the August Ones.

Yes, indeed, she thought. It's been quite a day.

Part 5

"About fifteen miles above New Orleans
the river goes very slowly.
It has broadened until it is almost a sea,
and the water is yellow with the mud of half a continent.
Where the sun strikes it, it is golden."

— Frank Yerby

31

While February thawed into a sunny March, the city buzzed with news that Mississippi Senator Jefferson Davis had been named President of the seven Confederate States of America and quickly formed a national government. Southern patriotism skyrocketed, but more sober souls prayed the audacious move wouldn't invite Union invasion. War would mean a blockade of New Orleans, the South's largest city and most important port, and cause cataclysmic damage to commerce. Breaths were held and hopes ran high until April 12 when a rebel army in Charleston, South Carolina, fired on Fort Sumter, a federal garrison in the city's harbor. President Lincoln's call for troops triggered secession by four more southern states--Virginia, Arkansas, North Carolina and Tennessee--and made war inevitable. The flag of the Confederacy flew defiantly in Jackson Square, atop City Hall and over the United States Mint on Esplanade Avenue as exuberant New Orleanians flooded the streets to reassure each other that the cowardly Yankees would throw down their guns and retreat at the first sight of the South's brave lads in gray.

Maddy knew better of course. She watched the sad madness from the balcony of her new apartment on Royal Street at Ursulines, regretting the knowledge that those star-crossed revelers were celebrating the beginning of the end of the Confederate dream. She didn't want to think about it, focusing instead on Félicité who was overdue for tea. She shaded her eyes from a brilliant morning sun and looked up Ursulines Street. She assumed her friend was delayed by the noisy, rambunctious crowd and was relieved when she spied Félicité threading her way through the masses. In her brilliant turquoise dress and bonnet, Félicité bloomed like a tropical flower as she edged along the drab, patinated walls of the old Ursuline Convent. Maddy waved and shouted over the din, and as Félicité approached the balcony she looked up and waved back. The happy moment ended when a drunken reveler grabbed Félicité's arm and pulled her close.

"Come here, gal! Give us a kiss!"

While Maddy watched in horror, Félicité's frantic struggle to push the man away only made him cling tighter. Maddy screamed for someone to help, but when the jostling crowd remained oblivious she took matters into her own hands. She rushed downstairs, skirts flying as she plowed through the mob and flew at Félicité's assailant from behind.

"Let her go!" she screamed, pounding his back with her fists. "I said let her go!!"

The bewildered drunk released Félicité and spun around, startled to learn his attacker was a fashionably-dressed white lady. He glared at Maddy, face red with fury and drink. "What's this nigger bitch to you?"

Maddy was so stunned by the vile epithet that she blurted the first thing that popped into her mind. "She's my sister, you drunken fool!"

The man roared with laughter. "The hell you say, lady! She's a whore from the balls!"

"How dare you?!" Emboldened by a temper she didn't know she had, Maddy slapped him hard across the face. Caught off guard, the man lost his balance and tumbled backwards, knocked cold when his head hit the curb. Unaware of what caused the fracas, the high-spirited crowd roared with laughter while Maddy grabbed Félicité's hand and dragged her home. They didn't stop running until they were safely upstairs in Maddy's apartment.

"Are you alright?" Maddy asked when she caught her breath.

"Thanks to you." Félicité sank onto a settee and fanned herself with a handkerchief.

"Eh, *bien.* Things could've been much worse."

"What do you mean 'oh, well?' That man was totally out of line."

"'Out of line?' What do you mean?"

Maddy curbed her modern slang. "I meant that he was behaving badly."

"*C'est vrai,* but it's nothing new. Once men see us at the *Salle d'Orléans,* they think they're free to say and do anything they wish, outside the ballroom as well as in."

They're like cat-calling hardhats, Maddy thought glumly. Some things never change. "That's outrageous!"

The green eyes narrowed. "You're acting very strangely today, Maddy. After spending so much time together, attending the opera and theater and sitting in the colored sections with me, I thought you understood my world better than most white people."

"I thought I did too."

"Then you should know my status as a free woman of color, and a courtesan to boot, makes me prey to all sorts of unpleasantness. If I had slapped that white man, I'd be thrown into the calaboose." She shrugged insouciantly. "That's the law, my dear."

Maddy kept still, fearing that her anger might expose her. She had seen many similar injustices these past few weeks, acts against the free people of color and reminded herself yet again to stop thinking like a liberated American woman while living in a nineteenth-century society where females remained chattel.

"Sometimes my temper keeps me from thinking straight," she said, relieved when Félicité's empathetic expression said she bought the explanation. "Now how about some tea?"

"I'd adore a cup." Félicité's voice trailed Maddy when she went to fetch the tea service. "For heaven's sake. When are you going to get a girl to help around here?"

Maddy knew that the idea of running a household alone

was anathema to this pampered princess, and that Félicité would be horrified to know modern-day Maddy not only cleaned her apartment but grocery shopped and cooked her own meals. "I told you I don't need anyone."

"Of course you do," Félicité insisted. "If nothing else, let me lend Zaza from time to time.

"She's not the smartest thing, but she's a sweet little creature and does as she's told."

And she's a slave, thought Maddy. That's more than I can handle. "I'll think about it," she lied, returning with the tea. "Now let's talk about something else. Remember I told you about visiting Madam Iris?"

"Of course. Did you go again?"

"Heavens, no, but I've been having strange dreams and have started wondering if she's truly a *voudou* priestess."

Félicité smiled enigmatically. "Don't be naïve, darling. How else do you explain those bizarre altars and bones you described?"

"Maybe I don't want them explained."

"Think what you like, but don't ignore her prediction."

"Does that mean you believe in voodoo?"

"It means I'm not a disbeliever. I've seen it work too often to dismiss it."

"So you think I should continue looking for this mysterious Spaniard?"

"*Pourquois pas?* I certainly would." She pursed her lips and looked naughty. "He might even be wildly handsome!"

Maddy ignored the jest and buttered a croissant. "There's another reason why I'm not quite myself today."

"Oh?"

She nodded toward an envelope perched atop a writing desk. "I had a letter from the friend who took me to see Madam Iris, the one with the same name as myself. She lives on a plantation outside Port LeBlanc. Poor dear is trapped in a dreadful marriage and begs me to come visit."

"This must be the day for disturbing letters. Mama wrote

that Papa is seriously ill and begged me to come to *Belle Rêve.*"

"After all you've told me about him, will you go?"

"How can I not?" Félicité's fair face clouded. "Although he may refuse to see me."

"Serious illnesses often change things," Maddy offered.

"Humph. You don't know my father." Félicité flicked an imaginary speck from a glove. "When will you visit your friend in Port LeBlanc?"

"I've set no definite date." She flinched when Félicité grabbed her hand and held tight. "*Mon dieu!* What is it?"

"I'm so frightened, Maddy. Please come to the island with me. I can't bear to make the trip alone."

Maddy was stunned by the intensity of her plea. "I'd be happy to help, but surely a stranger would not be welcome at such a difficult time."

Félicité offered a wan smile. "These days you're less a stranger to me than my father.

"Besides, you said more than once that you wanted to see the Isle Brevelle."

"I did indeed, but surely we could find a better time." When Félicité squeezed her hand harder, Maddy relented, knowing that, like Madeleine, Félicité would hound her until she got her way. "As you wish, my dear. When shall we go?"

"As soon as possible," Félicité said, brightening. "We'll visit the steamboat offices on Canal Street this afternoon and see what's sailing upriver. We'll have to book separate accommodations of course."

Maddy immediately grasped her inference. "I hate that we'll be apart during the voyage."

"There is a solution of course, but it depends on you."

"Oh?"

"We can be together as much as you like, unless you object to colored accommodations."

"You know I don't, but maybe we should try something different this time."

The green eyes narrowed. "Surely you're not suggesting—?"

"I'll book accommodations in the white section, and with you traveling as my companion, surely no one will challenge us." When Félicité looked aghast, Maddy said, "Good heavens, girl. You're as white as I am, and I don't see why—?"

Félicité shook her head. "Your naiveté never ceases to amaze me, Maddy. It takes only one suspicious soul to cause trouble. Once the authorities see my papers, I can be fined or arrested or at the very least put off the ship."

Alarmed once again by such harsh social realities, Maddy retreated. "I'm sorry. I should've known better."

"You need to curb your adventurous spirit, that's all."

"Alright then," Maddy said, eager to change the subject. "Who knows? Maybe I'll meet that mysterious Spaniard along the way."

Félicité chuckled." Not in the colored section, you won't."

32

Maddy leaned against the rail as the tiny steamboat *Thomas R* chugged up the Red River. She marveled at a pristine shoreline thick with willows and cypress, beautifully devoid of cell towers, gigantic billboards and highways. Félicité stood beside her, anxiety evident as she pointed out various landmarks. Maddy patted her gloved hand.

"Calm down, my dear. You're a nervous wreck and you're about to make me one too."

"Nervous wreck?" Despite her apprehension, Félicité smiled. "You have such a quaint dialect. What was that funny thing you said yesterday? Oh, yes. 'It is what it is.'"

Maddy ignored her latest trendy semantic slip. "Just take a deep breath and relax."

"*Tiens,* I'll try, but it's difficult since we're about to enter the Cane River and sail alongside the Isle Brevelle. *Belle Rêve* is only an hour away."

Maddy took her hand. "Don't worry, *bébé.* I'm here for you no matter what. I promise."

"You're a good friend." Félicité bussed her cheek. *"Merci."*

Félicité excused herself to regain her composure, leaving Maddy to recall her Louisiana studies and speculate about the extraordinary settlement she was about to visit. She knew the Isle Brevelle was thirty miles long by five miles wide and populated by a black dynasty begun in 1786 by Marie Thérèze Coincoin, a slave freed by Frenchman Claude Metoyer with whom she had ten children. Energetic and enterprising, Madam Coincoin found success by growing the finest tobacco in the colony, and when she died in 1816, her remarkable legacy was a degree of social, economic and political freedom unknown by non-whites anywhere else in the country. Sequestered in upper Louisiana, the Cane River colonists, like their Caucasian counterparts, raised gracious plantation homes, filled them with French furnishings, dined on elegant china and educated their sons in France. They also owned slaves. This ugly reality of African-Americans owning one another was often overlooked in the history books, and Maddy was unsettled by the prospect of seeing it first-hand. She was also anxious about being one of the very few white people on the island, and as the *Thomas R* approached the landing for *Belle Rêve,* she was overwhelmed with trepidation. Oh, Henri, she thought. How I wish you were here!

She felt better when Félicité rejoined her at the rail. *"Maman!"* she cried, waving excitedly as the prow of the riverboat ground roughly against the dock. *"Maman!"*

Maddy inspected the waiting crowd. Smartly dressed and radiating prosperity, they ranged in color from *café au lait* to near white. Prominent cheekbones and bronze complexions suggested Indian blood while more delicate features reflected French lineage. There was no mistaking Félicité's mother, Amédée, a striking older version of her beautiful daughter. She waved back and smiled, face streaked with tears as she welcomed her prodigal daughter. Félicité wept too as she hurried down the gangway to embrace Amédée and her entourage of family and friends, but Maddy discerned melancholy beneath the cheerfulness as everyone piled into carriages. Félicité's father Emile was mentioned only once when Amédée said there was no improvement and that he remained confined to his bed. Félicité said nothing, merely cozied against her mother during the short drive to *Belle Rêve.* When the carriages drew up before the two-story pillared home, Maddy was awed by the row of servants waiting on the veranda, and at that moment realized she was unprepared for the rural lives of the wealthy *gens de coleur libres.*

Dear Lord, she thought. It's *Downton Abbey* with an all-black cast!

The handsome house was as impressive inside as out. Decorated with restraint rather than extravagance, it reflected good taste and a secure social position. Like all arriving guests, Maddy and Félicité were given *cafe noir* before Amédée hustled her daughter down a hall, and a servant girl took Maddy's baggage and ushered her upstairs. Her room mirrored those she had seen on dozens of plantation tours, except that the furnishings were brand new. A *prie dieu* in the corner was identical to one she and Paige had seen in a Royal Street antique store last Christmas, as was a mahogany tester bed. When Maddy inspected its intricately carved posts and caressed the gauzy *mosquitaire,* she found the bed so inviting that she threw herself on the mattress and sank into an ocean of swan's-down.

"Heaven," she whispered, closing her eyes. "Sheer heaven." But her reverie was short-lived, vanquished by shouts down the hall and a crash followed by a soft tapping at her door. She hastily got up and smoothed her skirts. "Who is it?"

"Félicité. May I come in?"

"Of course."

The strain on Félicité's face said everything, but Maddy listened patiently. "As I feared, *Papa* refuses to talk to me, and *Maman* is devastated. She tried so hard to pave the way toward reconciliation and even dared remind him that our sainted Marie Thérèze Coincoin was herself a *placée* and that two of her daughters had white protectors."

"Then why does he object so strongly?"

"My father is so impossibly prudish he's embarrassed by the mere notion of *plaçage* and insists that our people have progressed too far for it to continue." Félicité paced the room, skirts swishing noisily. "He reminded me that our *placées* made their arrangements privately, here on the island, and called the balls glorified slave auctions. He even equates us with prostitutes. *Dieu me garde!*" she whispered. "My own father called me a whore!"

Maddy's heart went out to her dear friend. "I'm so sorry."

"Moi aussi," Félicité said. "But as you say, 'it is what it is.'"

Maddy tried not to smile at a nineteenth-century courtesan using twenty-first century slang. "So what will you do now?"

"Well, I'm certainly not going to run away like a scolded child. It's been two years since I've visited the colony, and there are old friends I would see before I leave."

"Good for you."

"As a matter of fact, I'm going to visit *Grand-mère* Mathilde this afternoon."

"May I go with you?"

"Merci, but she and I need time alone. I'll arrange for you to meet her before we leave."

"When might that be?"

"Two, maybe three days. Papa will be told I've gone back to New Orleans, and the servants will be sworn to secrecy. Being so ill and confined to his room, he won't know the difference, but I don't want to linger longer than necessary." She gave Maddy a quick hug. "Dinner is at five thirty. In the meantime, why don't you enjoy a stroll around the grounds? *Maman*'s gardens are the most famous on the island."

"That's a wonderful idea. Where shall I begin?"

"Come to the window and I'll show you."

Until then Maddy hadn't noticed the view. Her room overlooked semiformal gardens stretching from the side of the house toward a grove of live oaks. Their canopy of Spanish moss shimmered beneath a light zephyr. "How inviting."

"I suggest you wander to the river. It's cooler down there."

"Bon idée." After a moment she realized Félicité was staring. "Is something wrong?"

"It's your complexion. Your skin has such a wonderful glow in this light, and I've always envied the curve of your eyelashes."

"I inherited those things from my grandmother," Maddy lied. It wasn't the first time Félicité had commented on her grooming, and when they traveled together Maddy took special pains to keep her cache of L'Oreal well hidden. She reminded herself to keep her eyelash curler out of sight too.

"Then I'll see you at dinnertime?"

"Of course. *Mais*, are you sure you're alright?"

"Not quite," Félicité confessed tiredly. "But I will be."

33

Amédée's gardens were so lush and heavily perfumed that Maddy grew heady while exploring the profusion of roses, lilies and iris flanking marble statues depicting the four seasons. Taking Félicité's suggestion, she followed a winding path through Chinese fan palms and banana groves to the banks of the Cane River and a shallow cove ringed by weeping willows. Not used to so many layers of clothing, she began sweating and sought a cool spot under a luxuriant willow. Its long tendrils formed a living curtain between her and the water, and after a few minutes of watching the branches sway with the breeze Maddy began to drowse.

Her sleep was filled with images so soothing that she dozed for the better part of an hour. She might have continued if loud splashing hadn't prompted her to peer sleepily through the rippling willows. Maddy wondered if she were still dreaming when a nearly naked man splashed ashore, underdrawers clinging to skin as pale as her own, blackness leached away by generations of racial intermingling. Dark hair curled over his forehead, and a thick moustache drew attention to a sensuous mouth.

Good Lord, Maddy thought. The guy looks like the cover of a romance novel!

Believing he was alone, the stranger flung powerful arms wide, yawned contentedly, and stretched. Maddy was so mesmerized by the muscle play across his bare chest and belly that she didn't consider her vulnerability as a woman alone on an isolated river bank. She remained perfectly still while the man let the sun dry his skin and drawers before retrieving clothes stashed nearby. He donned dark trousers and a white shirt, and as he tugged on boots he cocked his head and turned in her direction. Seized by fear, she held her breath and prayed that her peach-colored dress was invisible through the swaying willow curtain. After a long, ponderous moment, the stranger turned away and disappeared along the weedy shore.

Alone again, Maddy scrambled to her feet and hastily brushed away the grass and twigs clinging to her skirts. Lengthening shadows told her hours had elapsed and that she should be getting back to the house, but a peculiar sound drew her attention back to the river. Rounding a curve came a skiff occupied by two men, one rowing and the other blowing a conch shell. When he spotted Maddy on the shore, he waved and sang out.

"*Grand danse le soir. Dimanche a huit heures! De la bonne musique, bon temps pour tous!*"

What a charming way to announce a community dance, Maddy thought, waving and calling back. *"Merci, m'sieur! Merci!"*

He smiled and blew her a kiss. *"No manquez pas de venire!"*

Maddy nodded and waved again as the other man rowed harder and shot the skiff around the bend where the stranger had disappeared. As she walked back to *Belle Réve,* she forgot about the dance and realized the handsome swimmer had unleashed a rush of desire making her think of Henri. Not for the first time she wished she could whip out her cell phone and call him, sharing the details of her day and asking if he missed her as much as she missed him. Since none of that was possible, Maddy was swamped by a painful wave of loneliness that deepened as she walked on. Her mood improved when she approached the veranda and heard Félicité call out.

"Did you enjoy your stroll, dear?"

"Very much." Maddy climbed the steps and settled into a white wicker chair. "Your mother's gardens are absolutely glorious."

"I'll tell her you said so." Félicité smiled, mood obviously improved. "Did you get down to the river?"

Maddy nodded. "It was so cool and soothing that I fell asleep under the willows. When I woke up I saw the oddest thing."

Félicité's eyebrows rose. "Oh?"

Her friend's curious tone warned Maddy against mentioning the sensuous stranger. Instead she described the boatman with the conch shell. "Such a quaint custom."

"One of many on our little island," Félicité said with pride. "I heard the boatman while I was visiting *Grand-mère.*"

"She's well I hope."

"She says so, but she has aged considerably since I left. It distresses me because we're so much alike I'm closer to her than *Maman.* You know how certain traits skip a generation."

Maddy thought of how much more she had in common with grandmother Aglaé than her own mother. "So they say."

Félicité smiled wryly. "She's so furious with Papa she threatened to come over here and beat him with her cane."

"I like her already," Maddy said.

"After all I've told her, she's anxious to meet you. She's a little bewildered at my having a white confidante but she will welcome you as she has all my friends."

Maddy smiled inside at the reverse racism. "When will I meet her?"

"Next time you accompany me to the island."

"But I thought—"

"I discussed things with *Maman* and decided it's best if we leave tomorrow. As patriarch, Papa has ways of finding things out, and I shouldn't upset him further. Besides, everyone I want to see will be at dinner tonight." She suddenly looked forlorn. "I apologize for dragging you all the way out here only to turn right around and go home."

Maddy felt the woman's pain at being shunned by her father. "No need to apologize. You warned me that things were unpredictable. At least I've met your mother and seen your childhood home."

"You're too kind," Félicité said. "God indeed works in mysterious ways, sending us friends when we need them the most."

Her words warmed Maddy's heart. "I feel the same way, *ma cher.*"

Félicité frowned. "I do hope dinner doesn't test those feelings."

"*Pourquoi?*"

"I doubt that I'll be able to steer tonight's conversation away from the war. *Grand-mère* says our young men talk about nothing but defending our island against the coming invasion. Two of our most vociferous hot bloods will be at dinner, so don't be surprised if they—"

"Again you needn't apologize," Maddy interrupted. "I assure you I look forward to their opinions and maybe even contributing my own."

Félicité was shocked. "*Sacrebleu!* Why would you be interested in war? It's such a dreadfully masculine topic!"

Be careful how you answer, Maddy thought. As an upper echelon courtesan, Félicité was trained to discuss politics but must not suspect it was one of Maddy's favorite subjects. Nor should she know Maddy would relish hearing how men of color talk would defend the Confederate cause and was eager to query them on that and other current events.

"By now you know I'm not like most women," she replied after a pause. "Many things interest me that most ladies choose to ignore."

Félicité turned serious. "But why think about something that may turn our world upside down? There will be time enough for that if and when it comes."

"*Alors,* so you have given the matter some thought after all."

"More than I'd like to admit. It's especially frightening given that I have no protector and no prospect for one. The truth is there's very little standing between me and starvation except the deed to that cottage in the Rue Rampart."

"I'm sure your mother would never let you end up in the street."

"I wish I could believe that."

"*Mais,* I thought she was your champion."

"She is indeed, but there's something you should know that I recently learned from *Grand-mère.*"

Maddy was alarmed by Félicité's grim tone. "Oh?"

"She says that Papa's finances are in tatters. The last two cane seasons were so ruinous he had to mortgage *Belle Réve* to stay afloat. It could be saved only under the best of circumstances, and with this war coming—" Félicité opened her hands, palms up. "Disaster is inevitable."

"*Bon dieu!*" Maddy gasped, hand drifting to her throat. She glanced across the lushly manicured grounds and up at the sturdy columns glowing white in the dusk. If ever a place was the picture of grace and plenty and built to last generations, the Chevalier home was it. "I would never have guessed anything was wrong."

"Nor would I."

"Why didn't you tell me before?"

"Because it would've ruined our conversation," Félicité replied airily, as if hiding bad news was the norm. Maddy was endlessly impressed by such exquisite manners, but fear lurked behind the genteel veneer and courageous smile. She took Félicité's hand.

"I'm so sorry."

"So am I, my dear, but to use your queer saying again, 'It is what it is.'"

Maddy had never hated those words until now.

34

The voluptuous feather mattress was not as restful as Maddy hoped. Accustomed to a firm bed, she tossed and turned before finding sleep. Far from being restful, however, it was punctuated by disturbing dreams set on a deserted stretch of levee. It was a blazing bright day, but thick clouds periodically erased the sun and cast dark, chilly shadows. Whenever Maddy shivered, sunlight flooded back to warm her, a peculiar cycle of hot light and cold dark that dizzied her. The light finally stabilized, and she floated toward a patch of soft, thick grass where Henri waited. As they embraced, a dome of branches closed overhead and shut the world away like a green cocoon. Maddy trembled as the verdant canopy surged in a great emerald wave, buoying them through a tangle of cane leaves that sawed her skin. She clung to Henri as they tumbled back to earth, but moments before impact he morphed into the stranger who emerged from the river. She cried out and surrendered to a ravishing *petit mort.*

"Henri!"

She awoke, shattering the dream, and for one terrible moment she was a lost child bewildered by unfamiliar surroundings. She sat up and struggled to orient herself, calming when she remembered she was at Félicité's house on the Isle Brevelle.

"Dear God," she whispered, tingling with guilt when she remembered the erotic dream. "What on earth was that about?!"

Maddy struggled to analyze what had happened but was too foggy to do more than listen to the night chirping of crickets. Through the gauzy mosquito net, the moonlit night was as unreal as her presence in a century not her own where she dreamed of a man also not her own. For the first time, she seriously questioned her decision to make this eerie time odyssey and ached for Henri to assure her that their love was real and unthreatened. Perhaps she needed to convince herself too after conjuring a stranger who had not only burned himself into her subconscious but seduced her dreams as well.

"I'm lost, Henri," she sighed, wistful and spent. "So very, very lost."

When a cool zephyr rushed through the window to stir the *mosquitaire,* Maddy told herself it was Henri's spirit and wrapped the breeze around her until her eyes burned with a desperate need for sleep. Exhausted, she fell back against the pillows and thought nothing more until someone knocked at her door.

"Who is it?" she called groggily.

"It's Félicité. May I come in?"

"Bien sûr." As Félicité slipped into the room, Maddy sat up and saw morning sunlight streaming through the window. "What time is it?"

"Almost eight," Félicité replied, tone reminding Maddy that country people rose with the sun. "You must have slept soundly." Maddy nodded, deciding not to discuss her restless night, much less her scandalous dream. "I wish I could say the same."

"You have a lot on your mind, *ma chère.* We can have a long talk on the boat if you like."

"You're sweet, but there's nothing to talk about." She kissed Maddy's cheek. "Shall I have breakfast sent up?"

"Please." Maddy decided it was best to give Félicité these last moments alone with her family. "What time are we leaving?"

"There's a boat in two hours that will take us to the Red River Landing. We can get another boat to New Orleans from there."

"I'll be ready," Maddy promised.

After indulging in broiled trout in cream sauce, potato croquettes, fresh plums and *café au lait,* Maddy packed and dressed for the trip. Per Félicité's instructions, she tugged a bell pull for a servant to take the luggage downstairs. When the small girl dutifully hefted the heavy portmanteau, Maddy fought the temptation to offer help and trailed silently, battling guilt with every step. She was halfway down the stairs when something froze her in place.

"Oh, my God!" she breathed.

In the vestibule below, conversing with Félicité's mother, was the stranger from the river. His dark hair was slicked back and he was formally dressed in black suit and tie with ebony boots polished to a high sheen. Maddy wondered why he wore a tuxedo so early in the day and what Madam Chevalier was telling him. Judging from her animated conversation and his responsive nods, theirs was an important discussion, and after ushering her onto the veranda, the man hurried in Maddy's direction. Seeing her on the stairs, he paused and bowed, silently inviting Maddy to continue down to the foyer. She did exactly that, pausing at the foot of the stairs to give him a smile.

"Bonjour."

He bowed again but avoided eye contact as he responded in a low voice. *"Bonjour, mademoiselle."*

With that, he walked briskly up the stairs and vanished. Maddy was shocked by his brusque dismissal, disappointed to learn her fantasy man was as ill-mannered as he was handsome. She ignored the affront and went outside where Félicité and her mother supervised the luggage being loaded onto the carriage.

"Send a telegram the moment you know anything," Félicité urged.

Madam Chevalier shook her head. "He was so bad off this morning, I may have news before you girls reach New Orleans."

"You know I'll catch the first boat back."

"I know."

As she turned to embrace her mother, Félicité saw Maddy. "Come along, darling. We must hurry if we're to catch the boat."

Maddy thanked Madam Chevalier for her hospitality, saddened to see the older woman's red-rimmed eyes. How terrible, she thought, for a mother to bid good-bye to a child ordered out of the house by her father. But Amédée Chevalier was the picture of grace under pressure and rested a hand on Maddy's arm as she spoke from the heart.

"I hope you'll come again to *Belle Rêve*," she said in a cool, steady voice. "When circumstances are more genial."

"I hope so too," Maddy replied.

"And please let me thank you for being such a good friend to my daughter."

Maddy nodded and for a moment thought she might cry, but she drew strength from these two stalwart women and climbed into the coach. Moments later, she and Félicité held hands as they jounced down the dusty road paralleling the Cane River. She noted Félicité did not look back when the road curved and her childhood home disappeared behind a stand of willows.

"Your mother is a great lady," she said.

"I wish I could be more like her," Félicité confessed. "But clearly it wasn't my destiny. No, as I said before, traits skip a generation and I'm much more like my grandmother."

"Me too," Maddy blurted.

Félicité faced her. "You must tell me about her sometime. *Tu sais,* you've never said much about your family."

"I don't mean to be mysterious. It's just that there isn't much to tell."

Félicité looked unconvinced. "Sometime," she repeated.

Maddy swiftly changed the subject. "May I ask you something?"

"Bien sûr."

"Who was the gentleman I saw this morning?"

"Gentleman? What gentleman?"

"In the vestibule. He was talking to your mother."

"Who on earth are you talking about?" The moment Félicité heard Maddy's description, she burst out laughing. "You're too wonderful, Madeleine. You know when to be amusing when I need it most."

"I'm so glad," Maddy said, more puzzled than ever by Félicité's next words.

"Who else but you would pretend Hector was a gentleman?" She laughed harder. "My father's manservant of all people!"

Maddy was stunned. "The man is a slave?!"

"*Mais,* why would you think otherwise?" Félicité's laughter stopped as realization dawned. "Ah! I suppose it's because you're from Natchez and wouldn't know about such things."

"What things?"

"White slaves, of course."

35

Maddy knew a little about white slavery but didn't know it existed on the Isle Brevelle. The phenomenon of blacks owning whites was as captivating as it was shocking, and she was eager to query Félicité. Again she reminded herself to act with restraint and not appear too curious as she pursued the conversation.

"I've certainly heard of them, but until today I'd never seen one."

"At least none that you knew of."

Maddy smiled. *"Touché."*

Félicité smiled back. "I must admit I was surprised to learn about them. My father brought Hector home from the slave mart in New Orleans the year I was born. He's the first white man I remember and the only gypsy, too."

"He's a gypsy?"

"Gypsy slaves are nothing new. Oliver Cromwell shipped them to the English colonies in the last century, and Spain sent them to the Caribbean long before that. Hector came from Cuba in fact." She gave Maddy a querulous gaze. "My dear, untold numbers of men, women and children were kidnapped from the streets of England and Ireland by press gangs working for white slavers who dumped their human cargo here in the New World. Those poor souls were worked to death on the plantations of Barbados long before slavers set their sights on Africa."

Maddy wondered how white slavery had flown under her radar when she researched this period. "How in the world do you know all this?"

"Despite his other shortcomings, Papa encouraged me to read from an early age and made his library available. History fascinates me."

"What else do you know about Hector?"

"Only that he's been my father's manservant since I was a child, and that Papa named him after a character in the Iliad, his favorite work of Greek literature. Hector is kind and good-hearted and enjoys freedoms permitted none of our other slaves."

"Such as?"

"He was taught to read and write and is allowed to wander the plantation freely."

That explains why he was off swimming by himself, Maddy thought. "Your father isn't worried that he might try to run away?"

Félicité thought the idea preposterous. "Hardly. Our island is small, and everyone knows Hector, including the dockmaster. Remember, white men are conspicuous because they're a tiny minority." She gave Maddy a peculiar look. "Besides, why would Hector surrender a pampered, privileged life superior to that of most people, black, white or otherwise?"

Because the man is a slave, Maddy thought grimly. Those in bondage who don't dream of freedom would be a rare breed indeed. Once again she was stunned by mid-nineteenth-century rationale. "Does that life include a family?" she ventured.

"We Chevaliers are his family," Félicité replied with a wave of her gloved hand. "If you're asking if Hector has jumped the broom, the answer is no. He's a man who cherishes his solitude, and when he's not tending to duty, he's in Papa's library. Reading seems to be his only real passion." She grabbed the leather strap when the carriage lurched hard to the right. "I wish they'd repair these dreadful ruts."

Maddy ignored the bumps in the road and kept the subject on course. "It's difficult to believe such a handsome, healthy looking male specimen would keep so much to himself."

"Did you say handsome?" Maddy nodded as a mischievous look crept into Félicité's green eyes. "Yes, I suppose he is, which reminds me of something I'd almost forgotten. A distant memory and a rather naughty one at that."

"Oh?" Maddy pressed.

"When I was growing up, one of my favorite pastimes was escaping from my nurse and running off to explore the plantation. I memorized the woods, swamps and cane fields as thoroughly as any overseer, and my favorite place was a willow grove down by the riverbank."

Uh-oh, Maddy thought.

"Late one summer afternoon, I was daydreaming under the willows when I saw someone in the river. It frightened me because I'd been warned a million times not to go in the water because of the current. I worried that someone might be in trouble, but this person swam toward shore with sure, strong strokes. It was Hector of all people." She leaned close to whisper her daring confidence. "And he was naked!"

"No!"

"He couldn't see me tucked in the shadows, and I certainly wasn't going to reveal myself since he was without clothes. I kept quiet as a mouse while he stretched out on the riverbank and dozed in the sun. I was scared to death he would discover me, but at the same time I was fascinated by seeing a naked man. And my dear!" She embraced the memory. "Hector was quite the sight!"

"I can only imagine," Maddy lied, trying to hide her excitement. "How old were you?"

"Sixteen. Certainly my mother had told me nothing about what happened between men and women, but I received an early education when I saw two slaves coupling in the woods." Félicité closed her eyes, as she conjured the memory of that long ago summer day. "I've never told this to a living soul, but I imagined myself doing the same thing with Hector."

Maddy gave her a conspiratorial smile. "Good for you!"

Félicité was delighted with Maddy's approval. "But I felt so wicked!"

"Being curious is merely a part of growing up, *ma chère*, especially when a supremely attractive man is the object of your curiosity."

Félicité chuckled. "And with Hector there was a lot to be curious about, if you know what I mean."

Maddy was a bit surprised by the frank remark. True, Félicité was a courtesan, but she had been strictly raised to be a chaste lady with fine manners. Her sexual inquisitiveness as a girl went against everything Maddy had read about high-born Southern women and was a refreshing revelation. Félicité's unexpected confession prompted her to make one of her own.

"Actually I do know what you mean. Sort of."

The pale eyebrows rose. "Oh?"

"I saw him in the river too, yesterday afternoon in fact." When Félicité gaped, Maddy hastily added. "He wasn't naked though. He was swimming in his underdrawers, and I must confess I wanted to see more. His wet drawers didn't leave much to the imagination."

Félicité's hat plume danced when she cocked her head. "So that's why you asked who he was!"

"Absolutely. To tell you the truth, I couldn't get him out of my mind. I even dreamed about him last night." Playing to Félicité's mutinous nature, she ventured into uncharted waters. "It makes me wish there was such a thing as reverse *plaçage*."

Félicité's mood darkened. "*Plaçage* is nothing to joke about. Besides, what you're proposing is beyond scandalous."

Maddy ignored the storm warnings and waded deeper. "I meant no disrespect, Félicité, but if men can have mistresses why shouldn't we enjoy the same privilege? Why must men make all the rules?"

"Because they can, I suppose," Félicité said resignedly. "It's the way it's always been."

"That hardly makes it fair."

Félicité sniffed. "If the world were fair I'd be enjoying a life of luxury on the Isle Brevelle with a husband of my choosing, not living alone in a little cottage in the Rue Rampart and looking for love at a public gathering." Something unpleasant flickered across her pretty face. "Even so, there are standards to be upheld."

"True, but they don't keep me from believing women should have more voice."

"I suppose not."

"Or daydreaming of a liaison with Hector."

"You can't be serious."

"Why not?" Maddy teased. "You did."

"Because I was a child with too much imagination," Félicité said dismissively.

"And now you're a grown woman. So what's wrong with being attracted to someone that's gorgeous and dashing and, according to you, kind and good-hearted?"

Félicité recoiled. "Are you forgetting who you are, Madeleine St. Jacques?!" Despite her status as courtesan of color, Félicité was ingrained with prejudices and caste dictates that would never change and so aghast that she cursed in Maddy's presence for the first time. "The man's a nothing but a damned slave!"

Not wanting to jeopardize a nineteenth-century friendship with twenty-first-century feminist arguments, Maddy dropped the subject. The remainder of the ride was silent, but Hector remained in her thoughts. In fact, Félicité's condemnation merely whetted Maddy's appetite for the man and she could think of nothing else.

Except, of course, her poor absentee Henri.

36

By the time they boarded the familiar little steamer, *Thomas R.,* Félicité had grown surly. She told Maddy she needed time alone and retreated to the colored section below decks her sharp tone warning Maddy not to follow. Maddy wandered the decks and tried to decide whether Félicité was worried about her father, annoyed by the ill-advised comments about *plaçage* or was simply being her mercurial self. Either way, she remained absent during the short downriver voyage and didn't reappear until the Ouichita & Red River Landing loomed off the starboard bow. Maddy was alone at the rail, relieved when Félicité slipped an arm through hers. "Feeling better, dear?" she ventured.

"A bit." Félicité sighed deeply. "Too much on my mind I'm afraid. Forgive me for being peevish." She nodded toward the landing where another steamboat waited to take them to New Orleans. "Look there. That must be ours."

"Oh, I hope so," Maddy enthused. "What a beauty!"

Once again she found herself thinking of Henri. The two shared a fascination for these long-vanished vessels, and she wished he could see this glamorous, gingerbread palace reminding her of the *Cotton Blossom* in the musical Showboat. A gilded palm tree was stationed between towering chimneys with lotus-shaped caps, and Roman gods and goddesses were painted on her paddlebox, embellishing the words *La Sirene.* The name rang a bell, and just as Maddy realized it was Jean-Noël's boat, he called from the top of the gangway.

"Mademoiselle St. Jacques! Up here! It's Captain Baptiste!"

Maddy smiled and waved back. "Look, Félicité. The captain is an acquaintance of mine."

"What a happy coincidence."

"Indeed it is." Maddy guessed it was no coincidence at all, merely the August Ones at work. "This certainly guarantees we'll be asked to dine at the captain's table." She realized her mistake immediately. "Oh, dear! Forgive me, Félicité. I wasn't thinking."

"You continually amaze me, Madeleine. Sometimes I think your social graces belong to another world."

How right you are, Maddy thought, trying to smooth things over as they disembarked. "Please forget I said that. We've booked cabins in the colored section, and we'll stay there as we did on the voyage up." Before Félicité could object further, she added, "Our being together is far more important than any silly dinner."

"The choice is yours," Félicité said, feathers still ruffled.

Further embarrassment was averted when Jean-Noël hurried down the gangway to greet Maddy in person. He touched the brim of his captain's cap and welcomed her aboard. There was no doubting the admiration in his eyes when they flickered discreetly to Félicité.

"Please introduce me to your friend."

"This is Mademoiselle Félicité Chevalier. Félicité, this is Captain Jean Noël Baptiste."

Félicité dropped a curtsy. *"M'sieur le captaine."*

"This is what I get for not checking the passenger list more closely," Jean-Noël said. "I could have been looking forward to this moment all the way from Memphis, knowing there would be not one but two beautiful ladies boarding here."

Maddy was embarrassed again when it was apparent he believed Félicité was white. Deciding to diffuse the situation before it became dangerous, Maddy took the captain's arm and asked for a moment alone. Once out of earshot, she played to Jean-Noël's sympathy as she explained their dilemma.

"One thing that your beloved Madeline and I share is our

frankness," she said. "That being said, I must tell you that my friend Félicité is a *femme de coleur libre.*"

"*Mais, non!*" Jean-Noël was clearly surprised.

"True enough. We have been traveling together in the quarters reserved for free Negroes. That's why you didn't see my name on the passenger list."

To Maddy's relief, Jean-Noël smiled. "What a generous thing to do for a friend. In fact, it sounds like something my Madeleine would do, and that gives me an idea."

"Oh?"

"I happen to know the bridal suite is available from here all the way to New Orleans. Might I suggest you and your friend make it yours as my guests?" When Maddy hesitated, he added, "It's the finest stateroom on *La Sirene.*"

Maddy was flabbergasted by the generous *beau geste.* "That's more than kind, but are you sure it will cause no problems?"

Jean-Noël drew himself up and spoke with imposing conviction. "I have authority over every inch of this ship and everyone on it. If anyone questions the arrangement, they will have to answer to me, and I assure you that's something they will regret."

Maddy resisted the urge to hug him, knowing it to be inappropriate. "I can't thank you enough. Now I must go to Félicité and present your proposition."

"Present?" Jean-Noël was bemused. "Are you suggesting she won't be pleased?"

Maddy laughed a bit nervously. "Oh, you know how fussy these high born women of color can be, Captain. Sometimes, speaking confidentially of course, they can have stricter standards than my own."

"Indeed. I've heard Madeleine say that a dozen times." He nodded at Félicité. "Since she's now in my charge, perhaps it would be best if I spoke to her."

Knowing how Félicité reacted to rich, dashing men, Maddy agreed. "I'm sure it would."

As Maddy expected, Félicité thawed the moment she heard Jean-Noël's princely offer and reacted with the utmost grace. "Your kindness is overwhelming, Captain Baptiste."

"Then please allow me to give you a tour of my beautiful lady before showing you to your quarters."

"I'd like nothing more," Félicité said, dimpling prettily as she boldly took his offered arm and nodded at the gangway. "Shall we?"

Wow, Maddy thought as Félicité turned on the charm full-tilt. Talk about pulling a one-eighty!

Félicité's performance continued as they explored *Mermaid's* fabulous appointments. They passed beneath stained-glass skylights and marveled at ceiling filigree as intricate as stalactites. There was a tunnel-like Grand Saloon teeming with marble statuary, potted palms and fine oil paintings, and a dining room for 160 passengers. The ship's statistics were equally remarkable, and Félicité seemed to hang on the captain's every word.

"She has a thirty-two foot beam and stretches two hundred and seventy feet from stem to stern, with the jackstaff adding another twelve feet," Jean-Noël explained. "She has eight boilers and a draft of eight feet. Those splendid chimneys are sixty-eight feet high, and we have a five-toned whistle which we will be hearing any minute."

"It takes my breath away," Félicité purred.

Jean-Noël beamed with pride, and Maddy smiled when his chest actually puffed out a bit. "Now, then. Are you ladies ready to see your stateroom?"

"If you please," Félicité replied, eyelashes fluttering.

Maddy's fascination with Félicité's routine continued as they entered a commodious suite dubbed the Cupid Chamber, named for a carved mahogany tester bed swimming with putti. Other lavish French furnishings gleamed with peach-colored upholstery, and matching silk draperies trimmed in silver bullion fringe puddled atop oriental carpets.

"It's breathtaking, captain." A wave of her fan enveloped the man in Félicité's rosewater perfume. "Absolutely breathtaking."

Jean-Noël's muttonchops flared as he smiled. "Then it meets your approval?"

Félicité tossed her head to make her garnet earrings dance. "Meets and exceeds, sir."

Good Lord, Maddy thought. Until then, she believed Hollywood movies only caricatured Southern women, but after watching Félicité's performance she decided they weren't far off the mark. Coquetting and "slopping sugar," as Grandmother Aglaé called it, were standard operating procedure for belles and courtesans alike, and she was disappointed when the ship's whistle lowered the curtain on Félicité's amazing act.

"If you ladies will excuse me," Jean-Noël said, "I must attend to my duties as captain. May I expect you to join me for dinner?"

"Indeed you may," Félicité replied.

"*C'est bon.* I usually dine in the officer's quarters, but I can't possibly keep so much beauty to myself. Shall we say seven in the main dining salon?"

"Seven it is," Maddy said. Once Jean-Noël bowed and exited, she turned to Félicité. "You were magnificent, my dear, but there's something I must tell you."

"He's unavailable, isn't he?" Maddy nodded as Félicité sank into a *fauteuil* chair and rearranged her skirts. "I was afraid of that."

"He belongs to the woman who lives on the plantation outside Port LeBlanc."

"*Mais,* didn't you tell me she was in a poisonous marriage? I should think Captain Baptiste would be an ideal husband."

"As do I, but she is married to someone else. The captain is, shall we say, the antidote to the husband's poison."

"*Ma foi!*" Félicité grunted and snapped the fan shut. "Why

is it all the good men are taken?"

"I don't know, my darling, but I promise if I were one, I would find you absolutely irresistible."

"*Merci, ma chère.* It's reassuring to know I can still summon a modicum of charm." Félicité sighed as she exhibited a rare moment of vanity. "After all, I must depend upon it for my very survival."

Maddy immediately thought of Blanche DuBois's tragic dependence on the kindness of strangers. Nor was it lost on her that Blanche and Félicité both lived in homes called *Belle Rêve.* She didn't know whether it was coincidence or the August Ones reminding her of home. Either way she turned her head and blinked away tears as the melancholy in Félicité's voice broke her heart.

37

After restorative naps, the women took special pains with their toilettes and evening dresses. Maddy chose silver brocade with black velvet trim while Félicité was far more daring in sky blue moiré, faille and satin showered with Chantilly lace and cut in extreme *décolleté*. Their efforts paid off when they entered the dining room and made their way to the captain's table with calculated slowness. All eyes, female and as male, monitored their progress, and Jean-Noël glowed with pride as he rose to greet them.

"Ladies," he said with a bow. "I'm the envy of every man on board."

"*Merci, m'sieur,*" Félicité said. "I assure you the honor is ours." Maddy noticed her coquetry was no longer in high gear.

While Félicité gazed around the room, nodding politely and basking in admiring gazes, Jean-Noël asked Maddy if she had received Madeleine's invitation to Five Oaks. "Her letter came right before I left for the Isle Brevelle," she replied. "I didn't have a chance to reply."

"I sincerely hope you'll accept." He lowered his voice. "I'm sorry to report things are getting desperate."

"How so?" When he glanced nervously at Félicité, Maddy said, "You may speak freely, Captain Baptiste. Thinking your paths would never cross, I discussed your dilemma with Félicité, and I can assure you she is not one to betray a confidence."

Jean-Noël looked uncertain but continued nonetheless. "Jules is more unbearable than ever, exploding with fits of temper and accusing Madeleine of outrageous things. The poor dear is absolutely miserable."

"What outrageous things? Surely he doesn't know—?"

"About us? No. We're especially cautious these days. His latest accusation is that she's a spendthrift. He even put her on a level with Natalie Benjamin."

"Who?"

"Even in Natchez you should have heard of her," said Félicité who had stopped surveying the room and was listening to the conversation. "Natalie is from New Orleans, and before she moved to France she was known as the most extravagant woman in the South."

"She's married to Judah Benjamin, the Confederate Attorney General," Jean-Noël added. "He once asked her to curb her spending, to which she famously replied, 'Oh, speak not to me of economic matters. I find it so fatiguing.'"

Sounds like a woman who needs her credit cards cut up, Maddy thought. "There's no truth to Jules's accusations, is there?"

"Of course not. Madeleine spends no more than any other lady of fashion and taste. Besides, it's her own money." Jean-Noël tactfully stopped speaking when the steward brought menus. He ordered whiskey for himself and *ratafias* for the ladies and told the man they would order directly. Alone again, he said, "St. Jacques has always resented Madeleine's family fortune, but it didn't keep him from moving into Five Oaks once they were married or buying a steamboat with profits from the plantation sugar crop. He secretly hates that it's his wife's fortune that brought him success."

"How ungrateful."

Félicité was more to the point. "He sounds like a *lunatique*,"

"A drunk lunatic at that," Jean-Noël lamented. "When Jules and I became partners, he was a smart, level-headed businessman. He was also charming and amusing which is how he captured Madeleine's heart. Alas, once they were married, he developed a taste for bourbon, and that's when the trouble began. Sober, he can be the perfect gentleman.

Intoxicated, he's a monster with a terrible streak of cruelty."

"Why don't you and your Madeleine run off to Mexico?" Félicité suggested. "Please don't tell me the notion has not occurred to you."

"*Au contraire, mademoiselle.* It's been our dream for years, but it's easier said than done."

"*Pourquoi?*"

"To be perfectly frank, money. Madeleine could never sell Five Oaks without her husband's knowledge, and because we're business partners my finances are thoroughly intertwined with his. Making matters worse, St. Jacques has recently begun association with the most disreputable of characters and engaged in any number of shady business deals. If he believed I was involved with his wife or wanted out of the partnership, he wouldn't hesitate to destroy us both and *La Sirene* too. You've no idea how pernicious and vindictive the man can be. Steamboat fires and explosions are all too common, and I know for a fact that some of these disasters were arranged."

"If he's so loathsome, what good will my visit do?" Maddy asked.

"I promise your mere presence will be a balm for Madeleine. For some strange reason known only to him, Jules behaves when there are guests at Five Oaks. I don't think he'd dare berate her with you under roof."

"Then I'll make arrangements after we dock in New Orleans."

"God bless you," Jean-Noël smiled, relief evident. "May I escort you to Five Oaks?"

"Won't Jules think that peculiar?"

"Not at all. Madeleine has taken the precaution of telling him that you two have been keeping company in New Orleans and that you and I are old friends. He'll be expecting us."

The plot thickens still more, Maddy thought. "Then I'll look forward to it."

Félicité made an effort to lighten the mood as she pe-

Still Time | 201

rused the enormous menu. "I trust you'll help us navigate these choices, Captain."

"It will be my pleasure."

While they considered their dinner choices, Maddy took inventory of her opulent surroundings and the dozens of fashionably dressed men and women. She glanced at one of the men Félicité acknowledged earlier, noting his knee-length broadcloth coat and ruffled shirt bosom with diamond buttons nicknamed "headlights." He caught Maddy's eye and, before she could look away, gave her a generous smile, and approached their table. She was surprised to discover she wasn't the only object of his attention.

"Captain Baptiste," he said in English. "William Mumford at your service."

"Good evening, sir." Jean-Noël rose to bow and shake hands. "I didn't know you were traveling with us."

"Indeed I am. I boarded at the Red River Landing and will be with you all the way to New Orleans."

"Splendid."

When Jean-Noël made introductions, Maddy noted that Mumford's eyes lingered a bit too long on Félicité's half-bared breasts. An uncomfortable shiver shot down her spine when he cocked his head and gave her an inquisitive look.

"You ladies look familiar. Do you all live in New Orleans?"

"Natchez," Maddy replied quickly. "Mademoiselle Chevalier is from New Orleans."

Mumford nodded, eyes narrowing. "I believe I've seen you before."

"It's possible," Félicité answered lightly. "At the opera or ballet. The theater perhaps."

"I fear my wife Mary and I don't patronize such places." Mumford paused before adding, "But no matter. I have seen you two somewhere, and that is enough for now."

What a strange thing to say, Maddy thought, praying Mumford didn't know Félicité from the *Salle d'Orléans*. She was relieved when he retreated to his table.

"What a peculiar gentleman," Félicité remarked. "I'm not sure he's trustworthy."

"You're very perceptive, mademoiselle," Jean-Noël said. "William Mumford is one of the most infamous gamblers on the river. His notoriety stretches from New Orleans all the way to Cairo, Illinois. Not all captains would allow him to pursue his livelihood aboard their vessels, but he's a genial sort and adds to the male passengers' enjoyment."

"He no doubt subtracts something too," Félicité joked.

Jean-Noël chuckled. "Clever, perceptive and beautiful. You're a deadly combination, mademoiselle."

"So I've been told," she said with a fluttering of eyelashes.

Given what Félicité knew about Jean-Noël and Madeleine, Maddy was concerned when she began flirting again. Perhaps, she thought, the woman can't help herself, but she was nevertheless glad when a waiter arrived for their order. "All this excitement has made me famished," she announced. While her companions listened in amazement, she ordered more *ratafia* along with *caviares sur canapés,* oyster soup, *pigeons sautés aux champignons,* asparagus and *cauliflower au buerre.* When she looked up, they were staring in disbelief. "Is something wrong?"

"Where on earth are you going to put all that?" Félicité asked with a laugh. "I'll barely manage half a dozen oysters and a bit of pompano."

Because you're too tightly cinched, Maddy thought. "Everything looks so irresistible I couldn't help myself. I'm sure I'll regret it later."

"Then perhaps a stroll around the Upper Deck after dinner is in order," Jean-Noël suggested. "The sky should be clear tonight with rivers of stars."

"'Rivers of stars,'" Maddy repeated with a smile. "Spoken like a true ship's captain."

Late, after *café noir* and *marrons glacés,* Jean-Noël escorted the ladies from the dining room. William Mumford smiled broadly as they passed, reigniting Maddy's fear that he would recognize Félicité. After their stroll around the deck, they repaired to their stateroom where Maddy asked about Mumford.

"We've both met him," Félicité said, fussing with the rows of buttons on her gown. "Seen him anyway."

"But where?"

"The night we met. You don't remember?"

Realization dawned as Maddy hastily reconstructed that unforgettable evening. "Was he one of the gamblers in that little room?"

"Indeed he was."

"Then if he remembers, he'll think I'm—"

"Like me. Imagine that!" Félicité gave her an impish smile. "Now please be a darling and help me with these silly buttons."

Maddy hugged her. "You're one of a kind, my dear."

Part 6

"The devil has a vast empire here."

— Sister Madeleine Hachard, *Personal Diaries (1728)*

38

The downriver voyage required only two days, but Maddy's nerves remained brittle for the duration. She lived in fear that William Mumford would recall seeing her at the *Salle d'Orléans* and presume she was a courtesan of color, albeit less concerned about social stigma than someone probing her background and presence in nineteenth-century Louisiana. Luckily the man stayed busy playing poker in private quarters, so they did not see each other again until they disembarked in New Orleans, nodding from a polite distance. Maddy was much relieved.

Jean-Noël waited at the bottom of the gangway and took her aside. "Please promise you'll come to Five Oaks soon," he urged. "Madeleine truly needs you. We both do."

"I promise, but I'll need a few days to catch my breath."

"*Bien sûr.* Perhaps dinner tonight at Antoine's would help." He nodded at Félicité waiting alongside the *Rue de la Levée*. "I mean no disrespect, but we have not had a moment alone on this voyage, and there are things I wish to discuss in private."

"In that case, I accept."

"*Bon.* I'll call for you at seven. *Au revoir.*" Jean-Noël tapped the brim of his captain's cap and excused himself to address other duties while Maddy joined Félicité.

"Shall we share a hack?"

"I was about to ask the same thing," Félicité replied. "I must watch my funds now that I know how desperate things are at home. I must also rest this evening so I'll be refreshed before attending the ball tomorrow night." She sighed, more with resignation than fatigue. "It's more pressing than ever that I find a protector."

"I wish I could help," Maddy said.

"I cherish your concern, *mon ami,* but as usual I must fend for myself. It's woman's lot, after all. At least women like myself."

The words bore such sad resignation that Maddy considered ignoring Jean Noël's request for privacy and asking Félicité to join them for dinner. Once more, protocol leapt like a panther when she realized a woman of color would be denied entrance at Antoine's.

"Shall we have lunch tomorrow?"

"Thank you, no. I have much to do and think about. If I'm unsuccessful at the ball, I must consider the alternatives."

Maddy noted an edge to her friend's voice. "Such as?"

Félicité feigned nonchalance. "Oh, nothing of importance."

"I know when you're being evasive, Félicité. Tell me. Please."

Félicité demurred. "It's nothing you need know about."

Maddy would not be put off. "You can't possibly mean *Le Salon Bleu?*"

Fire flashed in the lovely green eyes. *"Pourquoi pas?"*

Maddy was aghast. "Do you think I don't know about that place?"

"Je ne sais pas," Félicité was flippant. "Do you?"

"I do indeed and the very notion of you going there is unacceptable."

From her studies of the world of the *gens du coleur libre,* Maddy knew there were several ways for white men to arrange liaisons with females of color. The *Salle d'Orléans* was the *ne plus ultra,* of course, and below that were a series of venues where gentility and manners took a back seat to price. Indeed, women frequenting the *Salon Bleu* could be engaged for a single evening, not a lifetime. Occasionally beautiful and sometimes educated, they were the scarlet sisters of modern high-priced call girls.

"How would a white woman know of such things?" Félicité asked.

"You know by now that I'm an inquisitive soul," Maddy replied. "At home there's a place called Natchez-Under-the-Hill that offers carnal *divertissements* of every imaginable sort. It's so notorious that riverboat gamblers labeled it a hell's broth and some have even called it the wildest place on the Mississippi."

"I fail to see what this has to do with *Le Salon Bleu*," Félicité sniffed.

"You know what kind of women go there. Please don't make me say the word."

"I'll save you the trouble." Félicité struggled to be bold, but her voice wavered when she said, "Whore."

"Mon dieu," Maddy cried, further appalled. "I refuse to believe it has come to this, and I simply will not accept it."

"Non? Then what do you expect me to do?" Félicité demanded, mettle returning.

"For now, nothing. Perhaps if the two of us put our heads together we could come up with a plan that—"

"Time is something else I don't have, Maddy. I must confront the reality that I have a mountain of bills to pay and no way to pay them. In the past I could rely on *maman* for a few dollars, but those days are over, and the sound of the piper is deafening."

Dismayed and downcast, Maddy hushed when a hack finally responded to Félicité's waving handkerchief and drew his carriage to the curb. There was no conversation on the drive to their homes in the *carré de la ville,* and never, Maddy decided, had there been a heavier, more aching silence between them.

Félicité's woes continued to trouble Maddy that night, as did what she might encounter on the upcoming visit with Madeleine. Hector threatened to slip into her mind too, but she wouldn't allow him entry. When she crawled into bed, she was so emotionally exhausted that sleep came fast, bringing Henri with it. As before, his dream appearance was timed to bolster her spirits whenever the time journey left her frightened and adrift. Faced with so much uncertainty, and still plagued by lack of purpose, Maddy embraced his nebulous presence, drawing strength from it and his infusion of much-needed confidence. She remembered little of the dream when she awoke, but there was no doubting her newfound courage. When it was time to travel to Five Oaks, she welcomed the challenge.

39

As Jean-Noël hoisted the sail and deftly steered the small skiff from the dock, Maddy was both fascinated and unnerved by the chaos of the vast New Orleans waterfront. It was one thing to watch the spectacle from the levee and quite another to be thrust into the tumultuous, cacophonous harbor. Suitably impressed by Jean Noël's navigational skills as captain of *La Sirene*, she was further dazzled when he negotiated the slender passage between an incoming steamboat and outgoing Indiamen, enormous craft that could easily swamp the little boat. As soon as he found open water, Jean-Noël trimmed the sail and the short upriver voyage began.

"If this fair wind holds and we don't get run over by those big fellows, we should be in Port LeBlanc within the hour."

"I had no idea it was so close," she lied.

"So near and yet so far," Jean-Noël lamented.

"How much farther to Five Oaks once we put into port?"

"A half hour if Madeleine is waiting with the carriage." He grinned. "She'd better be!"

Eager to learn more about her ancestor, Maddy said, "How did you two meet?"

"Through Jules of course, but Madeleine's reputation preceded her," Jean Noël answered, warming to a favorite topic. "When she was a belle, more duels were fought over Madeleine Brasseaux than any other woman in the parish. There's even a grave attributing to her fatal charms."

Maddy experienced a peculiar mix of horror and pride. "Truly?"

"Truly. I first heard about her when a distant cousin attended a ball at the La Branche plantation near Five Oaks. My beloved was in attendance, and poor Raymond was so smitten he argued with some other hot-blood about Madeleine's coiffure."

"What on earth do you mean?"

"Raymond insisted the moonlight turned it silver while his rival contended that Madeleine's tresses were bluish. Insults were hurled, challenges issued, and they met at dawn under the Dueling Oaks. My cousin lived to tell the tale. His opponent did not. You know the old Creole saying, 'Pistols for two, coffee for one.'"

"Men and their eternal bloodlust," Maddy muttered, thinking of Rome's gladiatorial games and modern-day cage fighting. She was disgusted, but at least there was a certain honor at dueling's core. "How many duels did Madeleine inspire?"

"I've no idea, but I assure you the day Jules introduced me to his beauteous fiancée, a fever infected my heart that still rages today."

"Then it was love at first sight? How romantic!"

"For her too, I'm flattered to say. How we've wished we had met at an earlier moment in time, but such fantasies only bring heartache. There's no changing our fate, so we must grasp happiness whenever we can."

"How long has it been like this?"

"We dutifully fought our emotions and were successful until a moment at a Mardi Gras ball last year changed everything. Whoa! Hang on!" Jean-Noël swung the boom hard to starboard to avoid colliding with a sleek sidewheeler rolling at full steam. Maddy grabbed the sides of the boat as the huge vessel thundered by, rocking the skiff fiercely in her wake. Jean-Noël pointed and yelled. "Look there, Maddy! It's the *C.S.S. Ivy!*"

"Dear God," Maddy breathed as she registered the initials. *"Confederate States Ship Ivy."* With all that had happened in the past few days, the war had been shoved to the back of her mind. Reality returned when the steamboat-turned-warship swept past, and the day's excitement paled.

She called out once Jean Noël brought the skiff back under control and made safely toward shore. "Where's she going in such a hurry?"

"She's part of our new Mosquito Fleet," he called back. "Captain Hollins is converting our riverboats to gunboats to defend the downriver approach to the city. There's no doubt the Yankees will come from that direction."

"Will the defense include *La Sirene*?"

"Who can say? For now, most steamboats are needed for passenger traffic."

They continued in silence, earlier conversation vanquished by thoughts of war. So it's coming at last, Maddy realized grimly, and how long before it arrives in New Orleans? She racked her brain to remember the date when the Confederacy would stretch a great boom across the Mississippi River to block the Union Navy. Then would come the Battle of the Head of Passes and the Battle of Fort Jackson and Fort St. Philip, and after that was something she didn't want to think about.

"Captain Baptiste!" she called, surprising him with his formal title and pointing to a neat cluster of wooden buildings off the port bow. "Is that Port LeBlanc?"

"It is indeed, Mademoiselle St. Jacques, and we'll be there before you know it."

As they neared shore, Maddy was fascinated to see her hometown in its infancy. It was named for Camille LeBlanc, the French Minister of State who settled there in 1719, a year after the founding of New Orleans. She recognized nothing of the tiny settlement but nonetheless gleaned an inner glow from being there. Port LeBlanc's traffic did not compare to that of the downriver behemoth they left behind and provided easy dockage for Jean-Noël. He deftly secured the boat and was reaching for Maddy's hand when they heard Madeleine's voice.

"Maddy! Captain Baptiste! Over here!"

Madeleine was a burst of color among the drab crowd of

sailors, roustabouts and longshoremen working the small waterfront, reminding Maddy of a daffodil in her bright yellow day dress with printed cotton flounces and pagoda sleeves. She clapped a hand on her straw picture hat as she rushed to embrace Maddy like a long-lost sister. Aware that they were being watched, she politely nodded to Jean-Noël and offered her hand. Maddy could almost see desire crackling between the couple and felt the frustration of the requisite charade. She heard Jean Noël whisper as he bowed over Madeleine's gloved hand.

"If only these lips could rest where they belong."

"Soon," Madeleine whispered back. She beamed as she took Maddy's arm and spoke in her normal voice. "I can't tell you how much I've looked forward to this. It seems forever since we last saw one another. Where have you been keeping yourself?"

"As a matter of fact," Maddy replied, catching Madeleine's high spirits, "I'm only recently returned from the Isle Brevelle."

Madeleine's eyebrows rose as the name registered. "Oh?"

"I accompanied an acquaintance from there. She was visiting her sick father."

"Is she a woman of color, this acquaintance?"

"She is indeed," Maddy replied, wondering if Madeleine would question the unconventional friendship. Her concern was ill-founded as Madeleine smiled approvingly and indicated the waiting carriage.

"Jules is in the fields all morning but will join us for lunch. I hope you don't mind riding with the top back. It's such a beautiful day, and I have an extra parasol."

"It sounds wonderful."

As they piled into the open landau, Maddy felt a wave of trepidation that swelled as they left Port LeBlanc and jounced along a muddy road leading into the steamy countryside. Once she realized she was merely apprehensive over seeing her ancestral home, she relaxed and enjoyed the

scenery. Dark bayous and thick stands of cypress soon yielded to towering walls of sugar cane stretching to infinity on
both sides of the road. The deep green stalks rippled before
winds gusting off the Gulf of Mexico, shifting first one way,
then the other, and she wished for sunglasses when the glar-
ing sun was mirrored in a series of irrigation ditches.

"It's mesmerizing!"

"I never tire of looking at it," Madeleine confessed. "And
when they burn the fields the air smells like *crème brûlée.*"

Madeleine had been familiar with that peculiar marvel
since childhood, but pretended otherwise. "How delightful."

Madeleine smiled and twirled her parasol. "I hope you
feel the same about Five Oaks."

"She'll love it," Jean-Noël said as the driver flicked the
reins and urged the two horses into a faster pace. "You've
done wonderful things with the place."

"It's only a simple country home," Madeleine insisted,
gazing at her lover with a visible yearning. "Nothing like
Nottaway or Belle Grove with their dozens of rooms."

"I can hardly wait to see it," Maddy declared.

"Then keep an eye in that direction, and you'll get a
glimpse through those fields."

Sure enough, Maddy discerned a column here and a
roofline there before the carriage turned from the road onto
a robust *allée* of pine trees. Maddy immediately thought of
Oak Alley, the iconic antebellum home near Vacherie that
fascinated tourists with its twin rows of live oaks arching into
a natural canopy. Here, at the end of the alley, loomed a
Creole bungalow that might have been transplanted from
the West Indies. As she approached, an eerie rush of déjà vu
convinced Maddy that her blood had indeed been here before.

The prodigal daughter had come home!

"Five Oaks," she whispered, bathed in a wave of nostalgia.

"In case you're wondering, the trees giving the place its
name are over there." Madeleine pointed to a grove of enor-

mous live oaks shrouded in gossamer Spanish moss. Sheltered and shaded in their midst was a latticework gazebo. "That little summer house is my favorite spot on the plantation. We'll have coffee there this afternoon if you like."

"I'd like that very much."

Maddy was mesmerized as the carriage bounced to a stop before the two-story stucco house. Eight thick pillars with Doric capitals supported a second floor gallery with slender columns called *colonnettes*, and a steeply pitched roof deflected the intense sun and tropical rains of south Louisiana. Maddy noted that the ceiling of the first floor veranda was painted what the Creoles called *grand rouge*, a color made by mixing buttermilk and brick dust. The simple structure was given elegance with tall shuttered windows, French doors and potted topiaries between the columns.

"It's charming," she pronounced.

Maddy's imagination flourished as she conjured family tableaux, wondering which ancestors had romped on this lawn as children and played on that upper gallery when it rained and who was sired under this roof and pampered by wealth yielded from the cane fields. This endless speculation turned her breathing shallow as she was escorted into the house.

Madeleine, who missed precious little, said, "What we all need is a cup of coffee."

What I need more, Maddy thought, is a firm grip on my sanity.

40

After coffee, Madeleine insisted that Maddy nap before lunch and instructed Delphine, her personal maid, to take their guest to her bedroom. Still foggy with déjà-vu, Maddy let Delphine unbutton her dress and unhook her basque so she could rest unencumbered on a *chaise longue.* She'd barely stretched out when sleep brought dreams of Henri. It had been awhile since his last imagining, and she welcomed his appearance at the vanishing point of those infinite rows of sugar cane. Maddy's heart raced when he grew large enough to reveal a smile, but his countenance darkened as she slipped into his arms.

"What is it, darling? Why so serious?"

"Because we must speak of serious matters, *ma cher.* I know you have been yearning for me as I have for you, but you must now continue the journey as though I don't exist."

"No!" Maddy was alarmed. "There are times when thoughts of you are all that sustain me."

"I understand and love you more for it, but once again this is beyond my control." Further distressed, Maddy tried to withdraw, but Henri held tight. "I promise a time will come when you will understand this latest dictate."

"You're abandoning me!" Maddy wailed. "I'm far away in some lost universe and you're leaving me alone to fend for myself."

"You're never really alone, Maddy. Remember that."

"I may as well be," she protested. "I'm in the middle of nowhere with people I barely know, living every hour with the fear of discovery and with you as my only link to reality. Now you're telling me you're severing that link."

"You'll find ways to fill my absence," he insisted. "Embrace them."

That gave her unexpected pause. "Oh?"

"Besides, it's not forever."

"How long then?"

"I wish I knew." Before Maddy could protest further, Henri said, "You'll be fine, beloved. Look how you handled that man threatening Félicité, then sailed with her to the Isle Brevelle and now travel to your ancestral home."

"So it's true!" Maddy cried. "My first suspicions were right. Madeleine and I *are* family, and Five Oaks is my ancestral home!"

"True enough," Henri confirmed. "She is your great-great-grandmother."

"And Jules is—?"

"No matter the situation," Henri continued, "you've risen to meet the challenge."

Realizing the matter of family was closed, she dared consider Hector. "Do you know everything I've done?"

"Not everything. The August Ones keep certain secrets, and I suspect that's a good thing."

Maddy's pulse raced. "What do you mean?"

"I don't know everything you do in our shared universe in the present-day, so it's not unreasonable that the same is true of where you are now."

"Oh." Maddy was simultaneously relieved and discomfited.

"Besides, I trust you implicitly to choose the right paths, to take whatever opportunity presents itself and act on it."

Maddy trembled when Henri's hold loosened and he began to fade. "Please don't be too long in returning," she urged. "I don't think I could bear it."

"You can," Henri said, deep voice growing thin. "And you will."

As Henri receded into the infinite avenue of sugar cane, it trembled and heaved all of a piece, and Maddy drifted helplessly before being engulfed by the thunder of hooves. As she struggled free of the dream, she awoke to real hoof beats. She rushed to the window and looked down the *allée* to see a lone horse and rider racing beneath the piney canopy as though charging the house itself. Reined sharp and hard, jaws sawed by the bit, the horse whinnied and reared, struggling without success to throw off his tormentor.

"Hold, Brutus! Hold I say!" The enraged horse ceased bucking long enough for the rider to dismount and pass the reins to a terrified slave. He roared with laughter when the stallion reared anew, lifting the groom off his feet and dragging him away. He called after them. "Water him and rub him down, Bossa. I'll be out to the stables later to look him over." He turned toward the house and shouted again. "Madeleine! Are you back?"

My God, Maddy thought. Can this be my great-great grandfather?

The man below her window was nearly as wide as he was tall. Bull-necked and barrel-chested, he reminded her of a bantam rooster, and she watched, repulsed, as Madeline made to embrace her husband only to be ignored as Jules welcomed Jean-Noël.

"Good to see you, old man." Jules slapped his partner on the back and glanced toward the front door. "And where is your lady friend?"

"She's resting before lunch," Jean-Noël replied. "Auguste is here too."

Jules growled. "What the devil does he want?"

"Only to visit his sister," Madeleine replied wearily. "We'll have lunch as soon as you've cleaned up."

"I'm hungry now," Jules grunted. "No need to wait." Maddy was descending the staircase as he entered the foyer. "Ah! This must be the other Madeline St. Jacques."

"And you must be the other Madeleine's husband," Maddy retorted pleasantly. She was prepared to despise the man, but that didn't entitle her to rudeness. Not yet anyway. She curtsied when she reached the bottom step. "A pleasure, m'sieur."

"I assure you the pleasure is all mine." Jules bowed before kissing her hand. "Please allow me to welcome you to Five Oaks."

"Merci beaucoup."

Maddy grew uncomfortable when Jules scoured her with his eyes. "I come directly from the fields, mademoiselle, so please allow me a moment to refresh myself. I'll be back directly." He bowed again and was gone.

Maddy was wondering if she was the reason he changed his mind about cleaning up when Madeleine confirmed it. "Obviously you made quite the impression, my dear. He would never do that for me."

Maddy's face blazed. "*Mais,* I had no intention of—"

"Never apologize when Jules is involved," Madeleine said with a wave of the hand. "It's invariably a waste of time. You should also know the man has two personalities. One is charming and the other is monstrous. Hopefully you won't see the latter." She took Maddy's arm. "Now come along. I want you to meet my brother Auguste."

Maddy peered through the parlor doors and saw a tall, broad-shouldered man standing before the mantle. His back was to her as he studied a portrait of a handsome young couple in early eighteenth-century dress. "What a lovely painting."

Madeleine nodded. "Our parents, Céline and René Brasseaux. It was painted a year before their deaths."

"Goodness!" Maddy braced herself for more family revelations. "What happened?"

"Mama died in childbirth, and Papa followed a week later. He was thrown by his horse."

"Papa was the finest equestrian in five parishes including Orléans," Auguste said, overhearing his sister. "He'd taken that jump a hundred times and never fallen once. No one can convince me he didn't break his neck on purpose."

"That's hardly something to be discussed before guests," Madeleine declared.

Auguste turned toward Maddy. "Forgive me, mademoiselle. I'm afraid my manners were elsewhere."

"As usual," Madeleine teased. "This is the young lady I told you about, the one who shares my name. Maddy, this is my brother, Auguste Brasseaux."

As he approached, Maddy noted Auguste's arresting combination of black beard and ice blue eyes, but his clothes were equally notable. His rumpled shirt, buckskin vest and trousers and dusty boots announced he was a man of the outdoors, a hunter or trapper, perhaps. She also noted a startling resemblance to John Hamm, the star of Mad Men, her favorite television show. Wow, she thought, nearly swooning as Auguste brushed her hand with a kiss and cloaked her in the smell of tobacco and animal skins. She was further unnerved by a jolt of sexual energy she fought by reminding herself this was her great-great-uncle!

Conversation resumed when Maddy cleared her head and heard Jean-Noël say, "Auguste prefers spending his time in the bayous. He cares nothing for city life, or plantation life either for that matter."

"C'est vrai," Auguste said. "With animals, you know where you stand. With people—?"

He rolled his eyes when Jules bellowed from the dining room, summoning everyone to lunch.

"People are far less predictable."

"Please don't quarrel with Jules," Madeleine whispered anxiously. "Not today, with a guest under our roof."

"I promise, sister dear." Auguste bussed Madeleine's cheek and offered his arm while Jean-Noël escorted Maddy as everyone headed to the dining room.

Maddy found herself wishing it was her hand in the crook of Auguste's arm as she began yet another charade.

41

Jules's politeness paled against his fawning performance at lunch. It seemed to Maddy that he deliberately ignored everyone else while explaining the challenges of sugar planting and spinning vibrant tales of his exploits as a river captain. He occasionally asked Jean-Noël for confirmation of this story or that before turning his attention back to her.

"Might we hope you will extend your visit through the summer?" he asked with a smile.

"*Peut-être,*" Maddy answered. "I haven't thought that far ahead."

"I certainly hope you'll remain. Five Oaks belongs to its guests, and the longer you stay, the better. There's a great deal to do here."

"So Madeleine says."

When Jules grunted at the mention of his wife's name, Maddy guessed he was as volatile as Seth. Nor did she doubt he was as evil as Madeleine and Jean-Noël claimed, but for now she found him attentive and gracious. She tried not to stare, oddly fascinated as he finished eating and drained his wine glass. He extended it to the ever-mindful Cato and smiled at Maddy.

"Do you ride, mademoiselle?"

"I regret to say I do not," Maddy confessed. "I fell from a horse when I was a child. That cured all desire to ride again."

"I've yet to meet the horse I couldn't handle," Jules boasted. "Only this morning I had to curb one in to submission."

"Brutus shouldn't be ridden," Jean-Noël said. "He's too high-spirited to control."

Jules snorted. "Not for me. Brutus went to the stable with

a sore mouth today while I am none the worse for wear." When he stared at her, Maddy was compelled to respond.

"Remarkable," she managed, despite loathing all cruelty to animals.

"Not remarkable at all," Jules boasted. "It's simply a matter of letting the horse know who's master. Now then." He downed the second glass of wine and set it down with a loud thud. "Tell me, mademoiselle. Have you seen the workings of a sugar plantation?"

Maddy shook her head. "Cotton is king in Natchez."

"All the more reason you should permit me to give you a private tour."

Maddy didn't relish being alone with this human chameleon, but she wasn't about to miss another look at an age gone by. "I should like that very much."

"Then we'll be off."

"Now?"

"Now!"

No one said a word as Maddy was whisked outdoors where, for the next few hours, she explored every corner of Five Oaks and its vast emerald fields. Jules enthusiastically explained the steps involved in planting, cutting, processing, milling, refining and shipping the sugar and pointed out the buildings, machinery and men required to produce his "white gold." She met the overseer, a no-nonsense Irishman named Paddy O'Neill whose freckled face was coppered by the sun and wondered if he was responsible for a gaggle of freckled mulatto children playing outside the slave quarters. The oddly upsetting notion prompted her to end the tour.

"Might we find some shade?"

"We'll go to the gazebo right away," Jules said, offering his arm and dancing from one conversational topic to another as they walked. "You may think captaining a steamboat is romantic, but I assure you it's not. Danger comes from all directions, whether it's submerged tree trunks waiting to rip open your hull or shifting sand bars eager to run you aground."

"I'm aware of such perils," Maddy said, calling upon her carefully fabricated biography. "My parents died in a steamboat disaster when I was a little girl."

"Which one?"

"The *Black Hawk*. Have you heard of her?"

"Indeed I have. She was bound from Natchez to Natchitoches. The boiler exploded as she entered the mouth of the Red River. All the upper works forward of the wheels were blown apart, killing the pilot and engineer instantly."

"Along with fifty passengers," Maddy added.

"In 1835 I believe."

"1837," Maddy amended. She had memorized her story well. "Might we speak of something else?"

"Of course, mademoiselle. I apologize if I ventured into unpleasant areas."

Charmed yet again, Maddy smiled and changed the subject. "Tell me, sir. Do you consider yourself primarily a steamboat captain or a sugar planter?"

"I'm called both, but my preference is for the river. O'Neill is the true master of Five Oaks. He knows every secret of the cane business and how to get the most from the slaves."

"But you also seem knowledgeable."

"O'Neill taught me everything I know," he confessed. "My periodic inspections are only for my peace of mind. In fact, they're something of an unspoken joke between us."

"I'm sure you're being modest." Maddy's comment made Jules roar with laughter as they took seats in the shady gazebo. "What's so amusing?"

"I've been called many things, young lady, most of them unfit for your pretty ears, and I assure you 'modest' is not one of them." He was still chuckling when Cato came hurrying from the house. "Would you like something cool to drink, Maddy?"

"Eau de sucre, s'il vous plait."

"Sugar water for the lady and whiskey for me, Cato. And don't dawdle." Jules muttered something under his breath as the man rushed away, then turned toward a mountain of clouds building over the Gulf. His good spirits drained away, mood mirroring that of the coming storm. *"Mademoiselle?"*

His voice changed too, Maddy noted. Edgy and filled with foreboding. She wondered if she was about to see the real Jules St. Jacques. *"Oui, m'sieur?"*

"We've only met, but may I speak frankly?"

"If you wish."

"Tiens, it's about my wife and her increasingly frequent trips to New Orleans."

Uh-oh, Maddy thought.

"In fairness I will preface my comments by saying I understand it's difficult for Madeleine, being alone out here with me on the river for weeks at a time, but that hardly justifies her behavior in the city. At least what I imagine her behavior to be."

Fear crawled up Maddy's spine. "I'm afraid I don't know what you mean."

Jules expelled his suspicion with a ragged breath. "I think she may have a paramour."

Maddy's gasp was unfeigned, but for other reasons. *"Mais,* you cannot be serious."

Jules faced her squarely, eyebrows meeting in an ugly scowl. "Do you know otherwise?"

"I know nothing one way or the other, M'sieur St. Jacques. I only recently met your wife and have enjoyed her company on only a few occasions. Dinner, the theater, a few shopping sprees. I neither know her well, nor consider her a confidante, but I can truthfully say that Madeleine does not strike me as an unfaithful wife." She cleared her throat, hoping her lie wouldn't stick in her throat. "Perhaps these separations have made your imagination run wild."

"Perhaps," he conceded, "but when she returns from New Orleans, she seems somehow different."

"Because she's been indulged and rejuvenated," Maddy insisted gaily. "What lady doesn't derive pleasure from visiting the hairdresser and being fussed over by *modistes* and milliners as she tries on new gowns and bonnets? What woman doesn't enjoy dinner at Antoine's or a night at the opera and ballet?"

"You may be right, but the knot in my belly never forms unless something is wrong."

"It could be warning of something else," Maddy suggested.

Jules turned back toward the approaching storm. "I think the solution is to ensure that she is not alone."

"So you'll spend more time with her?" Maddy asked with trepidation.

"My schedule makes that impossible, but perhaps I'll ask Baptiste to keep eye on her when he's in the city. I know he would tell me if he suspected anything untoward."

Maddy's fears fled and she smiled at the irony. "I'm sure that's a wise decision, m'sieur."

"Do you now?" Maddy nodded as Jules stood and took her hand as the first fat raindrops began to fall. "If we hurry we can beat the storm."

Which storm? she wondered as they raced for the house.

42

Swiftly seduced by Five Oaks, Maddy experienced a soulful sense of belonging unknown in her modern existence. She was fascinated by plantation life, by neighbors met at soirées arranged by Madeleine and colorful river exploits traded by Jean-Noël and Jules at dinner. She was even more entertained by tales of the bayous spun by Auguste and was saddened when he returned to the swamps before they got acquainted. Jean-Noel also left when his sailing schedule called him back to New Orleans, and Jules followed in late May. Accompanying him to Port LeBlanc, Maddy and Madeleine found the tiny town in an uproar. Passing the reins to Madeleine and ordering them to wait in the landau, Jules waded into the crowd and managed to secure a newspaper with screaming headlines: *"Union Ships Enter Mouth of Mississippi!! USS Brooklyn Leads Blockade!!"*

"Looks like the Yankees are knocking at our back door," he said grimly as he tugged his portmanteau from the undercarriage. "I suspect it won't be long before the Confederate Navy will be after me to convert the *Madeleine* to a warship."

Maddy was surprised. "You named your steamboat after your wife?"

"*Naturellement.* What adoring husband wouldn't?"

"Should we be worried about the blockade?" Madeleine asked, barely masking her disgust with such hypocrisy.

"Not at all. It won't be long before Captain Hollins positions his Mosquito Fleet down around Fort Jackson. There's no armada in the world can get past him."

"When will you be back?"

"Two months, maybe more depending on how this

damned war goes." He blew a kiss in the general direction of the carriage. *"Au revoir, mesdames."*

"Au revoir!" Madeleine watched Jules shoulder his bag and head for the ferry to New Orleans. She gave Maddy a big smile and slapped the reins to set the coach in motion. "Two whole months of peace and quiet. *Ma foi!* What shall we do to celebrate?"

Maddy chuckled. "You don't waste any time, do you?"

"There's none to waste, my dear. Not with trysts to be arranged and the barbarians almost at the gates of Rome."

"Will Jean-Noël come to Five Oaks?"

"We've never risked it before, in Jules's absence I mean, but with you in residence it will appear perfectly proper." She reached over and patted Maddy's hand. "You will stay awhile longer, won't you?"

Remembering Henri's advice to welcome whatever opportunity arose, Maddy replied without hesitation. *"Certainement, ma cheri.* As long as you like."

Madeleine was so energized she hummed and sang a little on the drive back to Five Oaks. Her spirits remained high for several days, until a letter from Jean-Noël reported that war business would keep him away longer than expected. In a desperate effort to keep the lower Mississippi in Confederate hands, dozens of riverboats including *La Sirene* transported a steady flow of soldiers into New Orleans and ferried nervous passengers out. Madeleine passed the time by burying herself in her endless duties as mistress of Five Oaks, from balancing plantation ledgers to tending sick slaves, always with the devoted Delphine as her shadow. She also squired Maddy around the countryside and introduced her to more neighbors at White Haven, Magnolia Lane, and the LaBranche Plantation.

When Maddy was not being entertained or tended by Delphine, she spent her time reading novels from Madeleine's library. She had never read *Les Misérables* in French, but as compelling as it was it only reminded her that General

Robert E. Lee's beleaguered troops would be nicknamed "Lee's Miserables" toward the end of the war. It was a terrible burden knowing that the fall of New Orleans was less than a year away, and that the South was facing a firestorm of devastation. Worst of all would be the loss of over 600,000 soldiers, Union and Confederate, and untold numbers of civilians before Appomattox brought peace. Any hope of banishing the terrible truth from her brain came when Madeleine made a surprising announcement at breakfast.

"I want news of the war."

Maddy gulped her croissant. "*Pourquoi?* You've said repeatedly that it holds no interest for you."

"Because war is men's business, but Jean-Noël's latest letter changed that. He says the city is an absolute madhouse with everyone preparing for the worst, and I realized I was wrong to be an ostrich. After all, Union ships are now above the mouth of the Mississippi, and that's only seventy miles away. What if they make their way to New Orleans, and my beloved is caught in the crossfire?"

Maddy sliced open an orange picked that very morning. "We can only hope and pray for the best."

"That's not enough. We should also keep abreast of things. I told Cato to go into Port LeBlanc every morning for the latest newspapers. Don't you think that's a good idea?"

"Oh, yes. Knowing is definitely better than not knowing."

"*Exactement!*"

Madeleine's surprising change of mind spawned a morning ritual of reading the news aloud to each other while Delphine kept them supplied with coffee and sweets. An editorial in the *Daily Picayune* echoed Jules' sentiments that the city was safe. "'By land we are impregnable,'" Maddy read, "'and the coast and river's assailable points are susceptible to a degree of defense that floating wood or iron cannot make an impression.'" Another of Jules's predictions proved true when Captain Hollins, now a commodore, positioned his fleet 65 miles below the city between Forts Jackson and St.

Phillip which commanded opposite sides of the Mississippi. New Orleans sighed with relief as the *CSS Ivy* was joined by Confederate sister ships *Livingston, Jackson, McRae* and the flagship *Tuscarora*. To support this formidable flotilla, a massive chain was stretched between the forts to prevent enemy ships from sailing further north. Surely, everyone said, the Yankees couldn't penetrate such a powerful blockade.

More encouraging news arrived July 21 when Confederate forces at Manassas, Virginia, drove Union troops back to Washington, D.C. in shameless disarray, and on August 10 the Battle of Wilson's Creek was a Confederate victory for the formidable Missouri State Guard. The Battles of Dry Wood Creek and Lexington were two more wins for the heroic Guard, and Southern spirits soared higher still on October 12 when Commodore Hollins and his Mosquito Fleet made a daring raid on the Union fleet anchored at the Head of Passes. Supported by three fire rafts and the ironclad *CSS Manassas*, Hollins attacked after moonset, caught the enemy dozing and chased them into the Gulf of Mexico. The stunning triumph sent more chills throughout the Union and drove New Orleans wild with its first taste of victory. Caught up in the moment, Madeleine invited the neighbors for a celebratory dinner, requiring Maddy to again summon her acting skills as she shared their optimism.

What would these poor people say, Maddy wondered, if they knew that the monstrous downriver chain would be smashed and that the fall of Confederate New Orleans was only a matter of time?

43

Maddy was enjoying a cool November breeze on the second floor gallery when Delphine appeared with an envelope. "A letter for you, *maîtresse.*"

"*Merci,* Delphine." Maddy's hope that it was from Félicité was confirmed by the Rue Rampart return address. "Thank goodness!"

It was two months since Félicité's last letter, and Maddy was desperate for news. She sliced open the envelope with the tip of a fingernail and scanned her friend's elaborate script. "Gorgeous," Maddy muttered, wondering how much modern kids had lost with their relentless texting and insufferable penmanship. Félicité's words were as elegant as her script as she described a city braced for war and a renewed relationship with Joseph Moran. The liaison was tenuous due to Moran's eagerness to enlist in the Confederate Army, but thus far Félicité had kept him distracted. Maddy was relieved, more so with Félicité's postscript promising she had avoided "the S.B."

No *Salon Bleu*, Maddy thought. Thank God!

She was reflecting on Félicité's happy reversal of fortune when horse's hooves echoed beneath the *allée.* She stood for a better view and was thrilled to identify Jean-Noël. She waved and called from the gallery as Madeleine rushed to join her.

"My love!" Madeleine cried, hand flying to her throat. "He's here at last!"

Maddy laughed as Madeleine dragged her into the house and down the stairs. By the time they reached the veranda, Jean-Noël had dismounted and was waiting with hat in hand.

Madeleine was so excited she almost embraced him, but when Bossa appeared to tend Jean-Noël's steed, she remembered herself and curtsied instead.

"Captain Baptiste! What a pleasant surprise."

With servants' eyes and ears everywhere, the lovebirds acted out their usual polite charade with Maddy as a supporting player. Knowing they were desperate for a moment alone, she suggested coffee in the gazebo and promised to join them shortly. She went back inside and was giving food orders to Delphine when she heard another tattoo of hoof beats, this time from the rear of the Big House. Terrified that it might be Jules, she hurried to investigate and was relieved to see a figure in buckskins.

"M'sieur Brasseaux!" she called as Auguste swung easily from his saddle, boots hitting the earth with a soft thud. *"Bonjour."*

"Bonjour, Mademoiselle St. Jacques." He flashed a broad grin. "How nice that you're still keeping my sister company."

Maddy dropped a curtsy. "I thought it prudent to stay here since the city is in chaos."

"Oh, yes. The war."

She nodded. "Have you seen the madness for yourself?"

"Certainly not. I'm one of those rare souls who find the celebrated charms of New Orleans quite resistible. I much prefer the bayous and their people."

Maddy caught herself before using the term "Cajun," wondering if it existed yet. "You mean *les Acadiens*?"

"I do. If the bayous are good enough for the Cajuns, they're good enough for me."

"I see," Maddy said, question answered.

Auguste's eyebrows rose. "Truly you are a rare bird. You're the first city girl I've met who understands a man's passion for the country."

"Perhaps I spoke rashly, having never been there." Maddy was lying. She'd grown up working shrimp boats alongside her father and poling pirogues through the bayous. She thought of a painting she and Paige saw in the Museum of Southern Art last year. "But I've seen pictures of the swamps, one in particular by Charles Giroux. I admire their primeval beauty."

"You'd best admire snakes and 'gators too," Auguste laughed. "And more mosquitoes than you can shake a blade at." He yanked a Bowie knife from his belt and sliced playfully through the air. "Where's my sweet sister?"

"You're our second visitor today," she replied. "Captain Baptiste is in the summer house with Madeleine."

"Shall we join them?"

"*Bien sûr.* Delphine will be out in a moment with refreshments."

Auguste grinned again, white teeth gleaming against a black beard. "Good. I could use a cup of strong coffee."

Auguste offered his arm, and as they walked around the side of the house, Maddy suddenly wished Paige was there. She wondered what her friend would say about this giant of a man dressing somewhere between Davy Crockett and Jean Lafitte and looking like Jon Hamm. Blood kinship notwithstanding, Maddy found him hugely attractive, and, owing to the difference in multiverses, wondered if it were permissible to be more than acquaintances. Almost as quickly she wondered if she was losing control and why the nineteenth century continued to stir her libido. First Hector and now Auguste! Good Lord, she thought as another erotic wave washed over her. Was this what Henri wanted me to embrace in his absence? Wrenching herself back to reality, Maddy called out as she and Auguste approached the gazebo.

"We have another visitor!"

Auguste embraced his sister and Jean-Noël before settling in beside Maddy. She was braced for more role-playing when Madeleine eased her mind. "We can all speak freely, my dear. Auguste knows about Jean-Noël and myself."

"Oh, good," Maddy said, relieved. "That makes things so much easier."

"When does the devil himself return?" Auguste grunted, his loathing for Jules obvious.

"Another couple of weeks," Jean-Noël said. "We discussed our schedules for next month and have more business than ever, but I swear he's a man obsessed. He pretends to be committed to the war effort, but I know he's only interested in revenue from extra sailings."

"Did you tell him you were coming to Five Oaks?" Maddy asked.

"Actually it was his idea. He said he's worried about you ladies being left alone here and insisted I take time off to keep you company."

"But Commodore Hollins sent the Yankees packing, didn't he?" Madeleine asked.

"That he did, but you can be sure they'll be back with more men and more ships. It's only a matter of time."

You have no idea, Maddy thought.

"Jules is much more worried about the slaves," Jean-Noël continued. "O'Neill is an excellent overseer and keeps a tight rein on things, but there are ugly rumors on the Negro grapevine, wild talk of emancipation and so forth. They're getting restless, and we all know that's a dangerous thing."

Until then Maddy had considered Five Oaks the picture of peace and tranquility and never gave a second thought to her isolation. Now she recalled something she read while re-searching for her time journey. In Concordia Parish, across the Mississippi River from Natchez, the population was over 14,000, nearly 13,000 of which were slaves. Horribly out-numbered, the white planters and overseers and their fami-lies lived in constant fear of a slave rebellion, something that nearly happened only a few months ago. When a white boy overheard slaves plotting a revolt, the conspirators were identified and twenty-seven of them hanged.

"What if Jules is right?" she said. "It's definitely some-thing to think about."

"I've never worried about such things, and I'm not about

to start now," Madeleine sniffed. "Especially not with you two here."

"*Mais,* we won't be here forever, *ma cher,*" Jean-Noël reminded her.

Madeleine was unmoved. "You're here now and we must make every minute count." She gave Maddy and Auguste a pleading look. "Would you two please take a stroll?"

Auguste rose, bowed with exaggerated aplomb and offered his arm. "Miss Madeleine?"

"Please call me Maddy," she said as they left the quintet of oaks and entered the alley of pines. "It lessens the confusion."

"As you wish."

"And please tell me why you exchanged the life of a country gentleman for that of a trapper."

Auguste waved his hand at the magnificent *allée* and the jewel-like house gleaming in the sunlight. "Madeleine and I grew up here, and admittedly these plantation homes are beautiful, but they're filled with fancy manners and social rules I found stifling. I prefer hunting and fishing to waltzing some empty-headed coquette around the dance floor, so when I was sixteen I bolted into the swamps and never came back, except to visit of course."

"Madeleine understood this?"

"My sister understands me better than anyone. When we lost our parents, we formed an unbreakable bond, an alliance of sorts. It's something no outsider can touch, not even Jean-Noël and certainly not that monster, Jules." His face grew dark. "Pardon my language, mademoiselle, but I'd kill that bastard tomorrow if I thought I could get away with it."

"You needn't apologize for your language," Maddy said, squeezing his elbow. "I admire men who don't stand on ceremony and, besides, I assure you I've heard all the bad words."

"And how would a fine lady like yourself hear such things?"

"Perhaps I'm not the lady you think," Maddy ventured, feeling reckless enough to quote Oscar Wilde who was, in 1861, only seven years old. "Someone once said every saint has a past and every sinner has a future."

Auguste chuckled and seized the gauntlet. "Might that apply to you?"

Maddy fluttered her eyelashes and barreled into the lion's den. "Possibly."

He cocked his head. "You're a strange creature, just like Madeleine said."

"What did she say?"

"That you two were as alike as two bolls of cotton and that it scared her a little. You remind her of our Grandmother Solange, but I'm not certain I should tell you why."

"But you must! No woman in the world could ignore such a tantalizing remark."

"I'll tell you then, but remember the comparison was Madeleine's idea, not mine."

"I'll remember."

"Our grandparents, Pierre and Solange, came from Paris in 1799 and settled in New Orleans. Pierre was a commodities factor who quickly built a fortune and a grand mansion in the *carré de la ville* to showcase it." Auguste gestured at the house. "Five Oaks was a Christmas present for grandmother."

"How charming."

"Not as charming as you might think. It was merely a ruse to keep her out of the city."

"I don't understand."

"*Grand-mère* Solange was not a woman to bend to convention, a trait my sister and I both inherited." He took a deep breath. "Her illicit affairs caused endless gossip among the Creoles, until Grandfather could no longer bear it. He prayed that a country house would keep her away from temptation, but she still managed to indulge herself. Grandfather eventually gave up and began frequenting the *Salle d'Orléans.* I'm sure it's not a place you've heard of, but—"

"*Au contraire.* In truth, I enjoy a friendship with a lady who goes there on occasion."

Maddy stopped short of telling him she'd been there too.

"Mais non!" Auguste was as amused as he was shocked. "You're every bit as bold as Madeleine said. It's little wonder you remind her of *Grand-mère.*"

Maddy smiled. "Should I be flattered or ashamed?"

"You should only be yourself." A muddle of emotions danced across Auguste's handsome face as he studied her more closely. "There's one thing my sister didn't tell me though."

"What is that?"

"That you would sweep me off my feet."

Before she could comment, Maddy was drawn into his arms and kissed. Social taboos crumbled when she reminded herself Auguste was from another time and succumbed to the scent of leather, sweat and horseflesh along with a desire to feel him without the barrier of skirts and buckskins. She held tight and returned his kiss until he released her and stepped away. They stared at each other a long while.

"I...I don't know what to say," she managed finally.

Auguste laughed softly. "Say you meant what you said about men who don't stand on ceremony and that you'll let me come to your room after dark."

"Auguste, I—"

"Say it," he said, voice thick with desire.

"*Mais,* what will you think of me?"

"If you don't say yes, I'll believe you were coquetting like all those other empty-headed ladies."

"Then, yes!" Maddy cried, tilting her head back to invite another kiss. "Yes, indeed!"

44

"You'll find ways to fill my absence. Embrace them."

Henri's edict, which Maddy initially rejected, now soothed her soul as she waited for Auguste. Stirred by relief, she lit more candles and slipped naked into bed, the gauzy mosquito net making a soft whooshing sound as it nestled around her. French doors were flung wide to the gallery, admitting a warm breeze and flooding the cypress floor with moonlight. Coupled with the flickering candlelight, the room was bathed in gold and silver, and Maddy held her breath when she heard footsteps followed by a low voice.

"Maddy?"

"Auguste?" she whispered.

"Oui, ma cher. C'est moi!"

Maddy's heart raced as he stepped from the shadows wearing only a thin nightshirt reaching to his knees. When the flickering candlelight revealed his arousal, she eagerly opened her arms, and the *mosquitaire* rustled again as it was swept aside. The bed creaked with additional weight as Auguste settled alongside her. He reached beneath the sheets to pull her closer and gasped when he found bare flesh. He drew down the sheets and gazed hungrily.

"You're naked!"

She felt like she was channeling Félicité when she purred, "Would you prefer me otherwise?"

"Mais, non!"

Auguste yanked the nightshirt over his head and tossed it aside. He was a bear of a man, heavily furred on chest and belly, and because he was an outdoorsman, he dispensed with foreplay and took her fast. Maddy welcomed his blunt approach, meeting his challenge and mounting one of her own.

They were soon deliriously spent, and Maddy checked herself before blurting, "Wow!"

"You were magnificent," she said.

Auguste rolled free, propped himself on one elbow and studied her in the candlelight. "You amaze me yet again."

"Vraiment?"

"Truly. No woman has ever praised my…well, said such things to me. Nor have I known one to so thoroughly enjoy herself." He thought a moment. "At least not one of your station." When he saw Maddy's bemused expression, Auguste blushed. "I'm afraid I've put my foot in it again. I told you I was a man who spoke his mind."

Maddy smiled. "And I told you I'm not a woman to shy away from such talk."

"You're not offended?"

"Why should I be? You have your life as I have mine." She gave his beard a playful tug. "And why should you men have all the fun?"

"Sacrebleu!" Auguste's jaw dropped. "Madeleine said you had some unorthodox opinions, and I see that she is right again."

Maddy turned the tables further. "You're not offended?"

"By God, no! In fact, you may be the woman I've looked for all my life!"

Maddy hadn't expected that and beat a hasty retreat. "I'm deeply flattered, Auguste, but I could never live in the swamps."

He looked crestfallen. "I knew you were too good to be true."

"I don't know about that," Maddy soothed, "but I do know we should enjoy the here and now and not worry about tomorrow, especially with a war going on."

"I suppose you're right." August leaned close and gave her a tender kiss. "It's stifling under this mosquito net. Shall we go onto the gallery and see if we can catch a breeze?"

"Absolument. I was thinking the same thing."

Auguste reclaimed his nightshirt while Maddy slipped a chemise over her nakedness and followed him onto the gallery. It was only slightly cooler than the bedroom but yielded a refreshing zephyr. He put his arm around her shoulders as they gazed down the moonlit *allée*. The pines were silvered and surreal, an illusion enhanced by the twinkling of myriad lightning bugs. She smiled, utterly content.

"It's magical, isn't it?"

August nodded. "Nothing eclipses mother nature." He tensed. "*Mais,* who's that?"

"Where?"

"There. In the gazebo. Have they gone mad?!" Auguste gasped. Barely visible through the lacy trelliswork, Madeleine and Jean-Noël were locked in each other's arms. "Those fools! How can they be so careless?"

"Never mind about them, dearest." Maddy gave his arm a tug. "Let's go back to bed."

Auguste smiled. "You vixen!"

"Guilty," Maddy purred.

She gave the glorious, moon-washed night a final glance before following Auguste back into the house. Other, less sympathetic eyes watched too, and not for the first time.

45

With the keen ears of a trapper, Auguste heard the voices first. He was on his feet in a heartbeat, waking Maddy as he sprang from bed. It took her a groggy moment to remember why a naked man was standing in her bedroom.

"Auguste?"

"Trouble," he whispered, throwing on his nightshirt. "Stay here."

Maddy sat up when she heard the noise. "What is it?"

Gruffer this time. "I said stay here!"

Auguste melted silently onto the shadowy gallery and disappeared. Maddy held her breath until shouts propelled her outside too. Fear bloomed when she realized the commotion was coming from Madeleine's bedroom. The loudest voice belonged to Jules, and his slurred speech announced he was drunk.

"I've owned Cato since we were boys!" he bellowed. "Don't you think he tells me everything that goes on when I'm on the river? Everything!!"

Auguste remained frozen outside the bedroom windows. When he saw Maddy he motioned for her to keep back. She couldn't remember being so frightened.

"I've known about you two for weeks!" Jules yelled. "You fools were stupid enough to believe I wanted Jean-Noël to keep an eye on things. I was merely waiting to catch you red-handed, and now, by God, I have!"

Maddy heard Jean-Noël's voice, surprisingly calm and controlled. "Don't do it, man."

"To hell with you!" Jules roared. "To hell with both of you!"

Maddy screamed at the first gunshot and grabbed the

rail for support when she heard a second. Then came the crash of splintering wood and breaking glass as Auguste threw himself against the French doors and exploded into the room. She got to the ruined doors just as Auguste grabbed Jules from behind and smashed a huge fist against the man's head. The powerful impact sent Jules careening into Madeleine's armoire, bloodying his face and knocking him cold.

"Madeleine!" Maddy screamed. "Jean-Noël!"

She ran to the bed where the two clutched each other in a tangle of bloody bedclothes. Jean-Noël yanked the sheet down and cried with relief when he saw that Madeleine's upper arm was only grazed. "Thank God!"

Madeleine's voice was riddled with dread. "What about you?"

"Only a flesh wound I think." Jean-Noël put a hand on his shoulder where the bullet had passed through and splintered the headboard. "Thank God too much drink spoiled his aim."

"Thank God," Madeleine echoed in a thin voice. She was white as a ghost but managed to give instructions. "Wake Delphine and—"

"I'm here, *maîtresse*," came a voice from the doorway. Delphine slept in an adjacent room and, like the rest of the house servants, had been awakened by shouts and gunshots.

"Good girl. Now run fetch…fetch—" She slumped against Jean-Noël and fainted dead away.

Maddy knew first aid and acted swiftly. "Bring me towels and bandages and smelling salts, Delphine! Brandy too! Now hurry!"

After inspecting the two wounds, Maddy shredded a pillowslip and tied it tightly around Madeleine's shoulder to stanch the bleeding. She gave Jean-Noël a healthy dose of brandy, and with Delphine's help cleaned and dressed both wounds. The smelling salts brought Madeleine around and she mustered a wan smile as she squeezed Maddy's hand.

"Thank God you were here," she muttered.

"And thank God Auguste heard the noise." Not until then did Maddy realize Auguste was gone, and so was Jules. She gave Jean-Noël a fearful stare. "Where are they?!"

"I suspect Auguste is tending to unfinished business," he replied.

Maddy's voice shook as her imagination ran wild. "What does that mean?"

"Don't worry, my dear. Auguste knows what he's doing."

"But—?"

"Never mind," Madeleine interrupted. "I have something important to tell you."

Jean-Noël smiled despite the madness that had nearly killed them. "We both do."

"I think I already know." Maddy nodded at Madeleine's swollen belly. "When is it due?"

"In the spring, my darling. Along with the azaleas and lilies."

And the fall of New Orleans, Maddy thought grimly. "I'm so happy for you."

Madeleine's smile vanished when a sharp pain shot through her arm. "No need to ask whose child it is," she explained, as though reading Maddy's thoughts. "Jules came to my bedroom many nights but was always too drunk to...perform."

"That never crossed my mind," Maddy lied, cheeks coloring. At the same time, she was thrilled to realize Jean-Noël, not Jules, was her great-great-grandfather.

"Of course it did. You and I are so much alike that I know better." Madeleine patted the mattress. "You'll be with me when the baby comes, won't you?"

"Of course," Maddy said, perching carefully on the edge of the bed.

"Promise?" Jean-Noël said.

"Promise."

The three sat in silence, a moment filled with love and

devotion and gratitude for lives rescued from destruction. Madeleine and Jean-Noël began to drowse, prompting Maddy to extinguish all but one candle and slip back to her room. She was climbing into bed when she heard distant hoof beats. Going to investigate, she saw two riders tearing across the moonlit cane fields. One wobbled crazily in the saddle, while the other was steady and sure. As she watched them disappear, Maddy sought reassurance in Jean-Noël's words.

"'Don't worry, my dear. Auguste knows what he's doing.'"

Maddy slept fitfully, dreams punctuated by bloody images and the reverberating report of gunfire. Something settled heavily against her and she awoke with a start. "Auguste?"

"It's done," he muttered tiredly, snuggling from behind and wrapping his arms around her. "Now go back to sleep."

"*Mais,* I can't sleep without knowing what happened."

"As you wish." Auguste released a raggedy sigh. "Jules and I went for a midnight ride. His body will be found in an irrigation ditch tomorrow. The cause of death is a broken neck."

Maddy turned toward him, face warmed by the smell of whiskey as he supplied the details. He had carried Jules to the stable where he put him on his horse and saddled Brutus for himself. Auguste had ridden the excitable stallion many times and knew how to control him. Once they were deep in the cane fields, Auguste challenged Jules to switch mounts and have a race. Still half drunk and knowing Brutus was a faster steed, Jules seized the chance to humiliate his hated brother-in-law. When Auguste clucked softly to Brutus, the animal knew what was demanded and held still while Jules struggled into the saddle. Once he took the reins, the horse reared and whinnied and tore across the dark fields. Brutus was, as Auguste intended, headed for the widest of the irrigation ditches. It was an expanse the horse could easily clear, but one requiring great skill from the rider. Auguste listened with satisfaction when he heard a nightmarish scream and loud splash. In the stillness that followed, he trotted his horse to the ditch where Jules lay face-down in the water. The grotesque twist of his head announced his fate, and Auguste smiled with satisfaction when he heard Brutus galloping victorious into the moonlit night.

"It's done," he said again.

"Are you sure no one saw you?" Maddy asked.

"No one. Not even that vile Cato. He hated and resented Madeleine, you know, and was so rude that she often asked Jules to get rid of him. Jules invariably refused, and now I know why. Cato was his eager little spy."

"What will become of him?"

"He'll be taken into New Orleans tomorrow and sold."

"Dear God," Maddy gasped.

"Don't be sorry for him, *ma cher.* Like his hateful master, that black bastard has had this coming for a long time."

Part 7

"Death is everywhere in New Orleans, what of it?
Why go stare at it?"

— Anne Rice, *The Feast of All Saints*

46

A veil of secrecy was drawn over Five Oaks in the days following Jules's death. The shootings and, by association, Madeleine's illicit affair were taboo subjects for those few house servants who knew the truth. They understood their *maîtresse* meant business when Cato was abruptly dispatched to the slave mart in New Orleans, but in truth they were as relieved to have him gone as they were to see a cruel master dead and to be answerable only to the benevolent Madeleine. The Jefferson Parish sheriff was told only that Jules had gone for a midnight ride, that his body was found in an irrigation ditch the next morning and that, yes, he had been drinking heavily. With his violent alcoholic binges common knowledge, the matter might have ended there, but Jules's stature as a steamboat captain and wealthy planter demanded an interrogation of everyone from Madeleine to the lowliest house servant. With Maddy's help, Madeleine concealed her injury and received the authorities in her sitting room, propped on a pillow while feigning grief. To avoid implication, the wounded Jean-Noël simply hid in the attic. It didn't take long for the sheriff to reach what most people believed was a foregone conclusion: Whiskey and a runaway horse were the lethal combination causing Jules St. Jacques's death.

Everyone was relieved, and morale was given another boost as Madeleine and Jean-Noël steadily improved, the result of round-the-clock nursing from Delphine. The difficult situation left Maddy and Auguste no time for romance, but they recognized that their brief affair was that and nothing more. Deep affection had replaced desire, and they accepted that it was devotion rather than blind passion making it difficult to say good-bye and return to their respective homes.

"Will you visit me sometime?" Auguste asked as he swung into the saddle. "My cabin in St. Martin's Parish isn't anything fancy, but it has a very comfortable bed."

His insinuation made Maddy smack him playfully on the knee. "Remember your manners, m'sieur."

"*Mais,* it's so difficult with you around."

"For me as well," Maddy confessed, "but we both know our relationship is now as it should be."

Auguste nodded agreement. *"C'est vrai."*

"I'd like to think we'll meet again, but who knows what's waiting for me in the city?"

He tapped his vest pocket. "Remember I have your address. Perhaps I'll surprise you with a visit some time."

"As much as you loathe New Orleans?" Maddy laughed. "You're not fooling anyone."

"Stranger things have happened, my dear. War changes everything."

"I suppose." She stood on her tiptoes as Auguste leaned down for a final kiss. *"Au revoir,* Maddy."

"Au revoir, dear Auguste. And Godspeed."

The image of him disappearing at the end of the pine alley replayed in Maddy's thoughts as she promised Madeleine to keep in touch and boarded the afternoon ferry from Port LeBlanc to New Orleans. It was a bittersweet memory, and it didn't help that the Mississippi was choppy with whitecaps and swept by a December wind chilling her to the bone. She sought warmth in the passenger waiting room and pushed Auguste from her mind by concentrating on Félicité's letter bearing news of her father's death and hopes that Maddy would return soon. Félicité was anxious for her to meet Joseph Moran and hinted at other important news. Maddy couldn't help wondering if Félicité were *enceinte* by Joseph Moran but hoped that wasn't the case. One pregnant friend was enough for now.

The moment Maddy disembarked, she noticed major changes in the city. She didn't think it possible that the great

Port of New Orleans in 1861 could be busier, yet there was more water traffic than ever, boats coming and going in great profusion and producing a deafening din. Dozens of smokestacks blasted sparks and belched noxious black clouds prompting her to press a handkerchief to her nose as she hurried down the gangway. The wharves were as crowded and chaotic as the river with hundreds of men in crisp gray Confederate uniforms, their family and friends come to say good-bye, and civilians on any number of wartime missions. Attracting special attention was a company of Louisiana Zouaves, impossible to miss in their red tasseled caps and jackets and blue pantaloons.

After half an hour of failing to find a hack, Maddy hired a strapping Negro boy to carry her luggage and follow her from the waterfront to her apartment in the *Rue des Ursulines.* She paused only long enough to unpack a few things and freshen up, deciding to remain in her traveling ensemble as she walked to Félicité's house on Rampart Street. The sidewalks weren't so crowded here, and she was invigorated by a brisk walk in the cold. She smiled at the familiar little cottage with the blue door and orange trees and was warmed by the sight of smoke curling from the chimney. When she pulled the bell, the door swung open immediately, and Maddy faced someone she never expected to see again. She was too startled to speak but her inner voice murmured, "Hector!"

He bowed politely. "You are Mademoiselle St. Jacques, *n'est ce pas?*"

"Why, yes, but...but how do you know?"

"Mademoiselle Félicité spoke of you often, and of course I remember you from *Belle Rêve.*" He stepped aside. "Please come in."

Maddy had barely recovered from the shock of seeing Hector when a sweet voice called from the parlor. "*Ma cher,* Maddy! You're back at last!"

Maddy blinked away tears, realizing how much she had

missed her dear friend as Félicité hurried to embrace her. The two clasped hands as they sat together on a new *méridienne* with silk the color of a robin's egg. Maddy wondered if this were a gift from Joseph Moran when she noticed other luxurious additions to the parlor, but her attention soon reverted to Hector who stood watching from the doorway. She was suddenly uncomfortable, more so when she realized the air crackled with tension.

"Hector was just leaving," Félicité announced.

"If you please, mademoiselle," he said. "My name is Carlos. Carlos Mendoza."

"Of course," Félicité said icily. "Good afternoon."

He bowed to both women. *"Mesdames."*

Maddy frowned as he closed the door behind him. "'Carlos?' I don't understand."

"Of course you don't, and neither do I." Félicité waved a hand. "When my father died, a provision in his will granted Hector his freedom. He calls himself Carlos now. I suppose it's something to do with his gypsy heritage."

"That's wonderful!" Maddy blurted.

Félicité's face darkened. *"Mais,* why would you say such a thing?"

Maddy thought fast, reminding herself of Louisiana's complicated caste system. "Because you told me how fond of Hector your father was and because he obviously cared about the man's future."

"Bah!" Félicité snorted. "Papa would've been a lot wiser to keep the man part of *Belle Rêve's* inventory. Mama needs every cent she can get and will be lucky if anything's left after the place goes up for auction and her creditors come calling."

"Oh, dear!" Maddy cried, realizing that must be Félicité's important news. "How soon?"

"Next week."

Maddy squeezed Félicité's hand. "I'm so sorry. I do wish I could help."

"*Merci,* but there's nothing any of us can do except watch our family legacy disappear. Mama will go to live with *grand-mère,* who can barely support herself let alone anyone else." She shook her head with defeat. "I manage to send them a few dollars now and then, but if I didn't have Joseph I don't know what I would do."

"But you do have him, darling, and that's all that matters."

"For now." Félicité pulled away and rose, taffeta skirts swishing nosily as she paced the room. "You probably don't know that the balls have been permanently shuttered. If something happens and I need another protector, that option will no longer exist."

Maddy changed the subject before Félicité began talking about the notorious *Salon Bleu.* "You haven't asked about my trip."

"Forgive me in my selfishness." Félicité sat again. "Did you have a pleasant time?"

"Yes and no." Maddy delivered an edited version of the events at Five Oaks, saying only that Jules died accidentally and that Madeleine was expecting a child in the spring. She said nothing about her affair with Auguste or his role in Jules's death. Once Félicité digested all that excitement, Maddy broached the delicate subject of Carlos. "What was he doing here?"

"He wants help starting a new life in New Orleans, and I find it most inappropriate that he would involve me. In fact I find it downright brazen."

Maddy was upset by Félicité's harsh tone. "Is it so surprising that he came to you for help? The man was part of your household for years and probably knows no one in New Orleans."

"That hardly entitles him to come here and behave in such a fashion."

"What on earth did he do?"

Félicité fairly spat the words. "He acted as though he

were my equal!"

"But he's a free man now." Maddy immediately regretted the comment when she saw Félicité's green eyes narrow and was harshly admonished.

"Sometimes I think I don't know you at all, Maddy. For you to say something so outrageous, I can only think we must have been raised very differently indeed. *Mon dieu!*"

The intensity of her accusation and the complex protocol spawning it clouded Maddy's brain before the truth finally dawned. In Félicité's mind, Hector would forever be a slave and, skin color notwithstanding, the social equal of a lowly Negro house worker. His was simply a status that could never be elevated by a piece of paper declaring him a free man.

Maddy apologized, adding, "In my defense I can only say that things in Natchez are quite different and that I must constantly remind myself that I'm in New Orleans."

"It would be better for everyone if you did precisely that," Félicité sniffed.

"As you wish, my dear." Maddy smiled indulgently and changed the subject again. "Now you must tell me about your M'sieur Moran. My memory of him is scant you know."

"Of course." She glanced at the mantle clock. "He should be here any minute in fact."

Maddy was relieved when Félicité embraced a topic dear to her heart but registered precious little of what she heard about Joseph Moran. Instead she was suddenly consumed by a delayed reaction that rushed over her like the wind whipping whitecaps on the Mississippi. Hector was a white slave in a black household, she thought, and Carlos Mendoza is a free Spaniard I found in the last possible place I would ever think to look.

Oh, my God!

47

Stunned that Madam Iris's prediction had finally come to pass, Maddy only half heard Félicité reintroducing her to Joseph Moran. She remembered him immediately, a handsome, cherubic man with a shock of curly blonde hair and courtly manners. She was charmed as he kissed her hand and motioned for Zaza to bring him a whiskey.

"My darling Félicité talks of you constantly, Mademoiselle St. Jacques. Especially how much she missed you. I'm delighted to see you again."

"I'm delighted to see you again too."

"I'm also pleased to tell you how much I appreciated your little prank."

Maddy gave Félicité a puzzled look. "Prank?"

"I told him about you passing yourself off as a woman of color at the *Salle d'Orléans*," Félicité explained. "And I'm happy to say he had a sense of humor about it."

"You're hardly the first women to be so daring," Moran said, taking a healthy sip of bourbon. "A few years ago, a high-born woman named Justine Blancard costumed as a man and went to the balls with some male friends of hers. Of course most people were horrified, but I thought it was great fun." His shoulders rose and fell. "It was Mardi Gras after all."

Maddy looked self-effacing. "I know it was a mad thing to do, but as long as you're not offended by having your all-male territory invaded."

"Not in the least," Moran said with a smile. "Are you also daring enough to have a glass of whiskey with me?"

Maddy laughed good-naturedly. "I'm afraid I must decline, m'sieur. That daring I'm not."

Moran feigned shock. "I'm deeply disappointed."

Félicité patted his hand. "Dearest, you're embarrassing Maddy."

"Not at all," Maddy insisted, "but I confess that I'm suddenly wearied by my journey. I really must take my leave."

"Oh, dear," Félicité said. "Here you rushed over to see me and I've not given a thought to your travel fatigue."

Maddy stood and smoothed her skirts. "You'll forgive me for leaving then?"

"Not if you promise we'll spend all day together tomorrow. There's a new dress shop in the *Rue Royale* I'm perishing for you to see."

"I promise."

"And you must let Joseph's driver take you home."

"Thank you, but I prefer to walk. The cold air will do me good."

"Mind you, be careful," Moran insisted. "The city is quite dangerous now with all the wartime activity."

Félicité made a face. "This town is overflowing with new riffraff. It's absolutely appalling."

Maddy had no doubt Félicité was referring to Carlos. "I promise I'll be careful, darling, Will you come by in the morning?"

"Right after breakfast." Félicité gave her a warm hug. "*À bientôt*, dear friend."

"*À bientot.*"

Maddy finished her good-byes and hurried outside. The temperature had plunged while she was in Félicité's toasty little cottage and she snuggled her cape collar around her neck as she hurried down the Rue Rampart. She slowed when she approached Ursulines Street and saw a lone man standing on the corner. His hat was drawn low over his brow, whether against the cold or to hide his features she didn't know. Either way she wasn't taking any chances and was weighing an alternative route home when he called her name.

"Mademoiselle St. Jacques!"

She recognized the voice. "Carlos?"

"Oui, mademoiselle." His hat was in his hand as he approached and bowed. "I have been waiting for you."

She hadn't seen that coming. "Oh?"

"I was hoping I might accompany you home. I understand you have been gone for some time, and the streets are not as safe as they once were."

"So Mademoiselle Chevalier warned."

"I was also hoping to have a moment of conversation. May I?"

An awkward moment arose as Carlos hesitantly offered his arm. To the casual observer, it was nothing unusual, but after his long years of servitude Maddy was moved by the courage required to make such a bold gesture. She smiled and took his arm.

"Thank you. I live at the corner of Royal and Ursulines." An awkward silence descended as they walked, making Maddy wonder what the man wanted to discuss. Aware of his nervousness, she tried to defuse it by addressing the peculiar situation head-on. "This must be an extraordinary time for you, M'sieur Mendoza."

"Thank you for saying so. I must confess I'm still in a state of shock."

When he fell silent again, Maddy said, "May I speak frankly about the matter?"

Carlos muttered something unintelligible before answering. "That would be most refreshing, mademoiselle, as I have yet to meet a truly frank woman."

Maddy weighed the comment and decided she wasn't insulted. "Understandable, I suppose, but pleased consider me different from women you've known before."

"I think I already do." He coughed and cleared his throat. "What did you wish to say?"

"Only that I could never understand what it's like to be the property of another human being or to know what freedom feels like when it has been denied for so long. People like me take it for granted, which is a terrible thing of course."

There was no mistaking his pain when Carlos said, "Indeed it is."

Maddy retreated. "Am I making you uncomfortable?"

He nodded. "I'm afraid so, mademoiselle. I...I thought I was ready to discuss such things, but I know now that I am not. Your words are as unconventional as they are unexpected."

"I'm sorry."

"You are not who should apologize."

"Then what was it you wanted to talk to me about?"

"The same thing I tried to discuss with the young *maîtresse*."

He didn't realize his mistake, Maddy thought. "*Mais,* Félicité is no longer your mistress."

Carlos nodded. "Old habits die hard, mademoiselle. I was her father's manservant from the time I was sixteen, the year she was born." Maddy was dying to ask about his life beyond *Belle Rêve* but decided the moment wasn't right. "All I wanted was a little help," he continued sadly. "I would never ask for money of course, but I was in hopes she might know someone who could offer employment. I've been in the city for almost three weeks and can find no work."

"She made no recommendations?"

"Quite the contrary. She was clearly displeased that I presumed to call on her and asked me to leave. My hand was on the latch which is why I opened the door so quickly."

Maddy swallowed her annoyance. "How unfortunate."

"Indeed?" Carlos looked shocked. "You would not have reacted the same way?"

Maddy chose her words carefully, not wanting to impugn Félicité's behavior or sound too modern. "Mademoiselle Chevalier and I come from different backgrounds and hold different beliefs on a number of things."

He cleared his throat again. "Because you're white?"

"In part, yes." She took a deep breath and acknowledged the impact of her admission. "Truth is best, m'sieur."

"Agreed."

"Which brings me to your need for work. I'm from Mississippi and have spent little time in New Orleans since coming to visit last March. I have few friends and acquaintances but will be happy to ask if they can help."

"I will be most grateful for anything you can do, mademoiselle."

"De rien." As they got closer to the Rue Royale, the sidewalks and streets grew congested, and Maddy noted an increase in shady-looking characters. She decided the warnings were correct, and was grateful for the man's company as they stopped in front of her apartment. She slipped her arm from Carlos's elbow and said, "This is where I live."

He said nothing, only gave Maddy a peculiar, lingering look. A familiar shiver shot down her spine, the sort making her suspect the August Ones had a hand in the moment. She was encouraged to ask the man inside, but before she could act someone called her name over the din of carriages and the noisy crush of pedestrians. Over Carlos's shoulder she saw William Mumford with a plain looking woman some years his junior. When he saw a break in the traffic, the celebrated gambler hurried over.

"I trust you remember me, Miss St. Jacques?"

"Of course, Mr. Mumford. Captain Baptiste introduced us on *La Sirene.*"

"He did indeed." He introduced the woman on his arm as his wife, Mary, and looked at Carlos when Maddy introduced him. "William Mumford at your service, sir."

"Carlos Mendoza. Your servant, sir."

Maddy was surprised by Carlos's English, thinking he spoke only French and Spanish. She was also impressed by the ease with which he conversed with the Mumfords, chatting amiably as though he'd never been in bondage. No doubt Carlos's twenty plus years as a gentleman's gentleman had taught him to handle a wide range of social situations.

Mumford smiled broadly. "How fortuitous that we should encounter you, Miss St. Jacques. This is Mary's first time in New Orleans, and I was wondering where we might dine." He rolled his eyes. "I'm afraid when I come to town on business I don't frequent places appropriate for my wife."

"What is your line of work?" Carlos asked.

"Cards," Mary snapped with obvious disapproval.

"Now, now, my dear," Mumford said good-naturedly. "I haven't been a bad provider, have I?"

Mary bristled, making Maddy wonder if a steel magnolia lurked behind the dowdy façade. "This is hardly something to be discussed with strangers, William."

Maddy rescued the awkward moment by suggesting several suitable restaurants including Antoine's and the dining room at the St. Louis Hotel. She smiled at Mary. "I promise you won't be disappointed in either place."

"Thank you, miss," Mary said, voice softer.

Mumford's sharp eyes noted the keys in Maddy's hand and nodded at the building behind her. "Is this where you live?"

"Why, yes," she said, thinking quickly. "Forgive me for not inviting you in, but Mr. Mendoza and I have an engagement this evening."

"For which we are already late," Carlos added smoothly.

"Then perhaps we can visit another time," Mumford said. "Mary and I will be in town for a few weeks."

"I'd love for you to join us for dinner one night," Mary added a bit urgently.

"I look forward to it," Maddy said. "And now if you'll excuse us."

And just like that, Maddy was climbing the stairs to her apartment with her personal mystery man right behind her.

48

Maddy chuckled as she shut the door behind Carlos and began lighting gas lamps. "I must say you're a quick study, M'sieur Mendoza. You knew exactly what to say to the Mumfords."

"I assumed they were not people whose company you desired."

"Oh, they're harmless enough and who knows? Mr. Mumford might know someone who could offer you work." Maddy turned her back as Carlos helped her out of her cape. "I wouldn't mind dining with them, but not tonight. It's been a very long day."

"I'm sorry. I'll say good-night then."

"Nonsense." Maddy spoke so quickly Carlos gave her an inquisitive look. "The least I can do is offer a brandy after you took the trouble to walk me home."

"It was no trouble, mademoiselle."

"Nevertheless I insist." Maddy moved to help him with his hat and cloak but he stepped away. She tried not to sound exasperated. "I'm sure this is difficult, but please remember you are not my inferior. Since I don't have a servant, it is my duty to take your things."

Carlos's cheeks colored. "My apologies."

"And you must stop apologizing. We're both new at this."

"What do you mean?"

"That I've never known a white person in bondage, and that I'll surely make a few social blunders of my own." She was pleased with his hint of a smile. "You find that amusing?"

"Only because I've spent most of my life smoothing over people's social blunders."

"In that case, I suggest we dispense with formalities and address each other by our Christian names? I'd be pleased if you call me Maddy."

He looked stunned. "And you would call me Carlos?"

"I would indeed." She smiled. "Carlos."

He blushed and bowed a bit stiffly. "As you wish."

"Say it, please."

The blush deepened. "Maddy."

"Splendid. Now shall I get you that brandy?"

"May I help?"

Maddy put her hands on her hips. "My goodness! Have you never had anyone wait on you?" He shook his head. "Then it's high time you did, but we'll compromise."

"Oh?"

"I'll get the brandy and while you build a fire." She rubbed her hands together. "The damp is especially bad tonight."

The combination of brandy and crackling flames was perfect for taking the chill off the apartment and relaxing Maddy. Carlos seemed calmer too. Enough, she hoped, to talk about his past.

"May I ask you a few questions?"

"Certainly."

"Where were you before you became a part of the *Belle Rêve* household?"

"Cuba." Carlos took a draw from the snifter. "I was born there in twenty-three." Maddy did some quick math to determine he was thirty-eight. "My parents were born there too."

"Were they—?"

"Born into slavery? Only my father. My grandfather had been brought from Cadiz and sold into slavery. Surely you know that in Spain and elsewhere, gypsies are considered dispensable." He coughed and cleared his throat, as though strangled by the past. "In truth I am half gypsy, half Castilian. You see, my mother was niece of the Viceroy." Maddy's eyes widened when she realized Carlos had noble blood. Perhaps, she thought, that explains his pride and elegant bearing. "I never knew the details of my parents' illicit liaison, only that my arrival was the cause of great scandal that resulted in my mother being banished to a convent in Spain and my father being beaten half to death. He and I were sold at the slave mart in Havana when I was still a baby. Luckily a sugar planter bought us both so I remember Papa fairly well." Carlos stared into the flames. "They worked him to death in the fields, and he died when I was ten."

"Dear Lord." After a long moment, she asked, "Did you work in the fields too?"

"I escaped that awful fate only because the planter's wife wanted me for a house servant, but that was only a different sort of misery because I was bullied by the other slaves because of my white skin. I was sold again when I was twelve after catching the eye of a silk merchant visiting from New Orleans. He wanted me as a gift for a quadroon lady who lived here in the *carré de la ville,* only a block away in the *Rue Condé,* actually." He sipped again. "White slaves were always a novelty, especially sought after by the *gens de couleur libre.* With New Orleans's strange caste system, it's not difficult to understand why."

"No," Maddy said, still trying to register the horror and humiliation of being a gift for another human being. "I suppose not."

"My new *maîtresse* was a grand hostess who delighted in dressing me as a Venetian blackamoor and showing me off like a pet."

"Mon dieu!"

"Fate intervened again when M'sieur Chevalier attended a soirée at her house. His old valet had died and because he believed I showed potential he made the mistress an offer. By then she had wearied of her novelty, probably because I was sixteen and big as a full grown adult."

"So you were taken to the Isle Brevelle?"

Carlos nodded. "Where I was trained to be a gentleman's gentleman."

"And taught how to read and write and given access to M'sieur Chevalier's library." She smiled. "Félicité told me."

"Ahhh. Poor little Félicité. So beautiful and so doomed."

Maddy knew Félicité would be furious if she knew this man pitied her. "What do you mean?"

"She was the most rebellious child I ever saw. None of the nurses could control her, and her mother merely threw up her hands. Her father was the only one she obeyed, and much of that was because he showered her with endless gifts from New Orleans and Paris. She was spoiled beyond belief and did nothing that didn't please her. When her father arranged a marriage...well, considering where you met her, I'm sure you know the rest."

"I do and it's sad indeed."

Carlos drained his brandy snifter and stood. "I must be going, Mademoiselle—"

"Maddy."

"Maddy."

"As you wish." She was pleased when Carlos allowed her to fetch his cloak and drape it around his broad shoulders. Until that moment, she had not been close enough to inhale a blend of vetiver and his own pungent scent. "I'll need an address if I am to contact you. I was serious about speaking to Mr. Mumford. I have it on good authority that he is one of the most famous gamblers on the Mississippi. For better or worse, I suspect he has a wide circle of friends and acquaintances that might be able to help you."

"I'm indebted for anything you may do, but it's best that you stay away from my quarters on Gallatin Street. It's hardly fit for ladies such as yourself."

Maddy first heard of Gallatin Street in the old Bette Davis movie *Jezebel* and shuddered at the idea of Carlos living in such a notorious neighborhood. "Did M'sieur Chevalier give you nothing to start a new life?"

Carlos drew himself up. "There's no greater gift than my freedom, and I will be forever grateful for that. Unfortunately, the *maître's* finances are disastrous, and he had only this to offer." He drew a gold watch from his waistcoat and held it out. "Would you take this please, for safekeeping? I sleep on it every night in fear that it will be stolen."

"*Bien sûr.*" Maddy hefted the heavy watch and marveled at its delicate filigree work. "Hopefully your situation will change before long."

"Hopefully." Carlos took her hand and as he swept it with his moustache he raised his head and looked her directly in the eyes for the first time. A frisson down Maddy's spine made her feel vulnerable, so she was relieved when he smiled. "I have a confession to make."

"Oh?"

"This is the first time I've kissed a woman's hand."

Maddy smiled back, heart fluttering. "I'm honored."

"As am I."

Maddy withdrew her hand and lightly touched her throat. "Good night, m'sieur."

Carlos said nothing as Maddy opened the door. She watched him don his hat, descend the staircase and disappear onto the street. Suddenly empty and alone, she sank into the chair where he'd been sitting. The lingering warmth of his body seeped into her flesh and his scent returned to haunt her. It was precisely the premonition she needed.

"Vetiver," she murmured. "Henri's cologne."

49

By mid-December, much of New Orleans looked like a military training camp with the arrival of still more troops, volunteer companies and newly formed units. The usually glittering Christmas season and New Year's celebrations greeting 1862 were replaced by military parades and reviews and endless patriotic music. With war in the air, there were rumors that Mardi Gras would be cancelled, but like everyone else, Maddy refused to think about it and sought escape by attending concerts and theater. Sitting with Félicité in the colored section, she envied the fashionably dressed couples and yearned for a handsome gentleman to escort her around town. Sadly, the one she most desired was the one who could least afford it.

Maddy hoped that would change when William Mumford agreed to help Carlos find work, introducing him to a number of influential men and inviting him to his famous poker nights. Carlos didn't gamble of course, but the food and liquor were free, and he told Maddy it was a fascinating slice of life he'd never seen. Unfortunately, nothing resulted in gainful employment, and although Maddy had plenty of money, she knew Carlos would never accept a loan, much less charity. He dropped by every few days, his quiet masculine presence deepening her attraction and making her wonder if he had feelings too. Conversations remained respectable with Carlos acting the perfect gentleman and Maddy barely able to resist throwing her arms around him. She was sure the vetiver cologne was a positive sign of Henri's blessings, but when the stalemate continued she wondered if this were the wrong man or, worse, another sort of test. Either way, with Madeleine at Five Oaks, Félicité increasingly committed to Moran and, worse, Carlos unresponsive, she felt isolated and trapped in a life that was mundane and routine. New Orleans, even in the exciting turbulence of wartime, was losing its luster. As more weeks passed and she began wondering if the August Ones had forgotten about her, Maddy began contemplating a return to her own time. She went so far as to open her watch pendant and study the inside compartment, but instinct kept her from triggering the second hand. She tucked it back in her jewelry case and decided a more reasonable escape was shopping trip on Royal Street, but she got no further than the front door where a man sprawled across her doorstep. At first she thought him only a drunk, but closer inspection turned her blood cold.

"Carlos!"

He stirred at the sound of her voice. "Maddy?"

With her help, the big man struggled to his feet and managed to climb the stairs to her apartment. He offered no resistance when she steered him into her bedroom and tugged off his jacket. He managed a weak smile.

"This is most improper, mademoiselle."

"The devil with propriety," Maddy snapped, tossing the coat aside and easing him onto the bed. "You're hurt."

"Only a little bruised."

"Then why were you lying on the *banquette* like some derelict?"

"It's as far as I got. A gang of hooligans robbed the boarding house last night and tore the place apart." He touched a lump on his head. "I got away before things got too rough and managed to get over here. I...I must've passed out before I rang the bell."

"And you've been lying down there all this time? No one tried to help?"

Carlos struggled into a sitting position. "You know how New Orleans is these days."

"I'll get some cognac."

The brandy worked quickly, relaxing Carlos enough to allow Maddy to look for wounds.

When she opened his shirt, the badly discolored flesh revealed bruises much worse than she anticipated. She had seen enough.

"You're not going back to that horrible place, Carlos." When he started to protest, she touched his lips with a fingertip. "I won't hear otherwise. You can stay in the maid's room. All that matters now is that you'll be safe."

"I can take care of myself," he grunted.

"Don't be a child, Carlos. Nobody's impugning your damned manhood."

He looked shocked. "Did you say—?"

"Yes, I said 'damned' and I'll say a lot worse if you don't do what I tell you." Maddy poured another shot of cognac and shoved the snifter into his hand. "Now drink this and be still while I think."

"Think about what?"

"Arrangements to be made. First, you'll go back for your belongings."

"I'm sure whatever I had is gone."

"Then we'll get new things. Clothes and so forth."

"I won't have you spending your money on me," he grumbled. "It's not proper."

"Then what, pray tell me, are you going to do? Go back on the streets without a cent in your pocket and nothing but torn clothes on your back?"

"If I have to." He grimaced with pain as he struggled to sit up and fell back against the pillows. "You have my gold watch, and that's worth something."

"And what will you do after that's sacrificed to some pawnbroker? You're being ridiculous!"

Carlos bristled. "Who are you to call me names and order me about?"

"Would the situation be different if I were a man trying to help out a male friend?"

"Of course!"

"Give me one good reason why!"

"Because there are rules that must be obeyed, matters of propriety that—"

"Propriety! I loathe that stupid word!" Maddy struggled to restrain her temper as she paced the small room. "It's as meaningless now as it was before. Why should my gender matter now or at any other time? This whole system is antiquated and absurd!"

After a ponderous silence, Carlos asked, "Who are you, woman?"

Maddy froze. "What do you mean?"

He cocked his head and studied her. "You're like no female I've ever met, high born or otherwise. You befriend people of color and treat them as equals and you challenge the roles of men and women in society and you, an unmarried woman, think nothing of inviting an unmarried man, a former slave no less, to stay under your roof. Nothing you do makes sense!"

"Maybe not in this world," Maddy blurted.

Carlos's eyes narrowed suspiciously. "What do you mean?"

Maddy backpedaled. "I mean that a world that treats women like chattel and allows slavery is hardly a rational one." She perched on the edge of the bed and smiled. "Slavery is one reason we're fighting this war, isn't it?"

He set the brandy aside and opened his arms. "Come here, Maddy."

She had ached for this moment but something held her back. "What do you want from me, Carlos?"

"I don't know," he replied feebly. "What I *do* know is that I have never wanted a woman as much as I want you at this very moment."

"But you're in pain," Maddy protested, nodding at his bruises.

"I've been in pain as long as I can remember, dear lady,

and until I met you I never believed I'd find a way to end it."

The distance between them closed as though it had never existed.

50

Once Maddy and Carlos became lovers, they vowed to keep their relationship a secret. She knew Félicité in particular would never accept the unorthodox liaison and, determined not to let anything threaten their friendship, remained evasive whenever Félicité asked what was new. The secret was almost discovered one morning when Félicité dropped by unannounced, forcing Carlos to hide in the bedroom armoire. Maddy felt like she was in a screwball comedy with Carlos crammed in such a small space. When they were alone again, Maddy massaged his sore muscles and soothed him even more with some prolonged lovemaking.

"I truly wish Félicité would drop by more often!" he laughed afterwards.

January was a blissful month for Maddy, and, according to Carlos, the happiest of his life. Because of his self-education and access to Emile Chevalier's vast library, he was Maddy's intellectual equal in everything from literature to history, at least up until now. With winter howling outside, they huddled cozily by the fire and enjoyed hours of spirited discussions on a wide range of subjects. These interchanges were not without incident, however. Her mention of West Virginia's statehood, still a year away, required a convoluted defense, as did her praise for Jules Verne's *Journey to the Center of the Earth,* which wouldn't be published for two years. Luckily she managed to talk her way out of both dilemmas while reminding herself to be more careful about revealing events that had not yet occurred.

Much less stressful and more rewarding were the quiet talks after intimacy, those special moments between lovers when confidences are made and deep secrets shared. Carlos confessed that, except for some inept groping as a teenager, he was otherwise inexperienced with women. Considering his virility and passion, Maddy was surprised but seized the opportunity to teach him what she knew. His quantum leap from fumbling to finesse not only thrilled her but made her wish she had a female confidante. With Félicité and Madeleine out of the picture, she missed Paige more than ever and longed to pick up the phone and brag that Carlos exuded the sort of raw masculinity nonexistent in most men of the 21st century. Thoughts of the present naturally led to longings for Henri that made Maddy wonder yet again what she was doing with Carlos. To find peace of mind, she reminded herself what Henri said about forgetting about him and seizing the day and thus managed to soldier on. All, however, was not smooth sailing. She and Carlos entertained some fierce personal debates during which she fought to convince him to accept a small salary for his contributions to the household. He adamantly refused until she argued that he helped her dress, made excellent *café au lait* and served her breakfast in bed, all duties she would pay for if she hired a servant. Overwhelmed by such logic, Carlos finally capitulated albeit with a great deal of grumbling she found charming.

Like Madeleine, Maddy suggested that she and Carlos read the newspapers together, the French *L'Abeille* as well as the English-language *Daily Picayune* and *Republican,* weighing the latest war news and sharing their thoughts. They learned that on February 7, the Union Navy seized Roanoke Island from the Confederacy and chased them from Albemarle Sound to suspend war activity in North Carolina. At the same time, the Battle of Fort Henry opened the Tennessee River to the Union in their first major victory of the war, and the subsequent capture of Fort Donelson secured Tennessee's equally important Cumberland River. It also made a household name of a brigadier general named Ulysses S. Grant.

Toward the end of February, the seriousness of the war

struck the hearts of all New Orleanians with an unprecedented proclamation from Mayor John Monroe canceling carnival. "No masked individual is allowed to go on the streets on Shrove Tuesday," he stated, "and any disguise or fancy dress smacking in the least of Mardi Gras eccentricities, will be considered an offense." A week later an even more heartrending announcement appeared in the newspapers, placed by Comus, the King of Carnival himself.

"Whereas war has cast its gloom over our happy homes, and Care usurped the place where Joy is wont to hold its sway. Now therefore, do I, deeply sympathizing with the general anxiety, deem it proper to withhold your Annual Festival, in this goodly Crescent City, and by this proclamation do command no assemblage of the Mistick Krewe. Given under my hand, the first day of March, 1862, Comus."

Trying to forget Mardi Gras was officially dead, New Orleans refocused on the war only to reap more bad news. For all of March, ferocious fighting raged along the Mississippi from New Madrid, Missouri, to Island No. 10 with the North winning every battle and most skirmishes. Finally, on April 8, the Yankees were repulsed at Fort Pillow, Tennessee, forty miles above Memphis. With the upper Mississippi firmly in hand, Union strategists again turned toward the mouth of the great river and the South's richest prize—New Orleans. To protect the city, Confederate Major General Mansfield Lovell commanded six thousand troops while Commodore Hollins beefed up his Mosquito Fleet downriver. At the shipyards, men worked around the clock to complete the great ironclads, *Mississippi* and *Louisiana,* and the flagship *McRae* was filled with coal and dispatched to the forts. The populace breathed easier until rumors blazed that Yankee ships had reentered the mouth of the Mississippi with an enormous fleet and were steaming upriver to confront Hollins. Anxious crowds flooded the city streets, and churches were filled to overflowing with people praying to Our Lady of Prompt Succor who had led Andrew Jackson to victory over the British against impossible odds during the Battle of New Orleans in 1815. Of course Maddy knew the Blessed Virgin would offer no more help now than she did for Hurricane Katrina, and that the city was destined to fall on April 24, exactly two weeks from today. Since she couldn't tell Carlos the truth, she suggested they go watch history unfold.

"What do you mean?" he asked.

"How often do we get a chance to see a city prepare for invasion?" Maddy couldn't help humming a few bars of the old Joan Baez hit, The Night They Drove Old Dixie Down. "Jackson Square and the waterfront must be a sight."

Carlos welcomed her enthusiasm. "A splendid idea. It will be something to tell our grandchildren." His unexpected comment made Maddy pale. "What's wrong?"

"It's just that we never talked about...that is, I never thought—"

Carlos pulled her into his arms and nuzzled the top of her head with his chin. "I didn't mean to frighten you, dearest. It was presumptuous and foolish. Forgive me?"

"Think nothing of it," Maddy replied, still shaken.

In fact she could think of nothing else. She had been extremely cautious in matters of sex since pregnancy would complicate her two worlds beyond comprehension. That disturbing train of thought led directly to Madeleine's most recent letters. Her baby was due in a month and she was swollen and achy and miserably alone. Jean-Noël and Auguste spent as much time as possible with her, but like everyone else their lives were upended by the war. Madeleine begged her to fulfill her promise to return, something Maddy had selfishly put off because of Carlos. She's sent a letter last week announcing she would arrive tomorrow, April 11, and she stood on her tiptoes to give Carlos a kiss before telling him her decision.

"I must leave tomorrow to visit my friend Madeleine. I promised to be there when her baby comes."

"And when will that be?"

"Within the month. I'll be back before you know it."

"But what about the Yankees? The war could be in our backyard any day."

"Oh, I suspect that's a lot of saber rattling downriver, and besides I'm going the other way. Her plantation is upriver near Port LeBlanc."

"So you're determined to do this?"

"I've no choice, Carlos," she said impatiently. "I told you about her husband's death and how she's all alone in the middle of nowhere."

Maddy had carefully edited the truth about the shootings and murder at Five Oaks, believing that the less Félicité and Carlos knew, and everyone else for that matter, the better. But Carlos was unconvinced.

"I'm going with you."

"That's sweet, dearest, but this is something I need to do alone." Knowing the last thing she needed was a meeting between Carlos and Auguste, she smiled and embellished her lie. "It's strictly female business, and you'd be bored to death."

"So you don't want me to go then?"

"That's not what I said and certainly not what I meant."

"I think you're being selfish." Maddy bristled. "I hardly think it's selfish to fulfill a promise made to a good friend, especially one expecting a baby."

"Then go!" Carlos growled, grabbing his hat and cape and heading for the door.

"What are you doing? I thought we were going to Jackson Square to—"

"I'm going out!" he announced, with a dramatic flurry of his cape. "And I'm going alone."

Maddy was dumbstruck by Carlos's temper and listened in disbelief as he clomped angrily down the stairs. Because he had always been the perfect gentleman, she was all the more horrified by an ugly side she'd never seen. In an effort to analyze his behavior, she replayed what had happened. Was he upset because she was leaving him alone for a few days or was this about her negative reaction to his mention of grandchildren? Either way she was disturbed.

"Damn!"

Feeling the walls closing in, Maddy went onto the gallery. Jackson Square was only four blocks away, the river closer still. A dull roar came from both directions, the clamor of chaos and fear, of courage and determination, as the city braced for the unknown. She took a deep breath, as though she might draw strength from this great watery metropolis. New Orleans in 1862 was at its apogee of power and prestige it would soon lose and never realize again. Because Maddy knew the city's downfall was inevitable, it worsened her depression over Carlos. How she wished Henri would invade her dreams and offer guidance or that she could commiserate with Paige. Energy drained and spirits flagging, she sank into a chair and began to doze, even dreaming a little, until a deep baritone voice brought her back to reality. She jumped to her feet and looked down Royal Street, watching a lone figure weaving in her direction. Carlos was singing, of all things, Jeannie with the Light Brown Hair. Maddy was annoyed at his drunkenness but she chuckled when she heard him substitute her name for the woman in the song. Her anger and anxiety faded with each slurred chorus.

"Carlos Mendoza," she muttered to herself. "You're certainly full of surprises tonight."

Maddy opened the door and monitored Carlos's unsteady progress up the stairs. Still singing, he was unaware he was being watched until he reached the top step. "Uh, *bon soir, mademoiselle.*"

"*Bon soir,*" Maddy said cheerily. "Sounds like you enjoyed your solitary outing."

"In truth I did." He sat on the couch and gave her a lopsided grin. "But it would have been much more fun with you along."

"That's nice to hear." She decided he wasn't as drunk as she thought. "What did you do?"

"I went to the waterfront and ran into some old chums from the boarding house." He lowered his voice to a conspiratorial whisper. "We went drinking, and…well, I'm not much of a drinker, you know."

"So I see," she said indulgently.

Carlos was quiet for a moment, apparently trying to collect his sodden thoughts. He remembered a bundle inside his jacket. "Ah! For you, my dear."

Maddy couldn't imagine what was inside as she untied the strings and unwrapped the brown paper. "What on earth?!"

"Mariana plums, the very first of the season." He gave her another crooked smile. "You said they were your favorites."

"Indeed I did, and how thoughtful that you remembered." Maddy set the package aside and knelt at Carlos's feet. She took his hands and studied his ruddy face, amused in spite of herself. He looked like the quintessential bad boy caught in the middle of mischief, and it only made her adore him all the more. "Promise me something."

"Anything," he said, pulling Maddy into his lap and folding her in his arms. "Anything within my power."

"Promise that we'll never quarrel again."

He frowned. "Did we quarrel?"

Not knowing whether he was trying to remember or to define what happened, Maddy gave him a kiss. "For the sake of argument, let's say we did."

"*Pourquoi?*"

"Because it's the perfect reason to make up."

Carlos's chuckle suggested he understood perfectly. "In that case, milady, time's a-wastin'!"

Maddy braced a hand on the back of the couch as Carlos stood shakily with her still in his arms. He carried her to the bedroom, barely making it before the combination of his unsteadiness and her weight proved too much and the two toppled onto the bed. Their laughter was brief as Carlos reached for the buttons on Maddy's dress, and what followed was anything but quick. Because he was a little drunk, Carlos took his time and left Maddy so sublimely satisfied that the next morning found her humming Jeannie with the Light Brown Hair.

51

While Carlos slept, Maddy slipped from bed, dressed quietly and went in search of fresh beignets. She found a street vendor by the gates to the Ursuline Convent and, guessing Carlos would wake up hung over and hungry, splurged on half a dozen. Between the pastries and café au lait, he was soon as good as new and apologized again for last night's behavior.

"I'm afraid it was nothing more than the green-eyed monster," he said sheepishly. "I didn't want you to leave me, but now I understand why you must go."

"All is forgiven, my darling." Maddy mussed his sleep-tousled hair. "But please promise you'll behave while I'm gone."

"I promise." He drained his coffee cup and gave her a provocative stare across the breakfast table. "I'm wondering how I might prove my sincerity and devotion."

"Carlos!" Maddy cried with delight as he swept her into his arms and bore her back to the bedroom for more breathless lovemaking. Afterwards, she gave his bare thigh a playful swat. "Good heavens, man! If that was intended to keep me from leaving, you very nearly succeeded."

Carlos was amiably smug. "You can't blame a gentleman for trying."

"Indeed, I cannot." Maddy gave him a quick kiss and went to the wash basin, surprised to find her legs wobbly as she splashed water on her face. "Before I leave I must send a note to Félicité. I can't go without telling her where I am."

"I'll have one delivered for you, my sweet. Discreetly, of course."

She blew him a kiss. *"Merci, mon cher."*

Maddy was further pleased when Carlos insisted on seeing her to the ferry and vowed he would count the hours until she returned. Once aboard, she spotted him on the crowded levee and waved until the ferry pulled from shore. She watched his figure dwindle until a pair of southbound Confederate support ships erased her view. When they were gone, so was Carlos. She missed him already, but as she strolled the deck and enjoyed a warm spring breeze her excitement over seeing Madeleine buoyed her mood. The ferry made the trip faster than usual, and as it nosed into Port Le-Blanc she was happy to be back across the river. She scanned the waterfront for a familiar face and, finding none, worried that Madeleine hadn't received her letter, but as soon as she stepped ashore someone called her name.

"Miss St. Jacques! Over here." Paddy O'Neill, Five Oaks's overseer, waved from the carriage. When Maddy saw him, he leapt down and trotted over. "I'm mighty glad you've come."

"How is Miss Madeleine?"

He shook his head as he threw her baggage into the carriage. "She's having a pretty rough time I reckon. Mr. Baptiste and Mr. Brasseaux, they come sometimes, and Delphine does the best she can, but—"

"Oh, dear! The baby's not coming early, is it?"

"Not that I know of."

"Is there a doctor nearby?"

"One right here in Port LeBlanc," O'Neill said as he helped her into the carriage. "He's been down a few times."

"That's reassuring." Maddy tucked her skirts around her legs and looked at the overseer impatiently. "Shall we go then?"

O'Neill flapped the reins and the coach lurched forward. Because he was a man of few words, the drive to Five Oaks was without conversation. Maddy was excited about returning to her ancestral home, but suffered foreboding as they rode alongside the cane fields. The sensation deepened when O'Neill turned the carriage onto the *allée*.

"Mr. O'Neill?"

"Ma-am?"

"I have a peculiar feeling about this place. Is there something wrong, something you started to tell me back at the landing?"

He didn't answer until he reined the horse in front of the big house. "I reckon so, but I don't know if I should trouble you with it."

"Please speak frankly, sir," Maddy said firmly.

O'Neill shook his head, red face darkening. "It's the slaves, miss. I been an overseer over twenty years and I know damned well when they're unsettled and hiding something. You'll pardon my language."

"Bother your language. Have you given them reason to be unsettled?"

O'Neill turned prickly. "If you're asking how I treat them, ma-am, I got no taste for the whip. Now Mr. St. Jacques, he was a whip man, but I told him before he hired me that I either did things my way or he could find himself another overseer."

"Good for you, sir." She took his hand and slipped from the coach. "So what do you think is the problem?"

"Freedom, plain and simple. The slave grapevine's been working overtime ever since Louisiana seceded, and those fools probably think emancipation's right around the corner."

They're right, Maddy thought. "How many are there?"

"Seventy-three in the fields. Another twenty or so in the big house and quarters."

She looked him hard in the eye. "Are we in danger?"

O'Neill shook his head. "Every plantation has a troublemaker or two, ma-am, but I got a trustworthy lot of drivers to help keep things in line. My years in the fields tell me the slaves only want to run off, not do something crazy." He removed his cap and rubbed a sunburned bald spot. "Then again, a white man can never second-guess Negroes."

"Does Miss Madeleine know about this?"

"No, ma-am. Only the menfolk."

"Good." She followed him onto the veranda where he deposited her portmanteau. "I appreciate your honesty, Mr. O'Neill, and thank you for picking me up."

"Yes, ma-am." He touched his hat and was gone.

Maddy turned around as the front door swung open. "Oh. *Bonjour,* Delphine."

"*Bonjour,* mademoiselle." Delphine curtsied. "The *maîtresse* is waiting for you."

Maddy was so anxious to see Madeleine that she hiked up her skirts and ran up the stairs. When she entered the bedroom, however, she stopped cold and forgot everything she'd ever heard about pregnant women being radiant. With her red, puffy face, blotchy skin and misshapen figure, Madeleine looked utterly miserable. She managed a tired smile when Maddy kissed her.

"I thought you'd never get here," she sighed.

"I'm sorry I waited so long, darling." Maddy drew a chair close to the bed. "There's much to tell you, but first I want to hear about you and the baby."

Madeleine shifted uncomfortably. "I suppose we're well enough, but between the heat and the nausea and everything else, I'm a wretched lot most of the time. Thank God for Delphine. She's been a treasure, and of course Jean-Noël and Auguste visit when they can. Neither says much about the war, but I'm sure they keep things from me. Speak freely, Maddy. How are things in the city?"

"About as chaotic you'd expect." Knowing Madeleine deserved honesty, she saw no reason to sugarcoat the truth. "New Orleans is preparing for siege."

Madeleine winced. "I suspected as much. Dear Lord! What a time to have a baby!"

"Would it help if I suggested concentrating on the little miracle you and Jean-Noël are about to introduce to the world?"

Madeleine gave her a look. "No, it wouldn't, my dear, and

if you could change places with me you'd understand why." She leaned forward so Maddy could fluff her pillows and sank back weakly. "To be honest, I just want it to be over with."

"When are you due?"

"A month from tomorrow."

Uh-oh, Maddy thought. By then the Yankees will have taken New Orleans and there could be fighting all around Five Oaks. There was also the matter of the slaves when they learned the Confederacy no longer held the upper hand. She didn't want to think about it.

"Can I get you anything before I tell you my news?"

Madeleine nodded at the bedside table. "A sip of that water."

For the next half hour, Maddy explained her affair with Carlos, from the moment she saw him emerge from the Cane River and their brief meeting at *Belle Rêve* to his emancipation and appearance in New Orleans with a new name and identity. Madeleine was silent as she heard the improbable tale, not responding until Maddy revealed Madam Iris's prediction.

"So that's what that crazy witch told you! *Mon dieu!* I have got goose bumps." She pulled up her long sleeve. "Look at my arm!"

"I know. Me too."

Madeleine took another sip of water. "I suppose I should scold you for getting involved with such a man, but no doubt you'd tell me to mind my own business." A gleam danced in her eyes. "Especially considering my illicit liaison with Jean-Noël."

"Another thing we have in common." Maddy took Madeleine's hand. "That's enough gossip for now. I need to freshen up and have something to eat. I'm suddenly famished."

Madeleine groaned. "The thought of food makes me queasy." Maddy started to go, but Madeleine gripped her hand. "You've no idea how happy I am to see you. You're my best friend in the world, you know."

"As you are mine, *ma chère*." Maddy kissed her great-great-grandmother's damp forehead. "That's why I'm here."

52

Maddy was skittish as a colt. She didn't know if it was the hideous heat, war jitters, the baby's impending arrival, the restless slaves or a combination of all four. The only certainty was that time passed with debilitating slowness and that she was desperate for something—anything!—to happen. With damp clothes sticking to her skin, she yearned for air-conditioning as she and Delphine took turns tending Madeleine in the stifling bedroom. Throwing the French windows wide was no option since it welcomed hordes of mosquitoes and, besides, there wasn't a breath of wind to stir the heavy air. The heat and numbing routine gave Maddy headaches, and it didn't help that Madeleine's discomfort made her short-tempered and shrewish. Whenever Maddy thought she couldn't endure another temper tantrum, Madeleine would grab her hand, press it to a tear-streaked cheek and beg forgiveness. Grateful when Delphine insisted she could manage alone, Maddy retreated to the library to find escape via Hugo, Gautier and Stendhal. She was immersed in *Le Rouge et le Noir* when the thump of boots on the veranda jarred her back to reality. She reached the vestibule as Jean-Noël and Auguste burst through the front door. Jean-Noël saw her first.

"*Cher* Maddy!" he cried, throwing his arms around her. "When did you get here?"

"Almost two weeks ago." She was also warmly embraced by Auguste, but there was an undeniable edge to the moment. She stepped back and looked from one man to the other. "Something's happened. What is it?"

"Bad war news," Auguste replied. Maddy knew what was coming of course but feigned ignorance as he continued.

"Our troops down at Fort Jackson have been exchanging fire with the Union fleet for over a week. The fort has suffered serious damage but is holding firm, as is the boom stretched across the river. Word has it the Yankees will take a serious run at the blockade tomorrow night. We can't waste any time."

"What do you mean?"

"Madeleine has to be moved to Port LeBlanc," Jean-Noël said, urgency heavy in his voice. "We can't risk being caught in the country with marauding troops and no doctor."

"And agitated slaves," Maddy added.

"So O'Neill told you, eh?" Maddy nodded. "All the more reason to hurry. Storm clouds have hung over this place too long, and gut instinct warns me that they're about to break."

"Moi aussi," added Auguste.

Maddy nodded agreement. "I was thinking that very thing this morning. In fact, I was—" Maddy froze when a scream tore through the house. Without hesitation, she gathered her skirts and flew up the stairs, not caring if she gave the men a look at her pantaloons. She nearly collided with Delphine coming out of Madeline's room. "What's happened?"

"Her water done broke, *maîtresse.*"

"What does that mean?" Jean-Noël asked.

"It means the baby's coming, you fool," Auguste snapped. "I'll ride into Port LeBlanc and get the doctor."

"Baby won't wait," Delphine insisted. "Better send to the quarters for Sookie."

"Who's Sookie?" Maddy asked, heart racing.

"A midwife," Auguste answered. "I'll get her."

As Auguste raced downstairs, Jean-Noël went into the bedroom and took Madeleine's hand. Maddy hovered in the doorway, feeling like an intruder when she saw the glow of love between them. She whispered to Delphine who appeared with clean towels. "What can I do?"

Delphine replied with admirable authority. "Take Cap-

284 | Michael Llewellyn

tain Baptiste outside and keep him company." She dampened a towel in the washbasin, wrung it out and began sponging Madeleine's arms. "Sookie and me'll take care of everything."

"Do as she says," Madeleine muttered weakly. "Take the men and leave us alone." She grimaced when pain grabbed down below. "Go on now."

Maddy kissed Madeleine's damp forehead. "I'll be right outside the door."

The next few hours seemed interminable. Maddy had seen plenty of births on television and in the movies, but never the real thing. Madeleine's cries and moans were incessant as Delphine and the midwife worked with her while a third girl ran up and down the stairs, bringing fresh water and swapping stained towels for fresh ones. Frustrated and frightened, Maddy and the men took turns calling through the door, but the response never varied.

"Not yet!"

Jean-Noël was beside himself, drenched in sweat as he paced the hall and muttered prayers. Auguste was only slightly calmer, with Maddy's stress level somewhere in between. Tension remained constant until dusk when Madeleine unleashed a scream that iced Maddy's blood. The frightening silence was followed by a loud slap and a bawling baby.

"It's here!" Jean-Noël cried. "The baby's finally here!"

He embraced Maddy before leaning against the door and listening. The baby's cries continued for a moment and stopped. The ensuing quiet was broken by whispered conversation and then an agonizing wail from Delphine.

"Non, non, non!"

Maddy pushed by Jean-Noël and burst into the room, recoiling from a scene she would never forget. Madeleine's face was taut and as pale as Easter lilies. The bed sheets were soaked with blood, and the room was pungent with the odor of life and death. Maddy's legs gave out as she approached, and she sank into a chair beside the bed. Jean-Noël followed slowly, color draining from his tanned cheeks as he registered the tragic truth. In a voice so low Maddy strained to hear, he asked everyone to leave him alone. The servants hurried out, and Maddy dimly realized Auguste was helping her from the chair. Before Delphine closed the door, Maddy saw Jean-Noël crawl into bed beside Madeleine and cradle her lifeless body in his arms.

"Dear God!" She crumbled against Auguste and rocked with sobs, soaking his shirtfront with bitter tears. When he trembled against her, she knew he was weeping too.

"Like *maman*," he whispered. "When Madeleine was born."

Maddy remained lost in sorrow until she heard the baby gurgling nearby. Sitting with the child in her arms, Delphine wept softly for her lost *maîtresse*. Her dignity and devotion overwhelmed Maddy and prompted her to pull away from Auguste and touch the woman's shoulder.

"*Ma pauvre* Delphine," she whispered. "Is the baby alright?"

"Perfect," Delphine whispered back. She dabbed her tears with a corner of the baby's blanket before pulling it open to reveal a sweet face. "A fine baby boy."

"Thank God for that." Maddy looked at Auguste. "*Mais,* what should we do about Jean-Noël?"

"Leave him alone. He'll come out when he's ready." Auguste leaned close to see his newborn nephew and smiled when the infant looked back and gurgled again. "He'll need a wet nurse, Delphine. Is there one in the quarters?"

"*Oui,* m'sieur. Her name's Hagar."

How ironic, Maddy thought, that the woman was named for a freed biblical slave.

"Bring Hagar here and get the baby fed. After that, I want Captain Baptiste to see his son." Delphine pressed the precious bundle to her breast and slipped silently downstairs. "Are you alright, Maddy?

"I think I'd better go to my room for a while."

"*Bon idée*. And start packing if you like. We'll leave for New Orleans tomorrow."

"Alright, Auguste."

Maddy's feet were leaden as she walked down the hall and closed the bedroom door. Her mind was mush as she tried to comprehend what had happened, and so quickly! Little of it registered as she went through the motions of pulling clothes from an armoire and chest of drawers and stuffing them into her portmanteau. As darkness deepened, she knew she should be hungry, but her body was numb as she crawled into bed. The last of her strength left with one long, painful sigh.

"Dammit, Henri," she muttered. "I sure didn't sign up for this!"

53

The next morning, a priest was hurried from Port Le-Blanc, and in late afternoon Madeleine was laid to rest alongside her parents. Paddy O'Neill was in attendance along with the house servants and a large number of field hands who had special affection for their late mâitresse. The Brasseaux family plot lay only fifty feet beyond the quintet of oaks, but Maddy had never noticed it behind a curtain of towering bamboo. During the service, her eye roamed from one lichen swathed tombstone to another, silently memorizing her family history beginning with the oldest who had come from Paris.

Pierre Charles Théophile Brasseaux
Décédé a l'age de 78 ans le 5 Octobre 1848

Pierre's wife, the scandalous Solange, slept beside him, and Maddy wondered if it was coincidence that she died the same year as her cuckolded husband. There was also Gabriel Fantin Brasseaux, slain in a duel at age eighteen, and a number of infant graves, reminders that few of Louisiana's firstborns survived childhood. These were the forbearers who gave Maddy the blood in her veins, and as she watched one buried, the weight of times past was prodigious.

Her melancholy musing was interrupted by a distant rumbling toward the sea. Because wind had arisen from that direction, she suspected it carried the sound of naval gunfire, but she reconsidered when she saw a phalanx of fast advancing thunderclouds. She knew the Gulf of Mexico spawned storms with alarming speed, a reality prompting the vigilant priest to hasten the eulogy and bring the service to a close. All dispersed with the arrival of the first raindrops, excepting Jean-Noël who remained to watch the gravediggers commence their grim task.

Auguste took Maddy's arm and asked O'Neill to accompany them back to the house. Delphine was also summoned as they gathered in the library and waited for Jean-Noël. Auguste sat at a mahogany *escritoire* and produced a sheaf of official-looking papers which he identified as Madeleine's last will and testament.

"It was drawn up after Jules's death," he explained. "In the case of my sister predeceasing me without legitimate issue, Five Oaks is mine to do with as I wish. Jean-Noël and I discussed the matter this morning, and as neither of us want to return we've agreed to sell the property."

So, Maddy thought, this is how our ancestral home slipped through our fingers.

"You," Auguste told O'Neill, "will receive ample compensation for taking care of the land until it's sold and an extra sum because my sister and I appreciated that you treated our property well." He handed O'Neill an envelope. "We deeply thank you."

"I should be thanking you, sir," O'Neill said, humbled. "Your sister was a fine lady."

"Indeed she was." Auguste gave a second envelope to Delphine. "As of this moment, you're free. These papers certify that freedom and a small sum of money is included too."

Delphine's eyes glistened with tears, and her hands trembled as she reached for the precious document. Everyone in the room strained to hear her soft, *"Merci, m'sieur. Merci."*

"Tell Hagar she's free too, and have her pack because she's coming to New Orleans with us. We need a wet nurse for the baby." As Delphine slipped away, Auguste handed O'Neill a large packet. "These are documents of manumission for the rest of the slaves. Kindly distribute them before we leave. You'll drive us into Port LeBlanc to get the ferry."

The overseer frowned. "What about the cane, sir?"

"It can rot in the fields for all I care," Auguste said.

"Yes, sir."

As O'Neill left, Jean-Noël appeared with a small bundle in his arms. Maddy smiled when she saw how he held the baby close to his heart. "Is it done, Auguste?"

"It's done, *mon ami.*" Auguste held out a tiny box. "Except for this."

"Will you do the honors?"

"I will indeed." Auguste passed the box to Maddy. "This belonged to our mother, and because Madeleine said you admired it, I know she would want you to have it."

Maddy gasped when she saw the ruby and sapphire ring. Instinct and fear warned her she could not interrupt the path putting the ring on Grandmother Aglaé's finger, and she beat a quick retreat. "I'm deeply grateful, but you should save it for your daughter, Auguste."

"Suppose I never have one."

"Oh, I suspect you will."

"Then I have a confession to make. I honestly didn't want to let it go."

"Then you shouldn't," Maddy said, relieved that she had done the right thing. "But I thank you again, from the bottom of my heart."

Auguste smiled. "You can also tell me good-bye, my dear. I'm going back to the swamps where I belong."

"I presumed as much." Maddy gave him a lingering hug and, remembering their one passionate night together, was grateful for no incongruous emotions. "I'll miss you."

"And I you." Auguste embraced Jean-Noël as well and took a last look at his sleeping nephew. "Until we meet again, old friend." With that he was gone.

"It's time for us to leave too," Jean-Noël told Maddy. "Shall we have a drink first?"

"By all means. May I take the baby for a while?"

"My son's name is Louis," Jean-Noël said, passing her the child. "Louis Pierre-Barthélemy St. Jacques."

"Louis," Maddy breathed, mind reeling as she recognized the name and the final piece of the genealogical puzzle fell into place. She cradled the drowsing infant in her arms, again relieved that Jean-Noël, not Jules, was her great-great grandfather. "Hello, little Louis St. Jacques," she cooed.

Jean-Noël misunderstood her reaction. "I suppose the surname is a surprise, but Madeleine and I agreed calling him Louis Baptiste would be announcing his illegitimacy to the world."

"Indeed it would."

Jean-Noël was putting on a brave face, but Maddy knew that decision was breaking his heart. "May I suggest bourbon for a change?" he asked.

Maddy tried to lighten the moment by feigning offense. "Pray tell, why would you suggest strong spirits for a lady?"

His chuckle was as welcome as it was unexpected. "Because Madeleine enjoyed whiskey when we were alone and because you two were so very much alike. Also because I've long suspected you might appreciate something more potent than *eau sucre*."

Maddy chuckled too. "Your suspicions are right."

"C'est bon." He went to a credenza where a forest of decanters held fine liquors. The crystal bottles gleamed white when a flash of lightning illuminated indoors and out. Jean-Noël ignored it and poured two healthy shots of bourbon, then looked up as he waited for the thunder. As it broke overhead with enough ferocity to rattle the decanters, he passed the whiskey to Maddy. "I also suspect we're going to need this tonight."

Mister, she thought, you have no idea.

Part 8

"The paradise of the South is here, deserted and half in ruins.
I never beheld anything so beautiful and so sad."

— Lafcadio Hearn, Life and Letters, 1877

54

The core of the thunderstorm passed after dusk, breaking the heat but leaving a steady drizzle in its wake. Jean-Noël made sure his charges, Maddy with Louis and Hagar with her own baby, stayed dry as O'Neill drove them to the ferry. Maddy suspected they were in for a rough crossing, but found more to worry about when they reached Port LeBlanc. With the threat of war ever nearer, pandemonium and confusion swarmed through the little settlement like a yellow fever plague. The waterfront was choked with frantic crowds waving handfuls of Federal and Confederate money in a desperate effort to buy passage across the river to New Orleans where steamships and railroads could take them out of harm's way. O'Neill drove as close as possible before Jean-Noël told everyone to wait in the carriage while he waded into the mob. After half an hour he emerged with tickets.

"We don't leave until three in the morning," he lamented. "It was the earliest I could get." With sailing time six hours away, Maddy suggested returning to Five Oaks to wait, but Jean-Noël was adamant that they stay put. "Don't you know I can never go back there?"

Maddy understood and, like the others, huddled in the covered carriage to wait. She was tired and achy by the time they hurried through the rain and boarded the ferry. Jean-Noël got everyone situated inside the cabin and took a seat beside her, glancing repeatedly to make sure Hagar had the babies safe in hand. Except for quietly thanking Jean-Noël for her freedom, the woman hadn't said a word, and Maddy hoped she was the strong, silent type she seemed. With newborns to protect, Maddy needed all the help she could get with New Orleans promising even more chaos and danger.

She dreaded what lay on the other side of the river and her apprehension was confirmed minutes after they pulled away from the dock. Through a wall of rain, the eastern skies radiated an unnatural glow that grew brighter and more intense as they sailed toward it. Soon they were close enough to realize they were looking at the unthinkable.

The New Orleans waterfront was ablaze!

Maddy recoiled as fear erupted in the passenger cabin along with screams and hysteria.

"The Yankees!" an old woman cried.

"It can't be, miss!" a man shouted. "Hollins is still holding the forts downriver."

"How do you know, sir?" asked the woman's husband. "Maybe they broke through!"

Maddy tried to ignore the ongoing debate and sort through her Civil War knowledge. She turned to Jean-Noël. "What's today's date?"

"April twenty-fourth," he replied. "Why?"

"Just curious."

The Battle of Forts Jackson and St. Philip is going on this very moment, Maddy thought. The Union navy will break through the chain across the Mississippi, sail past the forts and be in the city by noon tomorrow. That much was clear, but no matter how far she plumbed her memory she recalled nothing about fire in the city. While others rushed outside, braving the chilly rain for a closer look, Maddy settled against the hard wooden seats. Hagar, she noticed, was a portrait of African stoicism, face a dark mask as she cradled the two babies against her bosom. Jean-Noël studied the approaching fire in silence, but Maddy knew he was calculating and after a few long moments he jumped up.

"Stay where you are. I'll be right back."

"Where are you going?"

"To speak with the captain." Maddy waited anxiously when Jean-Noël raced for the bridge. With his credentials as a riverboat captain he was sure to get some facts, and indeed he returned quickly with news. "The Captain's been shuttling back and forth all day and gets the latest reports from the New Orleans side. The last time he was there, the fire alarm bells struck twelve times and repeated four times, the signal that the Union fleet got past our forts. He says it's our boys who are burning up anything the Yankees might use. General Lovell ordered it as a precaution."

"What's Lovell doing now?" The question was feigned as Maddy remembered the facts.

Jean-Noël lowered his voice. "Evacuating his men."

Maddy knew this to be true, just as she knew this deed would haunt General Lovell the rest of his days. Intended to support the forts, his troops, ships, artillery and ammunition would be useless if the Union navy steamed past the protective boom, leaving Lovell no choice but evacuation. How, he reasoned, could he save a hopelessly low-lying city rung by levees and high water? Floating above the town, enemy ships could fire down into the streets and shoot people like fish in a barrel. Worse, if the Yankees chose to blow up the levees, New Orleans would be inundated in a matter of minutes. To avoid the inevitable, the Confederate general ordered all military stores, warehouses, and ships torched, loaded his troops onto trains and sent them north. He alone remained in the city.

"So invasion is imminent?" Maddy asked.

Jean-Noël nodded sadly. "So it would seem."

"What shall we do now?"

"The captain said both sides of the river are ablaze, and the closest safe dock is at Tchoupitoulas Street. We'll have to make our way to the *carré de la ville* from there." He took a deep breath. "The captain also reported that Lovell was ordered to seize all the river steamers regardless of who owns them. They'll be used to ferry the ordnance and commissary stores upriver to Baton Rouge."

"*La Sirene!*" Maddy gasped.

"The waterfront by Jackson Square was so crowded and

chaotic I docked her far upriver. I can only pray they've not seized her, but will see for myself as soon as I can."

Maddy lurched against him when the ferry pitched hard to port. She threw one arm wide and executed a soccer mom block to keep Hagar and the babies from pitching onto the deck. Everyone held tight as the brave little ferry rocked across foaming whitecaps and plowed toward the center of the river. The rains had little effect on the inferno as the sky remained ravaged by columns of flames with smoke billowing so thick that Hagar covered the babies' faces with their blankets. Wind occasionally parted the great wall of smoke to reveal what fed the flames. Mountains of sugar, salt, tar and thousands of cotton bales provided ample fuel, and the stench was as venomous as the smoke. Moored tugboats and gunboats also caught fire beneath the shower of sparks, and a ship laden with cotton, cargo blazing, had been cut free only to drift dangerously out of control. As the ferry captain desperately dodged the floating inferno and aimed for shore, an exploding steamer showered the water with hissing torches. With its blood reds and fiery oranges, Maddy thought the blaze as spectacular as it was lurid.

"Dear God," she muttered. "It looks like the burning of Atlanta in *Gone with the Wind!*"

"What?" Jean-Noël shouted as another violent pitch triggered screams of terror.

"Nothing!" Maddy yelled back, grateful that her careless comment was drowned in the noisy confusion. Taking a cue from Hagar, she pulled a handkerchief from her reticule and covered her nose and mouth. She closed her eyes as an additional precaution and found herself thinking again of *Gone with the Wind.* Like Scarlett O'Hara, she was traveling alongside the flames of a torched Confederate city in the company of a dashing Southern gentleman and a slave with a couple of babies. All that was missing was poor Melanie Wilkes.

55

Because the Tchoupitoulas dock was not a regular ferry stop, there were no hacks waiting for passengers. It took Jean-Noël half an hour to find a coachman willing to brave the streets of the terrified, unruly city. Twice the driver had to use his crop to drive away hooligans after his horse and carriage, and it was nearly five in the morning before they reached Maddy's apartment in the *carré de la ville*. The sky remained unnaturally bright with fires still blazing only three blocks away. Irritated by the smoke and noise, both babies cried nonstop, and she couldn't remember being so exhausted as she climbed the stairs. Her voice was a hoarse whisper as she called out for Carlos.

"Carlos?" Jean-Noël asked warily. "A servant?"

"Allow me to explain another time," Maddy pleaded. "I simply don't have the strength."

"I understand."

"Then you should rest here for now. The couch is comfortable enough, and I'll put Hagar and the babies in the maid's room. Tomorrow we can—"

"I can't stay," Jean-Noël interrupted, "and I must ask you a great favor."

Maddy guessed what was coming. "Oh?"

"I'll have no peace until I know *La Sirene* has not been commandeered. I was hoping you could keep Louis until I determine that my boat is safe and can make some arrangements. Could you find it in your heart to do that?"

"Of course," Maddy replied, welcoming the idea of spending more time with the baby. "In fact, I'd be delighted."

Jean-Noël smiled and tenderly kissed the baby's fore-

298 | Michael Llewellyn

head. "*Au revoir, mon fil.* Be a good boy and do what Hagar tells you." He slipped a gold coin into Hagar's hand. "You'll stay with us awhile, won't you?"

Hagar nodded. "Ain't forgetting the folks who set me free."

"Thank you." He embraced Maddy and stroked her hair, a gesture she found brotherly and sweet. "You were a brave lady tonight. Madeleine would have been proud of you."

"You're the one who was brave, Jean-Noël. I could never have made my way home without you. I promise we'll take good care of your son."

"I know you will, my dear, and for that I will be eternally grateful." He kissed her on the forehead and was gone.

Maddy immediately tended to Hagar and the babies, getting them settled in their little room before checking the kitchen for provender. Luckily Carlos had kept the cupboard well stocked, and what was lacking could be replenished with a trip to the riverside French Market. *If it hasn't burned down,* she thought glumly. She was so weary that she sat down to remove her wet clothes, shoes and stockings. A glance at the empty bed reminded her of Carlos's absence. He had promised to stay out of trouble, but his absence at this hour was troubling. She was far too exhausted to think of it further and fell asleep moments after turning down the gaslight. Her sleep was deep and dreamless and would have continued if noise from the kitchen hadn't roused her shortly after eight. She sat up groggily, needing a moment to realize she was back in New Orleans. She had left the bedroom door open to hear Hagar if she needed anything and looked toward the parlor when a long shadow fell across the carpet.

"Carlos?" she called.

"Maddy! You're home at last!"

"Yes, my darling! I'm home!" Maddy threw back the covers and hurried to him, but stopped short when she saw the wet, bedraggled creature at the end of the hall. Carlos's curly hair was matted and dirty, and a day's growth of black beard shadowed his cheeks and chin. His clothes looked slept in, and the shoulder of his filthy jacket was ripped and stained. He smelled heavily of sweat, grime and rum. Maddy's heart sank. "Oh, Carlos. You promised!"

"It's not what you think, my dear. I wasn't out carousing. I was at the waterfront like everyone else." He stepped closer, bringing his stench with him. "Don't I get a kiss?"

"Not until you've cleaned up." Maddy fanned the foul air between them. "You smell like the gutter."

Carlos burst out laughing. "Maybe because that's exactly where I've been."

"What are you talking about?"

"As soon as the fires started, everybody rushed to the docks to investigate. There was great confusion and general bedlam, and when people saw unguarded hogsheads of sugar and boxes of meat, they helped themselves."

"You don't mean looting!"

"Of course I do. There were hundreds of people down there, all of them loading up. Men threw hunks of meat over their shoulders, and women carried things off in their aprons. Barrels of molasses were smashed to smithereens, and pretty soon the gutters were sticky with molasses. It's the damndest thing I ever saw."

"Please tell me you weren't involved."

"Indeed I was, along with half the town. Why not? It made more sense than letting food burn up with the cotton. Just because our soldiers left it to rot doesn't mean we have to." He stepped aside and indicated a kitchen table piled with sugar, meat and coffee. "Look!"

Maddy tempered her disapproval by putting things into context. The man's not a real thief, she thought, and this isn't like the malicious looting after Hurricane Katrina. He was caught up in the moment, and he's right that it's better than letting things go to waste. People who are hungry would at least have something to eat.

"I suppose you're right."

"Of course I am," he said proudly. "There's enough here to last us a couple of weeks."

Maddy was now awake enough to take inventory. "Maybe this is propitious after all."

"What do you mean?"

"I mean for the next few days we'll have three extra mouths to feed."

"What are you talking about?" Carlos turned toward the sound of a bawling baby and saw Hagar emerge from the maid's room. "Who the devil is that?"

"That, my darling, is Hagar. It seems you are not the only one full of surprises this most unusual morning."

Carlos scowled. "You promised you'd never have slaves in this house."

"Hagar is not a slave. She's a free woman and a wet nurse that we very much need."

"Wet nurse?!"

Maddy nodded as she made an inspection of Carlos' haul. "While you're getting cleaned up, I'll brew some coffee and then we'll sit down so I can explain things."

"I'll hurry." Carlos was only mildly drunk, so the strong Creole coffee sobered him quickly, as did Maddy's revelation of Madeleine's tragic death. He reached across the kitchen table to take her hand. "I'm so sorry, dearest. I know how important she was to you."

"Thank you, Carlos. At least we'll have her precious baby for a while, and although I'm grateful for that I still haven't made peace with her loss."

"What can I do to help?"

"Be patient I suppose. It's not going to be easy living with two newborns. Hagar is an excellent nurse, but I'm sure the babies will make their presence known."

"When do you suppose this Captain Baptiste will return?"

"As soon as he learns his ship's fate, but who knows what's safe in this crazed city, especially since the Yankees will be here at noon."

Carlos frowned. "How do you know that?"

Another stupid slip of the tongue, Maddy thought. She blamed it on pure weariness. "Because...that's what the ferry boat captain said last night. He said the Union fleet passed the forts around two in the morning and that there's nothing to keep Admiral Farragut from sailing right into town." She checked her watch. "That should put them here in about three hours."

"Well, what do you know?" Carlos smiled. "New Orleans will be back in the Union!"

"I'm sure you're pleased," Maddy said wearily.

"Why shouldn't I be?!" he asked, temper flaring. "The South has meant misery to me as long as I can remember. Not only do I want the Confederacy to meet defeat. I want it to go down in flames."

"Calm down," Maddy said evenly. "I'll give you no argument because I believe you're entirely justified."

"Do you mean that?"

"Are you forgetting the times I railed against slavery and the mistreatment of women?" She sounded evasive and both of them knew it.

"Of course not, but that doesn't mean you want to see the South crushed. I know you're a Mississippian at heart."

The truth was Maddy didn't give a damn about the war, especially since she already knew the outcome, but the August Ones had called upon her to play a strict role. Earlier conversations and circumstances had convinced Carlos she was a Confederate, and since he would be suspicious if she suddenly changed sides, she had to make the strange situation work.

"What you say is true, my dear, but please remember this is a Mississippian who loves you too much to let politics come between us and that there are more important things to deal with."

"Such as?"

"Your anger and bitterness over the past. I truly believe it will help to talk about them. It could even help you begin a healing process." Dear Lord, she thought. You sound like one of those New Age fidelity consultants or whatever they call themselves.

"Maybe I don't want to heal. Anger can be good. It makes me feel alive."

"It can also *eat* you alive," Maddy offered a bit sternly. "You could start by telling me more about your past." When he didn't respond, she said, "When was the last time you had a good night's sleep?"

It was a brilliant sortie. She knew Carlos was constantly plagued by nightmares about his youth and would probably do anything to stop them. "Maybe you're right," he conceded.

She smiled. "At least try, darling."

After a long moment of silence, he began. "There's not much more to tell. You already know about the awful woman who dressed me up like a toy."

"I'd rather hear about your years with Félicité's family."

Carlos refilled his coffee cup. "It's true that the Chevaliers never mistreated me, and I'm grateful that the *maître* taught me how to read and gave me access to his library, but he still withheld that which was most dear to me."

"Your freedom."

"*Exactement.* And my loyalty and gratitude wasn't boundless. You should know I tried to escape twice, once by stowing away on a riverboat and another time by swimming."

Maddy recalled the moment when she saw him emerge from the water like an aquatic Adonis. She had, for reasons she didn't know herself, never told him about it. "Swimming?"

"I spent as much time as possible in the Cane River. The current is treacherous in spots, and fighting it made me strong." Maddy thought of the muscle play when he yawned and stretched while she spied from the willow grove. "Because white men on the island are rare and everyone knew I belonged at *Belle Rêve,* I was caught both times. Luckily I managed to explain myself, so Chevalier never knew what was in my heart. I was about to make a third attempt when the old master died and set me free."

"I'm glad you told me," Maddy said softly. "Among other things, I can see your looting as a way of getting back at the Confederacy."

"True enough," he said with pride, "and I promise it won't be the last time."

"What do you mean?"

Carlos waved away her question and helped himself to more coffee. "Now that I think about it, if the Yankee fleet is arriving this morning, I don't want to miss it. Do you?"

"I suppose not."

"*Alors*, you'll come with me then?"

"Of course." Maddy smiled. "I'll always want to share your moments of triumph."

"I hope you mean that, dearest."

56

Despite a steady drizzle, dozens of fires continued to smolder as Carlos and Maddy made their way to the Canal Street waterfront. Columns of gray smoke snaked upward, and damp ashes rained on crowds massed on the levee to stare, mesmerized, downriver. People were fearful and wary, moods cautious after last night's troublesome orgy of arson, pillaging and anarchy, but there was no denying they exuded a collective wave of pure hatred. Maddy could almost hear it crackle across the flat, gray water.

"Look there!" Carlos pointed excitedly as the first of thirteen Union ships rounded the great downriver bend in the Mississippi and glided silently past the *carré de la ville.* The fleet continued at a stately but menacing pace to the foot of Canal Street where it dropped anchor alongside a smoldering wharf and aimed two hundred guns at the city and its terrified populace. Carlos pointed at the *U.S.S. Hartford,* a heavily armed 225-foot sloop-of-war, by far the most impressive vessel in the fleet. "That must be Admiral Farragut's flagship."

"Talk about watching history unfold," Maddy said.

"It's sure as hell not the history I want to see," said the man behind her.

Maddy turned toward the familiar voice. "Mr. Mumford!"

Mumford nodded but did not remove his hat as the drizzle intensified. "It's nice to see you and Mr. Mendoza, but I do wish it were under better circumstances."

"As do I."

"Good morning, sir," Carlos said politely. He and Mumford may have been political opposites but he had not forgotten the man's efforts to help him find work. "Where is your wife?"

"Safe at home, sir. I was afraid for her to venture forth on such a dreadful day."

Mumford shook his head as officers aboard the ships began barking orders. "Who knows what those damned Yankees will do next?"

Carlos turned up his collar as the rain intensified. "Looks like they're coming ashore."

Horror and disbelief rippled through the restless multitude as a small boat was dispatched from the *Hartford* and rowed toward the levee. Maddy knew it carried two officers who would demand surrender of the city. She was close enough to hear men identifying themselves as Captain Bailey and Lieutenant Perkins and asking directions to City Hall. Their simple request triggered an explosion of rage from the shivering throng.

"Find it yourself, Yankee rabble!"

"Get the hell out of our city!"

"Where's your flag of truce, scum?"

"Barbarians!"

Bailey ignored the shouts and ordered his escort of armed sailors to close ranks as they made their way through the crowded streets. Maddy held her breath as the name calling got louder and nastier. It would surely have escalated into violence had not two highly respected citizens come to the rescue of the armed but vastly outnumbered invaders. William Freret, a former mayor, and city councilmen L.E. Forstall pushed their way through the hostile mob to insulate the soldiers and escort them to City Hall. Maddy, Carlos and Mumford followed until the storm moved full over them and disgorged heavy rains. Maddy tugged the hood higher over her head and yanked Carlos's sleeve.

"We'd better go home or we'll get soaked."

Carlos laughed loudly. "Hah! I don't mind getting soaked on a day like this." Ignoring Maddy's protests, he turned to Mumford. "Would you be kind enough to see Miss St. Jacques home, sir? I'd be forever grateful."

"Happy to," Mumford said. "I've had enough humiliation for one day."

"Thank you." Carlos jerked his head in the direction of City Hall. "I wouldn't miss this for the world!"

Maddy understood his eagerness to witness the official fall of the Confederacy's greatest city but was disappointed when he hurried away without a backward glance. She was further disheartened when she remembered his desire for more revenge on the South and prayed their political differences wouldn't become an unbreachable abyss. Mumford's words didn't help as they walked toward the *carré de la ville*.

"Perhaps your friend merely wants to witness history, but my gambler's gut tells me he's eager to see the city surrender."

"Not at all," Maddy lied. She knew Mumford was a rabid Confederate and did not want him to know Carlos's leanings. "He just likes excitement."

"Then today shouldn't disappoint him," Mumford said grimly. "Incidentally, my wife and I have long wanted to invite you to our new home on Esplanade. Surely you'd be amenable to a cup of tea on such a miserable afternoon." He winked. "Or a stiff shot of bourbon."

Maddy smiled. "Tea would be delightful." Since Mumford had no memory of their long ago meeting at the *Salle d'Orléans*, Maddy had enjoyed his friendship and especially welcomed it today. Carlos had upset her deeply, and she wasn't anxious to keep company with two babies and a wet nurse. She took his arm. "It's always nice to see Mary."

The angry crowds thinned as Maddy and Mumford left Canal Street behind and followed the *Rue de la Levée*. They were relieved to see that the steady rain was dousing the last of the fires, but that bit of good news was forgotten when they realized other Union ships were sending soldiers ashore. The vista of dark blue uniforms on the streets of New Orleans was more than a little unsettling.

"I'd like to shoot them all," Mumford growled as they

approached the old French Market. "Every last one of them."

"Let's hurry," Maddy urged, alarmed by his anger. "The rain is getting heavier."

They rushed on, maintaining a quick pace toward the Confederate Mint at the corner of Levee and Esplanade Streets. Operating as a United States Mint since 1838, it was seized after Louisiana's secession and now made coins for the Confederacy. As Maddy and Mumford approached Esplanade, a dozen Union marines trotted past, laughing and jostling as they headed back to the *U.S.S. Pensacola*. The reason for their high spirits was obvious when Maddy saw the crowds at the entrance to the Mint, shouting angrily and pointing toward the portico. Snapping in the wind and rain was a newly hoisted United States flag.

"How dare they!" Mumford grunted. "The city has not yet surrendered. The Mint is still property of the Confederacy!"

Mumford jerked away from Maddy with such force that she reeled into the iron fence surrounding the enormous structure. Shouting at the top of his lungs, he charged through the crowd and into the Mint itself. A group of equally outraged men followed and quickly appeared on the roof of the portico where Mumford, to thunderous cheers and Rebel yells, tore down the Union flag. He waved it triumphantly before returning to the sidewalk where a jubilant mob began snatching at it. Caught up in the moment, Maddy cheered and waved as Mumford clutched the remainder of the flag to his chest. Before he could get back to her, a crowd of Southern zealots intervened and spirited him away in the direction of City Hall. Mumford called out and motioned for her to follow, but she was cowed by the growing mob mentality and held back. Her excitement melted along with the crowd, and although wet and tired she still wasn't ready to go home. Félicité, she thought suddenly. I need to see Félicité!

With everyone in town either huddled indoors to keep dry or waiting in the rain outside City Hall for some sort of official word from Mayor Monroe, the streets and sidewalks were empty as Maddy rushed toward Rampart Street. As usual, she had a surge of warmth when she saw the little cottage, and the sensation deepened when Félicité heartily embraced her.

"Precious Maddy! You're home at last!" Félicité blinked away tears of joy. "I've missed you desperately."

"And I you, my darling," Maddy hugged Félicité back before handing Zaza her damp cape. "Are you well?"

"As well as I can be with the Yankees in New Orleans! *Mon dieu!* It's like the end of the world." Félicité sat on the *méridienne* and pulled Maddy down beside her. "And you? Are you alright? When did you return? What do you think of all this madness?"

Maddy smiled at the barrage of questions. "I'm fine, considering I spent all night traveling from Port LeBlanc and was up until five in the morning."

"Sacrebleu! Pourquoi?" Maddy gave her a quick recap of Madeleine's death and last night's treacherous flight from Five Oaks. Félicité's green eyes grew wider as each crisis was explained. "So you now have babies at your home?"

"Yes, and I wish you could see little Louis. He looks like a cherub."

"I'll see him soon enough. *Mais,* you must be exhausted. Did you venture out in the rain just to see me?"

"Of course." Maddy purposely made no mention of Carlos or Mumford. "And how is M'sieur Moran?"

"Poor Joseph has Confederate fever like every other young rebel in the city. I told you before that he had spoken of joining the army, and now that the city has fallen into enemy hands, I should be greatly surprised if he doesn't enlist."

"And how will this affect you?"

"Who can say? I'm praying he will remain my protector, but I must be realistic and accept that he will find me *de trop* once he goes off to war."

Maddy took her hand. "I know it's gauche to speak of such matters, Félicité, but I'm a woman of means after all and not someone to let her dearest friend suffer or go with-out."

"That's very kind, but you know a Chevalier could never accept charity." She gave Maddy a half smile. "*Mais*, it must seem to you that I'm always on the verge of some crisis."

"Not really. Your life is...well, it is what it is."

Félicité laughed softly. "There's that funny saying again. Oh, Maddy! Whatever would I do without you?"

Maddy had a chill that did not come from the damp out-side. I'm afraid you'll find out soon enough, she thought.

57

Maddy was dozing in the parlor, a sleeping Louis cradled in her arms, when the downstairs door slammed and woke her. Carlos stomped up the stairs and burst into the room, dripping wet and scowling. "What happened?" she asked groggily.

"Those damned Rebels don't know when to quit!" he barked.

"Calm down or you'll wake the baby. I just got him to sleep."

Carlos lowered his voice to a husky whisper. "I'm sorry, but what I witnessed is infuriating!"

Maddy pointed to the floor where a puddle was forming around his feet. "You're soaked, Carlos. Get out of those wet clothes, and I'll make coffee."

"Wait'll I tell you what happened!"

"In a minute." Maddy gave him a gentle push and went into the maid's room where she found Hagar napping. No surprise there, she thought. Tending to newborns is certainly no picnic. She carefully laid Louis on the bed beside the nurse, closed the door and tiptoed to the kitchen. As she ground the coffee, she realized this was a replay of that morning. Carlos comes home a mess and I calm him down, she thought. She was pouring the coffee when Carlos joined her. Before he said anything, she made him promise again to keep his voice down.

"I'll try, but it won't be easy."

"What on earth has you so upset? The Union took the city, didn't they?"

"Not yet, it hasn't." Carlos ignored the coffee and drummed his fingers on the table. "When Captain Bailey and

Lieutenant Perkins met the mayor, they demanded official surrender and ordered that the Louisiana flag be removed from City Hall, the Customs House and the Mint and replaced by the United States flag. Mayor Monroe refused on all accounts."

"Can he do that?"

Carlos shrugged. "He said he was a civil magistrate without the power to perform any military actions, and since the city is under martial law he instructed Bailey to meet with General Lovell. As for the flags, Monroe said the Mint and Customs House were federal properties of the Confederacy and that he had no jurisdiction over them. When Bailey repeated his request to lower the flag over City Hall, Monroe told him he could discuss that with the general too."

"Did Lovell show up?"

"I'll get to that in a minute. In the midst of the negotiations, your friend William Mumford stormed into the meeting and threw a tattered American flag on the floor. He and some other riffraff tore it down from the Mint."

Maddy was determined to keep things civilized but still spoke her mind. "He's not riffraff, and, what's more, I'm proud to say I watched him do it."

Carlos was appalled. "How can you say that when he desecrated the American flag?!"

"He desecrated an *enemy* flag," Maddy reminded him. "As Mumford said, until New Orleans surrenders, it's still a Confederate city entitled to fly the Confederate flag over Confederate property." Carlos merely scowled. "Now tell me about General Lovell."

"I suppose he arrived promptly enough when sent for, but matters only got more complicated. He also refused to surrender but promised to withdraw all Confederate troops. Naturally that dumped things back in Monroe's lap. He said he would discuss it with the Common Council and called for a meeting this evening at six."

"So things are at a stalemate?"

"They are indeed." Carlos shook his head. "I cannot understand how any sane individual, official or otherwise, can ignore the demands of an armed force anchored in their harbor."

Maddy smiled. "Of course you can."

Carlos frowned. "What are you talking about?"

"It's about honor, plain and simple. Certainly Mayor Monroe and General Lovell know New Orleans is lost, but they're obliged to put on a brave show for her people. Listen to the rhetoric that emerges over the next few days. I expect Monroe will heap great praise on the citizenry and demand respect for their courage and convictions."

"Such things are worthless when warships are aiming guns at your head."

Maddy was disheartened. "You sadden and surprise me, my love. After all the brilliant writing we've discussed, I was sure you understood the importance of honor."

"It works much better in books than in the real world, especially ours."

Maddy was shocked. "You don't mean that!"

"*Au contraire, ma cherie.* Do you not see what's coming?"

More than you can imagine, Maddy thought. Think and be careful how you answer. "I know it's a dark day for New Orleans, but—"

"Dark day? Bah! The whole of your beloved South is on the road to ruin, and that means the end of its economy and its ridiculous code of honor. Most important of all it means the end of the evil system that built it – slavery."

"The South was built on far more than slavery," Maddy said coolly. "Great and fine traditions from France and England, for example. Places where manners and gentility meant something."

"Manners and gentility built on human misery, you mean." Carlos waved a hand contemptuously. "Interpret it however you like, but there's no denying it's going to collapse." He began pacing the kitchen, face reddening with each step. "What's more, my darling, I'm going to give it a big push."

Here we go again, Maddy thought. When Carlos talked like this, he's spewing someone else's bile. Despite his intelligence, Carlos was a neophyte in emotional and social matters, a situation making him vulnerable to all sorts of predatory ideas. Maddy understood his hatred of a system that enslaved him, but she feared that his poisonous desire for revenge could destroy him and their relationship along with it. The abyss she worried about that afternoon loomed again.

"What are you saying?"

"I'm saying that I have friends of a similar mind and that we have discussed things that will bring us the satisfaction we want."

"Satsfaction or revenge?"

Carlos replied without hesitation. "Both."

Maddy's stomach turned over. "Precisely how do you plan to achieve these goals?"

"I wish I could tell you."

"Meaning you can't or you won't?"

"All of us took a vow of silence. Besides, it's too dangerous for you to know about."

Maddy's alarm sounded louder. "You frighten me with such talk, Carlos."

"Good God, woman! This is war, not the opera." When he saw Maddy's fear, he put his arms around her. "I don't like what's happening any more than you do, *ma chèr,* but for the first time in my life I have the power to make my own decisions and right some wrongs. Can you understand how important that is?"

"Of course I can, but the degree of your anger and a secret that's too dangerous to reveal terrifies me. What you must understand is that I don't want to lose you, over the Confederacy or any other cause." She looked deep into his eyes, past the rage and into something darker and more elusive. "You know that, don't you?"

"Yes, my love." The hardness in his handsome face softened, and the left corner of his lips curled up. "Where are Hagar and the babies?"

"They're sleeping in the maid's room. Why?"

She knew why of course and smiled when she heard his response. "I promised you I wouldn't raise my voice, but—"

Maddy touched a finger to his lips. "Shhh. I know."

She took his hand and led him into the bedroom smelling of his damp clothes and boots. She closed the door and turned around so he could navigate the galaxy of buttons, hooks and ribbons securing her clothes. One by one, they fell away. His clothes followed, and the two slipped naked into bed. A mutual lack of sleep meant their lovemaking was slow and, at times, labored, but Carlos eventually arrived. Maddy, however, was elsewhere.

"You weren't there this time," he said with disappointment.

"I'm just tired, darling. I had very little sleep last night and it's been a very long day."

"Then perhaps we might have a nap. Suddenly I'm tired too."

"Bon idée."

Carlos snuggled from behind. "When I lie with you like this, it's as if the universe has stopped."

Which universe, Maddy wondered, unexpected nostalgia for Henri dancing in her head as she drifted off to sleep.

58

As May wore on and the heat escalated, so did the war of words between Admiral Farragut and Mayor Monroe. Farragut still sought official surrender while the mayor responded with the florid rhetoric predicted by Maddy. When his letter was printed in the newspapers, she read it to Carlos as they breakfasted on the gallery.

"'The city is yours by power of brutal force, and not by any choice or consent of its inhabitants. It is for you to determine what shall be the fate that waits her. As to the hoisting of any flag other than the flag of our own adoption and allegiance, let me say, sir, that man does not live in our midst whose hand and heart would not be palsied at the mere thought of such an act; nor could I find in my entire constituency so wretched and desperate a renegade as would dare to profane with his hand the sacred emblem of our aspirations. You have a gallant people to administer during your occupation of this city, a people sensitive to all that can in the least affect its dignity and self-respect. Pray, sir, do not allow them to be insulted by the interference of such as have rendered themselves odious and contemptible by their cowardly desertion of the mighty struggle in which we are engaged, nor of such as might remind them too painfully that they are the conquered and you the conquerors.'"

Carlos scoffed and said such lofty speeches wasted everyone's time. He was far more pleased with Farragut's angry response and delighted in reading it to Maddy a few days later. "'The fire of this fleet may be drawn upon the city at any moment, and in such an event the levee could in all probability be cut by the shells, and an amount of distress ensue to the innocent population which I assure you I desire by all means to avoid. The election is with you. But it becomes my duty to notify you to remove the women and children from the city within forty-eight hours, if I have correctly understood your intention.'" He rolled up the newspaper and waved it at Maddy. "Now that's a letter that says something, my dear!"

"Indeed it does! It says the man wants to destroy our city!"

"Desperate times call for desperate measures."

"Spare me the platitudes!" she snapped, temper flaring at his smugness. "And please tell me you don't want more harm to come to the city!"

Carlos retreated. "Of course I don't. Nor do I think Farragut is serious."

"Oh, he's serious alright. And he's as fearless as he is serious. Look what he did in Mobile Bay? Sailing past the minefield blockade with himself lashed to the mast and shouting, 'Damn the torpedoes! Full speed ahead!' The man would walk into a lion's den unarmed!"

Carlos frowned. "When did Farragut attack Mobile Bay?"

Maddy's insides turned to jelly when she realized she had described a battle that had not yet happened. She plumbed her history facts and dredged up a desperate explanation. "I'm sorry. I was thinking of General Wilkinson in the War of 1812."

"You've been getting a lot of your facts confused lately," Carlos noted. "Perhaps it's time you got back to the history books."

"Perhaps," Maddy agreed. "Sometimes I get so upset I can't think straight."

Her latest slip of the tongue was forgotten, and she and Carlos had no more war discussions until Monroe responded to Farragut the next day. They read the letter together.

"Sir, you cannot but know that there is no possible exit from this city for a population which exceeds one hundred and forty thousand, and you must, therefore, be aware of the utter inanity of such a notification. Our women and children cannot escape from your shells, if it be your pleasure to murder them on a mere question of etiquette. You are not satisfied with the peaceable possession of an undefended city, opposing no resistance to your guns, because of its bearing its doom with some manliness and dignity; and you wish to humble and disgrace us by the performance of an act against which our nature rebels. This satisfaction you cannot expect to obtain at our hands. We will stand your bombardment, unarmed and undefended as we are. The civilized world will consign to indelible infamy the heart that will conceive the deed and the hand that will dare to consummate it."

Maddy's pride in her hometown soared. "What do you think of that, Carlos dear?"

"Words, words, words. Nothing more than words. Do you honestly believe that Monroe truly reflects the sentiment of the citizenry?"

"I not only believe it," Maddy retorted, grabbing her plumed hat and gloves. "I know it."

"What do you mean and where are you going?"

"Mary Mumford and some other ladies have drawn up a petition supporting Mayor Monroe's stand. We already have hundreds of signatures, and I'm off to Félicité's house to get hers as well."

"That will accomplish nothing," Carlos scoffed.

"Of course it will. Our petition will keep morale high and present a united front, and if you can't understand that, I'm sorry but I'm too busy to explain." Carlos chuckled. "Now what do you find so amusing?"

"You, my darling. Doing battle with Admiral Farragut armed with feathers and finery."

"I suppose you'd rather I stayed home?"

"I would indeed." He caught her elbow as she reached for the door. "I can think of much better ways for us to pass the time."

"Carlos—!"

318 | Michael Llewellyn

"Hagar and the babies will be over at Mademoiselle Chevalier's all day. We have the place to ourselves."

Maddy was disarmed by his suggestive tone but wouldn't be deterred. "I'll only be gone a couple of hours, my sweet. Hold your naughty thoughts and perhaps we can renegotiate plans when I return."

"If I'm still here," Carlos teased.

Maddy feigned indifference. "Honest to goodness, I've no idea why I care about you."

"Sure you do," he said with a naughty wink.

"You're impossible!"

Maddy gave Carlos a quick kiss and a saucy toss of her head before dashing downstairs, smiling when his laughter followed her to the sidewalk. A thick cloudbank held the sub-tropical sun at bay, making the morning so cool and inviting she took a leisurely detour along the Mississippi. As she walked along Levee Street and saw the steamboats, she naturally thought of Jean-Noël. It was almost two weeks since he wrote that he had found *La Sirene* safely berthed where he left her and volunteered her for an emergency mission he did not explain. He pleaded for her to keep baby Louis until he returned. Maddy didn't mind although she wondered how much longer he would be gone. The truth was that a servant and two infants interfered with her already strained relationship with Carlos, and she prayed that Jean-Noël would come soon so the household could return to normal.

She glanced downriver and smiled when she saw the French warship *Milan* drop anchor near the Union fleet. Just like the history books say, she thought. The sleek man-o-war had come to protect French citizens, and Captain Alexandre de Clouet would soon be aboard the *Hartford,* vigorously protesting Farragut's ultimatum to evacuate the city. Clouet, never a man to mince words, would call it a "barbarous act" and cite the hundreds of innocent French residents who couldn't possibly leave in such a short time. For Farragut, it would be the final thorn in his side, and by the end of the day he would write Mayor Monroe stating that he was turning the city over to Major-General Benjamin Butler and leaving New Orleans for good. Believing themselves triumphant, the citizens would rejoice, but Maddy shuddered as she conjured the difficult days to come. Far more worrisome than Farragut, Butler was a petty, thieving, small-minded brute destined to become the city's worst nightmare. His most hateful abuses would be directed toward, of all people, the women of New Orleans.

"Fasten your seatbelts, girls," Maddy said to herself, paraphrasing Bette Davis in *All About Eve.* "It's gonna be a bumpy month."

She took a final look at the sleek, graceful *Milan* before turning up Hospital Street and continuing down Rampart. Félicité was especially ebullient that morning, greeting her with kisses and hugs and spinning around to show off her forest green taffeta dress.

Maddy smiled, catching Félicité's high spirits. "A gift from Joseph, no doubt."

"That's only part of what he did, the dear, dear man." Félicité stopped spinning and sat.

"He promised not to enlist in the army, at least not any time soon. I was so afraid he'd go running off, like so many of our brave boys in gray."

"I'm delighted to hear it." Maddy produced the petition and explained its purpose. Félicité happily signed but her mind was clearly elsewhere. "What are you thinking about?"

"I'm thinking about how many heads I'll turn in my new dress," Félicité laughed. "Shall we go for a stroll?"

"I'd like nothing better, my dear. It's a lovely day."

"Wonderful." Félicité happily clapped her hands. "I have a new parasol too!"

"*Mais,* it's so overcast you won't need it."

"Since when do I let weather interfere with fashion?" Félicité chirped.

Moments later, the two strolled arm-in-arm from Rampart Street to glamorous Esplanade Street, the wealthy Creole's undisputed thoroughfare for fashionable promenading. Félicité adored it, especially when some unsuspecting white gentleman tipped his hat. Her mood remained bubbly as they passed one mansion after another and she positively beamed when Maddy insisted the dress did wonderful things for her eyes.

"Merci." Félicité fussed with the elaborate kimono sleeves. "I know it's a bit much for morning wear, but I couldn't help myself."

"It's such a pretty day we should've brought little Louis along."

"C'est vrai. I do adore playing with him. He's such a sweet-natured child."

"And I appreciate you letting Hagar bring him over. I never suspected you would find a baby so entertaining."

"Joseph enjoys him too, but I'm certainly not encouraging him to start a family. The times are simply too precarious."

"I should think so."

"Mais, how much do you know about Hagar? I've never met anyone who's so quiet, especially a woman."

"Only that she belonged to Five Oaks plantation."

"Does she ever talk?"

"The most I ever heard her say was to thank Captain Baptiste for her freedom."

"And her baby? It's so fair! I don't suppose you know who fathered it."

"I've no idea." Maddy didn't want to think it might be Jules. "What does it matter?"

"Oh, it doesn't. I was only making conversation, but I must say she's absolutely wonderful with the babies. They almost never cry, and when they do she knows how to quiet them down." Félicité stiffened her hold on Maddy's arm. "Do you see what's coming our way?"

"You mean those soldiers?"

"Exactly!" Félicité hissed. "Let's show those dirty Yankees what we think of them."

"What do you mean?"

"You'll see."

Actually Maddy knew what was coming. When the soldiers were within a few feet,

Félicité glared as she yanked her long skirts aside with dramatic flurry and made a great show of preventing her hem from touching the enemy. The performance had precisely the desired effect, prompting the soldiers to mutter obscenities as they hurried by.

"I believe I made my loyalties clear," Félicité said with satisfaction. "Oh, I meant to tell you. I've been talking to a woman who is making Confederate cockades and ribbons to be pinned on hats and dresses. I ordered some for both of us."

"That's very thoughtful."

"She's also compiled a list of things Confederate ladies should do upon encountering the enemy."

"Such as?"

"Oh, crossing the street if there is a crowd of soldiers, and, mind you, being quite obvious about it. She also recommends getting off omnibuses and streetcars if soldiers come aboard and changing pews if they venture into our churches. And of course we should sing Southern songs, especially 'Dixie' and 'Lorena.'" When Maddy didn't respond, Félicité asked, "You do think it's a good idea, don't you?"

"Bien sûr, ma chère."

Maddy was lying. She knew all about the consequences of obeying these new Confederate etiquette rules, and that the patriotic, well-meaning lady suggesting them could never have imagined she would trigger an explosion of outrage traveling halfway around the world.

59

Another week passed with no word from Jean-Noël.
Maddy was worried but directed her concern to General Butler who wasted no time in seizing control of New Orleans
and ruling with an iron hand. His first act was trumping up
conspiracy charges against Mayor Monroe, the chief of police
and a prominent city judge. After dispatching them to Fort
Pickens, Butler appointed General George Shepley as Mayor
and named his provost marshal, Captain French, chief of police. The citizenry fumed at such underhanded tactics and
flagrant disregard for the law, but "Beast Butler" was only
getting started. With city government firmly in his pocket,
he turned his spiteful eye on the people themselves. He im-
prisoned William Mumford for tearing down the flag, seized
$800,000 from the office of the Dutch consul, censored the
local newspapers, forbade churches from fasting for the Confederacy and arrested clergymen who refused to pray for
President Lincoln. He acquired another nickname, "Spoons
Butler," for confiscating the silver of a New Orleans woman
trying to cross Union lines, but the worst abuse came when
his men complained of insults from not just the town's le-
gions of prostitutes but also its high-born ladies. Irritation
grew when he heard of dirty dishwater tossed from balconies
as soldiers passed beneath, and women like Félicité drawing
their skirts aside as though his men were contaminated. Annoyance turned to outrage when he saw a chamber pot with
his likeness painted inside, a great favorite, he was told, in
the town's many bordellos. His response came May 15 with
Order No. 28, quickly nicknamed the "Woman Order." Nailed
onto buildings and wrapped around lampposts throughout
the city, Order No. 28 gave soldiers the power to act against

any woman they deemed disrespectful, which could lead to arrest, overnight detention and a fine of five dollars. It naturally triggered public indignation from the elite uptown Garden District to the downtown brothels of Gallatin Street. Maddy already knew a great deal about its ramifications, but was angered anew when she saw it freshly printed and fluttering from her building.

"As officers and soldiers of the United States have been subject to repeated insult from women calling themselves the ladies of New Orleans, in return for the most scrupulous non-interference and courtesy on our part, it is ordered that hereafter, when any female shall by mere gesture or movement insult, or show contempt for any officers or soldiers of the United States, she shall be regarded and held liable to be treated as a woman about town plying her vocation."

Maddy made sure no one saw her tear down the offending poster before hurrying inside to show Carlos. Thus far he had said only that he thought Butler's actions were questionable, but he conceded this was inexcusable.

"I suppose the old boy's gone too far with this one."

"You suppose?!" Maddy was seething. "Do you realize this means I can be arrested for prostitution simply by snubbing some silly soldier?"

"Maybe Butler won't try to enforce it once he hears how outraged everyone is."

"To the contrary, my dear. Outraging people is what that monster does best. After this, I venture to say there's no limit to his abuse. I wouldn't be surprised if he suddenly...oh, no!"

"What is it?"

"Félicité!"

"What about her?"

"I'll bet she hasn't seen this!" Maddy told him about Félicité's interaction with the soldiers on Esplanade Street and her firm commitment to displaying Confederate loyalties. "She plans to spend the day shopping and, knowing how much she hates Yankees, she's bound to get into trouble." Maddy

324 | Michael Llewellyn

checked her pendant watch. "Maybe I can catch her before she leaves."

"I'm going with you."

"*Mais,* our relationship is a secret."

"She'll find out sooner or later, dearest, and, besides, you need to take a man along. The city's mood will be especially hazardous once that order circulates."

"Alright." She gave him a quick kiss. "Let's hurry!"

Carlos tugged on his jacket and grabbed his hat before trailing Maddy down the stairs. As they rushed up Ursulines Street, they saw knots of people on street corners and balconies, standing in front doors and leaning out windows. They didn't need to overhear conversations to know everyone was discussing Butler's newest offense. When they rounded the corner of Rampart and looked toward Félicité's house, they knew they were too late.

"Oh, no!" Maddy gasped.

Félicité was heading in their direction, elbow in the firm grip of a Union soldier. Her face was flushed with anger, and she struggled to break free every few steps. She screamed when she spotted Maddy.

"For the love of God, help me!" she cried in French. "This fool is trying to arrest me!"

The young private understood not a word. "You'd best keep still and come along, miss."

Carlos stepped forward. He was a good deal taller than the soldier and spoke with authority. "What seems to be the problem?" he asked in English.

The soldier scowled. "It's none of your concern, rebel!"

Carlos laughed heartily. "You assume I'm a Confederate, young man, when in fact I'm a citizen of France departing tomorrow on the *Milan.*" Maddy duly noted his exaggerated French accent. "I assure you my loyalties lie with His Imperial Highness Napoleon III, and that I am most anxious to leave this wretched Southern pesthole."

"What's that got to do with this wench?"

"Wench?" Carlos feigned shock. "Good heavens, lad. This is Madam Félicité Chevalier, *La Comtesse d'Petit Fours!!*" Maddy knew Carlos was making this up as he went along and suppressed a smile at the soldier's befuddlement. "She is a friend of mine and a French citizen as well. May I ask the nature of her offense?"

"She crossed the street when she saw me coming," the soldier said, embarrassed to state the ridiculous offense. "That's, uh, a violation of Order No. 28."

"I don't believe I'm familiar with such an order," Carlos lied. "It must be new."

"Yes, sir. General Butler issued it this morning."

Carlos turned to Félicité and told her in French to play along. Being a courtesan had taught her plenty about acting, so she spoke a few words and stopped struggling. Afraid she would laugh, Maddy looked away when Félicité conjured a few real tears.

"Merci, Madam La Comtesse," Carlos looked back at the solder. "She says she knows nothing about the new law and was merely crossing the street to visit a friend."

The man cocked his head. "Are you sure?"

"Oh, absolutely. Like me, the lady is a French citizen who cares nothing for American politics. Surely, under these circumstances, a gentleman with esteemed judgment such as yourself can make a timely exception."

The private was annoyed by the flowery language. "Ignorance ain't no excuse, sir. Now get out of my way."

Carlos didn't budge. "One moment, young man. I assure you if you arrest a French countess you will expose yourself and your superiors to a great deal of embarrassment. The wise thing would be to forget the whole unfortunate incident." While Carlos talked he extracted his wallet and produced a sizable roll of bills. Maddy's eyes widened as he peeled off a few dollars and passed them to the soldier's free hand. Knowing enlisted men were always looking to augment their meager pay, he was not surprised when the youth eagerly pocketed the money and released Félicité's arm. "You are a gentleman and a scholar, young sir," Carlos said, bowing politely.

"And the perfect example of everything Northern," Maddy added with a syrupy smile.

The soldier was hopelessly bewildered. "Alright, but from now on you people better pay attention to our laws. This is the United States and I don't care if you are foreigners."

"By all means," Carlos said, tipping his hat before the boy scurried down the street. He looked at the ladies. "That was close."

"Indeed it was," Maddy said, love and admiration dancing in her eyes. "Perhaps chivalry is not dead after all."

Félicité looked thoroughly confused, but to Maddy's relief didn't ask why she and Carlos were together. "I'm very grateful for what you did, Hector, but I don't understand what happened with that soldier."

"We shouldn't talk about it in the street," Maddy warned. She turned back to Carlos. "And for heaven's sake put that money away before someone sees it and knocks you in the head. Where on earth did you get such a sum?"

Carlos grinned mischievously. "Same place I got this." When he tucked his wallet back inside his jacket, he flashed an elegant gold pocket watch. "Brand new too."

"It must've cost a fortune," Félicité said, well acquainted with costly things.

Before Carlos could respond, Maddy said, "We shouldn't be discussing this in the streets either. We'll talk about it at home."

Carlos checked the time before pocketing his watch again. "I'm afraid it will have to wait, my dear. I have business meetings all morning." He gave Maddy an apologetic smile. "I'll explain everything this afternoon."

"Alright, darling."

When he was out of earshot, Félicité asked, "What were

you doing with Hector and for heaven's sake why did he call you 'my dear' and why did you call him 'darling'?"

"Let's go to my apartment," Maddy said. "We need to have a long talk."

Félicité's eyes were wide with wonder. "Indeed we do!"

60

It took Maddy the better part of the morning to explain, and, at times, justify her liaison with Carlos. As she feared, Félicité's prejudices rendered her shocked and skeptical and would surely have been worse had Carlos not come to her rescue that morning.

"I appreciate the man's valor," she conceded, "but he was still a slave."

"Through no fault of his own," Maddy reminded her. It needled her that a courtesan, albeit originally high-born, haughtily disdained a self-educated man like Carlos, but she knew there was no challenging the ingrained caste system or defusing Félicité's attitude with the revelation that the man's grandfather was a Spanish viceroy. The most she could hope for was some sort of emotional détente.

"Rules are rules, and his circumstances are not of my making," Félicité declared. When Maddy merely stared, Félicité threw up her hands in dismay. "Oh, dear. It's all so complicated, isn't it? This convoluted world we live in."

"True enough. It's also one where we should seize love and happiness wherever we find it, don't you agree?"

"I suppose," Félicité conceded. "Although it was doing that very thing that forever trapped me in a life I despise."

"I know." It was a discussion they'd had many times, but Maddy pursued it in hopes of making peace between her lover and dearest friend. "I admired your gamble and hoped you would admire mine too."

"Gamble?"

"*Mais, oui.* You gambled on happiness with Philippe, like I'm gambling on happiness with Carlos. He came into my life like a bolt of lightning, and we don't choose who we fall in love with, do we?"

"No, I suppose not."

"And we want others we love to share our happiness, do we not?"

Félicité gave her a long look. "I understand your argument, *mon ami.* I want nothing but happiness for you, but this particular man is so…so very difficult for me to accept. Our histories are so long and intertwined."

Maddy made one last attempt at breaching the void. "Then I want you to do something for me."

"Anything, *ma chère.*"

"Imagine you know absolutely nothing about Carlos, nothing about his background or history or especially that he belonged to your father."

"But that's impossible."

"It shouldn't be. Not for someone who so often lives in a world of fantasy."

The reference to Félicité's profession was a frantic arrow, but it hit the bull's eye.

"Go on," Félicité said coolly.

"Imagine a dashing Spaniard approached you in the *Salle d'Orléans* and—"

"Please don't ask me to do this, Maddy."

"But I want you to see what can happen when we look beyond social stereotypes and racial profiling."

Félicité frowned. "I don't know what those words mean."

Maddy quickly replaced her modern terminology with a timeless albeit stale adage. "You mustn't judge a book by its cover."

"Agreed, but, again, you must understand how difficult this is when I've known the man all my life."

"I'm only asking that you try. For my sake, and his too of course."

"Then give me a moment." Félicité closed her eyes and grew still. Maddy became increasingly anxious, and when she thought she couldn't bear the tension another moment, Félicité broke her silence.

"Alright, my dear. I'm going to tell you something Hector once said, something I've never told another living soul." Maddy's heart clutched hard. "Please remember that talk between us was strictly limited and never, ever included anything of a personal nature. There was one exception, and I've never forgotten it." Félicité fiddled with a lacy cuff. "The night before I was to run away with Philippe, Hector told me he knew about our plans. I never knew how he found out, but everyone knows house servants are the eyes and ears of plantation families." Maddy thought ruefully of Cato. "I fully expected him to tell Papa, but he said only that he wanted to wish us well. I couldn't have been more shocked."

"But that's wonderful!" Maddy cried.

"It seems so now, but then it was all so frightening and confusing. Something forbidden had been breached with his unexpected confidence. I was grateful but at the same time felt vulnerable and somehow obliged."

"Would that be such a bad thing?" Félicité shook her head no, embarrassed as they both thought of her refusal to help Carlos find employment. "And was that not a glimpse behind the book cover?"

"Yes, I suppose it was, and I now understand what you mean. His was an act of pure human kindness and caring, of wishing for someone that which he could not have himself."

"Happiness and love," Maddy finished.

Félicité looked slightly stricken. "I know you'll find this impossible to understand, but I never thought a slave could experience emotions the way we do. I had suspicions of course but always dismissed them."

Maddy couldn't imagine the social indoctrination and caste biases drummed into this woman since she was a child. "And now?" she pressed gently.

"Now I feel terrible for thinking such a thing."

Maddy wished Félicité would say she was sorry or wrong,

but she praised what she knew was a heroic effort. "I'm very pleased to hear you say that."

"Then you do understand me?" Félicité asked a bit breathlessly.

"Much better now. Like Carlos, you were forced into circumstances not of your choosing and you handled them as best you could."

"I never thought of it like that, but, yes. You're right."

"Thank you, darling. I know that was a difficult admission."

"In that case," Félicité continued, "I may as well make another one."

Maddy noted a mischievous tone creeping into her voice. "Oh?"

"If I had never known Hector and he had come into the *Salle d'Orléans* and offered to be my protector, I would have accepted him in a heartbeat."

Tears of joy burned Maddy's eyes as she rushed to embrace her friend. "You've no idea how happy that makes me!" After a moment she added, "But please call him Carlos. The name Hector died with his slave life."

Félicité looked grim. "Like my life died that first night I attended the balls." She thought a moment. "Perhaps he and I have more in common than I realized."

"Including someone who loves you both very much," Maddy said.

"In spite of my beliefs?"

Maddy chuckled. "In spite of everything." Félicité tried to look hurt, but the twinkle in her eyes said she was amused. Maddy hugged her again. "My goodness but we're an odd pair."

"The oddest." Félicité's visible relief told Maddy she was glad the awkward conversation was over. "Ah, look who's here."

The women smiled as Hagar appeared with Louis freshly fed, bathed and diapered. Every day at noon Maddy took charge of the baby to give Hagar time with her own child, but today Félicité insisted on taking him. Maddy couldn't resist a little teasing as Hagar slipped Louis into Félicité's arms and returned to her room.

"Aren't you worried about your new dress?"

"Don't be silly." Félicité reconsidered and rolled her eyes. "Well, maybe a little."

"What on earth?!" A woman's scream sent Maddy rushing onto the balcony. In the streets below she saw early signs of the bedlam that would trademark the day as the ladies of New Orleans began their battle of wills with Yankee troops. Maddy knew it was inevitable, but her liberated sensibilities made it difficult to register an utterly surreal scenario. Félicité was less reticent when Maddy called inside to explain the disturbance.

"I want to scream too," Félicité called back, shifting the wiggling baby to make him more comfortable. "I can't imagine what President Davis will say about this outrage."

"I'm sure we'll find out soon enough."

Maddy was appalled by the spectacle of another Southern lady being manhandled by a pair of Union soldiers. She recognized the unfortunate woman as a neighbor and held her temper to keep from shouting and suffering the same fate. Although she knew she had nothing to fear, she was nonetheless alarmed when someone rang the downstairs bell. She was relieved to welcome someone she never expected to see again.

"Auguste!"

"Hello, Maddy." He kissed both cheeks and followed her upstairs. "You're well I trust."

"I am indeed." She stepped back and looked at him, disturbed by the dark circles under his eyes. "And you?"

Auguste didn't answer, distracted by his nephew and the beautiful woman holding him. "Who is this?"

"My friend Félicité Chevalier. You've heard me mention her."

"Of course."

"This is Auguste Brasseaux, Félicité."

Félicité smiled at the rugged visitor dressed in trapper's gear. "A pleasure, m'sieur."

Maddy watched Auguste kneel beside Félicité and inspect the bundle in her arms. One look at little Louis and he began weeping. When he buried his face in his hands, Maddy was instantly at his side.

"Auguste! What is it? Tell me what's happened!"

"Please forgive me," he muttered. Auguste walked away and kept his back to the women until he regained his self control. He turned around slowly, as though forcing himself to face Maddy. His face was a mask of anguish. "I'm sorry to have to tell you this, dearest Maddy, but Jean-Noël has been killed."

Maddy's hand flew to her mouth, and, without realizing it, she sank onto the couch.

"Mais, non!"

"Poor Captain Baptiste!" Félicité cried.

Auguste sat beside Maddy and took her hands. "Since bringing you here, he has been operating *La Sirene* as a ferry between Baton Rouge and Vicksburg, transporting troops and arms and supplies before the Yankees press north from New Orleans and cut our supply lines. Three nights ago he was running by Natchez when *La Sirene* struck a snag which ripped through her hull. According to eyewitnesses, she capsized in minutes. Most of the crew and passengers made it to shore, but Jean-Noël was lost along with his ship."

"Lost or dead?" Maddy asked anxiously. "Is there a possibility that he—?"

Auguste squeezed her hands. "His body washed up on the Louisiana side of the Mississippi the next morning. He was buried where he was found, beside the river he loved." He gave Maddy an agonized look. "I wish he could rest forever beside Madeleine, but no one knows exactly where he was laid to rest on that muddy levee."

334 | Michael Llewellyn

Maddy nodded slowly. "I understand."

The room was deadly still for a moment before erupting with wails as Louis began to cry. "It's as if he knows his papa is gone," Félicité said, rocking him and clucking to quiet him. "Hush, my angel. Hush."

Auguste went to her. "Please give him to me, mademoiselle." Félicité slipped the bawling baby into his uncle's arms and, like Maddy, watched, puzzled, as the man began whistling a tune. To their amazement, the baby stopped crying and gurgled as though singing along with the melody. Auguste smiled sadly and turned to Maddy. She knew what was coming before he said the words.

"I'll take the boy to the bayous and raise him as my own. My neighbor's wife has a newborn and she can nurse him."

Maddy nodded agreement. "I'll have Hagar pack his things."

"Thank you for keeping him all this time. I know Jean-Noël was also grateful."

"De rien."

Maddy had another big surprise when she found Hagar had already stashed Louis's things in a carpetbag and was herself packed and ready to go. "I'll be leaving too," she said quietly.

"But where will you go?" Maddy asked.

Hagar glanced skyward. "I reckon He'll guide me."

Maddy experienced a twinge of loss as the last ties with Five Oaks began unraveling. "I won't let you leave unless you let me give you a little something."

Hagar drew herself up. "I got my freedom and my gold coin. Don't need nothin' more."

Maddy fought tears as she hugged this enigmatic woman with whom she had been through so much. "Thank you, Hagar," she whispered. "For so many things." Hagar nodded silently and was gone.

Moments later, Maddy steeled herself for another goodbye and walked Auguste downstairs where she embraced him and kissed the baby a final time. She understood now that this had been the child's destiny all along. More importantly, as little Louis headed for bayou country, she understood why she had been repeatedly told that her Creole ancestors were Cajun.

61

Maddy slept badly, little wonder since June 7 was a day she greeted with great dread. She stood on her balcony and sipped coffee, wary of morning skies resembling tarnished pewter and air heavy enough to feel. They were appropriately foreboding, as was the loud pounding of nails reverberating four blocks away. A scaffold with a strange horizontal flagstaff was being erected before the newly renamed United States Mint, the stage for an execution scheduled for eleven o'clock. Maddy's heart hurt every time she heard another nail pounded into place.

The more she thought about it, the less she could believe William Mumford was headed for the gallows, nor understand why the August Ones had set the poor man in her path. It was another cruel twist on a journey peppered with personal tragedy and, of late, more evildoing by General Butler. When Butler ordered Mumford arrested for tearing down the Union flag the day New Orleans fell, she thought the Beast would merely humiliate the man. Mumford was a bonafide folk hero after all, but Butler, determined to make an example of the man, had him convicted of treason and sentenced to death. As news of the verdict spread, the argument arose that New Orleans was a Confederate City at the time of the deed and that Mumford was only doing his patriotic duty. Crowds gathered at city hall demanding to know how such an act could be considered treasonous. Threats were made against Butler's life, and with rumors of insurrection to prevent the execution, New Orleans was unbearably tense. "Good morning, dearest." Maddy jumped at the sound of Carlos's voice as he joined her on the gallery. "I didn't mean to frighten you."

"I've been jumpy since I got up. Poor Mary must feel like Calpurnia on the Ides of March."

"Calpurnia?" he asked sleepily.

"Julius Caesar's wife." He gave her a quizzical look. "You haven't forgotten what's happening today, have you?"

"I wouldn't miss it. Now, are you coming with me?"

"Of course not!" Maddy knew public executions were well attended spectacles, but found them as repulsive as slave auctions in the St. Louis Hotel. "The whole idea is barbaric."

"Only because you have such strange sensibilities. Don't you realize that the great majority of the spectators will be there to honor Mumford and pay their respects?"

"A peculiar way to honor an innocent man if you ask me." She cocked her head. "And what do you mean I have 'strange sensibilities'?"

"It's not important." Carlos headed inside the kitchen and looked for coffee as Maddy followed.

"It must be important or you wouldn't have mentioned it."

Carlos filled his coffee cup and sat at the kitchen table. "It's good with Hagar and the babies gone, eh? Don't you like having the place to ourselves again?"

Maddy bristled. "You're changing the subject."

"Actually, what I'm doing is avoiding an argument."

"We don't argue. We discuss." When Carlos sipped silently, she gave him a verbal push. "All relationships need to grow, my love, ours included, and keeping things from each other is a step in the wrong direction."

"I'm not keeping things from you, Maddy. It's just that—"

"That what?"

"Sometimes you say peculiar things."

Maddy wondered if it was more peculiar than lacing nineteenth-century speech with twenty-first-century slang. "Such as?"

"Calling public executions barbaric when they've been around for hundreds of years."

"That doesn't make them any more civilized than Rome's gladiatorial games."

"Those gladiators are something I wish I could have seen," Carlos confessed.

Too bad you can't rent the Russell Crowe movie or watch the HBO series on Rome, Maddy thought. "That's beside the point."

"No, it's not. I appreciate your opposition to slavery but I don't understand your objection to the treatment of women. They're worshipped and adored and—"

"Put on pedestals?"

"Exactemente."

"And left on those pedestals while men go elsewhere for amusement, *n'est-ce pas?*"

Carlos looked shocked. "Maddy!"

"Is this not true?"

Carlos pursed his lips. "For some men, I suppose, but not I."

"Lucky for me, you're an exception to the rule, but do you think that's right and fair?"

"Maybe, maybe not. What matters is that it's the rule. It's accepted behavior. It's normal."

"Normal is a setting for a hair dryer, that's all."

"A hair dryer?" Carlos grimaced. "That's exactly what I'm talking about. These strange words and phrases that go unexplained. Selfohn. Blahg. Google. Sometimes it's like you're speaking a foreign language, and when I ask for a translation you change the subject or say you meant something else." He shook his head. "Since I've never been anywhere except Cuba and Louisiana, I've wondered how Natchez could be so different, but even that doesn't make sense. In some ways you're downright mysterious."

"Nonsense."

"Then explain what a hair dryer is."

"Someone who fans wet hair," Maddy replied, "and they're perfectly normal in Natchez."

She didn't know if Carlos accepted her ridiculous explanation but she was relieved when he picked up the morning newspaper and read. "*Mon dieu!* President Davis is so angered by the Woman Order that he's put a price on Butler's head."

"The President should take a number," Maddy blurted.

"What did you say?"

"I meant that a number of people would like to kill Butler. That's an execution I'd gladly witness."

Carlos chuckled. "You little hypocrite."

"Not at all," Maddy retorted. "Some executions are justified. Mumford's most definitely is not, while Butler's demise would be a service to mankind."

"No argument there."

"Thank you." Maddy was grateful that they didn't disagree further. Despite his strong Union sympathies, Carlos concurred that the occupied city didn't deserve Butler's cruelty and corruption. "What else does the paper say?"

"The Order has been condemned overseas too. Lord Palmerston in Parliament called it 'infamous,' and U.S. Secretary Seward apologized to the British chargé in Washington for Butler's 'perverted' phraseology. The French called it 'an unpardonable affront to womanhood.'"

"As Butler is an unpardonable affront to mankind." Maddy sneered. "This hanging is indefensible."

"Perhaps someone will intervene."

"How is that possible when Butler has announced there will be troops everywhere?"

"Surprises are nothing new in this town." Carlos sipped his coffee and added more sugar. "And the biggest is yet to come."

"Meaning what?"

"Meaning nothing."

"Now who's being mysterious?" When Carlos buried his nose in the newspaper, Maddy wondered if this was another reference to his secret pact for taking revenge against the Confederacy. She didn't want to think about it on such a mis-

340 | Michael Llewellyn

erable day. "Go if you like," she said, seized by a new wave of revulsion. "I can't bring myself to watch a friend murdered."

"Alright, my dear." He finished his coffee. "I promised to meet some people, so I'd best be on my way."

"What about your breakfast?"

"I'm meeting them at Café Fernandina and will get something to eat there." He leaned across the table and kissed her. "Will you be alright?"

"I don't know," she admitted, "but don't worry yourself."

"I'll stay here if you want me to. I mean it."

Maddy smiled. "I know you do, and that's why I love you." She kissed him back and waved her hand. "Now, shoo!"

With Carlos gone, the next few hours dragged. Maddy wandered the apartment and repeatedly went onto the gallery, as though she might hear or see something announcing that the deed was done. She couldn't stop thinking about Carlos's insistence that attending public executions was a show of respect. As that notion took root, Maddy decided she was doing Mumford a disservice and understood what she must do. She grabbed her bonnet and quickly covered the short distance to the Mint.

"My God!" she gasped as she approached the corner of Levee and Esplanade Streets. The crowd was huge, spreading like a wave from the front of the Mint across the two traffic lanes and neutral ground of the broad Esplanade. Maddy wound her way through the throngs, trying to get a view through the forest of towering top hats and a heavy detachment of infantry with fixed bayonets. The best spot she could find was on the steps of a mansion across the boulevard. From there she discerned the scaffold, the makeshift flagstaff and a lone figure in white. Maddy began to weep when she recognized the tropical linen suit Mumford so often wore.

She listened to a Negro officer read Mumford's offense and watched a priest mount the platform and huddle with the accused. She wished she could hear Mumford's brief address but turned away when the noose was put into place. She closed her eyes and wept harder when the wooden drop fell with a resounding crash. A few women screamed and wailed before a collective groan rose from the Mint and spread across Esplanade like a bitter cloud. The drums began a steady beat as Maddy joined a crowd dispersing in silence. The drumbeat followed her down the street and continued until she reached her front door.

"Farewell, William," she whispered skyward, face streaked with tears. "And Godspeed."

Part 9

"If I am pressed to say why I loved him,
I feel it can be explained only by replying:
'Because it was he; because it was me.'"

— Montaigne

62

Maddy had never been prone to depression, but as the days passed following the loss of Madeleine and Jean-Noël and Mumford's execution, she was plagued with sadness. It hardly helped that Félicité was mourning the loss of her protector. Like many other steadfast Confederates, Moran attended Mumford's hanging only to succumb to patriotic fever and visited Félicité just long enough to say good-bye before rushing to Mississippi to enlist in the Rebel army. Maddy had scarcely finished comforting Félicité when she learned Mary Mumford, left almost penniless after her husband's execution, had been evicted. She rented Mary a small apartment in the Rue Rampart and discreetly ensured that the poor woman had food on the table. Maddy entertained a certain amount of Southern pride when she heard Mary's new quarters had become a gathering place for Confederate loyalists, but it did not ease her ongoing melancholy. She remained drained and emotionally detached, a situation that worsened when Carlos began spending his evenings out and coming home at all hours. Maddy knew it involved his secret enterprise but didn't have the strength to question him and remained helpless as their lives continued to diverge.

One morning when she awoke so exhausted she couldn't get out of bed, Carlos brought her a cup of strong black coffee. "What's wrong, *mon cher?*"

"This dreadful heat," Maddy lied, not wanting him to know the real source of her insomnia. "I tossed and turned all night."

"I know, dear. I was there."

"Mmmm."

"Maybe we should take the train to the lake," he suggested. "There's usually a breeze on Pontchartrain, and, if nothing else, it will get you out of this stifling apartment."

"You're sweet, but I think I'll stay in bed. I'm so tired I'll surely fall asleep."

"You're certain?"

"I'm certain."

"Shall I tend to some errands then? You could probably use the peace and quiet."

"I think that's a fine idea."

"As you wish then." Carlos kissed her damp forehead. "Pleasant dreams."

The truth was Maddy needed to be alone to sort her thoughts, a prospect that seemed increasingly remote as the sun soared and turned the place into an oven. Bathed in sweat, head aching with despair, she shut her eyes and spoke to the heavy heat.

"I hope you can hear me, Henri, because I'm totally lost and confused. The war and all this death and misfortune have exhausted me and made personal relationships difficult too." She took a breath and wondered if the August Ones still withheld knowledge of Carlos from Henri. "For five days, since poor William was hanged, I've had no energy to continue my life here. Is it possible that my work is finished and that it's time for me to come home? If so, I am bewildered as to the purpose for my journey. Perhaps it was learning the truth about my family origins, and if that's the case I'm deeply grateful." She stretched and yawned. "But I can't help wondering if I'm destined for something more, and it's the not knowing that exhausts me so. I'm still yours to command, but if I don't hear something soon I'm afraid I'll lose my mind." She yawned again and turned onto her side. "Please, Henri. Please tell me what to do. I'm so…tired and…so…lost."

"I'm here, Maddy."

"Henri?" she cried. Caught in that netherworld world between sleep and wakefulness, she didn't realize she was dreaming. "Is it really you?!"

"*C'est moi, mon cher.* Talk to me."

"I'm frustrated and depressed," she confessed. "You know that's not like me."

"They're both signs that things are about to come full circle. Indeed, the reason you must rest today is to gather strength for what's to come."

"And what...what is that?" she asked slowly.

"Your mission of course."

"Can you please tell me more?"

"I'm told only that the next few days are crucial and that you will know what to do when the situation arises."

"I'm frightened," she whispered in a small voice.

"You shouldn't be. You've proven your mettle time and again, learning from each challenge and moving on to successfully confront more. I had no idea you would encounter so many obstacles and doubt I could have handled them as well. I'm still amazed that you attended Mumford's execution."

"At least tried to. Frankly I amazed myself that day." Maddy coughed softly and rolled onto her back. "But now I'm filled with apprehension."

"Don't be. Keep courage in your soul and me in your heart, and you'll be fine."

"Oh, Henri. You're forever in my heart."

"As you're in mine."

"But when can I come back to you?" When Maddy got no answer, she repeated herself again and again until another voice woke her up.

"Come back to who?"

"Carlos?" She squinted at the blurry figure in the doorway. "I...I thought you were gone."

"I came back for my watch."

"How long have you been standing there?"

"Long enough to hear you say those bizarre things."

She sat up and rubbed her eyes. "I must have been dreaming."

"A dream you have often enough. I've repeatedly heard about this Henri and your hopes for returning to him" Carlos glowered. "The man is more than a damned dream, Maddy."

"No, he's not," she insisted.

"Do you think I'm a fool?

"Of course not."

"Then who is Henri?"

"Someone from another life." Lord, she thought. Did I really say that? "He's certainly nobody you need be concerned with."

Maddy slipped from bed and went to the washstand, hoping a splash of water would help clear her head. Carlos lunged like a panther and grabbed her wrist. "Stop lying to me, woman.

You're seeing another man!"

"I'm not lying, and let go of me!" Her reaction was so fierce, he obeyed. "You always know where I am, Carlos. How could you possibly imagine there could be anyone else?"

"Félicité, of course."

"What has she to do with anything?"

"You say you're visiting her when in fact you're secretly—"

"Don't bother finishing that sentence. It's beyond ridiculous."

"You're the one who's ridiculous, you and your ideas about a woman's place in society. What was the stupid word you used? Liberated?" He laughed cruelly. "You know what I say to that? I say *merde!*"

Keep your cool, Maddy thought as she dipped both hands in the wash bowl and splashed her face. "I don't want to quarrel with you, Carlos, especially over something as silly as a daymare. They're worse than nightmares you know."

"I know nothing of the sort."

Maddy dried her face and hands and faced him squarely.

"This argument is about something else you know."

"What do you mean?"

"You've been brooding for days. Something's wrong."

"I've acted no stranger than you," he countered.

"Touché," Maddy conceded, wanting things to cool. "It's all understandable, you know."

Carlos's voice was softer now as he caught her mood. "How so?"

Maddy waved a hand. "The war and this dreadful occupation. Like everyone else, our lives are in turmoil. We're both rudderless, you more than I since you still can't find work."

"Perhaps."

"But that doesn't entitle us to take our frustrations out on each other."

"No, it doesn't." Carlos took her hands and kissed them both. "I'm sorry I shouted and grabbed you like that. You know I didn't mean it."

"I have to believe that, Carlos. The one thing I hate above all else is one human being hurting another, especially when they profess to be in love."

"Point taken, my darling." Carlos folded her into his arms. "You know what would cheer us up immeasurably?"

Maddy smiled. "Does it require my getting dressed?"

Carlos smiled too. "Well, I was about to offer buying you a new chapeau at Madam Poché's and lunch at the Hotel St. Louis, but if you have other ideas—"

63

Maddy welcomed Henri's reassurance, but it was a double-edged sword once she and Carlos made peace. They ignored the turmoil swirling around them as they took long walks during the day and enjoyed nights filled with sweet lovemaking. The only blight on their happiness was her knowledge that she would eventually leave him, so she greeted each morning as though it was their last. Then, as quickly as their ecstasy returned, it vanished, and Carlos along with it. When she awoke one morning and discovered he hadn't been home all night, she hurried to Félicité's house and spilled her fears.

"He's stayed out late before," she said, "but never all night. You know how dangerous New Orleans is these days. I'm terrified something awful has happened."

"I don't suppose you'd consider going to the police."

"Hardly!" Maddy snorted. "I can't imagine anything lower on their priority list than some Confederate woman who's lost her paramour. I'd be laughed out of the station house."

"I suppose you're right." Félicité took another bite of croissant and changed the subject. "What do you hear from M'sieur Brasseaux?"

"He's well, and the baby thrives."

"Do you suppose he'll join the army?"

"I know only that Auguste is his own man and definitely not one to follow the crowd. He was set to inherit Five Oaks but he gave it to his sister and chose the bayous instead."

"*Mais,* why on earth would he do that?"

"Freedom I suppose. He loathed plantation life."

"Did he loathe its comforts too?"

"He said the protocol strangled him and that he derives much more joy poling a pirogue through the swamps than dancing the Virginia reel in a ballroom."

Félicité was appalled. "What peculiar priorities."

"Perhaps, but I could easily have loved him."

"Madeleine St. Jacques! Do you mean that?" Félicité listened raptly as Maddy told her about her brief fling with Auguste. "Why did it end?"

"It was one of those liaisons not meant to last," Maddy explained, catching herself before calling it a one-night-stand. "I knew from the beginning that he would go back to the bayous and I would come here."

Félicité pursed her lips, eyes dancing mischievously as she sipped her coffee. "You are deliciously wicked, mademoiselle!"

Maddy smiled. "I prefer to think of it as deliciously free."

"How I envy you."

"You shouldn't. I know my relationship with Carlos will also end soon."

"What?! Why would you say such a thing?"

"Because it's time for me to move on."

Félicité's high spirits plummeted. "Please tell me you're not going home to Natchez!"

"I don't know yet." Maddy hadn't planned on revealing any future departure that particular day, but the moment seemed to warrant it. She moved to comfort Félicité when she saw the dread on her friend's pretty face. "I won't be leaving for a while."

"*Mais, non,* Maddy! I couldn't bear it!" Félicité stood so suddenly her full sleeves sent the coffee cup flying. She ignored it and threw her arms around Maddy's neck. "I won't let you go! Do you hear me? I won't let you leave me!"

"I don't want to leave either, darling, but there are circumstances beyond my control."

"What circumstances? Surely it's not something you can't tell your best friend."

"It's not that simple, my dear. If I could tell you I would, but it's a sort of secret."

"A secret?!" As Maddy suspected, Félicité's curiosity went into overdrive. She pulled away and stared, eyes widening. "It's something to do with the war, isn't it? You're going on some kind of secret mission!" Before Maddy could respond, Félicité's flight of fantasy soared higher still. "Aha! I have it! You're going to spy for the Confederacy!"

Maddy ignored the absurd notion and decided to let Félicité think whatever she liked. Anything, even something that far-fetched, was preferable to the truth. She took her friend's hands and held tight.

"You won't tell anyone, will you?"

"Of course not! Oh, Maddy! How selfish of me. Here you are, going off to help the Confederate cause, and I'm thinking only of myself." Maddy ignored a rush of guilt as Félicité hugged her again. "When will you return?"

"Promises are unwise during war time, Félicité. You know that."

"I do indeed." Félicité went back to her chair. "After Joseph left, I thought about going home to Isle Brevelle, but Mother writes that I should stay here." She looked helpless. "The planters have been ordered by the government to switch from cotton to food crops, provender for themselves and the army, but there's a terrible drought. *Maman et grand-mère* barely have enough to eat. I'm worried sick about them, but she insists they're alright and says I'd just be another mouth to feed. I feel so helpless."

"I'm so sorry. Forgive me for asking, but how are you for money?"

"Joseph left me a little something, but it won't last forever."

"Please promise you're not considering *Le Salon Bleu*."

"I promise. In truth I would never have been able to do such a thing, but especially not now with the place patronized by Yankee soldiers and other rabble."

Maddy had a sudden brainstorm. "*Écoute!* Maybe there's another way to make the Yankee presence work for us."

"What do you mean?"

"When I was trying on her hats at Madam Poché's shop, she mentioned she was desperate for help. Her girls all quit because they refuse to wait on the Union officer's wives, and—"

"And you think I wouldn't refuse?"

"Hunger and patriotism make strange bedfellows, Félicité." She thought of Carlos's words, "This is war, woman, not the opera."

"Oh, I don't know. So much has changed that I can't think straight any more."

"Think about keeping the wolf from the door," Maddy said.

Félicité gave her a half smile. "Now why would I want to do that, Maddy dear? It would be like losing an old friend."

64

Back home, Maddy was distressed to find Carlos still missing. She grabbed her copy of Balzac's *La Comédie Humaine* and went onto the gallery. She tried to divert her worries by immersing herself in the book and was welcoming a cool summer breeze when Carlos came up the stairs. She didn't know whether to be angry or grateful, but emotions won out as she threw herself in his arms. He kissed her sweetly and touched her lips before she could speak.

"Before you say anything, please let me explain," he said. "First, I'm very sorry I didn't come home last night." Maddy kept quiet as he ushered her to the couch and drew her down beside him. "I've been up all night, but before I tell you why I must ask you to promise to keep what I say a secret. You must tell no one, not even Félicité, because the consequences could mean life or death."

"Good heavens, Carlos!" Maddy trembled as he squeezed her hands, wondering if this began the final act of the August Ones. "Is it really so dire?"

"Promise me!"

"Alright then. I promise."

Carlos expelled his plan in one long breath. "We've found a way to end the war quickly."

"What?!"

"My time with William Mumford, shall we say, paid off in a most unexpected way. As you know I accompanied him to several card games, and things could get interesting toward the end of the evening. Men who drink too much talk too much, and Mumford's rich Confederate friends were proof positive."

Loose lips sink ships, Maddy thought.

"According to them, a great store of gold bullion was seized when Louisiana seceded and took over the U.S. Mint. Those federal workers swearing loyalty to the South were allowed to stay on as employees of the state, and the Confederate government began minting its own coinage, mostly half dollars. Nobody knows how much was put into circulation, but the bulk was stored in vaults at the Mint." Carlos stood and paced the room, excitement growing. "When the Yankees began closing in, naturally there was a rush to get the gold out of the city. Some was dispatched to Jackson on a train protected by the Confederate Guards and some was stashed with foreign consulates here in town, but nothing was done with those surplus gold coins. No one knows why the Confederate government waited so long, maybe because there was a collapse in communication when things got chaotic. The point is, the coins are still here."

Maddy was shocked. "You learned all this from Mumford's acquaintances?"

"Most of it. The rest I learned from the man who headed the mint operation." He smiled coldly. "When Louisiana seceded, I assure you he swore allegiance to the Confederacy only to save his job."

"How did you meet this man?"

"His name is Archie, and you need know no more than that. Suffice it to say there are places in every city where desperate men gather to commiserate. When such men have certain needs and goals in common, they make plans together. Do you understand?"

"I'm guessing this is the revenge you've hungered after," Maddy said evenly.

Carlos beamed. "Your guesswork is superb, my dear. When the mint ceased operations last fall, the Confederate government dismissed all employees except Archie and used the building to quarter troops. Archie collaborated with the government on a plan to move the gold coins in case of an emergency, but no one anticipated the waterfront being in flames. They were loading the gold onto a wagon when the wind shifted, and the fires blocked their escape route through the Faubourg Marigny. They got trapped on New Levee Street, so they drove the wagon into an empty lot behind the warehouse. When wind carried the fire there, Archie fled along the Pontchartrain train tracks, but the other men were killed when the warehouse collapsed. They're buried under the wreckage along with the gold."

Maddy's pulse quickened. "So you and Archie are the only ones who know its location?"

Carlos nodded. "The rains finally extinguished the fires, but by the time Archie found the coins, Union soldiers were under Butler's orders to stop anyone trying to flee the city. Carriages and wagons were searched along with their passengers, so there was no choice but to leave the treasure where it was."

Treasure, Maddy thought suddenly. Dear God! This must be the famous lost gold of the Confederacy! She'd heard the legends of course. One claimed it sank with a Savannah ship bound for France and another that it was lost in a train robbery in north Georgia. Still another said it was buried somewhere outside Richmond. Had she stumbled onto the truth?

"The city fell over a month ago. Why hasn't your friend moved the gold?"

"Because Yankee troops commandeered the warehouse next door for a storage facility. We spied on the place last night, and although only one soldier keeps regular watch, he'd notice anyone scavenging next door, much less loading that much cargo onto a wagon."

"It sounds like an impossible situation."

"Not with a decoy." Carlos sat again and looked hard into her eyes. "Especially a woman decoy."

A dull ache gripped Maddy's heart. "You can't be serious!"

"Of course I am, darling. You're absolutely perfect, brave and sure of yourself. I know no one better suited for the job."

Maddy tried desperately to reason. "Have you lost your mind? If you get caught you'll go to jail. You, Carlos, who's been a prisoner all your life!"

He ignored her argument. "There's more to it than that, Maddy. Much more. This isn't like robbing a bank, you know. It's about saving lives and entire cities. Without this fortune, the Confederacy can't finance the war much longer. With such limited resources and their ports blockaded, this will hasten the inevitable."

"If that's truly your goal, simply let General Butler have the gold."

Carlos snorted. "I may be a Unionist but I wouldn't give that bastard the time of day."

"Oh, I see. The truth is that you and your fellow thief want the gold for yourselves. For heaven's sake, man! Why all the grand pretense? Why not admit it?"

Carlos growled as his pious claim crumbled. "Alright then. So what if we keep the loot? You can't deny it would still be a great triumph for the Union."

While Carlos argued on, Maddy couldn't help weighing the overwhelming merit of ending the war three years before Appomattox. Hundreds of thousands of soldiers would not die and almost as many women would not be widowed and their children orphaned. Sherman would not burn Atlanta, Columbia and Richmond or execute his infamous March to the Sea. The South's economy would not be devastated for decades to come, and yet—

And yet, she thought, such a deed would change history and that was something she dared not allow. She was so lost in thought that she didn't realize Carlos had stopped talking.

"Well?"

"I'm sorry, Carlos. It's out of the question."

"But you don't even know what we need you to do. It's nothing more than a bit of acting."

"Carlos, I—"

He waved a hand, unhearing. "We'll go to New Levee

Street at two o'clock in the morning. All you have to do is go over to the officer standing watch and strike up a conversation. Once you have him talking, simply insult him."

"What?!"

"With Butler's Woman Order, he's duty bound to arrest you and that means leaving his post. Even if he takes you to the calaboose and comes right back, that will give us enough time to load the gold and make our getaway." When Maddy stared in disbelief, Carlos said, "It's absolutely foolproof."

"If it's so foolproof, find another girl. I'm sure there are plenty of local ladies who would be happy to insult the enemy, especially with payment involved."

Carlos grunted. "Archie and I have discussed this at length. There's a great fortune at stake and no one else we can trust with our plans. No one. Don't you understand?"

"I understand perfectly, Carlos. And you must understand that there's nothing you can say that will change my mind."

"Are you sure?"

"Positive. Now can we please talk about something else?"

Carlos studied her for a very long minute before reaching into his jacket pocket. "Perhaps this will change your mind."

Maddy's heart plummeted when he held out her L'Oreal lipstick, "Where did you get that?"

"A much more important question, my dear, is where did *you* get it?"

65

"I'm waiting, Maddy."

She struggled to remain calm and defuse the potentially explosive incident as deftly as possible. "Oh, there it is. I've been looking everywhere." She opened the lipstick and touched up her mouth. "Wherever did you find it?"

"On the bedroom floor," Carlos said, momentarily distracted. "When I was shaving yesterday morning I saw it lying by the washstand."

"Thank goodness." Maddy thought of her lie to Madam Poulard about the zippered bustier. "These lipsticks—"

Carlos snarled the word. "Lipsticks?"

"Yes. They're called lipsticks and they're very difficult to come by. An aunt bought this one in London some years ago, and I've never seen one since."

Carlos's next words chilled Maddy's soul. "I know damned well they're not available anywhere, mademoiselle. At least not in these times."

Maddy willed herself to stay cool. "What on earth are you talking about? There's a little shop on Regent Street near Picadilly Circus that—"

"Stop lying!" Carlos snapped. "I've been suspicious of your behavior for months,

Madeleine St. Jacques, or whoever you are. People from Natchez don't use all those peculiar adages, and much of what you say and do doesn't add up, especially when it comes to politics and history. Whenever I questioned you, there was always an explanation, but finally I began asking myself why your odd behavior continues."

Maddy folded her arms across her chest and looked out the window. "I've no idea what you're talking about."

"What about the time you mentioned a world war? No, not just a world war. A second world war! There is no such thing. What does facebook mean? And nine-eleven?" When she didn't respond, he said, "It's as if you're living in some sort of fantasy world with this Henri person or, I don't know, maybe another world altogether, and I'm not the only one who thinks so." He snatched the lipstick away. "I showed this to Archie last night. The man worked at a mint, Maddy. He's a metallurgist, and he said he had never seen anything like it. Not so much the metal but this other alien material!"

Plastic, Maddy thought. In the madness of the moment, she flashed on the scene in *The Graduate* when the man tells Dustin Hoffman his future lies in one word. Plastics. She smiled in spite of herself.

"I'm glad you think it's funny!" Carlos grunted. "I think whatever you're doing is dangerous and I also think you're in a lot of trouble."

"This is ridiculous, Carlos. You're making a mountain out of a molehill."

"We'll see about that. I count a number of Yankee officers in my new circle of friends and I want them to see this thing. Archie believes this peculiar material has potential in warfare."

Plastics in warfare, Maddy thought with dread. Dear God, man. You have no idea,

Carlos sat down and got right in her face. "You'd better listen to me and listen well. You have until tomorrow to come to your senses and start explaining yourself."

Maddy's temper awoke. "Who are you to give me ultimatums?"

"Someone who simply doesn't believe you're who you claim to be. We may be at war, but it's not impossible to telegraph Natchez and get the facts about you and your family." Carlos laughed when Maddy's face blazed. "Those red cheeks say you're hiding something, and the sooner you tell me the truth, the better."

360 | Michael Llewellyn

Maddy made a frantic stab at calming the storm. "Do you still love me, Carlos?"

Carlos pulled back, face undergoing a hideous transformation as he spat words that would brand her forever. "I never loved you, woman. You were nothing more than a convenience."

It took a few seconds for his awful pronouncement to register. "What are you saying?"

"That I used you, my dear, plain and simple. From the moment I saw you at Félicité's house, I suspected you could be of service. I was heady with my newfound freedom, you see. At first I sought only to use your connections for finding employment, but when I saw the opportunity for more—" His shoulders rose and fell as an evil leer crawled across his face. "Who was I to turn down a free place to stay, especially since it included such a warm, deliciously furnished bed?"

For a moment Maddy thought she might be sick. "I don't know who you are," she declared. "You can't be the Carlos I know and love."

"*Au contraire, ma chère.* I'm more myself now than ever before. It was all an act, you see, and believe me I was taught acting by the masters. How to say, *"Oui, m'sieur,"* and *"Mais, non, madam!"* when I truly wanted to tell all of them to go to the devil. I suppose you could say I was never off stage, until now, here, with you."

Maddy's gorge rose. "This isn't happening!"

"No? Then, consider this. Remember the morning you found me on your doorstep, all bruised and bloody? That was all carefully staged with a little help from Archie. Like that fanciful tale I told you about being dressed up as a blackamoor. Truth be told, that lady treated me quite nicely. Maligning her was an easy play for sympathy and, thanks to your big gullible heart, here I am." He tossed the lipstick in the air and caught it behind his back. "That's a little trick I learned as a child in Cuba."

Maddy shook her head, trying frantically to process all

this and wondering if the August Ones could be so cruel. "No!"

"While I'm being honest, I should also tell you I didn't spend all of last night watching that army warehouse. Most of the time I was with Charmaine."

Maddy could barely say the name. "Char...Charmaine?"

"My mistress, darling. Ask Félicité about her. They both worked at the *Salle d'Orléans* before it closed its doors. Oh, and I must tell you the most difficult part of this charade was pretending I was a virgin. Good God, woman. When I was at *Belle Rêve*, it was a rare night indeed that I didn't go carousing in the slave quarters. Why wouldn't I, especially when I was given extra privileges by the *maître* for every yellow bastard I sired?"

"I don't believe you!"

Carlos laughed callously. "I don't give a damn what you believe."

Maddy struggled for reason. "But Félicité said you were so kind to her and her family."

"And I suppose she told you I encouraged her to elope and even wished her well." Maddy nodded. "Ah, yes. That was the sweetest revenge of all. I knew Félicité's departure would break the old man's heart and split that damned family right down the middle. Her lover's death was merely *lagniappe,* driving her into a life of prostitution and her father to an early grave."

Maddy was speechless as Carlos clasped his hands behind his back and strutted like a prosecuting lawyer concluding his case.

"I strongly advise you to reconsider your decision not to help in tonight's adventure, unless you want me to contact the officials in Natchez and find out if you're who you claim to be. If you think about it, it's not really asking so much, and after it's over I'll disappear from your life forever. You can even keep all your strange secrets because I won't care any more, not that I ever did. Oh, and if you think you can knock me in the head and run away I have someone watching this house. You'd never get past the front door."

Maddy barely made it to the bedroom before retching violently into the washbasin.

The miserable day continued after Carlos disappeared, leaving his hideous revelations to haunt her. Her misery deepened when she went onto the gallery and identified her watchdog down in the street, a roguish sort who grinned and waved at his prisoner. If ever there was a time when she needed a cell phone to call for help, it was now. Maddy felt so powerless that she took off her pendant watch and stared at it, fingers trembling when she reached for the hidden compartment. As much as she wanted to flee home, she knew in her heart that her mission remained unfulfilled. She lay down in bed, desperately trying to fall asleep and conjure Henri, but her dreams were ugly daymares swirling around Carlos and his web of lies.

The terrible heat lingered, even as the sunlight began to fade and the air took on a thick dusty glow. She knew she should be hungry, especially after her bout of nausea, but the idea of food was repugnant. She realized she had nothing to do but wait for Carlos to return and put his plan into motion. Another long hour passed, and she watched shadows grow across the bedroom walls and disappear under the cloak of darkness. By now, respectable people would be home and the criminal element would emerge from the woodwork to work their evil magic. Carlos, she had no doubt, was with Archie or Charmaine or perhaps both. The stillness consumed her, so heavy now that Maddy jumped when she heard footsteps on the stairs. Thinking it was Carlos, she remained in the dark bedroom, silent and quaking with fear.

"Mademoiselle Madeleine!"

"My God!" she cried, sitting up so fast she grew dizzy. "Is that…Hagar?"

"Oui, mademoiselle. C'est moi!"

Maddy leapt from the bed and rushed into the living

room, almost knocking the woman down when she grabbed her by the arms. "I was never so glad to see anyone in my life!"

"What's wrong?" Hagar asked. "And why are you in the dark?"

"No reason," Maddy lied, pulling the woman down on the couch beside her. "How did you get in?"

"Still have my key," Hagar said. "I suppose I should've rung the doorbell, but since the place was dark I didn't think anybody was home."

Maddy's mind sped as she theorized what had happened. The man across the street obviously didn't think twice about a black woman entering the building, perhaps even thought Hagar was going to another apartment. Either way, a golden opportunity had presented itself.

"I need you to do something," she whispered. "Something that's a matter of life and death."

66

Encouraged by her talk with Hagar, Maddy felt good enough to eat a little bread and cheese and fortify herself with a couple glasses of Madeira. Sleep was an impossibility, so she tried to continue reading *La Comédie Humaine,* but gave up when the words repeatedly swam together on the page. She could concentrate on nothing other than wondering when Carlos would come for her and if Hagar had succeeded on her desperate mission. How much of the world's destiny, Maddy thought wildly, rests with an illiterate ex-slave woman!

She was wide awake in the parlor when, at the stroke of midnight, Carlos and Archie appeared, smelling of liquor and eager to get on with their crime. Maddy didn't know what she expected Archie to look like, but it certainly wasn't this jowly butterball with pinched nostrils and a head of unkempt gray hair.

"I see you're dressed and ready to go." Carlos nodded approvingly. "Good."

"I just want to get it over with."

"So do we," Archie said, his homeliness enhanced by a grating voice.

Maddy didn't even try to hide her revulsion as she turned to Carlos. "Have the plans changed? Is there anything else I need to know?"

"No. Our wagon is waiting downstairs. We'll ride over to New Levee Street and approach the warehouses from downriver. We'll park several blocks away. When you see the guard, you know what to do, and we'll get busy the moment you two walk away."

"Wait a minute," Maddy said. "Who's going to pay my fine?"

"I am of course." Carlos peeled a five dollar bill from a wad in his pocket and passed it to her. "So you see, my dear. There is such a thing as honor among thieves." He checked his watch.

"We're wasting time, Archie. Let's go."

Maddy was in such a state that the ride was more dream-like than real. Streetlights in this end of town were scarce, throwing large areas into deep shadow, and a full moon was playing hide-and-seek with high flying clouds. As the wagon drew to a halt, Carlos pointed down the street, indicating two soldiers chatting in front of a warehouse. Everyone watched tensely until they realized one guard was merely relieving another.

"Thank God," Carlos whispered as the extra soldier walked away in the direction of Esplanade Street.

"Okay, girly," Archie muttered. "Get to work."

Faced with the moment of truth, Maddy's courage wavered badly and, despite the awful heat, a shudder shot down her spine. "Carlos, I...I don't think I can do this."

"You damned well better," he growled, patience gone. "If you know what's good for you." He gave her a rough shove, nearly knocking her out of the wagon. "Now get over there and do as you're told!"

Again, Maddy thought she was in a dream. The soldier was watching his friend walk away and didn't hear Maddy approach until her feet crunched on the oysters shells covering the dirt road. He spun around, rifle cocked and aimed.

"Who's there?"

"It's only me, officer," Maddy answered in English, noting the private's uniform and flattering him with an advancement in rank. He didn't look a day over eighteen. "May I have a word please?"

"Yes, ma-am." He lowered his gun and cocked his head when he got a better look. He smiled. "What's a pretty girl like you doing in this part of town? You look lost."

"I'm afraid you're right." Maddy took a deep breath, struggling to bring her nerves under control. "Lost and alone."

The soldier's smile broadened. "Is that right?"

"Oh, yes." Maddy sashayed past the man, turning his gaze so he faced upriver. Over his shoulder shadowy figures slipped from the wagon and darted into the alley. In minutes Carlos and Archie would begin scavenging the gold. "You look a little lost and alone too, sir," she purred.

"Blevins," he said, "Private Mickey Blevins."

"May I call you Mickey?"

"I wish you would." Knowing no superior was watching, he jauntily pushed his cap back on his head. "What's your name, sweetheart?"

Maddy blurted the first thing that popped into her brain. "Angelina Jolie."

"That's a mighty pretty name."

"Thank you, Mickey. And now, may we speak frankly?"

"You go right ahead, Miss Jolie."

Maddy took a deep breath and stepped back, putting her hands on her hips in a posture of defiance. "I think every Yankee soldier is a yellow, lily-livered coward, and I'd like to spit right in General Butler's face!"Her insults were so totally unexpected it took a moment for Blevins to register them. "What...what's that you said?"

"I said you Union soldiers aren't fit to lick Confederate boots."

"You little Rebel bitch!" Blevins spat, grabbing Maddy's arm and pulling her into the street. "Maybe you'll think different after I haul you off to the calaboose."

"You're not hauling me anyway!" Maddy screamed, fighting to wrench free. "Filthy Yankee!"

The pushing and pulling continued along with the insults as the irate soldier dragged Maddy toward Esplanade eight blocks away. They were almost to the railroad tracks when cracking sounds erupted behind them. Blevins froze.

"What the devil was that?" He jumped at the sound of more gunfire. "It's coming from the warehouse!" Maddy was silent, paralyzed with fear as he turned on her. "And I'm betting you're the decoy to make the coast clear! Goddamned rebels!"

Blevins gave Maddy a vicious shove that sent her reeling backwards. She tripped and tumbled across the train tracks, grateful when layers of clothing cushioned her fall. She struggled to her feet and watched Blevins race back toward his post, and when the moon burst free of the clouds, it illuminated a scenario she would never forget. She held her breath as a figure darted from the shadows, grabbed Blevins from behind and knocked him in the head. Maddy hoped he wasn't badly hurt when he screamed and collapsed, but she wasn't about to investigate. She slunk into the shadows as the soldier's assailant climbed into the driver's seat of Carlos's wagon and grabbed the reins. More feet crunched on shells as three more men burst from the alley, heaved bags into the back and scrambled into the wagon. None appeared to be Carlos, and premonition coursed through Maddy's soul as the driver snapped the reins and the wagon vanished down New Levee Street in a cloud of moonlit dust. Ignoring Blevins, she crept into the alley, footsteps breaking an ominous stillness when her shoes crunched on shattered glass and more oyster shells. As she cleared the alley and emerged into a vacant lot, she heard a rustling noise and a low, agonized moan. There was no denying the source.

"Carlos!"

Following the terrible sound, she spotted him sprawled atop a pile of charred debris. He was groaning and clutching his chest. "Dear God!" She hiked her skirts and cautiously picked her way through treacherous piles of debris, snagging her pantalets on twisted nails and broken boards, nearly stumbling over Archie's lifeless body. When she reached Carlos, she saw his eyes were wide open and gaping at nothing.

"Oh, Carlos!" she cried.

As she knelt beside him, he whispered her name. "Mad...Maddy?"

"Yes, it's Maddy." She winced when she saw the blood. Bullet wounds in his neck and chest gushed red, a warning that he wasn't long for this world. "I'm here."

"I can't...see you."

"I'm here," she said again,

Carlos's hand trembled violently as it reached into empty space. Maddy pressed it to her cheek. At that moment, all hatred and disappointment melted away and she saw only a man whose life had never been his own. She understood that Carlos's tragic fate was preordained, just as she knew her mission had led her to this moment, to protect the stolen gold and keep history on course. In the process, this poor, blameless soul had to be sacrificed.

"I'm—ungh!" Carlos choked suddenly, coughing black blood on Maddy's bodice.

"I'm...I'm sorry."

"I know you are, my darling, and I'm sorry that fate tore us apart, but there was no way to stop it. Do you hear me?"

With no response, Maddy didn't know how much Carlos comprehended, but when the moonlight burst free again, she knew his life was ebbing away. He tried to talk, but the words were so faint she leaned closer, so close that her lips brushed his cheek as she strained to hear.

"Who...are...you?" he whispered.

Tears seared Maddy's eyes and great loss stirred her soul as she whispered the truth. "Someone who loved you with her heart." Still clutching his hand, she ignored the stink of whiskey and carnage to kiss Carlos's lips. "Now go to sleep, my angel, and find peace at last."

There were no more words as she waited for Carlos to die. When the moment came, Maddy bathed his forehead in tears before laying his hands gently atop his chest. As she leaned back and erased her shadow from his body, something caught the moonlight and gleamed brightly against his silk waistcoat. Oh, Carlos, she thought. Even while committing robbery, you're dressed like a gentleman. She took his new watch as a memento and got slowly, shakily to her feet. Only then did she say her final good-bye.

"I'm glad it was you who freed me to go home." She blew him a kiss. *"Au revoir, ma cherie."*

67

Peeking into the street, Maddy saw Blevins staggering toward Esplanade and trailed him from a safe distance. She wanted to help the poor man but knew not to involve herself in an assault on a Union soldier, much less two murders and the disappearance of a fortune in gold coins. She hovered in a dark doorway, relieved when Blevins was spotted by other soldiers and taken into a nearby building. Only then did she fly way home where she tumbled fully dressed into bed and welcomed her deepest sleep in months. She woke at ten, groggy but refreshed, and downed a cup of strong coffee before hurrying to Félicité's house. She had to tell her friend what happened to Carlos, an edited version anyway, before she could return to the twenty-first century. Félicité hung on Maddy's every word, sweet face registering everything from horror to relief as she heard about Carlos, Hagar, Mary and the missing Confederate gold. It took a moment for her to find her voice.

"So you gambled that Hagar could get word to Mary who would arrange some way to ruin the heist?"

"Mary's home is a haven for Confederate spies and loyalists, so I knew I could trust her with my desperate plight. It was my only hope for getting the gold to its rightful owners."

Félicité shook her head. "What a frightening story, and what a brave girl you are!"

"Believe me I wish it hadn't happened, but—"

"It is what it is," Félicité finished, sighing as she quoted Maddy. "Oh, darling! I'm so sorry I ever introduced you to that awful Hector. I knew in my heart of hearts that he was not as he seemed."

"Perhaps I did too, but in any case it's finished." She knew she could never reveal the circumstances driving Carlos to his unfortunate destiny or explain that she had forgiven him everything. She put all that from her mind and noticed Félicité sported a deep blue silk day dress trimmed with blonde lace. "You're looking especially fetching this morning, my dear. Is that a new frock?"

"This old thing? Heavens, no. You know I no longer have money for such things."

"Perhaps not, but—" Maddy smiled as the truth dawned. "I know you too well, my dear. Are you expecting a caller?"

Félicité looked coy. "As a matter of fact I am. He came into town a few days ago and paid me a call, but only after discovering you weren't home." She paused, waiting for Maddy's reaction.

"Someone was looking for me?" Maddy thought fast. "Auguste!"

"Yes, my dear. Auguste. He had some legal matters in the city to tend to. It seems Captain Baptiste left his estate to Louis, and Auguste will hold the money in trust while raising the child as his own."

"In the country, no doubt."

"Oh, yes." Curls danced as Félicité shook her head. "You were right about him eschewing plantation life. Auguste is committed to spending the rest of his life in the bayous."

"And waiting out the war there I suppose."

"As I understand it, his loyalties are familial, not political. He plans to stay home and defend his little settlement up in St. Martin Parish."

"The man is no coward," Maddy said, remembering Auguste's ferocious intervention with Jules. "I admire him enormously."

"As do I, but...oh, Maddy! He says the place where he lives is so small it doesn't even have a name."

Maddy chuckled. No matter how dire her circumstances, Félicité would forever be the pampered belle. "Why should that matter to you?"

Color rose in Félicité's cheeks. "Because I'm going with him."

"What?!"

"Oh, dear." Félicité snapped open her fan and waved it so hard Maddy felt air moving five feet away. "It's all happened so fast I'm not sure I understand it myself. When Auguste came here looking for you, he ended up staying the entire afternoon and much of the evening." Her blush deepened. "In the course of the conversation, he confessed being attracted to me the one time we met. You remember. When he came for the baby." Maddy nodded, warmth seeping into her heart as she anticipated the rest. "As we talked, I realized I was attracted to him too, especially when I thought of Louis and how desperately he needs a mother. You know I adore that sweet child."

Maddy knew Félicité spoke the truth. "Yes, I do."

"With you going away and me left alone in a town full of Yankees and the Isle Brevelle in such dreadful straits, one thing led to another, and it seemed the right thing to do."

Maddy worked to digest what she heard. It was a serious stretch to imagine this spoiled beauty stuck in the swamps, riding pirogues instead of fine carriages, dining on raccoon instead of foie gras, and wearing cotton instead of silks and satins. She was thrilled with the match but felt obliged to ask Félicité if she was up to the challenge.

"You know it will be difficult, *bébé*. Very difficult and unlike anything you know."

Félicité stopped fanning herself and smiled. "You're a dear friend to be concerned, but perhaps you don't know me as well as you think. If nothing else, I understand survival and, as you once put it, keeping the wolf from the door. The girl you refer to, the selfish, indulged courtesan, is no more."

Maddy was incredulous. "Do you mean that?"

"*Ma chère,* I swear on my life she disappeared the moment Auguste asked me to go with him, and lest you think it's only another arrangement of convenience, I assure you I will not only love the man but will spend my life making him happy. Whether at the balls or in the backwoods, giving pleasure is the one thing I do well. Surely you understand that by now."

"Of course I do!" Maddy cried as this wonderful reality finally registered. She gathered Félicité in her arms and they shared tears of joy until Félicité dabbed her eyes with the handkerchief she loaned Maddy the night they met.

"Now you must see what Auguste gave me." She slipped away and returned with something sparkling on her finger. "I've been perishing to show you!"

Maddy's heart sang when she saw Grandmother Aglaé's ruby and sapphire ring, relieved to see it was back on course. How totally fitting, she thought, that it should find a home on the hand of this lovely woman of color. "It's gorgeous."

"I think so too. Don't you adore the butterfly design? I've never seen anything like it."

"It's as unique as yourself." When their eyes locked, Maddy knew they shared the same thought, that Félicité's black blood, however scant, prevented her from marrying a white man, and that this ring would be a public declaration of their love and devotion. Maddy hugged her again. "I can't tell you how happy I am, for both of you."

Félicité looked relieved. "I was hoping to hear you say that because I remembered you once professed feelings for Auguste, and I would hate to think that—"

"Kindly put that out of your mind, Félicité. The girl who fell for Auguste has also disappeared, and now that I know you're leaving New Orleans I'm ready to go too."

Félicité frowned. "Are you still undecided about where you're going?"

"I'm afraid so."

"But how will I know where to find you?"

"You needn't worry about that, my dear," Maddy lied, "because I know where you and Auguste will be."

"Then you'll promise to stay in touch?"

"Bien sûr," Maddy said, lying again and ignoring the ache in her heart. "When are you joining Auguste?"

"He's coming for me at noon." Félicité glanced at the clock on the mantle. "Will you wait until then?"

Maddy smiled. "I'd never miss the chance to see him one more time."

"C'est bon. He'll want to see you too."

Maddy looked up when she heard a crash in the bedroom. "What on earth—?"

"That racket is Zaza packing. I promised it would be the last thing I'd ask her to do."

"What do you mean?"

"I wanted to take her with me, but Auguste disapproves of servants. I think that's when I began realizing what I was getting myself into. You know. How different my duties will be and so forth. Anyway, I thought about selling Zaza, but I simply can't imagine her belonging to anyone else."

"So you're setting her free?" Félicité nodded. *"C'est merveilleux!"*

"Tiens, we're all starting new lives so I decided it was appropriate. In fact she'll be staying with Hagar."

"Hagar?"

"Apparently they've known each other for some time. Part of the slave grapevine I suppose. And that reminds me—"

"Of what?"

"You said that Hagar appeared out of nowhere when Carlos was holding you prisoner, but you never said why she came."

"She never said," Maddy confessed. "And in the madness of the moment, I guess I forgot to ask."

"It sounds like divine providence to me," Félicité said with a touch of excitement.

"Yes, I suppose it does at that," Maddy agreed.

Or, she thought, the August Ones.

68

"It's wonderful to see you, Maddy." Auguste released his bear hug and stepped back. "You're looking wonderful."

"As are you." She beamed when he slipped an arm around Félicité's tiny waist. "I've heard your good news."

"You approve I hope?"

"I couldn't be more pleased. Now I can stop worrying about Félicité."

"But darling!" Félicité cried, pretending offense. "You know I can take care of myself."

"Oh, I do indeed," Maddy conceded, "but I'll sleep better knowing you have Auguste to help with the job."

"A job I will relish every day." Auguste grinned.

"You two make me sound absolutely frightful," Félicité protested.

"Nonsense," Auguste said. "If my beloved Madeleine were here, she would tell you I could never resist a challenge."

Everyone laughed good-naturedly while trying to avoid thinking about farewells. Poor Zaza only made matters worse when she made her tearful good-byes, but once she was gone Félicité shifted attention elsewhere by urging Maddy to tell Auguste about last night's daring adventure. He listened intently, face darkening with anger when he learned of Maddy's ill treatment by Carlos.

"If the man weren't already dead, I swear I'd do the job myself."

"Thank you, Auguste, but the matter is best forgotten. In fact, I prefer that we not mention it again."

"Of course, my darling," Félicité said. "We've much better things to discuss."

For the next few minutes they made small talk with both women sneaking glances at her watch. When he realized neither wanted to say good-bye, Auguste reminded them it was time to walk Maddy home.

"You're right," Maddy said. "I have packing of my own to do."

"Oh?" Auguste asked.

"She's also leaving New Orleans," Félicité explained. "She's being very mysterious about her destination but promises to stay in touch."

"In that case, I won't try to dissuade her."

Auguste locked the door to Félicité's cottage and positioned himself between the two women as they took their final walk together. No one spoke because the moment weighed so heavily, but when they reached the corner of the Rue Ursulines and the Rue Royale, Maddy froze, grip tightening on Auguste's arm.

"Look there! At the door of my apartment."

"What on earth—?" Félicité hissed.

"Police," Auguste said. "Keep walking, straight ahead!"

Doing their best to feign disinterest, they continued across Royal to the corner of the Rue Condé where Auguste told them to wait. He walked back to Maddy's apartment building and boldly addressed the two men guarding her doorway.

"Excuse me, gentleman," he said in English. "I'm here to visit my friend Madeleine St. Jacques. Is she at home?"

"If she was, we wouldn't be waiting out here," grunted the older policeman, a red-faced, grizzled sort who'd seen too much of the world. "What's your business with Miss St. Jacques?"

"I told you she's a friend. Is something wrong?"

"She's wanted for questioning," the other cop answered. "She was—"

"I'll handle this, Perkins," his partner grunted. "I'm Lieutenant Caruthers, sir. The lady in question was co-habiting here with Carlos Mendoza who was found dead early this morning along with a certain Archibald Cook. A soldier near the crime scene reported conversing with a belligerent Southern female and hearing gunshots. Since his description matches the woman living with the murder victim, we need to talk to her."

"But she couldn't possibly be involved in such a thing," Auguste insisted. "I know the lady well and can assure you she is a model citizen."

Caruthers snorted. "Model citizens often lead double lives, sir, especially in this town.

Last week, one of the most prominent Garden District ladies was caught spying for the Confederacy, and a priest at St. Roch's is under suspicion for dealing in contraband. A priest! Who's to say this St. Jacques woman isn't doing things you know nothing about?"

"Perhaps you're right," Auguste conceded. "In that case I'll be on my way."

"Hold on a moment." Caruthers pulled a pad and pencil from his breast pocket. "Your name, sir?"

"Auguste Brasseaux."

"Address?"

"St. Martin Parish." When the policemen waited for more details, Auguste indicated his buckskins and added, "I live in the bayous, sir. A trapper by trade."

"What brings you to New Orleans?"

Auguste wanted to reply that his visit was none of the man's business, but since the New Orleans police force was a tool of the ruthless Butler he forced a smile. "A country boy can always use a trip to the wicked city, sir." He nudged the man with an elbow. "If you know what I mean."

To his relief, Caruthers smiled back. "I do indeed, Mr. Brasseaux. Thank you for your cooperation."

"Your servant, sir." Auguste touched the brim of his cap and strolled nonchalantly away. Although he was eager to tell Maddy his news, he detoured around the block to find

her and Félicité where he left them. "The police want to question you because they found Carlos's body and know that he lived with you. You'd best stay out of sight, and under no circumstances go back to your apartment."

"Oh, God!"

Maddy's mind sped with possible solutions. She was desperate to return to the future, but where could she make a safe departure? Suddenly she knew.

"I need a hack."

"Where are you going?" Félicité asked, voice thin with anxiety.

"I have a friend uptown who can hide me a few days, until I decide what to do next."

"*Mais,* why not come with us?" Auguste asked. "They'll never look for you in the bayous."

"You're sweet, but this is best," Maddy insisted. The determination in her voice warned there was no use arguing. Auguste moved toward the curb and scanned Condé Street for a cab. "You two have no idea how much I'll miss you, and baby Louis too."

Félicité's upper lip quivered, but she seemed determined not to cry. "It's still hard to grasp that you're departing my life as quickly as you came into it. I'll never forget you."

"Nor I you, my dear, dear friend." Maddy saw a cab drawing up to the curb and embraced Félicité one last time. "And now I really must say *au revoir.*"

"*Au revoir,*" Félicité and Auguste said together.

Auguste had barely helped Maddy into the cab when it lurched hard and pulled away. She stared straight ahead, unable to bear watching her friends shrink to nothing. Her eyes teemed with tears which she made no effort to wipe away, but she was so lost in fear and gloom that she barely heard the driver ask for a destination.

"Uptown," she replied. "Number Twenty Five Orange Street."

69

Maddy had composed herself by the time the cabbie crossed Canal and cut over to Magazine Street. She felt safer as she put more distance between herself and the *carré de la ville*, but also more alone. She was exhausted by these last forty eight-hours, and as corny as it was she related to Dorothy Gale at the end of her Oz adventures and couldn't help thinking there was no place like home.

"Home," she whispered to herself. As the driver turned onto Orange Street, she eagerly watched for the house Henri would occupy a century and a half later and was bewildered when the driver drew up in front of a vacant lot. "Why are you stopping here?"

The driver pointed to the picket fence surrounding the house next door. "You said number twenty-five and that one there is twenty-three. See for yourself."

"But I don't understand. There should be a house here."

The driver was less than sympathetic. "You want to go somewhere else, lady?"

"No," she said, paying the man. "I'll get out here."

Maddy felt even more alone when the cab left her on a deserted sidewalk. The day's heat was peaking, driving everyone out of the sun, and thunderheads were mounting over the Gulf. She knew it was only a matter of time before New Orleans got the usual afternoon storm, and when she saw a distant flash of lightning she searched for cover. Knowing better than to seek shelter under the sprawling live oaks, she had no choice but to knock on someone's door or stand on their porch until the storm passed. She continued down the block, hoping to find a friendly-looking house, when she heard a woman calling out.

"Jane! Jane. Time to come home!"

It was the first sign of life on Orange Street, and Maddy followed it to a woman on the front porch of a neat little cottage, a worried look on her face as she called for her missing child. A simple iron fence separated house from sidewalk, and as Maddy reached the front gate, she was overwhelmed by of déjà vu. She grabbed the gate for support when she recognized Henri's house!

"But how—?" As she collected her thoughts, she remembered the city had reorganized its street numbers in the early twentieth century. The house was here all along. "Thank God."

"Look out!" She turned as a freckle-faced girl of four or five came racing down the street, rolling a hoop ahead of her. The girl laughed as the hoop crashed into the fence and stopped herself just short of running into Maddy. "Hello. Are you looking for my mother?"

"Well, I…I'm not sure."

The girl screwed up her face. "That's a funny answer."

Before Maddy could respond, the woman left the porch and strode angrily toward the gate. "Where on earth have you been, Jane? You were due home ten minutes ago."

"I'm sorry, Mama. I was playing over at Eloise's house and—"

"Never mind. Come inside before it starts raining." Maddy stepped aside as Jane opened the gate and hurried toward the cottage. The girl's mother gave her a sympathetic look. "You look lost, dearie."

"I suppose I am," Maddy said, unsure of what more to say. She looked up as fat, cold raindrops splashed her face. "I was—"

"Never mind. You better come inside too until this thing blows over."

"Thank you!" Maddy closed the gate and barely reached

the porch before as the skies opened. "My goodness!"

The woman gave Maddy's smart plaid silk day dress an envious look before motioning her inside. "I'm Sophie Buckner, and you look like you could use a cup of coffee."

Maddy shook her hand. "Madeleine St. Jacques, and you're very generous. Coffee would be wonderful."

As she followed Sophie inside, Maddy couldn't resist looking for similarities to Henri's house. Her pulse jumped as she paused before the room that would become his library with its fabulous first editions and myriad clocks and watches. Her hand absently strayed to the watch pendant around her neck as Sophie called down the hall.

"In here, dearie!"

Maddy entered a sun room overlooking the grounds behind the house. It bore no resemblance to Henri's miniature jungle with its great Chinese fan palms and white wicker furniture. A kitchen outbuilding stood some twenty feet away, and the well-worn path beside it no doubt led to a privy. The path was already turning to mud as the rain came in heavy sheets.

"Looks like I made it just in time," Maddy said as she sat at a table for two.

"In more ways than one," Sophie said.

Maddy was about to ask what she meant when Sophie approached with cups and saucers and a plate of fragrant pralines. She wore her hair swept high atop her head, exposing her ears and neck, and when she leaned across the table Maddy couldn't believe what she saw.

"But that's impossible!"

"What's impossible?"

She pointed with a shaky hand. "Are those—?"

Sophie nodded and took her seat. "Plastic surgery scars? Yes, they are."

"You mean—?"

"I'm a Courier too."

Maddy was reeling. "But how could you...how did you

know about me?"

"The August Ones of course," Sophie replied evenly. "When it was time for you to leave the century, they sent you here to me."

"I don't understand."

"Simple. That little escapade last night put you in grave danger, dearie."

"You know about that, too?"

"Last night's dreams. I suspect the cops will be looking for you before the day's out."

"They already are," Maddy said, grimacing when she remembered how close she came to being arrested. "When I saw them outside my apartment, I grabbed a cab and got the hell out of Dodge. That's why I'm here."

"Good girl." Sophie gave her a reassuring look. "You're safe now."

"I understand that, but—"

"But what? Are you alright?"

Maddy grew dizzy as she struggled to process what was happening. Meeting another time traveler was almost too much on top of everything else.

"I think…I think I need a minute."

"Some fresh air should help." Sophie cracked the French doors enough to admit some cool storm air. "Better?"

Maddy nodded as the truth finally sunk in. "So you're also from the future."

"I've been here nine years, since 1853. Back home I was a nurse at the DeLorca Clinic, specializing in tropical diseases, and my mission was to keep someone from dying of yellow fever. You probably heard about the big epidemics here in '53 and '58."

"I have." Maddy thought of Félicité's lost husband. "Were they as bad as I've heard?"

"Beyond bad, honey. Like something out of a horror movie. I'd researched it thoroughly, but I still wasn't prepared for the awful reality. All those bodies turning black and piled in the streets, the bonfires and booming cannons. And of course the stench." Sophie closed her eyes and rubbed them with the heels of her hands. "I still have nightmares."

"And I thought I had it rough." Maddy shook her head. "Did you succeed in your mission?"

"Well, I saved the woman I was assigned to help but fell in love with her son. He died in the fifty-eight epidemic but not before getting me pregnant." Sophie nodded toward the contented sounds of Jane's playing. "Our daughter."

"Dear Lord," Maddy breathed.

"The August Ones told me I could leave Jane behind or stay with her in the nineteenth century. I'm here because abandoning my child wasn't an option." She chuckled wryly. "And please don't make any jokes about *Sophie's Choice.*"

Maddy smiled, warmed by the reference to something from her time. "I promise, but why can't you take Jane to the future?"

Sophie's face clouded. "Because her aging process is fixed in the nineteenth century and she'd be long dead by the twenty-first."

"What about you?"

"My aging process, like yours, is fixed in the twenty-first. While you and I are here, we won't age." Maddy remembered Henri saying she would return the exact same age as she left. "It's a bitch, isn't it? I discover the damned fountain of youth, and what good will it do me? I'll end up watching my daughter die along with my friends and everyone else around me."

"That's horrible."

"Yes, it is."

"But won't you ever—?"

"Die? Not until I return to my real time." Sophie pushed back a wayward strand of hair. "I'm sure you can understand I don't like thinking about it, so let's get back to your mission."

"As best I can determine, it was to keep Carlos from absconding with the gold of the Confederacy."

"Why was that so important?"

"It would've ended the war three years before Appomattox."

"Which would've altered history of course."

"Exactly."

"Looks like that coffee will have to wait until I can get out to the kitchen." Sophie glanced at the driving rain. "So tell me what things are like in your time."

Maddy thought before responding. "When did you leave?"

"May 6, 2001."

"And you know nothing of what happened after that?"

"How could I?"

God, Maddy thought. She doesn't know about the Trade Towers or Hurricane Katrina or the first African-American President or a dozen other historical milestones. "Are you sure you want to know?"

Sophie hesitated. "Judging from the look on your face, maybe not. Maybe we better concentrate on getting you home instead."

Home, Maddy thought again. She flinched as something tickled her cheek. It was like a man's caress and she wondered if it was Henri's presence or only wishful thinking. "Did they tell you anything about this house?"

"Only that it's to be your launching pad." Sophie chuckled. "Is this your home in the future?"

"It's my boyfriend Henri's house."

"Wow." Sophie chuckled. "This unending synchronicity is amazing, isn't it? The August Ones weave one damned amazing web."

"You can say that again."

"What's this place like in your time?"

"Loaded with charm. It's been beautifully restored and updated. In fact, this room is the kitchen."

"A real honest-to-God kitchen?" Sophie looked around the room. "That's what I miss the most, after indoor plumbing and air conditioning of course."

"Me too." Maddy munched a praline. "Along with cell phones and charge cards."

"You don't regret coming here, do you?"

"Not for a minute. In spite of a few rough patches of course."

"Such as?"

"For starters, how about betrayal and duplicity, several deaths and a few murders?"

"Sounds familiar," Sophie muttered wearily. "Goes with the territory."

"But still the experience of a lifetime."

"More like several lifetimes." Sophie cocked her head and gave Maddy a long look. "Something tells me you're anxious to put it all behind you."

"More than anxious," Maddy confessed. "Do you mind if I skip the coffee?"

"Of course not." Sophie took a bite of praline and savored its sweetness. "I hate to see you leave so soon, but believe me I understand."

"Thanks." Maddy took a deep breath. "So what do we do now?"

"I've been instructed to take you to a room down the hall, the one where you paused when you came in."

"It's Henri's library, full of clocks and books on time travel. In the future anyway."

"I figured it was something special." Sophie stood. "It's an empty bedroom right now. I manage okay on my nursing salary, but I rent it out to boarders when we need extra cash."

Maddy remembered her money. "Sophie, I've got a wad of bills I'd like to get rid of."

Sophie's eyebrows rose. "Are you kidding me? Don't you remember that old adage about saving your Confederate money? Almost all of it will be lost or destroyed when the war ends so it'll be worth lots more in your time."

"I know, but since it's not really mine I'd like you to have

386 | Michael Llewellyn

it." Maddy put the bills on the table. "Please take it. For all your help."

"Thanks, dearie. That's very generous." Sophie tucked the cash in an apron pocket. "I swear those August dudes work in strange ways, don't they?"

"Indeed they do." Maddy followed her down the hall. The guest room was furnished with good mahogany pieces that would someday be worth a fortune in Royal Street's antique stores. "What a pretty room."

"Thanks." Sophie seemed suddenly edgy as she looked at the watch pendant around Maddy's neck. "Is that your ticket back?" Maddy nodded. "Then I guess I'd better leave you to it. Do you need anything else?"

"As they say back home, I could use a hug."

Sophie grinned and opened her arms. "Sure thing."

"Thanks for everything," Maddy said. "Good luck to you."

"You too, dearie." Sophie stepped into the hall and grinned at the ceiling. "Beam her up, Scotty."

She closed the door and was gone.

70

Left alone, Maddy went to the window and looked outside. The storm was breaking up with shards of sunlight slicing through the black clouds. Steam rose from streets and rooftops as the rains slowed, lending an air of unreality to the scene. Maddy lingered, knowing this was her last look at the nineteenth century and wanting to commit every detail to memory. She smiled as a carriage clip-clopped by, spinning wheels reminding her it was time to leave.

"Au revoir, La Nouvelle-Orléans," she whispered as she moved away from the window. "Good-bye."

Maddy started to stretch out on the bed until she remembered it occupied the space where Henri's watch cabinet now stood. She racked her brain to remember what was positioned where and decided the space by the door was the best choice. That way she could avoid colliding with furniture when she ended her journey. She took one final look before popping open the compartment in the watch pendant and, with no more hesitation, pushed the stem to set the second hand spinning. She gripped the pendant tight, took a deep breath and waited. Nothing happened. She continued staring at the watch face, heart racing. Still, nothing.

"What's wrong?" she whispered. Why am I not...oh!"

Maddy smiled as reality dawned and she realized the August Ones were giving her a final test. The pendant was dated 1861, but this was 1862 and she understood now what prompted her to take Carlos's new watch from his dead body. She retrieved it and pressed it to her chest while looking back at the spinning hand of the pendant watch. It was soon a blur along with everything else. The floor began trembling, then delivered a powerful shudder that shook the walls and rattled the windows as the years began speeding by. The noise of change grew deafening, and night and day switched places with fast flashes reminding Maddy of a strobe light. Weather changes were apparent too as winds slammed the house, sometimes rocking it with hurricane force gusts. Furniture in the room came and went, along with wallpaper, paint colors and light fixtures. Maddy watched, fascinated, as the gasolier was replaced by an electric chandelier, and shelving climbed the walls. She grabbed the doorknob for support when the carpet was yanked beneath her feet, holding tight until the room resumed its present appearance. The terrible din died away, replaced by heavy stillness and then the faint sound of song. Maddy's heart soared when she rushed into the hall heard Henri singing in the shower.

"I'm home!" she cried, hugging her arms tight and weeping with joy. "I'm really home!"

Her first impulse was to toss off her fancy nineteenth-century day dress and join Henri in the shower. Deciding that might scare him to death, she chose a more subtle approach. She crept silently into his bedroom, stripped to her chemise and crawled into the tester bed. As she lowered the gauzy *mosquitaire,* she glanced around the room and was exhilarated by its familiarity. She caressed the mahogany headboard to reassure herself she was back, excitement growing until she saw a silver tray with champagne on ice and two glasses. Making matters worse was the clock beside the tray.

"One in the morning," she muttered. Then, "Oh, God! Why is Henri showering at this hour and what if he's not alone?!"

Maddy's pulse quickened when the shower stopped. She listened for a woman's voice, fearing what she might do if she heard one. Henri seemed to be taking forever to dry off, but finally the door opened and he stood there naked as the day he was born. He looked at the bed and smiled.

"Welcome home, darling."

Maddy was in shock. "You...you're not surprised?"

"Of course not. I knew you were coming." He nodded at the sideboard. "Why do you think I have champagne on ice?"

Maddy was still trying to piece things together. "At one o'clock in the morning?"

"That's the time you left, my love, so naturally it's the time you would return."

"Oh, my God! You're right."

Henri came closer, arousal growing with every step. He parted the mosquito net. "My, don't you look fetching!"

Maddy's emotions surged as she tugged the chemise over her head and tossed it aside. "What are you waiting for, man? An engraved invitation?"

71

Maddy awoke with a start. It took her a moment to shed the cobwebs of time and realize the naked man sleeping beside her was Henri and not Carlos. She propped herself up on an elbow and looked over his shoulder at the clock.

"Ten thirty," she breathed. "Good heavens."

She knew why she slept so late of course. She and Henri had been up until all hours, drinking champagne, getting intimately reacquainted and discussing her adventure. He wanted every detail, and while she debated how much to tell him about Carlos, Henri revealed that he already knew. He reminded her that what she did in another multiverse was separate and self-contained and had no bearing on their relationship in the here and now.

"Sort of like, 'What happens in Vegas stays in Vegas,'" he explained, kissing her forehead to seal the deal.

Maddy felt much better, but there were still plenty of unanswered questions. All in good time, she thought as she padded naked into the kitchen and made coffee. Suddenly ravenous, she ate a banana and devoured a container of peach yogurt. She had a chill while waiting for the coffee to brew and remembered it was no longer August but February, the month when she left on her journey. Shivering, she hurried down the hall and, careful not to wake Henri, raided his armoire for a long-sleeved sweater and a pair of socks. She chuckled when she saw herself in the full-length mirror. Quite a difference from the layers of underwear and girly silks and satins she'd worn this past year and a half. She glanced at Henri, still sleeping and snoring softly in the big tester bed.

Yes, she thought. It's good to be home.

Maddy followed the smell of the rich Luzianne coffee back to the kitchen, poured a cup and sat at the kitchen table. She experienced a Möbius strip sort of déjà vu when she realized she had eaten pralines on this very spot in 1862, only yesterday with Sophie, and wondered if she might have more such moments. It was simultaneously comforting and disconcerting, but she welcomed both sensations. Besides, she thought, what choice do I have? Still, in Henri's absence she needed some sort of anchor and tingled with anticipation as she reached for the phone and punched Paige's number.

"Hello."

Her smile bloomed at the sound of Paige's voice. "Hey, you!"

An intake of breath was followed by a brief silence. "Darling girl! Is it really you?"

"Alive and in person."

"How are you and where are you and what in the world have you been doing?" Paige gushed. "Tell me everything in twenty words or less."

"Same old Paige," Maddy said, wiping away tears when she realized how much she had missed her dearest friend. "Promise me you'll never change."

"And promise me you'll stop referring to me as 'old,'" Paige laughed. "My God, it's good to hear your voice. You alright?"

"Couldn't be better. You?"

"Peachy. When did you get back?"

"At one in the morning. I'm at Henri's house."

"No surprises there, dear. Now tell me when we can get together. Your adventures are hardly something to be discussed over the telephone. How about cocktails at the Sazerac Bar? For old time's sake, no pun intended."

"That sounds wonderful. I can't wait to see you."

"Ditto, kiddo. But tell me one thing. Was it everything you expected?"

"And then some," Maddy said with a laugh.

"Did you by any chance find out anything about your family?"

"You could say that."

"Splendid. Shall we say five-ish at the Roosevelt?"

"I'll be there with bells on and my hoopskirt off."

"Ciao, darling!"

Maddy hung up, warmed inside from the sound of Paige's voice. The sentiment deepened when Henri appeared in the doorway, rubbing his eyes, curly hair sticking out in all directions. She rushed to hug him.

"Good morning, *bébé.*"

"*Bonjour, ma chérie.* Did you sleep alright?"

"The first deep, dreamless sleep I've had in months." Maddy kissed him and poured his coffee. "You?"

"My sleep was deep but not without dreams. I don't remember them though." He scratched his head and took the steaming cup. "I heard your voice. Were you talking to Paige?"

Maddy nodded. "She wants to meet me at the Sazerac at five. Do you mind?"

"Not if I can spend the day with you."

"I'm counting on it," Maddy said. "In fact I have an adventure planned for us."

"I'm all ears."

"Remember last night when I told you about Five Oaks plantation?"

"Is that where we're going?"

"If you don't mind. It's below Westwego and we can stop and visit *Grand-mère* Aglaé on the way. After what I learned about my family, I've got some questions for granny dear."

"Didn't you say she refuses to talk about family history?"

"Yeah, but I've got some tricks up my sleeve. You'll see."

Henri coughed and cleared his throat. "I hate to tell you, darling, but I honestly don't know if Five Oaks is still standing. Then again I could be confusing it with someplace else. So many of those old plantations had 'oaks' in the name."

"Only one way to find out." Maddy sipped her coffee thoughtfully. "Regardless of what's left of the place, I owe the August Ones a debt of gratitude. Oh, I know foiling the plot to steal the Confederate gold and keeping history on track was the main reason they sent me back, but what they revealed about my family history is something I'll cherish forever. I never expected such an incredible voyage of self discovery."

Henri smiled. "You're not disappointed by what you learned?"

"Not a bit." Maddy chuckled. "For heaven's sake, Henri. Who wouldn't want adultery, duplicity and murder in the family?"

"Your grandmother, that's who."

"Mmmm. I'll get to the bottom of that soon enough."

72

Aglaé St. Jacques was a petite woman who bore more than a passing resemblance to her granddaughter. Aside from physical appearance, she had also bequeathed Maddy a certain feistiness and determination, and even at 85, was not one to trifle with. She ushered Maddy and Henri into a sun room reminiscent of Henri's back porch.

"It's been way too long since you visited, *ma petit.*" Aglaé eased herself onto a settee and patted the seat beside her. She gave Maddy an approving nod. "I like that you're wearing your hair loose and free these days. Buns are better suited to old ladies like me." She smiled and smoothed her tidy coiffure as she looked at Henri. "And how nice of you to bring this gentleman along. I never get to meet any of your friends."

"I apologize for that, *grand-mère*, and I promise you'll be seeing more of us both."

White eyebrows rose as Aglaé turned toward Henri. "She sounds so serious."

"She is indeed, Madam St. Jacques."

"But that's not why we're here," Maddy interjected, hoping to divert her from probing the relationship with Henri. "I want to talk about the St. Jacques family."

Aglaé looked disappointed. "Now why do you want to bring that up again, *chère?* I've told you time and again that I only know so much about them."

"I know, but please hear me out." Maddy took her grandmother's hand and felt a jolt of déjà-vu when the ruby ring pressed against her palm. If only you knew where that thing has been, she thought. Then she began her lie.

"Last week at the research center I stumbled upon a brand new genealogical website. As you know, I tried to trace family history before but never got further back than great-grandfather Louis. It was as if the family didn't exist before him. Anyway, this new site enabled me to trace the St. Jacques family back to a plantation near here called Five Oaks." Aglaé was silent. "That was quite a surprise since I was told our people were Cajun when in fact they're Creole."

"Je suis Cajun," Aglaé insisted with an edge to her voice. "I know nothing about this Creole business."

"Certainly you're Cajun, dear, but I'm apparently a mixture of both." Maddy took a deep breath and continued her lie. "According to this new source, two of my great-great grandparents were Jules and Madeleine St. Jacques. Madeleine's grandfather was Pierre Charles Théophile Brasseaux, and he came from France in 1799." She gently squeezed her grandmother's hands. "Didn't grandpapa ever mention any of this?"

Aglaé gave Henri a wary glance. "You don't know what you're asking, Madeleine."

"I believe I do," Maddy insisted. "And if you're worried about Henri—"

"I promise that nothing you say will leave this room," he said.

"And I promise that Henri is a man of his word," Maddy added. Something unreadable crossed Aglaé's face before she rose unsteadily and ambled to a marble-topped table. For the first time, she looked frail, making Maddy wonder if this confrontation was wise. "*Grand-mère*, if this is upsetting you, then we can forget the whole thing."

Aglaé ignored her and inspected the tabletop. It was covered with family photos, blurred Polaroids and daguerreotypes, all of which Maddy had seen before. Her grandmother picked up one of the oldest and opened the back. She removed a faded photo and held it up. Maddy shuddered inside when she recognized Jules, a benign expression masking his evil soul. "This is Jules St. Jacques," Aglaé said, "but I assure you he is *not* your great-great grandfather."

Maddy played innocent, not daring to reveal she knew the truth. "But how is that possible?"

"Simple," Aglaé said with a weary sigh. "Several people in your father's crazy family are not who they seem, and I was sworn to secrecy when I married into it. Until now I never imagined I would have to renege on that vow, nor imagine how this computer research business could change everything." Aglaé sighed again and leaned against the table. "Lord help us all."

Maddy rushed to take her arm. "Maybe you should sit, grandma."

"Nonsense!" Aglaé pulled away and flashed the fire Maddy so admired. "I always figured this would be a deathbed confession, but I want to speak my piece standing on my own two feet. *You* go sit."

"Yes, ma-am." Like an admonished child, Maddy obediently perched on the arm of Henri's chair and waited.

"This...this is very difficult, you understand." Aglaé pushed a wayward wisp of white hair back into place and smoothed her bun. "All I know is what your grandfather Armand told me." Maddy nodded and took Henri's hand. "To begin with, Jules was a terribly cruel man who mistreated your great-great-grandmother Madeleine, the lady you're named after. They did indeed live on a plantation called Five Oaks."

"Forgive me for interrupting, *grand-mère,* but do you know if it's still there?"

Aglaé shook her head. "I'm not even sure where it is. Somewhere south of here is all I was told. Anyway, Jules's abuse eventually drove Madeleine into another man's arms. His name was Jean-Nöel Baptiste and it was he, not Jules, who fathered your great-grandfather Louis. Your grandfather claimed he didn't know the particulars, only that someone murdered Jules and convinced the authorities that he died in a fall from his horse. Louis was born some time after that, but poor Madeleine died giving birth."

Maddy fought to keep from swooning against Henri, mind sagging with the weight of what she had witnessed first-hand. I already know all this, grandma, she thought. I was there!

"I don't know what happened to this M'sieur Baptiste," Aglaé continued, "but somewhere along the line he dropped out of the picture. I only know that little Louis was taken up to St. Martin Parish by Madeleine's brother, Auguste Brasseaux, and was raised in the country. That was the beginning of the cover up."

"Cover up?"

Aglaé nodded. "Since his Uncle Auguste was a trapper living in a Cajun settlement, Louis grew up believing he was Cajun, not Creole. Not long after Louis was born, Auguste took up with a woman from New Orleans, a real beauty by all accounts and high born too." Maddy squeezed Henri's hand and braced for what was coming. "She and Auguste had a daughter named Heloise whom they raised with Louis. Louis and Heloise fell in love as teenagers and eventually married. They were your grandfather's parents. They were also first cousins, but such unions weren't taboo upon in those days."

Maddy's throat was so dry her voice cracked. "Do you know this woman's name, the one who was Heloise's mother?"

Aglaé thought a moment before replying, "Félicité." The nape of Maddy's neck burned and her face blazed hot when she realized Félicité was another great-great-grandmother. Aglaé frowned. "Is something wrong, Madeleine?"

"No, no," Maddy managed, thrilled by the extraordinary revelation. "Please go on."

"Once Louis and Heloise married, the tangle of lies and deceit deepened. The problem was that Heloise's mother was a woman of color. A very light-skinned one, mind you, but back then there was the 'one drop' law."

"Meaning one drop of black blood identified someone as black," Henri offered.

"Correct. Under the law Heloise was considered colored, and since miscegenation was illegal in Louisiana, she and Louis couldn't marry. Louis wasn't about to let this stop him though. Because St. Martin Parish was dirt poor and he was rich, he had no problem altering certain court house records and destroying others. Over the years, the truth about Heloise's bloodlines was forgotten. I suppose that's why you were never able to find out anything, until now that is. In any case, Louis and Heloise moved to Westwego to start new lives. I married their son Armand and you know the rest."

"Did you meet Heloise or Louis?"

"They died long before I met your grandfather. You must remember he was twenty years older than I." Aglaé had a pained expression as she returned to the couch and settled against the cushions. "Come sit with me, *bébé.*"

Maddy hurried to her side. "Are you alright?"

"I'm fine. It's just that I truly hate what I have to tell you next." She took a deep breath. "I'm ashamed to say Armand was a terrible bigot. In my own defense I never knew it until your father was born, and although Armand was careful about what he said and did around me, I knew he was involved in some awful things."

Maddy was horrified. "You don't mean the Klan?"

Aglaé nodded sadly. "That and more, I'm afraid. He was tormented by the fact that he had black blood, and I suppose this was his way of denying it. It was right after the war, and those were awful times for race relations. Those awful Jim Crow laws were the rule, and even when they were thrown out in 1965 and desegregation began, Louisiana fought it. Laws against interracial marriage stayed on the books until some landmark case in 1967."

"Loving vs. Virginia," Henri said softly.

"That's the one."

"What prompted grandfather to tell you the truth?" Maddy asked.

"When Heloise died, I was going through her things when I came across letters between her parents. It broke my heart to read about Auguste and Félicité and their forbidden love and how they desperately yearned to legalize it by marriage. Of course I confronted Armand. You know I can be like a dog with a bone sometimes, Madeleine. I wanted answers and I didn't stop pestering your grandfather until I got the facts."

"I'm so glad you did. Isn't it a relief to tell the truth after all these years?"

"Relief doesn't begin to describe it," Aglaé replied. "There were several times I wanted to 'fess up, but I decided it was a Pandora's Box best left closed."

"Not because of the race thing I hope."

"Heavens, no. I'm sure you consider it as unimportant as I do, especially since we know half the people in Louisiana have a touch of the tar brush." When Henri chuckled at the archaic adage, she added, "I'm sure that's politically incorrect, young man, but I'm too old to learn all this new terminology. People my age don't like going back to school, you know." She smiled at her favorite granddaughter. "Have I answered all your questions?"

"All but one. You said Louis was a wealthy man. What happened to his fortune?"

"You can thank Armand for that," Aglaé said grimly. "What the great depression didn't take, his gambling did. That's why your father ended up on the shrimp boats. Remember Auguste had been a hunter and trapper, so things sort of came full circle."

"So they did," Maddy said with a nod.

"Do you forgive me for keeping secrets all these years?"

"There's nothing to forgive, *grand-mère.*" She hugged Aglaé close. "I'm thrilled to know the facts, especially about this Félicité person."

"Funny you should say that because she intrigued me too. One of her letters mentioned a privileged childhood on the Isle Brevelle. I couldn't help wondering what brought her first to New Orleans and then to remote Cajun country. That's a very circuitous journey."

"I guess we'll never know, but maybe that's as it should be." Maddy glowed inside with a favorite memory, smiling as she heard Félicité's sultry French imitating her favorite expression.

"It is what it is."

EPILOGUE

Maddy's heart sank as Henri turned into the *allée* leading to Five Oaks. The drive was badly rutted with most of the ancient pines dead or dying, and, as they approached road's end, her dread was confirmed. Savaged by fire, vandals and time, Five Oaks was an absolute ruin. The roof and second floor *colonnettes* had long ago collapsed, leaving eight Doric columns to support nothing but sky. Subtropical jungle curtained what remained, and the odor of decay and loss hung overhead like a miasma.

"Dear Lord!" Maddy whispered as the car jounced to a stop. "It's more like a grave than a house."

"Do you still want to get out?" Henri asked.

"I have to, darling. You know that."

"Of course I do."

Maddy took Henri's hand as they explored the wrecked, overgrown driveway. The crunch of oyster shells underfoot reminded Maddy of the fateful night when Carlos died, and more memories rich and tragic, of Madeleine, Jean-Nöel and Auguste, hurtled from the empty space once occupied by the upstairs bedrooms. She silently acknowledged them and continued across the lawn. Not a single board remained of the gazebo, and a thick carpet of roiling weeds nearly prevented Maddy from locating the family cemetery. She found it only after tripping over the plot belonging to her scandalous ancestor, Solange. From there, it was easy to find Madeleine's grave under a blanket of dead vines. She pulled them aside to expose a tombstone.

"Look at this, Henri," she said, caressing the name etched in marble. "I wonder who installed it."

"Perhaps Auguste and Félicité returned at some point."

"Perhaps." Maddy sat back and stared at the stone. "I wish I'd thought to bring flowers."

"Those are morning glory vines, darling. Your beloved Madeleine will have flowers most of the year."

"That's comforting to hear. Thank you." As she knelt in the soft earth, Maddy was overcome by more memories. She lost herself in them before pulling the watch pendant over her head and speaking more to the grave than to Henri. "Perhaps I'll leave this instead."

"Let me show you something first, something I found when I replaced the daguerreotype with the watch." Henri took the pendant and popped out the watch to reveal an inscription he read aloud. "To my beloved Madeleine. Yours eternally, Jean-Noël.'" He slipped it back into Maddy's hands. "Don't you think Madeleine would want it to stay in the family?"

Maddy didn't hesitate as she clutched the watch to her breast. "Yes, I do," she whispered.

"I'm glad." Henri smiled. "Do you want some time alone here?"

"You're sweet, but I've seen what I came to see." She took his hand and pulled herself up. "We can go." Henri draped an arm around her shoulders as they left the cemetery and crossed the ruined lawn. Maddy gave the sad ruins a last look. "I wonder what caused the fire."

"Who knows? Arson. Lightning. Mrs. O'Leary's cow kicking over a lantern."

Maddy gave him a playful swat. "That was Chicago, silly."

"I know. I was there."

"What are you talking about?"

"The Great Chicago Fire of 1871." He gave her an impish grin. "That's how my back got burned."

"What?!" Maddy stopped walking and faced him. "Henri Chabrol! Why didn't you tell me?"

"As I told you once before, you Couriers are the stars and

we Marshals are merely the supporting cast." He smiled. "Now let's focus on the present, my darling, and forget about traveling back to the past."

"Alright." Maddy gave him a quick kiss. "At least for the time being."

THE END

AUTHOR'S NOTES

No American city claims a more omnipresent past than New Orleans. At times as invasive as the notorious humidity, its combination of ancient ambience and spirit of place proves the potency of locale. I was enjoying dusk on my French Quarter gallery when I experienced the tableau ascribed to Madeleine in the first chapter, and I admit that being beguiled by a moment lost in time is as unsettling as it is unforgettable. That fragile, intoxicating reverie inspired me to write this book and, once I began, it proved to be the tip of a nineteenth-century iceberg.

New Orleans' wildly exotic history is ideal for conjuring spirits of the past and evoking intense nostalgia. A society including white slaves, black masters, courtesans and a caste system based on skin color seems like fantasy nowadays, but it was reality in antebellum Louisiana. Under that state's peculiar *Code Noir*, if slaves demanded to buy their freedom, their master could not refuse, and the results were astonishing. In 1860, New Orleans's population of 168,675 included 13,385 slaves and 10,689 free people of color. Only 6% of the population, these *gens du coleur libre* owned over a quarter of the city's houses and the great majority were women! These remarkable people achieved a degree of liberation, wealth and culture unequalled by their counterparts elsewhere in the country, including the free states. They became bankers, architects and musicians, published newspapers and wrote poetry, boasted their own schools and often educated their sons in Paris. They attended Mass at St. Louis Cathedral, patronized the French Opera, where they had box seats in the second tier, and made the Quadroon Balls an international tourist attraction. Their rural counterparts, notably on the

Isle Brevelle, developed vast plantations, raised majestic Greek Revival homes, and adhered to a rigid, highly refined social code. Like their city cousins, they owned slaves.

While black bondage in America is well documented, white slavery often masquerades under the broad labels of "indentured servitude" and the "convict trade." In the 1600s, thousands of the so-called "surplus poor" were snatched by press gangs from the streets of England, Ireland and Scotland for enslavement, many of them children. (The word "kidnapper," first recorded in 1678, derives from "kid" and "napper," an obsolete word for "thief," and usually meant English children stolen for slavery.) Oliver Cromwell, as Félicité tells Maddy, captured hundreds of Irish and Scots from 1649 to 1655 and dispatched them to the colonies where they were worked to death on the plantations. Gypsies were shanghaied by the British and Spanish alike, so it's plausible that Carlos was born into Cuban slavery and taken to New Orleans before ending up on Louisiana's Isle Brevelle.

Maddy's journey incorporates a number of real life personages, notably William Mumford, who became one of the Confederacy's earliest martyrs after Major General Butler executed him for an impulsive act of patriotism. The outrageous "Woman Order" was also fact, and although Butler imposed great hardships on occupied New Orleans, he at least ensured that the city did not starve.

The "lost gold" of the Confederacy is also real. In May, 1865, with defeat inevitable, Confederate President Jefferson Davis emptied his nation's treasury and ordered it returned to France who had loaned it to support the Southern cause. Over $90,000 in gold was loaded into a wagon along with monies from a Virginia bank. En route from Richmond to Savannah, where it could be shipped to Paris, the money disappeared in a robbery near Chennault Plantation in Georgia and has never been found. No one knows if the treasure was divided by the robbers or buried elsewhere and forgotten, but digs in the vicinity turned up nothing.

Tennessee Williams lived in the French Quarter in the winter of 1938-9, and, as a struggling playwright, occupied a number of cheap garrets, including one on Royal Street. It was actually his place on St. Peter Street where he heard and wrote about "that rattle-trap streetcar named Desire" in 1946. Maddy's apartment is a combination of the two. I also took liberties with the seasons to infuse summer torpor as a possible cause for Maddy's supposed hallucination.

Not all mysteries are solved, of course, and not all questions have answers. I don't yet know if Maddy and Henri will live happily ever after or if the August Ones will dispatch her to another multiverse. Time will tell…

— Michael Llewellyn, New Orleans

Acknowledgments

Thanks are due to artist Bob Bush for his handsome cover design, to editor Jan Smith Patterson for tackling a complicated manuscript, and to A Thirsty Mind Book Design for another superb formatting job. I'm also indebted to Gary B. Mills for his book, *The Forgotten People: Cane River's Creoles of Color,* without which I could never have brought Félicité to life, and to author Arturo Pérez-Reverte who wrote something in *The Seville Communion* that inspired the title for this book: "*Still* is an adverb of time."

About the Author

Michael Llewellyn is the author of eighteen published books under various pen names in historical fiction, adventure, contemporary fiction, mystery and nonfiction travel. *Still Time* is his first time travel book. A native of Fountain City, Tennessee, Michael comes from a long line of Southern writers and memoirists. His maternal grandmother, Eula Lankford Brooks, was a published novelist, and a cousin, James Agee, won the Pulitzer Prize for his novel, *A Death in the Family*. Michael is married and lives in California Wine Country. Visit his website at http://michael-llewellyn.net/

Made in the USA
San Bernardino, CA
17 April 2015